BRYANT & MAY
Hall of Mirrors

www.penguin.co.uk

BRYANT & MAY
Hall of Mirrors

CHRISTOPHER FOWLER

Doubleday

LONDON · TORONTO · SYDNEY · AUCKLAND · JOHANNESBURG

TRANSWORLD PUBLISHERS
61–63 Uxbridge Road, London W5 5SA
www.penguin.co.uk

Transworld is part of the Penguin Random House group of companies
whose addresses can be found at global.penguinrandomhouse.com

First published in Great Britain in 2018 by Doubleday
an imprint of Transworld Publishers

A CIP catalogue record for this book is available from the British Library.

ISBN 9780857523440

Typeset in 11/13 pt Sabon by Jouve (UK), Milton Keynes
Printed and bound in Great Britain by Clays Ltd, Bungay, Suffolk

Penguin Random House is committed to a sustainable
future for our business, our readers and our planet. This book
is made from Forest Stewardship Council® certified paper.

1 3 5 7 9 10 8 6 4 2

For Margaret, big in the sixties

'In the sixties, everyone you knew became famous. My flatmate was Terence Stamp. My barber was Vidal Sassoon. David Hockney did the menu in a restaurant I went to. I didn't know anyone unknown who didn't become famous.'

MICHAEL CAINE

DRAMATIS PERSONAE

TAVISTOCK HALL

Beatrice, Lady Banks-Marion, the owner of Tavistock Hall
Harry, Lord Banks-Marion, the owner's son
Melanie, Donovan, Victoria, assorted hippies

GUESTS

Monty Hatton-Jones, businessman
Donald Burke, millionaire
Norma Burke, Donald Burke's wife
Vanessa Harrow, singer
Slade Wilson, designer
Revd Trevor Patethric, vicar
Pamela Claxon, novelist
Toby Stafford, lawyer

BELOW STAIRS

Alberman, the butler
Mrs Bessel, the cook
Mrs Janverley, the housekeeper
Parchment, the valet

Nigel 'Fruity' Metcalf, the groundsman
Elsie, the parlourmaid

DETECTIVES

Arthur Bryant
John May

HOUSE ROOMS

Snowdrop – Billiard Room
Lavender – Dining Room
Rose – Reception Room
Hawthorn – Drawing Room
Lupin – Library
Iris – Reception Room
Primrose – Breakfast Room

1

GET BACK

'Considering they're written by an elderly police detective with a faulty memory,' Arthur Bryant's editor said as he perused the cheaper end of the wine list, 'your memoirs have sold rather well.'

'Not well enough to earn me any money,' Bryant replied, cleaning his fork on the end of his tie.

Simon Sartorius ignored the jibe. He was a gentleman of the old school. The phrase 'hale and hearty' might have been coined for him. He favoured striped shirts from Turnbull & Asser, cufflinks, blazers and comfortable Oxford toecaps, and probably owned a straw Panama for his holidays in Provence. His spectacle-clad eyes always smiled and his face appeared naturally cheerful in repose. It was why Bryant had selected him. Such a man, he felt, would always be honest and patient, or at the very least polite.

For his part, Simon was already starting to regret taking his author to lunch today. It wasn't that he disliked Bryant in any way; he simply could not understand what the fellow was about. There was an air of devilry surrounding him that made you want to keep checking on the cutlery.

Wedged in the gloomiest corner of an alcove in a Chelsea restaurant that validated its shabbiness by being French, Bryant had reluctantly parted with his overcoat but had managed to outwit the waiter and hang on to his immense rainbow-striped scarf. The thing was draped around his neck like a shedding boa constrictor.

'Of course,' Simon said, 'some less charitable critics have suggested that your first volume should have been filed under Fantasy.'

Bryant shrugged. 'What is reality?'

'Well, it's the state of things as they actually exist, as opposed to an idealistic or notional sense of them.' The editor liked to be clear about these matters.

'That's easy for you to say.' Bryant checked his huge white false teeth in the blade of his knife. 'My memories are like patches of old road that have to be repaired now and again. Everyone knows that memories become real over time.'

'Nevertheless, if readers buy your memoirs expecting a realistic account of life in one of London's special detection units and find themselves with a volume of speculative fiction, they should really be informed,' said Simon, not unreasonably.

'I don't see why,' Bryant replied. 'They happily believe the tabloids.'

Simon understood that cheeriness would always achieve more than antagonism, so he ploughed on. 'I *do* think that telling them you were investigating crimes during the Blitz is pushing it a bit.' He searched in vain for a waiter. 'Perhaps a tad more honesty next time?'

Bryant mimed affront. 'I'll have you know I keep detailed notes. Mistakes sometimes occur in translation.'

'Why do your notes need translating?'

'I write them in Aramaic. It's a three-thousand-year-old language so I have to make up a lot of words.'

'But you change things around,' said Simon helplessly. 'The Leicester Square Vampire, for example. I've read at least three accounts of that particular investigation, all of them quite different.'

'That's because there's my version, the official version and the truth.'

'And you hold information back.' Simon raised his eyebrows and index finger to a waiter who, being French, ignored him. 'For example, why won't you admit your age to anyone?'

'Because at my age you only admit it to your doctor. It takes me so long to scroll down to my year of birth on computers that I start to wonder if they'll actually have it. Are you sure there's still a market for my memoirs?'

'Oh, absolutely,' said Simon with conviction. 'These are strange times, and readers need to be taken out of themselves.'

'I suppose in a world of clickbait and slut-shaming my little anecdotes are charmingly anachronistic.' Bryant didn't actually know what those things were; he had heard someone at work mention them.

Simon felt a frown furrowing his brain and fought it back. 'Then I dare say we'll soldier on with another volume if you can stand it. It was terribly unfortunate that your previous biographers had such rotten luck . . .'

'What with one being murdered, you mean,' said Bryant. Slouched back in his chair, he appeared about to vanish beneath the table. His fringe was white and vertical, his azure eyes as round as buttons. The editor felt as if he was having lunch with a teddy bear.

'Ah, the murder. That was a bit of a sticky wicket.' Simon caught the waiter's eye again and tried to magnetize him. 'None of us expected her to up stumps and retire to the pavilion like that. Still, the innings isn't over yet, is it?'

'We never played cricket at school,' said Bryant, who had hardly ever attended school, let alone played a competitive sport.

'Oh, right.' Simon assumed everyone had played for their county at least once, so Bryant's remark made no sense to him.

'I can't write the memoirs myself,' said Bryant. 'I tend to wander off.'

'We'll have to find you someone who can.' He returned to the safer ground of the wine list. 'They do a rather pleasing Crozes-Hermitage here. Young but robust,' he added before realizing that his lunch companion was neither.

The waiter finally dragged himself over and took the wine order. Bryant looked about while his editor discussed the wine in flawless French. The restaurant was a mahogany funeral parlour swathed in brocaded crimson curtains, dimly lit by art nouveau lamps. It served its steaks rare and its puddings well done, and if you didn't like it you probably went to a comprehensive school and jolly well needed to learn some manners.

Simon tucked in his napkin immaculately but somewhat prematurely, an indication that he had attended a boarding school. 'I was wondering if you had a subject in mind for a follow-up volume, something that would really raise your batting average? You must have a nice juicy crime up your sleeve, an investigation that you've never been able to talk about. One of those cases that took place in the days before psychological profiling or counselling.' He broke open a pensionable bread roll. 'If you can come to the crease with a first-class game we might take the Ashes with this one.'

'Phones,' said Bryant, exploding his bread and swathing it in butter.

'I'm sorry?'

'You said "before psychological profiling or counselling". For us it was phones. They changed everything. Policing is about evidence. Finding out what's real or false, who's telling the truth, who's withholding information. Back in the 1970s we were taught to shout at crime-scene bystanders: "Did anyone see what happened?" I don't need to tell you how that turned out. We used to rely on public requests, sightings, interviews, till receipts, bus tickets. As soon as people started using mobiles they left a trail wherever they went. We didn't have to trust hearsay any more. Before, we had to rely on finding a telephone box. Now we search online records.'

'Yes, but it's not terribly dramatic,' Simon pointed out, 'running through phone numbers on a screen.'

'It's still more interesting than life in the Met,' said Bryant cheerfully. 'Their crime scenes end up looking like film sets. Too many officers hanging around with nothing to do. The annual London murder rate is too low, always around the one hundred mark in a city that's heading for nine million residents. Pathetic. So naturally everybody wants to attend one. A lot of coppers never get the chance any more. It's like signing up for a safari expecting to see a lion roar and coming back having seen two monkeys and something scratching itself in a mud pool.'

'That's a good thing, though, isn't it? Surely one doesn't want murderers to score more than a century?'

'Knife culture has left every disenfranchised teenager with a chip on his shoulder thinking it's acceptable to carry one of these.' Bryant twanged his knife on the table for emphasis, making nearby diners look over. 'Stabbings are banal trage- dies committed over trivialities. Even George Orwell bemoaned the declining quality of English murder.'

Simon's brow knitted. 'But the Peculiar Crimes Unit spe- cialized in cases liable to cause public disorder, no? Wasn't there ever an investigation that changed you, perhaps when you were younger?' He stared at his luncheon guest and tried to imagine what he had been like as a young man, but the effort was too demanding.

'Funnily enough I was thinking about one such case just the other day,' said Bryant. 'Although it was a bit of an oddity, even for us, and the outcome wasn't at all what anyone expected.'

'I wouldn't worry too much about that,' said Simon hope- fully. 'I'm sure we can find a biographer who'll spice it up a bit, give our readers a bit more bang for their buck, so to speak.'

'That's not normally necessary. We've come across some

killers who've made Titus Andronicus look like Rupert Bear. But now that I think back, this one *did* play out rather like an Agatha Christie novel.'

'Unguessable?'

'Unbelievable. Not that there's anything wrong with that. The beauty of Christie is that beneath all the rubbish about strychnine and vicars there's usually a simple unconscious truth.' Bryant's aqueous blue eyes searched the ceiling as he ransacked his memory. 'It was the sort of thing that could only have happened in the 1960s, when everything was less *examined*. We were young and naïve. There was so much that was new to us. By today's standards the situation was utterly absurd, of course. In those days we were academics, mainly working on abstract scenarios. If we'd been more experienced in the field and had taken everything a little more seriously, I imagine the outcome might have been different.'

'It sounds promising.' The wine arrived. 'Ah, Chateau Screwtop.' Simon gave a small wince of apology that said, *Publishing margins are tight and you don't shift enough copies to warrant something with a cork.*

Bryant was oblivious. 'The investigation began and ended in a single weekend, although I suppose its roots went back further than that. It was at the end of the summer of 1969, an extraordinary time to be young. I dare say you recall that year . . .'

For a brief moment Simon's naturally cheery face clouded. 'I'm not actually old enough, Mr Bryant.'

'Really?' Bryant peered closely at him. 'You do surprise me. You must be married. Of course it's hard to explain just how strange the sixties were to people who weren't around then. What is it they say? "If you can remember the sixties you weren't there." Mind you, I can't remember going to the barber's yesterday. I looked in the mirror this morning and got quite a shock.'

'I was just starting prep school,' said Simon helplessly.

'Back then I was not the wrinkled wreck you see before you,' Bryant continued, oblivious. 'I was young and lithe. Young, anyway. I've always been a tad portly.' He prodded his stomach with his knife. 'Luckily, waistcoats were fashionable. I had energy, zip, get-up-and-go. It was a thrilling time to be alive. Everything was fresh; everything was new. I bought a kipper tie. I met a girl. I punched a capitalist. I smoked my first joint.'

'I think we can leave out that part,' said Simon.

Bryant loosened a coil of his scarf and raised his hands as if framing a picture. 'Let me set the scene for you. Overnight the country went from monochrome to Technicolor, from austerity to abundance. The Rolling Stones. The Kinks. David Hockney. Mary Quant.'

Simon wondered if he was going to get one of Bryant's lectures and tried to head him off. 'I went through a bit of a David Bowie stage myself – "Can You Hear Me Mister Spaceman". Rather jolly.'

It didn't work. Bryant was on a roll, ticking names off on his fingers. '. . . James Bond. *The Avengers*. Monty Python. Julie Christie. Peter Cook. It was the era of affirmative action, self-expression, free love, political commitment. Did you know that Woodstock, the moon landing, the Manson murders and the My Lai massacre trial all happened within a few weeks of each other?'

Simon thought hard. 'I think we studied the period—'

'Then something went horribly wrong. The Beatles went mad. Kissinger a war criminal, Nixon a crook, the end of social liberalism, the birth of monetarism.' He gave a chesty sigh. 'For a moment we blossomed and anything seemed possible. But it didn't last. John Lennon's song "God" contained the line "The dream is over", and of course he was right. Britain had thought it could manage alone, but it couldn't. Swinging London was a commercial flop. The idea of a new egalitarian nation hit the old barrier of class, and the dream turned into a ghastly nightmare. Rising inequality, industrial disputes, deregulation. The seventies.' Bryant gave a shudder. By now his good mood had completely dissipated. He took a livening slug of wine.

'I wasn't thinking about a socio-political history so much as a good gory murder,' Simon interjected. 'We find readers are quite happy to swallow a bit of serious stuff so long as we feed them some sex and violence every now and again.'

'In that case,' said Bryant with a secretive grin, 'I think I have the perfect case for you.'

'Lovely, although perhaps a little more accuracy in the telling this time, eh?' Simon was concerned that his author's biographical outings had elevated unreliability to a mission statement. 'If you do a good job on this and sell well, there's no reason why we can't cover the rest of your cases chronologically, right up to your retirement.'

'I haven't retired,' Bryant replied, nettled.

Simon mentally checked his notes. 'Oh, I assumed—'

'John and I are still working. You're still working, aren't you?'

'Yes, but I'm much—'

'Back then being in a specialist unit was very different,' Bryant recalled. 'Typewriters sounded like lawnmowers. Reports were filed with carbon copies. We knocked off at six. Telexes took forever to send. Most specialist units were shut at the weekend. If we were outside and needed to call in we had to use public telephone boxes, because we weren't issued with two-way radios and weren't allowed to use the Met's police boxes. But I'll give it a shot. Or, to use your parlance, I'll drop-kick it over the, er, net.'

Simon looked at him uncertainly. 'Super,' he decided. 'Let's get the case written up. Just so long as there's a nice horrible murder at the beginning.'

'There isn't. In fact, for a while I didn't think there was going to be a death at all.'

'Oh. I was rather hoping for a whodunit.'

'This case was more of a when-is-someone-going-to-do-it-and-to-whom. To utilize our technical parlance.'

'Look, Arthur—'

'Please, call me Mr Bryant.'

'I trust you to find something that will please your readers. Clearly they're interested in hearing about the strange investigations you've handled at the PCU.'

'I think they must be,' Bryant agreed. 'One of them followed me home and shouted through my letter box. But I think that was because I called him a murderer. It was a misprint.'

'Perhaps we could have ninety thousand words by September?'

' "Strawberry Fields Forever",' said Bryant.

'I'm sorry?'

'The Beatles track. It's four minutes, three seconds long.'

Simon was nonplussed. 'Not sure I'm quite following you.'

'It took fifty-five hours of studio time to record that brief track,' Bryant explained. 'If I write my own memoir it'll take a lot longer, exponentially speaking.'

'Oh dear.'

'Luckily for you, I've already taken the problem into account.' He smiled at Simon with wide innocent eyes. 'You can have the book in a couple of days.'

'Er . . . ah . . .' Simon managed, now completely flustered.

'Shall we order?' said Bryant, rubbing his hands together. 'I'm starving.'

2

CONCRETE AND CLAY

Jackie Bushell checked the clock on the mantelpiece and realized that her daughters should have been home half an hour ago.

They had told her they were going to play with school friends at the end of Columbia Road. They knew that they always had to be back by six, but now *Dixon of Dock Green* was about to start – not that their TV picked up much of a signal. The tea things had been laid out ready for the girls' arrival. Paul liked to say goodbye to them before he went off to work at the Kardomah restaurant, where he was a waiter.

Jackie prepared tea as her mother did, standing the loaf on end and buttering it before slicing. On the transistor radio Cilla Black was singing 'Anyone Who Had A Heart'. Jackie blew the ash off her cigarette without removing it from her lips. A whimpering came from under the table. She reached down to the Yorkshire terrier. 'Ratty, go to your basket, you're not allowed in here at mealtimes.'

The dog remained where he was. Something was bothering him. His eyes were turned up at her and he was shivering, but the room was warm.

'Go on, you big soft thing, go and see if they're home.'

Ratty did not move. His eyes rolled up at hers piteously, as if he was frightened of being beaten.

'If you don't stop that noise I'll have to put you out.' She took another look at the dog. She hoped it wasn't distemper. A lot of the dogs in the neighbourhood were feral, and she knew the disease was highly contagious. His nose felt cold enough.

Jackie rose and squared off the china, putting the spoons straight. Since moving into their new flat on Hackney Road she had become extremely house-proud. The neatly pebble-dashed block was prefabricated and had balconies and picture windows. It was only a few months old. She had never lived in a new house before. The family had always rented a room from Paul's parents in Bow. They had been lucky to get their names on to the list.

It was a maisonette, and had come with a built-in top-loading washing machine that looked as if it had been delivered direct from the Ideal Home Exhibition. The paint-work and wallpaper were still fresh and clean, oranges and yellows, and she was determined to keep them looking bright, even though Paul still insisted on leaving his bicycle in the hall.

She looked at the clock again. The girls were trustworthy. They knew better than to talk to strangers, but they weren't usually late for tea. Violet was headstrong and tomboyish, and gentle Daisy followed her sister everywhere, so there was a chance Violet had taken her to the bomb-site. It occupied an entire block on one side of Hackney Road and was full of half-collapsed walls and razor-sharp sheets of corrugated iron. Heaven knew who hung around there in the shadows, or what they got up to after dark.

'Ratty, please stop making that awful fuss.' She glanced under the table again. Whatever was up with him? Usually he only got like this just before a storm.

She was just wondering if she should go over to the bomb-site and start looking for the girls when the front door opened. Ratty stopped whining for a moment but stayed hidden behind the chair legs, crouching low.

'Where have you been?' she called, untying her apron. 'Your dad's got to get off in a minute.'

'Sorry,' Daisy called. 'It wasn't my fault, it was Vi.' They stood in the doorway in matching blue summer frocks and cardigans, their hair tied back in plaits, peas in a pod.

'Violet, you're supposed to keep an eye on the time. Did you go over to the bomb-site? Tell the truth and shame the devil.'

'No, Mum—' Violet began, but Daisy cried, 'Yes we did, Vi.'

'Vi, you know it's not safe over there, remember what happened to Percy at number thirty-three, they had to make him a new ear. Show me.' She examined Daisy's hem. 'You've put a tear in that. It'll need a stitch.'

Violet was looking under the table at the whimpering Ratty. They had found him abandoned as a puppy under the station arches and had mothered him, turning him soft – at least, that was what Paul said. 'Mum, what's wrong with Ratty?'

'Nothing. Now go and wash your hands, both of you, and hurry up.'

Jackie nipped out to the kitchen and returned with sausages and beans just as the girls came back and slid into their chairs. On inspection, Violet's hands were clean but her knees were covered in smudges of dirt and one cardigan sleeve was snagged. 'Look at the state of you,' said Jackie, appalled. 'Nanny Kath knitted you that top. It'll be lovely once you grow into it.'

'My arms aren't going to get a foot longer, are they?'

'No backchat. You're supposed to set an example to your sister.' She went to the doorway and called, 'Paul, it's on the table, come and eat.'

When she reached down to the dog it backed away from her, still whining. 'Ratty, what's come over you? You know the rules.'

'That dog's been on my sleeves,' said Paul, appearing at the dining-room door with his waiter's jacket over his arm. 'Have you got the brush?'

'He wouldn't fall asleep on it if you hung it up occasionally,' she said, locating the brush. 'Give it here. The dog's under the table. Can you get him out? But eat something before it gets cold. Tell Violet off for ruining her cardie.'

'You been on that bomb-site again?' said Paul, squeezing to the end of the laden table, trying to find the dog at his feet. 'Nanny Kath can't see well enough to knit, you know that, Jackie.'

'Support,' Jackie mouthed at her husband, casting an eye at the girls.

'You shouldn't get your clothes dirty, either of you,' said Paul dutifully. 'Your mother has eczema.'

'Then she should wear rubber gloves when she washes them,' said Violet defiantly.

Daisy didn't appear to be listening. She was squinting and looking up at the ceiling. Ratty howled again, in a higher and more plaintive register.

'What's the matter now?' asked Jackie, fork raised in one hand.

'There's something in my hair,' Daisy said. She shook her fringe and white dust sifted out. Violet laughed.

'Not over the table!' Jackie cried. 'That does it. That's the very last time you play on the bomb-site. They're supposed to be building houses on it soon and then you'll have to find somewhere else.'

Daisy was sitting with her knife pointing upwards. 'It's not me, it's coming from the ceiling,' she said.

'Don't be daft,' said Paul, cutting into his sausages. 'That's your bedroom up there.'

'She's right,' said Jackie, half rising. 'Look.'

Floury blooms of dust were falling on both of the girls. As they looked up at the ceiling the centre light began to swing in a gentle arc like a Foucault pendulum.

'What the bloody hell is causing that?' Paul asked, jumping up. 'It's not trucks going past, is it?'

'A cobweb,' said Jackie.

'What?' Paul looked at her in puzzlement. He followed her eyeline and saw a feathery black line appearing across the ceiling. He was about to make a joke about her cleaning skills when one side of the ceiling split and fell down.

It wasn't just lath and plaster, though, it was a great triangle of concrete, followed by a square-cut beam of grey stone. A second crack produced another loose section. One hovered above their heads at an angle, then seesawed down on them with a bang.

Daisy screamed as Violet vanished in a dense cloud of cement dust. The next beam fell squarely across the table, slicing it clean in half. Ratty was crushed and silenced. More and more debris dropped through the hole. The whole ceiling was coming down now.

With a terrible tired groan the bricks in the outer wall of the flat began to move away by themselves, exposing the gloomy interior of the room to the sunlit street. There was a bang in the kitchen next door. The crack had spread and brought down that ceiling too.

Jackie jumped up but could barely see her hands in front of her face. Behind Paul more of the street appeared, and then the dining-room window was buckling inwards, shining like a great soap-water balloon. Moments later it exploded as if it had been fired from a cannon. There were screams and yells beneath the roaring fall of stonework.

Jackie tried to find her daughters in the blizzard of plaster and cement. She saw a sandal-shod foot and pulled at it, but there were long slabs of concrete on top. The rubble was frosted with crystal fragments that looked like sprinkled diamonds.

'Paul,' she cried out. 'Give me a hand.' It was absurd, she thought, like something from the Blitz, but the war had ended over twenty years ago. 'Paul,' she cried again, 'the girls.'

But when no answer came she saw that Paul was folded up on the linoleum floor, covered in shards of glass and dark blood like splashes of paint, and a great concrete beam stood where his head should be.

I can get them out of here, all of them, she thought. *I've always been able to fix this family.*

But then the kitchen gas main ruptured, and that was the end of that.

3

YELLOW SUBMARINE

'All right, here's another one,' said Arthur Bryant. 'Fish.'
' "Fish",' John May repeated. 'Any particular fish?'
'No, just generic fish.'
'OK. Ready?'
'Go.'
'From Russia With Fish.'
'Fishfinger.'
'The Good, the Bad and the Fish.'
'A Fishful of Dollars.'
'A Fish for all Seasons.'
'The Charge of the Fish Brigade.'
'Link?'
'Historical.'
'Accept. Thoroughly Modern Fish.'
'Half a Fish.'
'What's that meant to be?'
'Sixpence. *Half a Sixpence*. Musicals.'
'Damn. Accept. Twenty Thousand Fish under the Sea.'
'Snow White and the Seven Fish.'
'Link?'

'Walt Disney.'

'Bollocks.'

'Now let's do "Carburettor".'

'No, you're too good at this,' May complained, flipping him a coin. 'Here's my tanner.'

'You still owe me two bob from yesterday.'

'I'm not playing any more stupid games with you. I always end up broke before payday.'

On a muggy, overheated Saturday afternoon in September 1969, the detectives met up for a pint in Camden Town, a nondescript neighbourhood imprisoned between smoky railway lines and rubbish-filled canals in North-West London.

For as long as anyone could remember, the impoverished, treeless brick terrace of Camden High Street had been stained the colour of stewed tea, but now it was being transformed, painted over in bursts of sunflower yellow, tomato red and ocean blue. Its drainpipes were entwined with tangerine sunflowers, its awnings shaded in candy-stripes. The old fruit and vegetable stores had been plucked out like bad teeth and replaced by boutiques selling Indian kaftans, ruffle-necked shirts and brocaded waistcoats. Butchers, bakers and coffin-makers were being turfed out to make way for gaudy emporia selling military tunics, Victrolas and Crimean helmets.

The area was still in a state of flux; fashionable little antique shops and hippy bookstores were sandwiched between old-man cafés and nicotine-rinsed betting shops. The art students who had brought this about were a peculiar mix, nostalgic for empire and war, experimenting with futurism and optical art. This nascent oasis was hardly bigger than a couple of football pitches; it began where two old pubs named after witches, the Black Cap and the Mother Red Cap, stood diagonally opposing each other, and ended just after the bridge over the Regent's Canal.

The old Irish families complained about the influx of mods and their dolly birds; young money was flooding in but precious little of it got into the surrounding streets, which were as shabby and rivalrous as they had ever been. Besides, the swinging scene wasn't here, not really, but over in Carnaby Street and the King's Road; you needed money to be a dedicated follower of fashion and there was precious little of it in this part of North London.

John May stepped aside to let two girls pass. In matching white knee-boots, lime-green sunglasses and sunburst minidresses they left behind them a beaming trail of turned heads. May stared as they clambered on to the back seat of a Mini Moke painted all over with a cartoonish military band. They were sharing a private joke, or perhaps laughing from the sheer pleasure of knowing that they were young and pretty and being stared at.

'I feel sorry for those young ladies,' said Bryant disapprovingly.

'Why?'

'Having you leer after them. You're like one of those creepy paintings whose eyes follow you around the room.'

'I'm appreciating the female form, you bookworm,' said May, his eyes continuing to follow the girls as their car headed across the lock bridge. 'I'm interested in them intellectually as well, you know.'

'You're not looking at their brains.'

May was still hypnotized. 'God, Arthur, look around yourself! Don't you ever stop to stare at girls?'

'No,' said Bryant firmly. 'I can't afford to. They distract the mind and muddy the senses.'

'But they're everywhere and willing! You're a bit of a panda about sex, aren't you? Don't you like them? I mean, that's cool too . . .'

'They don't like me. I'm the wrong shape or something.' He hopped out of the way to avoid some prancing twerp in an Adam Adamant cape and top hat.

'There's a lid for every teapot.'

'By which I take it you mean I should be happy with a

horrible one. It's a matter of timing. Girls are never around when I need them, and I never need them when they're around. I'm waiting until they invent robot companions.'

'Did you never——?'

'I had a soulmate once.'

'What happened to her?'

'She fell off a bridge.'

'Oh.' May hardly knew what to say. He caught sight of his profile in the window of Totally Gear and mentally gave himself the thumbs-up. His chestnut hair tumbled over his Regency collar. His flared jeans and Edwardian boots looked good on his long legs, and the woven leather belt emphasized his slim waist. Perhaps leaving the neck open on his thong-tied paisley shirt was too much. Next to him he saw a shorter, chunkier fellow dressed like other people's fathers. Bryant wasn't just uninterested in buying fashionable shirts, he couldn't be bothered to iron the handful he owned.

It's hard to imagine London's oldest detective as a young man, isn't it? An unlined face, an unclouded eye, an unjaundiced viewpoint, a 32-inch waist, just one chin. His good points then were pretty much unchanged: naïvety, an ill-concealed sense of amusement, a willingness to believe in almost anything that fought the tide of popular opinion. His bad points were in evidence too: a determined refusal to take life seriously, a disregard for rules, a taste for the incendiary, a tendency towards anarchy. Not the off-the-peg anarchy of the times, though: an altogether more personal and peculiar form of rebellion. He was immune to the tidal pull of popular opinion.

'Finding the right partner', Bryant continued, 'is like buying a car. You either try all sorts of flashy vehicles and drive them at high speed or you keep one in the garage that never goes anywhere, which you keep polished and cherish for ever.'

'What a peculiar mind you have.' May shaded his eyes and

pointed to a poster pasted to a pub wall. 'Look, it's today – the Canal Carnival.'

'The Regent Regatta.'

'The Pontoon Procession.'

'The Maritime Motorcade.'

'The – er . . .'

'Hesitation.'

'Bollocks.'

'Sixpence.' Money changed hands. They ran to the side of the bridge that passed over Camden Lock and looked over.

A flotilla of tugs and barges was queuing to get through the lock, each craft decorated in a different style. As clouds of confetti drifted over the revellers, trumpets, drums and guitars clashed in a cacophony of noisy merriment.

One barge was painted as the Yellow Submarine, crewed by Blue Meanies and girls in shaggy purple mini-furs. The one behind it was populated entirely by pregnant women. Along its hull had been painted the words: 'Our Bodies – Our Choice'. Several of the chanting mothers-to-be had their bare bellies daubed with slogans: 'Burn Your Bra', 'Baby Love', 'We Can Do It!' Further back, a blue and white Royal Naval Lifeboat bobbed about, its slickered crew collecting donations from the crowd.

'This is so groovy,' said May.

'Can you not say that?' asked Bryant, wincing. 'I don't know where you pick up these ghastly neologisms.'

'But it's change, Arthur! You can smell change in the air.'

'I can smell hot dogs, incense and marijuana.'

'Just take a look around you. Remember how grey everything was when we were kids? How everything had to be shut down, closed at five, turned off to save money? Half the time you couldn't even get a cup of tea.' He looked over at a knot of Jamaicans openly smoking cannabis. 'And now it's all so—'

'Don't say it,' Bryant warned.

'—turned on.'

'You had to, didn't you?'

May shrugged happily. 'This is freedom.'

'This is a few people openly using drugs in the street, John. It's all fun and laughter now but where will it end? Smoke a little weed, snort a little cocaine, inject a little heroin?'

'What's wrong with a little idealism?' May asked. 'You admire free thinking in others so long as you don't have to get involved.'

'In what, exactly?' asked Bryant heatedly. 'How are this lot going to change the world?'

'Try reading Castaneda – it'll blow your mind.'

'I don't want my mind blown,' Bryant replied grumpily. 'These hippy writers are selfish and irresponsible. I'll tell you what made our nation the bastion of patrician morality it is today: the ability to be profoundly miserable. It's one of our greatest strengths, to be ranked beside shutting the boozers at ten thirty and regarding the waterproof mackintosh as an acceptable item of clothing. Where is all this irresponsible fun going to lead? To nihilism, ignorance and— Burlington Bertie.'

'I'm not playing another game.'

'No, down there, on the Yellow Submarine. It's Burlington Bertie from Bow.'

May leaned over the side of the bridge and peered down. 'I have no idea who you're talking about.'

'Do you never look at the *Police Gazette?*' Bryant cantilevered further over. 'He was once the East End's most notorious hitman – until he went bonkers. He carried out a double murder in Burlington Arcade and pleaded insanity. The press called him Burlington Bertie. What on earth is he doing here?'

'Are you sure that's him?'

'You have a look. Directly below us on the barge, shaven-headed. Don't let him see you.'

May located the man just as he passed underneath them.

He was wearing a black leather jacket and jeans, riding the prow of the boat with his legs wide apart and his back to them. A sore-looking stitched scar ran across his crown like the join on a baseball, so deep and poorly attended that the plates had knitted badly. His head appeared to have been assembled from skulls of two different sizes.

'Agh, that's horrible,' said May.

'I don't know his real name and I've never seen his face, only the back of his head. That's all they showed in photographs. How did he manage to escape?'

'Are you absolutely sure that's him?'

'There can't be anybody else with stitches like that.'

'Do you think we should take him in?' May hoped the answer was no. 'It's the Met's job, they're better trained to—'

But Bryant had already gone. May saw him pushing his way through the crowd towards the steps that led down to the canalside, but it seemed that every imaginable obstacle was in his way. With a helpless shrug, May set off after him.

The steps were blocked by teenagers dancing about with banners and balloons, fathers balancing children on their shoulders, girls armed with sugar drinks and pink candy-floss. May became embrangled with a pair of white-faced mimes strumming banjos, but shoved past and eventually reached the bottom, leaving behind a trail of disgruntled revellers.

Bryant hopped, trying to see. 'The barge can't go anywhere, not until the lock is reopened.' Olivine water was gushing through the gap in the old wooden gates as the lock filled.

'We're not armed,' said May. 'You can't just tackle him if he's dangerous.'

'So we're supposed to let him get away? There are women and children everywhere.'

'You're right.' May suddenly changed direction, running back towards the bridge.

'Where are you going?' Bryant called, but between them was a ragged marching band, clattering and booming chaotically.

A string of firecrackers exploded and thick yellow smoke drifted over the crowd. When it had passed he saw May climbing off the RNLI lifeboat with something bright red and metallic clasped in his hands.

'It'll have to do.' He pulled at his partner's sleeve. 'Come on.'

Bryant tried to slow him. 'You can't fire a flare gun in these crowds, with all these kids around.'

'Stay cool, I'm not going to flip out.' May caught sight of his target. 'If you're right, these people are standing beside a homicidal maniac.'

'Do not fire it,' Bryant warned.

'Don't worry. I'll only pull it on him if I have to. It'll hold him still long enough for you to cuff him. You *do* have handcuffs on you?'

'Yes, but I've never used them. I don't even have a key.'

They pushed their way on to the Yellow Submarine barge. Bryant's unassuming appearance worked in his favour. He was already within a few feet of their target when he saw May manoeuvring further ahead, squeezing past several Blue Meanies to reach the barge's bow.

The arrest flashed through his brain: confrontation, shock, cuffs on, guilty party led quietly off the barge and up the path into Arlington Road towards the cop shop, the carnival continuing without interruption, no harm done.

4

WE CAN WORK IT OUT

'But we all know what happened next, don't we?' said Roger Trapp.

He ran a hand through his Brylcreemed hair, releasing a flurry of dandruff. There were already snowdrifts on the shoulders of his wide-lapelled pinstripe jacket. Trapp's hypochondria made him paranoid about a thousand imaginary minor ailments, except the two from which he actually suffered: scurf and industrial-strength halitosis. He was red-eyed, sore-faced, short-tempered, small and unprepossessing, all of which made him prone to grandiloquence. He also had a small birthmark on the back of his neck shaped like a question mark, but because he never saw it he was always puzzled by the uncertainty it created as he was leaving meetings.

The detectives stood before his desk like sixth-formers hauled up before the headmaster.

'He didn't mean—' began Bryant.

'I didn't mean—' added May.

'It wasn't meant to go off,' they both said.

Trapp looked out of his second-floor window at the queue opposite, squeezed under the canopy of the Royal Opera

House, trying to avoid the rain. All he saw was a sea of grey: grey hats, grey raincoats, grey faces. Bow Street on a wet Monday evening. No sign of Swinging London down there.

'It didn't just go off, though, did it?' Trapp said through clenched teeth.

'A fluke,' said Bryant. 'A chance in a—'

'The engine hatch had been left open,' said May.

'You sank a barge.'

'Technically we blew it up,' said Bryant. 'The water wasn't deep enough to sink it. The people on board were surprised more than anything.'

'By that I take it you mean "surprised to find themselves flying through the air with their clothes on fire"?'

'The water—' May began.

'– it put everything out,' finished Bryant. 'Nobody was injured.'

'Badly,' added May. 'Nobody was injured *badly*. They just sort of – ended up somewhere else.'

'I lost part of an eyebrow,' Bryant pointed out, looking for sympathy.

'And this mythical bogeyman of yours? Where did he go?'

'We don't know—'

'—don't know, sir.'

The detectives shifted their weight from one foot to another uncomfortably.

'Shall I tell you where he went?' Trapp bared his long yellow teeth at them. 'Nowhere. Burlington Bertie didn't go back to Bow. He never left Broadmoor. His real name is Cedric Powles. A criminally insane pathological liar with an IQ of 152 who particularly enjoys messing with people's minds, which is probably why he appeals to you, Mr Bryant. I have a letter here from the Head Nurse of E wing.'

'The average stay at Broadmoor is only six years,' said Bryant. 'It's a psychiatric hospital, not a penal institution. He must be due for release by now.'

Trapp rattled the letter at him furiously. 'Are you going to argue with this as well?' He caught sight of himself in the mantelpiece mirror and realized that his head had changed colour. 'You just can't accept responsibility, can you? This is it, the very last time. You two are out.' He flapped his hand at the door.

'What do you mean, out?' asked May.

Trapp stuck his little finger in his ear and wiggled it, suddenly worried that he was hearing things. 'You – you both – have personality flaws. Separately you might have made half-decent officers but together you're a nightmare. I'm not putting up with it any more. The sheer anxiety I feel every time you begin an investigation by doing something completely illegal – well, it's happened for the last time.' He tasted his tongue, worried now about acidity. 'I'm on tablets.'

'You've only been here three months,' Bryant pointed out. 'Most of our bosses last up to a year before leaving.'

Trapp looked innocent. 'I'm not leaving. You are.'

'You can't do that,' said Bryant. 'It's our unit. We inherited *you*.'

'We'll go to arbitration,' May threatened.

'Yes, I know all about your little tricks with arbitrators, and it's not going to happen again.' Trapp ill-advisedly shook his head and was forced to dust down his shoulders. 'You must take me for an idiot.'

'Well, yes,' said Bryant.

'Now look here, your ex-MOD pals in Whitehall are not going to cover for you this time because I have a little deal of my own to offer.' He yanked open his desk drawer and produced two sheets of type, placing one before each of them. 'You're not leaving the office without signing these.'

'Resignations?' said Bryant, clearly appalled. 'Oh come *on*.'

'We're entitled to an independent evaluation,' said May. 'You can't force us to sign anything before an official inquiry into last Saturday's events.'

'Fine,' Trapp agreed with grateful celerity. 'I can arrange for a private tribunal to handle your case at Scotland Yard.'

'Wait, what's the alternative?' asked Bryant.

'The alternative, Mr Bryant? It's putting your belongings, including that revolting Tibetan skull on your desk, all those weird dusty books and the thing that looks like a grenade into some cardboard boxes and taking them home on the bus.'

'We'll get a taxi, thank you,' said Bryant. 'Cheapskate.'

'We'll take the inquiry,' said May.

On Wednesday morning they walked from St James's Park tube in saturating rain and climbed the slickened steps to Metropolitan Police Headquarters. 'Out of the frying pan,' Bryant complained. 'Now we face a kangaroo court that's already been briefed on how to get rid of us. Are there any names on that slip?'

May consulted the hand-delivered letter. 'Kasavian. First name Horatio.'

'Horatio. Have you ever wondered why we remember Napoleon by his first name but Nelson by his last?'

'No.' May turned over the page. 'No rank given, some kind of Home Office-appointed intermediary by the sound of it. Shall we call Gladys and find out if she's heard of him?'

'You could have suggested that earlier,' said Bryant. 'We'll never find a phone box around here. Besides, I haven't got any change.'

'I gave you that two bob I owed you.'

'I bought a book. *Belman's History of Bavarian Fire Engines*. The revised edition. Such are the small pleasures of my life. Who would I be if I gave up being a copper?'

'Someone proper.' May caught his partner's eye. *I dare you.*

'Farmer?'

'Someone calmer.'

'Writer?'

'Someone brighter.'

27

'Vicar?'

'Someone quicker.'

'Concierge?'

'Bollocks.' May handed over a sixpence as they entered the marble hall. 'How do you think we should handle this?'

'Don't know, don't care. The decision has already been made. I'm more concerned about Burlington Bertie. How can he be in Broadmoor and on a barge in Camden Town at the same time?'

'There's only one answer to that,' said May. 'We saw someone else who happened to have a similar kind of scar. Maybe it wasn't even a scar but a tattoo. You admitted you never saw his face.'

'I'm not good with faces,' said Bryant. 'I've studied scars. I wrote a thesis on them.'

'I know, you showed it to me. I couldn't make head nor tail of it.'

'Neither could I. I need new glasses.'

They made their way to the reception desk, where a uniformed old soldier stamped their names on to passes.

'When we outgrew the old Whitehall Place building,' said Horatio Kasavian, lighting a Piccadilly, 'a new HQ was constructed on Victoria Embankment. The workmen found a body while they were digging out the foundations.'

Kasavian stood before an immense glazed-cotton map of London, thoughtfully drawing smoke up his nostrils. There was something ethereal about him. Premature greying and a deficiency of melanin had leeched him of all colour, so that he appeared to be a phantom of himself, and yet Bryant found that something appealing remained. He had a deep-eyed intensity that could not be as easily dissipated as his pigmentation. When he asked questions he leaned forward, keenly curious for answers.

'The dismembered torso of a woman. A murder on the site of the nation's criminal investigation headquarters. It became known as the Whitehall Mystery, and was never solved.' His silver-grey eyes remained fixed on Bryant. 'That's the problem here at Scotland Yard. The truth is always partial and never absolute. There are things which we simply cannot know. I foresee a time when our every movement is watched, recorded, catalogued and annotated. Only those who break the law will have anything to hide. On the day this comes to pass, all crime will cease.'

'And you'll be out of a job,' said Bryant.

'Many people are already out of their old jobs, Mr Bryant, and it's mostly for the better. What about the executioners, the miners who drowned in tunnels beneath the sea, the children who worked with mercury and died at thirteen with bright green bones?' He studied the glowing end of his cigarette. 'Consigned to history. That's no bad thing.'

'No,' Bryant agreed, 'of course not.'

'Then is it so terrible to imagine a time when everyone is watched and there are no detectives?'

'So long as we don't become a totalitarian state. People will always need some kind of privacy.'

'Perhaps the only people who say that are the ones who get up to bad things in private.' He turned and ran his fingers along the yellow map line that marked out Piccadilly, as if reminding himself of a lover's contours. May shifted uncomfortably in his chair, wondering when he would get to the point.

Kasavian smiled at some private thought. 'This city means everything to me. I was born at its centre and will probably die no more than two or three miles from the same spot.' He held out an index finger. 'I've been watching you two for some time. The city's got to you as well, hasn't it?'

Bryant suddenly sensed that the tide had turned in their favour. 'We care' – he cleared his throat – 'we care very much.'

'That's what I wanted to establish,' said Kasavian, grinding his cigarette into an onyx ashtray. 'So, Cedric Powles, aka "Burlington Bertie", feral, intelligent, dangerous. He killed an antique dealer and his "male companion" – I think that's the correct terminology nowadays – in the Burlington Arcade, and because Powles told the court that he rose at ten thirty that morning the press gave him a nickname. He killed the pair with a samurai sword that was on display in the shop. If the murders had occurred in Manchester I don't suppose they would have made the papers, but, as I'm sure you know, Burlington Arcade is just off Piccadilly and therefore popular with tourists. Powles never denied committing the crime. No real motive emerged from the trial, even though we know that the dealer was selling valuable antiques through the Chinese black market. We assumed Powles did it for money, but also because he liked doing it. He conducted his own defence. Here's part of his summing-up speech.'

Kasavian unfolded an onion-skin page and handed it across. Bryant read: ' "England is a country of peasant stock. Although it has a tiny intellectual elite, most of its people are credulous, witless, socially inept sheep so obsessed with feeding themselves that they fail to notice when a wolf moves among them.'

Bryant looked up. 'Classic illusory superiority complex,' he said. 'What did the judge make of it?'

'Powles was declared medically unfit to continue the trial and was packed off to Broadmoor. I suppose the only strange part is that you should have thought you saw him on a carnival barge in Camden Lock. Especially since you say you've never seen his face.'

'I recognized him from behind. He was badly scarred, sir. I understand that the antique dealer fought back.'

'Yes. Powles suffered brain damage in the fight, which paradoxically helped his case. So you clearly identified his scar.'

'Yes, sir.'

'From the bridge. A distance of what, sixty feet?'

'I am long-sighted, sir,' Bryant explained.

'So it appears. Where was he exactly?'

'Standing on the prow of the barge, on the flat part, facing away from us.'

'And what was he doing on it?'

'The barges were heading towards Regent's Park in a procession but they were stationary, waiting for the lock gates to open. Anyone could step on board from the towpath.'

Kasavian was thinking ahead. 'I mean, what was he actually *doing* on it?'

'I don't know,' Bryant admitted. 'Neither of us knows.'

'So, having positively identified this man as a psychopath from his unusual – let's say unique – scars, you decided not to inform a Metropolitan Police officer but to act outside of your jurisdiction.'

'It would have been impossible to locate an officer. We thought if we waited he would get away.'

'Of which, I imagine, there was a strong likelihood. How did the flare gun come to be fired?'

'There's a pin that prevents it from being activated by simply pulling the trigger,' May explained. 'When I raised the gun I discovered that it was missing.'

'So the detonation was an accident.'

'Yes.'

'But you were aiming it.'

'Yes, because I was about to call out to him. He still had his back to me.'

'And what happened?'

'Another barge ran into the back of us and I slipped. The gun went off and the flare passed into the engine housing.'

'I see. You were lucky that the hull was metal and contained most of the explosion. I hope you're not going to make a habit out of blowing things up.' He looked almost amused.

Bryant studied Kasavian's translucent features but could not read his thoughts. He shot his partner a look. *What is happening here?*

'What did you see after that?'

31

'Someone on the towpath had let off firecrackers and there was a lot of smoke drifting about,' said May. 'The barge's engine caught fire and exploded. Some people fell into the water. When the air cleared we couldn't find him.'

Kasavian grunted. The room fell silent and grew cold.

'I have a seven-year-old son,' he said suddenly. 'For a child of his age Oskar holds surprisingly conservative views. He thinks we should round up all the bad people, lock them in cells and throw away the keys. Where did he get that from? Not from his parents. I fear that his views may become more extreme, that he may have inherited the worst of me. A vocational peril, I suppose. He doesn't care for London. I need people who do.' He sighed. 'Roger Trapp has a letter from Broadmoor.'

'He told us about it, sir,' said May.

'I take it he didn't let you study the contents.'

'No, he didn't.'

'He got it from Cedric Powles's file. It's over a year old, written in answer to a government request. Burlington Bertie went before a medical board and was released nine months ago. He is originally from Camden Town. So you see, there's a very good chance that you really did see him.'

'Could this make any difference to our current position, sir?' asked May.

Kasavian tapped out another Piccadilly and lit it. He turned back to study the map once more. 'What you did was unforgivable, Mr May. It went directly against the grain of your unit's remit. You endangered the public; you put women and children at risk. The press reported that you fired a gun. What if the public lost faith in the police because of this? England sets the world an example by not allowing its police to carry firearms.'

'We acted in the public interest,' said Bryant.

'After the smoke cleared you stayed to pull people from the water. Why didn't you go after him?'

'Instinct, sir,' said May. 'It was more important to make sure that there were no civilian casualties.'

'You chose innocent people over a guilty man. Well, that's acceptable.' Kasavian searched the wall map as if looking for answers. 'It would sit badly with me if we simply threw you out on the street, and it wouldn't be healthy for the department if the newspapers picked up the story. But you can't go back to the Peculiar Crimes Unit. Mr Trapp is quite adamant on that point. He's not the sharpest knife in the drawer, but I suppose you both know that.'

'Then what's going to happen to us?' asked Bryant.

Kasavian released a slow, smoky breath through his nose. 'There's a chap at the CPS with a problem, name of Farthingshaw. He's a bit of a jobsworth but if you agree to help him out, I can push Trapp to put you on the assignment. It'll give me time to think of something more permanent for you both.'

'Why would Roger Trapp allow us to take a freelance job?' asked May.

'Because there's no one else to do it, and he thinks I'll be in his debt.'

'Will you be?'

'Good Lord, no.'

'Who would we report to?'

'Do you have a fellow officer you trust?'

'Yes,' said May, 'at the unit, Gladys Forthright.'

'Then liaise with her. It's better that I deal with Trapp. You two seem to rub him up the wrong way.'

Kasavian opened the door, indicating that the interview was over. 'It's not what you're used to but it's better than nothing, and I have a feeling it may call for a bit of smart thinking. There'll be a lot of tiresome paperwork to fill in, I'm afraid. Go home and wait for a call.'

The detectives thanked him and walked to the tube station together. There was no point in heading back to Bow Street.

Their belongings had already been transferred: Bryant's to Whitechapel, May's to Soho.

'What was all that about?' asked May. 'Funny, talking about his son. As if he trusts us somehow. Why should he give us a break?'

'I think it's some kind of test,' Bryant replied. 'I've heard that they're going to start giving specialist officers psychological examinations.'

'What a daft idea.'

The evening rush hour had started. The station's hanging globes threw yellow light on the office workers as they folded their wet umbrellas and began queuing at the ticket machines.

'I don't know what to do now,' said May, beating the raindrops off his jacket. 'Are we out of work or aren't we?'

Bryant looked at the golden-hued tube entrance, the dark sky, the orderly pulse of commuters, and hesitated. 'I was just thinking about what Kasavian said. "The truth is always partial and never absolute." You know how I hate inconclusiveness. Just once I'd love to head an investigation in which everything leads to a single unequivocal solution.'

'I'm sorry you won't get your dream, old chap.' May clapped him on the shoulder. 'It's been a strange week. You should go home and get some rest.'

'I'm not tired.' Bryant shook his head. 'I think I want to walk for a while.'

May watched as his friend headed back out on to the rain-glossed street and lost himself in the home-going crowds.

Three agonizing weeks passed before they got the phone call.

5

HELLO, GOODBYE

'Name?'

'Arthur Bryant.'

'I meant your full name.'

'Arthur St John Aloysius Montmorency Bryant.'

'Bit of a mouthful.'

'My mother liked to get value out of the vicar.'

'Marital status?'

'Spinster.'

'Age?'

'I can remember ration books but I'm still unable to grow a full beard.'

'Any serious conditions?'

'Yes. Financial.'

Mr Farthingshaw drummed impatiently on the desk. Thanks to the Pall Mall smouldering in his ashtray, his fingers were the same colour as the wood. 'Perhaps it would be possible for you to treat this interview with a touch more gravitas, Mr Bryant?'

Arthur Bryant looked around the court official's office. The only wall that wasn't beige was magnolia. In the centre of it was a calendar for an exhaust-pipe company featuring a girl in a red bikini sprawled across the bonnet of a Ford Cortina. There was one small window overlooking a tiled stairwell full of cigarette ends and old copies of the *Daily Mirror*. One headline read: 'Guilty of Murder: The Krays will be sentenced today'.

'It could do with a lick of paint in here.' Bryant waved away the ashtray's smoke. 'It's like a sorting office. I thought you legals always worked out of lovely old Victorian chambers.'

Farthingshaw ignored him. 'You do understand the gravity of your situation, don't you? This is all that's left on the table. The unit will never take you back. While you sit here making jokes your boss is filling your old position.' He looked down at his notes. 'I see from your report that you've suffered a few accidents. It says you blew up a barge.'

'In the course of a pursuit. Not the first time it's happened. Well, the barge part was new. Usually it's buildings or cars.'

'But you're fully recovered? No mobility problems?'

'I recently had trouble going through a turnstile with an accordion, but no.'

'So you're up to this.'

'How hard could it be?'

'You've not much experience in the field.'

'I'm sure we'll manage.'

'We?'

'My partner, John May. We always work together.'

'Ah yes. There were two of you involved in the carnival – ah – incident.' The court official ran a nicotine-stained digit down his notes. He sported a large-tooth combover and wore tiny rimless spectacles that must have been hard to see out of with such narrow-set eyes. 'My information must be wrong. I have you down as being posted in the detective division of Bow Street Police Station, Covent Garden.'

'That is correct. We ran a specialist unit housed within the station.'

'I don't have anything about that here.' He flipped through his pages in puzzlement. Cigarette ash cascaded over the sheets. 'There should be a pink form.'

'You wouldn't have one. John and I belonged to the Peculiar Crimes Unit. We weren't technically part of the Met.'

'Really? Science-wallahs?'

'At first, yes. One of seven specialist agencies formed by the wartime government. We – that is, they – handle more general civic stuff now.'

'Just the two of you?'

'There have been others helping out,' Bryant explained. 'We were going through a bit of a lean time when this happened. You obviously know our current boss, Roger Trapp. There's also a detective sergeant, Gladys Forthright.'

Mr Farthingshaw gave up trying to see through his glasses and pocketed them. 'Have you ever done anything like this before?'

'We looked after Coatsleeve Charlie when the East India Dock mob were after him.'

'The bookie? I thought they caught him and broke both his legs.'

'I fed his whippet while he was in hospital. If you're concerned about our suitability, perhaps you should talk to "Nipper" Read.' Bryant dug out his pipe to combat the stench of cigarettes.

'I don't think we need to disturb Mr Read,' the court official decided. 'He's become a bit of a celebrity since the Krays. I imagine your name came up because this prosecution is being brought out of Bow Street. I must say, given the circumstances, I thought you'd be keener.'

'We're very keen, Mr Farthingshaw, but our unit was not set up to act as a safety net for the cases the Met fail to catch. For the past three weeks I've been going mad with boredom.'

'We're not there to provide entertainment for you, Mr Bryant.

This – little project won't go through the PCU. I can't allow you anywhere near your old unit, do you understand?'

'Yes, sir,' said Bryant glumly.

'Does the name Sir Charles Chamberlain ring a bell?'

Bryant searched the ceiling, performing a theatrical imper-sonation of somebody thinking. 'The Berkshire-based Liberal peer, wife is Lady Henrietta Somerset, a philanthropist work-ing in the Belgian Congo if memory serves.'

'Clearly your memory doesn't serve. He's a millionaire prop-erty developer who lives in Belgravia.' Farthingshaw gave his interviewee the kind of suspicious look one gives a plumber who tells you that a year-old boiler needs replacing. 'He got himself into a bit of hot water recently and covered it up smartish, but not before one of his clubroom pals decided to turn whistle-blower on him. A chap called Monty Hatton-Jones is prepared to give evidence against him at the Law Courts in the Strand on Monday morning. He's been fully briefed and is expected to push the prosecution through for us.'

Bryant was intrigued. 'Why would he do that?'

'What do you mean?'

'You said "one of his clubroom pals". If Chamberlain was his pal, why would he turn state's evidence?'

The question irritated Mr Farthingshaw. He didn't expect colleagues to parse his sentences. 'Well, I don't know, Mr Bryant, he just is. We're more concerned about making sure that he stays in one piece until then. Think you can manage that?' He transferred his upright cigarette from one hand to the other, mindful of the long ash that had formed.

'So it's babysitting?' Bryant looked disappointed. 'It's not in our usual realm but I suppose beggars can't be choosers. I hate being on leave, wandering around museums all day wait-ing for it to stop raining. It feels like you don't exist any more.'

'Just answer the question, Mr Bryant. Can you do it?'

'What, keep him alive for a weekend? I imagine so. Are you expecting someone to have a bash at him?'

'Chamberlain is far too high up the ladder to have any known criminal associations, but after the Krays' trial we're erring on the side of safety. Mistakes were made and lessons must be learned. All you have to do is make sure that the witness turns up for his court appearance on Monday.'

'Sounds like a piece of cake. We'll do it.' He slapped the table cheerily, causing Farthingshaw's ash to collapse.

The court official irritably screwed out his cigarette and folded his paperwork away into his briefcase. 'One other thing. We'd like you to sound him out about Sir Charles. It would be useful to know if Chamberlain spoke to anyone else.'

'You want to know whether he bribed other officials.'

'Let's just say that it would be advantageous to see how far his network extends.'

'Won't that come out on the witness stand?'

'Perhaps, but one doesn't want any nasty surprises.'

'In other words you want us to do your job for you.'

Farthingshaw's face hardened. 'I read your full history, Mr Bryant. You had a cushy little number going at the PCU. They let you get away with murder. It's a shame you had to go and muck it up.'

'I never saw it as a "cushy little number", Mr Farthingshaw, I felt I was dedicating my life to the performance of an essential public duty.'

A look of smugness crept across the court official's unappealing features. 'Did you now. Then you might make this more than just a babysitting job. As you'll discover when you meet Hatton-Jones, there's been a bit of a snag.'

'Wait, what do you mean?' Although he was still young enough to prove eager, Bryant knew that when a pen-pusher downplayed an easy-sounding assignment it was because there was something horribly wrong with it.

Farthingshaw rose, ready to beat a hasty retreat. 'I'm afraid he has us over a bit of a barrel.'

'The witness?' Bryant's eyes narrowed. 'In what way?'

'If we don't co-operate with him, he won't play ball with us.'

'You mean he won't testify unless . . . What exactly does he want?'

'I think you had better talk to him,' said Farthingshaw. He handed over a manila envelope with the relieved look of a clairvoyant selling his berth on the *Titanic*. 'And jolly good luck to both of you.'

6

20TH CENTURY MAN

The bowler-hatted man in the scarlet ringmaster's jacket rode past a huge painting of Jean Harlow. He was balanced precariously atop a penny-farthing and wobbled against the kerb, his knees thrust out, only just managing not to fall off when a taxi nosed past. Nearby, somebody was singing an old vaudeville song through a megaphone. Bryant would rather have caught up with his partner on Waterloo Bridge, where they usually met, but May had wanted to buy a shirt on the King's Road.

'You understand I have no desire to stand around in a boutique while you try on tasteless clothes,' Bryant said, bouncing along the pavement beside his partner. 'Why you should wish to become some kind of ambulatory coat hanger is beyond me. I still remember those ghastly purple bell-bottoms you bought.'

'My hipster loons, what about them?'

'Don't you remember wearing them to the Black Raven? The thread in the turn-ups got wound around the girl next to you. She wasn't very impressed when you walked away and pulled her off her stool. I agreed to come here because I thought you had better be briefed. Ever hear of a chap called Sir Charles Chamberlain?'

'Concrete,' said May. 'He's a great fan of it. A very fashionable architect.'

'I don't care for this new brutalist style. The term is a French word meaning raw, you know. It was used by Le Corbusier to describe his choice of material – *béton brut*, raw concrete.'

'Trust you to know that.'

'I've never been down the King's Road before.' Bryant looked around. A pretty girl in a white Biba minidress and sunglasses was coming out of Granny Takes A Trip with shopping bags, but for every young trendsetter there were at least two old men in raincoats and caps. 'I thought it would be more exciting somehow. You hear so much about it. It's just shops, isn't it? Sir Charles Chamberlain made part of his vast fortune by experimenting in concrete. There was an article on him in *The Sunday Times*.'

'I reckon it's the way forward,' said May. 'Have you been to the new Hayward Gallery? The whole thing is made of great stone slabs.' He tore his eyes away from the passing girl and turned his attention back to his partner. Bryant, he felt, was a stranger to the joys of summer life in London.

'I've seen photos of the Hayward. It looks like some kind of bottling factory,' Bryant complained. 'There are quite enough ugly buildings in London already. Why would we want any more?'

'I think you misunderstand what he's trying to achieve,' replied May. 'Sir Charles Chamberlain is the man of the moment. His companies were the subject of a BBC *Man Alive* programme. He's a civic-minded modernist who advocates an egalitarian approach to community design. He's worth millions.'

'Not for much longer.' Bryant sidestepped an Afro-haired beanpole in octagonal glasses, canary-coloured loons and amber love beads. 'He's up before the beak on Monday morning, Law Courts on the Strand. I was supposed to give you a letter to sign from the CPS but I forgot to bring it.'

'On what charge?'

'Corruption. Chamberlain's people were caught offering bribes to a Westminster Council official. Apparently we're too junior to be granted access to the full details of the case. I quote.' Digging into his Harold Wilson raincoat (waterproof, wool-lined, deeply unfashionable) he produced a folded square from the *Daily Sketch*. ' "Says Sir Charles, 'It's time for London's mean little Victorian houses to be demolished and replaced by all-concrete homes.' The *Sketch* says let's have houses in the sky. That's where the city's future is, in sunlit flats of up to one hundred storeys high. Building upwards will safeguard London's green belt for future generations. Sir Charles may prove the saviour of British town planning, and is currently in top-level negotiations with the new Greater London Council." It's a sure sign of dirty work when the press start praising a captain of industry.' He tucked the article away.

'It doesn't make sense,' said May. 'Why would he have allowed himself to get caught up in a grubby bribery scandal?'

'Maybe he was a bit too impatient to get things done.'

May was disgusted. 'This country is so philistine when it comes to change. That clipping of yours is right. Most of us are still living in poky little Victorian boxes. Every time we're offered something new we shake our heads and retreat into the past.' He had to raise his voice as they passed a shop blasting out psychedelic rock.

Bryant put a finger in one ear. 'Chamberlain may be building for future generations, but not for me. I prefer Victorian houses, thank you. They're cosier.'

'And colder and draughtier and darker,' May countered. 'Wouldn't you like to live in a place that has a separate bathroom and an inside toilet?'

'Not really. The former seems wasteful and the latter unhygienic.'

'You can't stop progress, matey. We're scraping the soot off this city and going psychedelic. Haven't you seen Carnaby Street? They're planning to stop traffic going down it and pave the whole thing over. Soon the entire city is going to look like that. Concrete and plastic and glass instead of boring old bricks.'

Bryant glanced doubtfully at the shower of three-dimensional op-art stars that fell across the window of a former fish shop. 'It'll take more than a lick of paint to change things.'

John May had lately moved to a stylish split-level flat above a strip club in Brewer Street, Soho, but Bryant was back in Whitechapel at his widowed mother's damp rented house. The death of her husband had prematurely aged her, and the state had failed to rehouse her in the blank new flats springing up around Petticoat Lane. Mary Bryant had been told she could not stay in her property for much longer as it was technically a slum, having no indoor toilet or separate bathroom. Her entire neighbourhood had been earmarked for demolition. Even though her friends loved their new modern flats, she refused to look at them.

She had cried for days after receiving the notice to quit; she had lived in the same tiny house all her life, and her brothers still lived in the next street. Bryant had petitioned the council to no effect. In a few weeks' time his mother would be moved to a new prefabricated maisonette at the top end of Columbia Road.

Bryant accepted that life would never be as easy for him as it was for John. There was a class gap between them, not much more than a crack really, but enough to separate their lives and cause a tingle of resentment after a few drinks.

May stopped before a shop called Hippy Hippy Shake that sold Afghan coats, navy drill tunics, Boer War uniforms and Indian kaftans in an array of eye-watering colours, all arranged beneath a huge dayglo poster of a pointing Lord Kitchener. The scent of patchouli oil wafted out on a tinny arabesque of sitar music. 'Look at those fittings,' said Bryant indignantly. 'You can tell it used to be a barber shop.'

'You can get your hair cut anywhere, Arthur! This is with-it gear, baby.'

'Please stop sounding like somebody on *Juke Box Jury*. And don't tell me this is where you buy your clobber. Look at the prices!' He tried to read the tag on a tie-dyed granddad shirt. 'You could spend ten guineas on an outfit if you weren't careful.'

May glanced down at his own wide-lapelled denim jacket, orange polo neck and flared jeans. 'About sixteen pounds ten, actually.'

'On your wages? Stone the crows. Bell-bottoms were designed so that sailors could roll them up, not so you could parade around London hoping to impress birds. You won't catch me in a fez and a cape. These are my old man's demob trousers. My mum got a draught excluder from the leftover material.' He stopped to light his Lorenzo Spitfire.

'How did this Chamberlain chap get caught, anyway?' May paused to consider a shop dummy modelling a collarless aubergine velvet suit and matching floral scarf.

Bryant sucked another match flame into his pipe bowl. 'I'm assuming you read the notes I posted to you?'

'I couldn't decipher your handwriting.' May had been going out with a wild-eyed waitress from Lyons' Corner House and had lost a couple of days, judging by the amount of washing up in his sink. Last night the vaguest recollection of a party in the Post Office Tower had surfaced.

'You know the hardest part of my job?' said Bryant. 'Holding your attention. Now, flibbertigibbet, try to concentrate while I paraphrase. Chamberlain is connected to a number of European trade fairs where his staff struck suspicious deals with councillors under his direct orders, but the evidence is mostly hearsay and flimsy. The prosecution reckons that part of the story is still missing.'

'You mean there's no paper trail and his defence lawyer might get him off the hook.'

'That's what they're afraid of, so the Home Secretary ordered the CID to look for a whistle-blower. Step forward one Monty Hatton-Jones. He used to work in an auction house and now owns a number of UK companies, including a construction plant in Dagenham. He reckons that within five years this whole city could be rebuilt, but he's reliant on Chamberlain for contracts. He has to be careful about who he signs up with; mistakes cost more than just reputations. Look what happened to the residents of Ronan Point. That was over a month ago and they're still waiting to be rehoused.'

In East London the corner flats in a newly opened twenty-two-storey prefabricated block had collapsed from bottom to top, killing four and maiming many more. There was already talk of the disaster destroying public confidence in affordable high-rise homes.

'That was a tragedy,' May admitted.

'It was down to poor design and corner-cutting,' Bryant responded. 'The country's in the middle of a building boom, and no matter how good Chamberlain is, he can't be allowed to get away with bribing officials. The trouble is, Sir Charles casts a long, dark shadow over this city. He owns segments of the entire housing supply chain. He buys up the land and demolishes the old buildings, and his architectural practice designs the new flats that go in their place. Now this fellow Monty Hatton-Jones is willing to testify against him.'

'Because he has some part of the missing paper trail?'

'He has something much better. He was present at a crucial trade show in Berlin, where he managed to record a damning conversation between Chamberlain's people and the Westminster planning officers.'

'Why would he do that?'

'It may not have been deliberate. Apparently he was tinkering with some equipment on the display stand next door. They were demonstrating a thing called a "compact cassette". It's a sort of—'

'I know what it is,' said May keenly. 'They were developed for dictation. Phillips are planning to introduce a high-fidelity cassette deck for home use next year. It'll use volume compression and expand high frequencies to boost low-level treble information—'

Bryant raised his pipe. 'You know I offered to warn you when you were being boring? The point is that it was on the stand where Chamberlain's chaps were chatting with their cronies, and the microphone picked up their deal.'

'What, accidentally, just like that? A bit convenient, wasn't it? Was Chamberlain set up?'

'That's what we don't know. The point is that the so-called "cassette"—'

'Do you have to put inverted commas around everything that strikes you as new-fangled and undesirable?' asked May irritably.

'—may not be admissible in court, so Hatton-Jones is prepared to back it up with full testimony.'

'What does the tape actually say?'

'We can't have access to it, but I understand it details payments that will be made to the councillors if they give priority to Chamberlain's tender.'

May was puzzled. Something didn't ring true. 'Wait, how does Chamberlain know this Hatton-Jones fellow?'

'I believe they go back a long way.'

'How far? Business, university?'

'School.'

'Then why on earth is Hatton-Jones prepared to hang him out to dry? Don't these chaps stick together?'

'That', said Bryant, 'is what we've been asked to find out. Trust me, there'll be plenty of time, more than forty-eight hours. He's being delivered into our care this afternoon. He'll remain with us until we reach the Law Courts with him on Monday morning for his appearance at ten thirty sharp.'

'What are we going to do with him?' May wondered. 'We can't lock him up at Bow Street.'

'I don't see why not,' said Bryant. 'Not in a cell, obviously. More like under house arrest.'

'Perhaps we should bring him toast and marmalade and the morning papers too.'

'No, Gladys can do that. Look out.' Two young men in Second World War army uniforms painted with 'Ban The Bomb' slogans were arguing with a pair of Chelsea Pensioners who clearly did not take kindly to seeing military outfits worn by trendy pacifists. They were briefly joined by a girl wearing a British sailor's uniform with a giant iridescent fish on her head. She ducked into an Aladdin's cave filled with rainbow-coloured neckerchiefs and brightly dyed lace shirts.

'Really,' Bryant complained, 'how much longer do we have to put up with this ludicrously self-conscious we've-all-run-away-to-join-the-circus-in-silly-hats peace-and-love maharishi nonsense? This wouldn't happen in Newcastle. Try poncing about with a crystal walking stick and a feather boa up there and you'll get your eye poked out.'

'I think you're taking a bit of high spirits rather too seriously, Arthur.'

'Am I? Swinging London is a con,' Bryant raged as more boys in military jackets and decorative medals pushed past. 'Most of the country is still trapped in the fifties. It hasn't got two halfpennies to scrub together. We're not continental. In Great Britain *coitus interruptus* means the man getting out of bed to put another shilling in the gas meter. This lot can pretend the sun will shine for ever while they dance around blowing bubbles with flowers in their hair, but really we're a nation of carpenters, shopkeepers and mechanics. All this optimism and glamour and pretending you're creative is already on the way out.'

'What a prematurely senile old misery guts you are,' said May indignantly. 'What are you going to be like when you're middle-aged? I'd rather have this than what we had before: petrol rations and utility furniture. It's nice to see some bright colours and hear pop music for a change. Get off your soap box and tell me something more about Chamberlain.'

'The point is, it isn't just a babysitting job.' Bryant squinted up into the sunlight. 'If we get more information out of Hatton-Jones maybe we could widen the investigation to include the Westminster planning committee. At the moment it's not our case that's going to trial. They're after the man at the top, so only Chamberlain is on the stand. But if we can get definite proof that others are on the take, we could really make a name for ourselves. The unit isn't going to survive much longer without a couple of high-profile arrests under its belt.'

They had stopped outside the yellow Formica and chromium fascia of an ABC café. May checked his Timex. 'Lend us a bob; I'll get two teas. Then we have to get to Bow Street.'

'We're not picking him up from Bow Street,' said Bryant. 'We're collecting him from a coffee bar in Belsize Park. He won't go anywhere near the West End.'

'Whyever not?' May asked.

'He thinks Chamberlain is going to send someone after him,' Bryant explained.

'Really? This fellow is a knight of the realm, not a Kray.'

'Your naïvety is really quite charming.' Bryant flagged down a taxi. 'I imagine Sir Charles will make sure that his own hands stay clean this time.' He opened the door and ushered May in. 'Our Mr Hatton-Jones reckons he's in fear of his life.'

7

LES BICYCLETTES DE BELSIZE

The Belsize Park coffee bar was called Sweet Suzy Sunshine. Its floorboards were woozily painted in diagonal green and yellow stripes. On the bare brick walls gig posters for Jethro Tull and the Moody Blues vied for space beside Cleo Laine and Anthony Newley. The café was the brainchild of Sweet Suzy, a well-spoken girl in a strawberry-blond hairpiece who was waiting on the tables. Since the juke box was playing Jimi Hendrix's 'All Along The Watchtower' rather too loudly, Monty Hatton-Jones had perched himself at a white wrought-iron table outside on the sunlit pavement.

He was hard to miss. Bryant first spotted a vast flabby face as maroon as mutton, atop some kind of public school tie that looked as if it was strangling him. This vision of epicurean indulgence was dressed by Savile Row but not too recently, its copperish hair waved and shaved in the Bond Street manner, its moustache ends waxed to points. Hatton-Jones seemed born to loll in a gentleman's club wingback, but his bulk made him appear positively Brobdingnagian when balanced upon a minuscule wire-framed chair.

'Forgive this ghastly venue,' he said, half-heartedly rising to greet them. 'I thought I'd be safe here. No one I know would ever imagine me visiting such a place.'

'It's just a lick of bright paint, hardly a den of iniquity,' said May.

'You know what I mean – all these long-haired layabouts and their chicks. I had to come out here because it's all jungle-bunny music inside.' Hatton-Jones was a picture of florid indignation. He had the look of a man who always went where he intended to go, and damn everyone else. 'There's one chap in there wearing Distinguished Service medals from the Great War on a bandsman's tunic,' he complained. 'Decent officers died for those gongs. The government should bring back conscription. That would teach them some bloody respect.'

'So that another generation of young men could needlessly die for their country?' asked May.

'Look here, that's conchie talk,' warned Hatton-Jones. 'I live in Greenwich, where we still respect the value of a decent bloody navy.' His eyes glistened like angry marbles and gave him energy, but also a hint of incipient lunacy. Right now, he didn't seem much like a man in fear of his life.

Bryant had already decided that he would let his partner deal with Monty. He sat back and felt the sun on his face. A woman in a brown tea-cosy hat and tartan overcoat walked past. She was holding on to a girl in a yellow minidress that had a circular hole cut out of the front. Mother and daughter were so firmly locked in different eras that it seemed hardly possible they could co-exist. Lately he saw the same disjunctions wherever he looked: Victorian workhouses next to glass tower blocks, E-type Jaguars passing horse-drawn rag-and-bone carts, mods standing beside pensioners. Transitional times.

Hatton-Jones was still droning on about how awful today's young people were. Bryant could hear children laughing. There was a school playground nearby. What would the next

London be like for them? The city transformed itself like an actor changing costumes in a play, now a hero, now a fool, now a tyrant.

He turned his attention back to May. His partner looked as if he was about to attack Monty. His hot-headedness had increased of late. John was three years younger. He couldn't yet see how everything fitted together. His wild energies needed to be directed into his work, not his weekends.

'Let's concentrate on the matter at hand, shall we?' Bryant suggested. 'I think perhaps we should be on first-name terms, seeing as we're going to be spending so much time together.'

'Fab,' said May, eyeing their charge venomously. 'We can all be chums.'

Hatton-Jones sent him the kind of look that might cross the face of a vet waiting for a dog to die. 'I don't know you,' he said finally. 'You're policemen. My family never socialized with anyone in public service. I suppose in our brave new world we're all required to be comrades.'

'I thought you were in trade,' said May, refusing to concede the point.

'I'm a company director,' Hatton-Jones elucidated. 'If I were in the army, that would make me a general. One of your colleagues, a chap called Farthingshaw, told me I needed to be accompanied until my court appearance.' He waggled an index finger between them. 'That is the only reason why you and I are speaking.'

Sweet Suzy arrived with a tray. 'Two cappuccinos. That'll be one and fourpence.'

'I only want to drink the coffee, not buy the cup as well,' said Bryant, digging out change.

'I say, she's a delicious little dolly bird,' murmured Hatton-Jones, watching Sweet Suzy's bottom as it undulated away. For one horrifying moment Bryant thought he was going to lick his lips. A weekend in Monty's company was suddenly starting to feel as though it might be a very long time indeed.

'You don't seem too worried about your situation,' said May, echoing his partner's thoughts.

'Of course I'm bloody worried, that's why I asked you to meet me all the way out here in bedsit land,' Monty steamed. 'Chamberlain knows some very unsavoury characters. They could well be looking out for me in London.'

'I understand you're staying at the National Liberal Club, is that right?' May asked.

'Well, under normal circumstances that would be the case.' Hatton-Jones twisted a tiny sliver of lemon into the remains of his black coffee. 'However, I've been invited to spend the weekend with a business acquaintance, so I'll be travelling down to Kent tonight and staying until Sunday night. It's invitation-only.'

'I'm afraid you can't do that,' said May.

'I've already accepted.'

'We have to be with you at all times.'

'I do understand the concept of accompanying a witness,' said Hatton-Jones. 'I discussed it with the prosecutor. Clearly we'll have to come to some arrangement.'

May stood his ground. 'There's no arrangement to come to. It's absolutely out of the question. You'll have to cancel.'

Hatton-Jones flicked his lemon peel on to the pavement. 'I shan't be doing that. No one needs to know, old chap. I'll be back in plenty of time.'

'You really think that a highly respected architect and knight of the realm would come after you like a common thug?' May asked.

Hatton-Jones looked him over. 'How old are you? What do you think happens when men who stand to make millions of pounds see it all going down the drain? You think they reach gentlemen's agreements over cups of tea? The war put an end to all that. You chaps can take the weekend off. I got through a war; I can manage this. You'll only be a hindrance. Go on, bugger off and I'll come to collect you first thing Monday morning.'

'We're responsible for your safekeeping,' May pointed out. 'If you wish to leave our sight you have to sign a form.'

'Very well then, give me the form and I'll sign it.'

'I don't think you quite understand,' said Bryant. 'The waiver allows you to go to the lavatory, not hare off to Kent.'

Hatton-Jones's features were suffused with an alarming rush of blood. 'Look here, you little oik, I'm booked on the five thirty from London Bridge so we'll obviously have to work something out.'

'Absolutely not,' said May, catching his partner's eye. 'You're staying here with us.'

Hatton-Jones pushed his crimson face so far forward that May could count the broken veins in his nose. 'I think you've got yourself a little confused about which of us is the criminal. I'm going into the witness box because someone has to stop Charlie from destroying the already shaky reputation of our industry. You heard what happened at Ronan Point, I presume?'

'That wasn't his building.'

'It could easily have been. I expect some support from the police, otherwise I'll have to reconsider my offer to appear for the prosecution. Now, listen to me carefully. I'm staying with Lady Banks-Marion and her son Harry, Lord Banks-Marion, at Tavistock Hall. They're having a weekend party. It's the last weekend party they're ever likely to hold. The hall was once one of the nation's grandest country houses, and I have important business to conduct with someone there, so I'm afraid you'll just have to come with me.'

'How did you wangle an invite?' asked Bryant.

'I didn't need to *wangle* one, as you put it. An invitation was naturally forthcoming. I suppose I could ask for it to be extended to you two. Our fathers were friends.'

'My father was friends with all sorts and never got invited anywhere.'

'I don't suppose they throw weekend bashes in Wapping. Dinner will be a formal affair. You'll need to pop home and have someone pack your wardrobe, assuming either of you owns such a thing as a decent jacket.' He smirked fiercely at each of them in turn.

May pushed back. 'You're telling me that you're prepared to conduct your business affairs with a pair of common police officers in tow? That would put a bit of a crimp in your style, wouldn't it?'

Hatton-Jones rolled his eyes. 'Obviously you wouldn't be able to announce your professions. You'll have to be incognito.'

'How are you going to introduce us?'

'I'll say we were in the army together or you were employees or something. Anyway, no one will be interested in you. There are always a couple of invisible guests invited as ballast at these weekends.'

'He's insufferable,' May said while Hatton-Jones was away from the table. 'We can't let him do this. We have to insist that he stays in town.'

'And risk having him pull out before the trial? He could collapse the entire case, and he knows it.' Bryant looked around to ensure they weren't overheard. 'I'm afraid I was sort of warned about this.'

'What do you mean, *sort of* warned?'

'I forgot to tell you. Roger Trapp said if he absolutely insisted on going to Kent we should go with him. He knows someone there who can help us.'

'What are you talking about?'

'The groundskeeper at Tavistock Hall is a chap called Brigadier Nigel Metcalf, "Fruity" to his friends. He happens to be an old army pal of Trapp's who owes him a favour. Trapp says he'd trust him with his life. Metcalf was a career soldier, but was badly injured at Arnhem during Operation Market Garden. Lost an arm and a leg. After the war he couldn't get a job as anything but a liftman, so when he was offered a position looking after the hall he jumped at the chance. Now he's got his own accommodation in the gatehouse and is taking care of the grounds.'

'How do you know all this?'

'It was in the notes you were supposed to read. I imagine the war taught him to stay invisible and keep to himself, so he'll be a good observer. He can help us keep an eye on our witness.'

Hatton-Jones was back. From the irritated look on his face, Bryant surmised that he had tried chatting up Sweet Suzy and had been rebuffed.

'We'd better get a move on if you're coming with me,' he snapped. 'Let me do the talking when we get there. It's bad enough me having to pretend that I actually know you. You'd better invent new names for yourselves just in case anyone asks. Keep it simple and don't do anything that will draw attention.'

'Like what?' asked May.

The director eyed May's fashionable get-up with distaste. 'Try not to speak, mind your manners and find something less vulgar to wear,' he suggested with a weary sigh. 'I look at you two and wonder, what was the point of beating the Germans?'

8

MAGICAL MYSTERY TOUR

It was a question that many had asked themselves.

After the war, austerity had dragged on for another decade. In railway stations it was impossible to buy a cup of tea without queuing. Stores were more shut than open. Shelves remained empty, meals stayed small and fruit came in tins. Coal was rationed. Sweaters and socks were darned. Even hotel sheets were patched. Across the capital, the cheapest option was exercised without consideration. Cracked church steeples were demolished instead of being repaired, bombsites were boarded up instead of being built upon and prefabs sprouted like mushrooms where proud family homes had once stood. Stone and mahogany were replaced with asbestos and plywood. Stop-gap measures became so permanent that soon no one could remember how life had been before.

The war's warriors had died to make way for an army of lovers; nearly half of all Londoners were now under twenty-five, and an aura of unwarranted confidence lit up the capital. For kids with credit, contraception and cool, the city was suddenly sexy. And those who had fought were forced to confront the first generation of people who did not need to know the meaning of obligation.

Arthur Bryant could see that although London had exploded like a brilliant rocket across a winter sky, the flare path was now fading. The liberated women and feminized men who constituted that tribe known as the Beautiful People pointed out that ravaged battlefields were filling with wild flowers, but the idea proved a little disingenuous.

Still, optimism lingered; opportunities still existed for anyone with talent and determination. To John May the sixties meant a fresh start, money in the bank and promotion to a fully independent police unit. He was able to move his parents into a new flat in the relatively cheap student neighbourhood of Belsize Park. It was a time when he fell in and out of love, and took his first holiday in Spain. Suddenly there was money to spend and life was good.

His partner remained less impressed. Bryant watched the streets fill with happier people in brighter clothes, driving smart new British cars bought on instalment plans, but the streets themselves were still black with soot and gap-toothed from bombing. He had never possessed the right kind of mind or physical shape to be fashionable. His wispy hair had mostly vanished in his mid-twenties and his neck had thickened so that he was starting to look prematurely middle-aged. As a consequence he remained imperceptible to the long-legged girls who made John May stop and gape.

While everyone else became enraptured with new music, art and fashion, Bryant remained convinced that the city's primary-coloured vibrancy would evaporate almost as soon as it had begun, and, as always, it was because he had done a little more homework than anyone else. He could see that the nation's balance of payments was already causing concern. Britain was still shut out of the Common Market. *It won't make any difference that we won the World Cup or that our pop singers invaded America*, he thought gloomily. The seeds of Swinging London's collapse had been borne on the winds of its arrival.

'Just a load of barrow-boys with pudding-basin fringes and wide-collar shirts, and a few rich nobs cashing in,' Bryant had sniffed, and perhaps he'd had a point. As May adjusted his paisley-print kipper tie and squirted himself with Aqua Manda, ready for another night out in Soho, he'd decided that his partner probably had reason to be downbeat. But what was the point of being young and in London if you weren't going to enjoy it?

Now, as he quickly folded a purple nylon dinner shirt into a suitcase, he wondered how much of a liability Arthur would prove over the coming weekend.

They had never gone undercover before. The witness didn't seem to think he was at risk in the countryside, so perhaps it was wrong to worry. Hatton-Jones would be at ease among those of his own class. Arthur was another matter; he tended to become obstreperous when surrounded by ladies and gentlemen of the upper echelons. May remembered their assignment to provide security at Lord Beaverbrook's charity ball. After an argument about hereditary peers Bryant had accidentally knocked an earl into a fishpond. His unrepentant response ('They were both only ornamental') did nothing to placate their host.

The detectives met up again at London Bridge Station. It was rush hour, and the place was unbearably crowded. Bryant had a porter with him, pushing a huge cabin trunk on a trolley.

'Good Lord, Arthur,' May exclaimed, 'how much stuff are you taking with you?'

'I don't have any actual weekend clothes,' Bryant explained, 'so I asked the amateur theatre group next door if I could borrow something. They're running a Noël Coward season at the moment, so I was able to cadge some togs from *Cavalcade*. There's a thing called a shooting jacket and a sort of horse-riding hat, along with some plus fours, spats, tails and a top hat from the 1935 London Gang Show. I haven't actually looked to see what else is in there. I suppose you already own the right gear, what with your habit of going out.'

'Look, there's Hatton-Jones,' said May, pointing through the crowds. 'Come on.'

'I haven't been on an electric train yet.' Bryant beckoned to the elderly porter, who tried to keep up. 'I suppose they'll be cleaning this place now.'

He pointed up to the darkened station roof, its glass canopy still stained sepia from coal dust. The last steam train had made its final run, but the acrid smell of burning coal still hung in the air. It lurked in blackened corners, walkways and corridors, as if it had been absorbed into the bricks and tiles.

Hatton-Jones flicked away his cigarette end. 'Look out, here come Sooty and Sweep again. I thought you weren't going to make it. I hope you bought first-class tickets.'

'No, third, I'm afraid,' said Bryant, secretly delighted to see his face fall.

'On the way you can fill us in about Sir Charles Chamberlain,' said May, 'starting with why you're turning him in.'

They boarded and made their way along a corridor, finding some empty seats in a compartment acrid with stale smoke. Bryant insisted on giving Hatton-Jones a hand with his luggage. He didn't trust their charge, and took the opportunity of checking out Monty's case, which was peculiarly heavy.

'Let me explain something to you,' said Monty. He checked that the seat was clean before seating himself opposite Bryant and May. 'I'm fifty-two years old. My parents were Victorians. I was born in one world war and survived another. When you wonder why I find you both so annoying, try to bear that in mind. Ask me what you will.'

'How did you . . .' Bryant began.

'. . . meet Sir Charles Chamberlain?' May completed their question.

'We met at St Paul's.' Hatton-Jones watched the platform passing as the train pulled out.

'What, the cathedral?' asked Bryant.

'The school. We both went to Brasenose and followed our fathers into the Foreign Office. Charlie and I were due to inherit our families' respective estates, as generations had before us.'

'What went wrong?'

'We were hit by the cost of the war and rising death duties. Taxes became crippling, just as they had been after the Great War. Charlie's grand family home had been designed by Robert Adam, but it was demolished.'

'Why?' asked May.

'It would have cost too much to repair, and his family was stony broke. It was one of the reasons why Charlie decided to train as an architect. Our family home was sold to a foreigner.' He virtually spat the word. 'Britain's great country houses are being knocked down at a rate of one a week, and this has been going on for the last fifteen years! The damned Labour government was determined to dismantle England's upper echelon.'

'So what did you do?' asked May.

'What *could* I do?' Hatton-Jones sucked his moustache, remembering. 'I went into business, invested in new technologies. Charlie completed his training and spent the next decade helping to rebuild Berlin. Not directly, of course – it was hard to get tenders without being part of the market there – but the post-war years were good to him. He told me that the future of building lay not in bricks but in concrete, and when he returned I agreed to supply him with materials.'

'So at this point you were obviously still friends,' said Bryant.

'I saw him in the season, of course, but yes, I suppose you could say we still had much in common.' As the train clattered over the points, he allowed his Brylcreemed head to loll back against the seat. 'Clubs, sporting events – and our wives were cousins.'

'You say they *were* cousins.'

'I'm divorced now. Charlie's wife died in Germany. Three years ago we built the Harrington Centre for Applied Sciences in—'

'—Coventry, yes, I know about it,' said May. 'The auditorium collapsed. Something about it having been built over a wartime bomb?'

'That story was invented by Charlie's public relations officer.'

'So what happened?'

Hatton-Jones looked out at the passing bomb-sites, factories, back gardens. 'I don't know for sure. Charlie had a friend on the council. To get the budget signed off, they needed to start work within days of approving the contract. The land survey hadn't been completed but they decided to go ahead anyway. Charlie has a signature design he uses in all his buildings, a simplified cross-beam pattern that replaces interior structures. The external walls are pre-stressed and have these steel rods running through them so they can't crack. You'll find the same design in every one of his projects; it's cheaper than putting up more internal walls. It's innovative, but it's also experimental. There was a new building in East London that had previously suffered bomb damage, so it was torn down and replaced with the design developed in Charlie's practice. I think that's what caused the collapse.'

'Wait, you're not talking about Ronan Point now,' said May. 'This was a separate case that barely made the headlines. A block of maisonettes in Hackney subsided, killing two little girls and their parents. So you decided to turn him in.'

'The Ronan Point designers will probably escape jail,' said Hatton-Jones. 'The DPP doesn't want to see the same thing happen with Chamberlain.'

'Forgive me: your company is supplying his, so if he's found guilty won't you lose your client?'

'Any man of Charlie's stature who goes to trial is tainted for ever, regardless of the outcome.' Hatton-Jones searched his pockets for his cigarette case. 'Charlie is already being closed out. There are many who will have nothing more to do with him. Some of us still follow a code of conduct.'

'So you decided to speak out because he broke the rules.'

'On Monday morning I have to announce to the court that my oldest colleague has been corrupted.' He lit a Pall Mall and blew smoke above him. 'Do you have any idea how painful that will be for me?'

'Then why do it?' asked May. 'Why sell one of your own down the river? I can't believe it's out of moral obligation.'

'I'm glad you decided to do the right thing, Monty,' said Bryant solicitously.

Hatton-Jones nailed him with a cold stare. 'I did not agree to first-name terms.'

'When you speak to the court, you'll have the thanks of the entire police force. And they'll be listening intently to your witness statement for any discrepancies.' May patted him on the knee. 'Monty.'

The train was heading for Canterbury, so they had to transfer to a branch line. 'Why did you let him off like that?' May asked Bryant angrily as they disembarked. 'You always kow-tow to toffs but you don't have to, you know. Monty and Sir Charles grew up together and intermarried, and suddenly Monty decides to ignore the old school tie and sacrifice his pal? That makes him a rat in my book.'

'You're younger than me, your blood runs hotter,' Bryant replied, looking about for a porter's trolley. 'We're stuck with him for the whole weekend. Why reveal your hand now? Let's wait and see what happens.'

'Why, do you really think something's going to happen? Won't we just be sitting around all weekend reading newspapers and waiting for the rain to stop?'

Bryant had a secretive look about him that his partner had

lately come to recognize. 'Haven't you noticed? Monty keeps disappearing to make phone calls. And what's in his weekend case? It weighs a ton. I keep asking him who he's meeting and he won't tell me. This little trip isn't what it seems. He's up to something.'

Another concern was occupying Bryant. His mother was about to move to a newly constructed maisonette only streets away from the home that had collapsed. If she was at risk, he needed all the information he could gather.

The porters came forward to collect their valises and Hatton-Jones led the way between the platforms. While they waited for their connection, May jiggled the change in his pockets and paced about. He had a skittery energy that could barely be contained. Bryant needed to find a way of slowing him down so that he would think more dispassionately. 'Have you decided yet who you're going to be?' he asked.

'I thought I'd improvise,' May replied. 'I went to the Establishment Club the other night and saw some comedians doing it. What about you?'

'I've got the whole thing worked out to the finest detail,' said Bryant. 'Seeing as I'd borrowed the clothes I was going to be a Noël Coward character, but I can't do the funny voice. "Very flat, Norfolk." See? I'm from the East End. I'm bound to end up sticking in a swear word.'

'You heard what Monty said. They won't even notice us if we stay in the background.'

Bryant checked the information board for their onward connection. 'Fine by me,' he said. 'I'm getting paid for a weekend of – what, exactly? I'm bound to end up having dinner next to some old bird who looks like a cross between Miss Havisham and a haunted boat. God, I'm not going to have to ride a horse, am I? I'm terrified of them. When I was ten I was thrown off our milkman's carthorse, then it trod on me. I was never happier than the day it was shot.'

'Why did your milkman have it shot? Was it ill?'

'No, he'd been offered a van.'

'Perhaps not riding then,' said May. 'Billiards.'

'That's just posh snooker.'

'Bridge.'

'Snap.'

'Clay pigeon shooting.'

'Funfair ducks.'

'Piano recitals.'

'Pub songs.'

'Er—'

'Hesitation.'

'Bollocks.'

'A tanner.' Bryant held out his hand while May reluctantly dug into his pocket once more.

9

HOUSE OF THE RISING SUN

Lieutenant Coultas was looking confused again. His spectacles had misted over, his face fell slack and his grey eyes lost focus. If he'd scratched his head with the tips of his fingers he would have looked like Stan Laurel. It usually meant that he had committed the kind of error made huge and insoluble by its simplicity.

Captain Debney could tell he was about to be made party to the error, and in his book a problem shared was two people in trouble. He touched his trimmed moustache, watching impatiently as Coultas attempted to unfold an immense wax-paper Ordnance Survey map on the table without tearing it to bits.

Outside the tent over a hundred men were awaiting orders, ready for the start of Operation Britannia, although as it looked to be a nice evening they were happily smoking, lounging about on the grass and telling each other filthy jokes.

'I can see where the problem has arisen, sir,' the lieutenant began. 'The sergeant and I thought that we were taking our co-ordinates from the main road that passes around the edge of Mulberry Wood, whereas in fact we should have been taking it from the village green at Knotsworth.'

Captain Debney massaged the bridge of his nose. 'Just tell me how far out we are,' he said, wishing that, like the map, he was somewhere he wasn't supposed to be.

'Four and a half miles, sir.' Lieutenant Coultas thought that if he gave a brisk, confident answer it would somehow lessen the mistake.

'Four and a half *miles*?'

'Yes, sir.'

Debney looked down at the map, which had a continuous red line drawn through fields and forests, forming a cross-hatched patch of empty land that had been specially selected for the coming weekend of manoeuvres. 'So what I'm looking at is wrong.'

'Totally, sir.'

'And where should it be?'

'Here.' Lieutenant Coultas produced his marker and drew a new line on the map that ran across several roads, two villages and through the middle of a pub.

'So we now have to tell everyone inside this new demarcation zone that if they so much as stick their heads out of a window they could get their ears blown off.'

'Not quite that but they shouldn't use the roads, sir, because our tanks have to cross them. They don't exactly turn on a sixpence and the lads can't see what's coming because the lanes are below the hedgerows.'

'So we could flatten a busload of orphans.'

'Not sure there's an orphanage in the area, sir.'

'I meant theoretically.'

'We could cancel the exercise, sir.'

Captain Debney turned to give his lieutenant the full benefit of his withering stare. 'And how can we do that with six armoured vehicles, a minesweeping squad, a signals corps, two platoons carrying live ammunition and a French major general taking notes? This exercise is supposed to be hush-hush. And now you tell me it'll be passing through civilian areas.'

Debney's idea of hush-hush was perhaps optimistic, but in the days before the country was strangled by health and safety regulations its armies were far more cavalier about military manoeuvres. With the war still in living memory, nobody took much notice of explosions emanating from any of the unmarked firing ranges that dotted the English countryside.

'See your point, sir.' Lieutenant Coultas studied the map furiously. 'There are only two villages affected, Knotsworth and Crowshott, and they're linked by a single narrow lane, so I don't suppose there'll be much traffic. Anyway, it's too late to apply for closure.' He checked his watch. 'It's Friday afternoon. The council officials will have all gone home by now. We could post signs warning vehicles to proceed at their own caution and be on their guard.'

'So they'll be creeping along nice and slowly when a Chieftain tank suddenly lands on them,' said Debney. 'Put barriers up. If anyone needs to get through they'll have to call us.'

'We'll be on the move, sir, so there's not much likelihood of anyone being able to get through on the field line.'

'Even better. They can phone the local constabulary, which is – where?'

'There's PC Wermold in Crowshott but he has trouble walking, and another one who lives in Dimmington, nine miles away, but after that the nearest proper station would be Canterbury.'

'And what's this?' The captain stabbed a forefinger at a shaded grey rectangle on the map.

'Tavistock Hall, sir,' Lieutenant Coultas replied. 'Country pile. The local authority used to billet schoolchildren there during the war. I read that it's being sold to some wealthy businessman. He hasn't taken possession yet.'

'So there's no one there to alert about the exercise?'

'No, sir, been empty for several weeks by the sergeant's

reckoning. We have seen some activity beyond the house but it looks like a hippy encampment.'

'Sounds like a legitimate target. Perhaps we should send the chopper over just to make sure.'

'Can't do that, sir, it's been requisitioned for use by Major General Giraud.'

'Very well.' The captain continued smoothing down his moustache, which had a tendency to bristle around Lieutenant Coultas. 'Give the lads the evening off but don't let them go into the village. I don't want them turning up in front of Giraud with black eyes.'

Lieutenant Coultas thought about trying to refold the map but decided to beat a hasty retreat. He hadn't had time to double-check that Tavistock Hall was empty, but if anybody was still there it would probably only be the mad old hippy who had sold it, and a few exploding shells might wake his ideas up.

Their ancient taxi still had running boards and had been pensioned off from London. It took them from a by-pass to a B-road and then to the narrow high-hedged lane that linked Knotsworth with Crowshott. As the detectives passed through the first village they saw soldiers climbing from the back of a lorry, their arms filled with striped poles.

'Are they closing the road?' asked Bryant, looking back.

'Probably just helping out with some repairs,' said May.

'On a Friday evening? Seems a bit unlikely.'

The squaddies were setting up trestles on which to fit the poles. One of them was carrying a sign that read 'Halt!'. Bryant was suspicious. 'I don't like the look of that. I hope we can get out again.' He looked over at Monty but found him still asleep.

Their route extended beyond the second village, and then passed beneath a dense canopy of trees. The lane narrowed and eventually petered out. It became an uneven track and finally a dead end, beyond which the high brick wall of the estate could be seen. They stopped before a pair of black iron gates that had to be pushed apart.

'I'm not goin' any further,' said the driver firmly.

'My dear fellow, this is not a Dracula film,' said Bryant. 'It's Kent, not Transylvania.' He glanced at his trunk, which had been lashed to the running board.

'All right, but it'll be another five bob.' He got out to open the gates.

Their first glimpse of the hall was strobed through the regularly spaced cypress trees that palisaded the gravelled drive. An immense cream-coloured Palladian pile with Venetian pillars, steep mansard roofs, uncountable chimney stacks and an impossible number of windows stood at the top of a gentle slope, above a semi-circle of lawn. Bryant noted that the grass had only been trimmed near the house; the owners were saving money on gardeners.

The taxi drew up between a dribbling fountain and a set of sweeping limestone steps. This first impression was calculated to inspire awe, but on closer inspection many of the marble façades were cracked and uncared-for, and weeds were pushing their way through the damaged steps.

A servant, sallow, melancholy, prehistoric, descended and removed their valises from the taxi. He and the driver had trouble releasing Bryant's great trunk.

'Who am I again?' Bryant asked, balking at the foot of the steps.

'I thought you said you'd come up with an identity,' May said from the side of his mouth.

'I did, but I've forgotten it.'

'Well, you'll have to think of a new one then.' He tilted his head back and squinted. 'What on earth is that thing on your upper lip?'

'I've just put it on, it's part of my disguise,' Bryant said, proudly stroking his black pencil moustache.

'It's ridiculous – you look like Terry-Thomas. Take it off before anyone else sees.'

'I can't. It's glued on with spirit-gum.'

'Well, make sure it doesn't fall into your soup.' May stepped back to admire the house. 'Will you look at this place? It can't be all one building, can it?'

Tavistock Hall had been designed to house artefacts lifted from the treasure temples of the ancient world and provide a grand home to their privileged pilferers, along with a profusion of aunts, uncles, nieces, nephews and, somewhere around the back in narrow-windowed gloom, servants, but it had clearly fallen upon hard times. Plasterwork was patched, bricks had crumbled out, tiles were missing and even a few high windows were broken.

Taken as a whole, though, and from a distance, it was still impressive. The south-facing frontage of soft grey brick and buttery plasterwork filled Bryant with wonder. His excited eye travelled to the elegantly proportioned windows that provided a grandstand view of the grounds. 'It must be early nineteenth century,' he said. 'I wonder who it was built for?'

'Look up there,' May exclaimed, pointing to the granite lions, unicorns and basilisks adorning the façade. 'What is that thing?'

A stone creature sat precariously close to the edge of the balustrade. It looked like a carved ostrich with scaly legs.

'A gryphon, I think,' said Bryant.

'I bet they have a maze.'

'Topiary.'

'A folly.'

'A lake.'

'A gazebo.'

'A pergola.'

'Swans.'

'Peacocks.'

'Er—'

'Hesitation.'

'Bollocks.'

'That's another tanner.'

May forked over sixpence, laboriously and reluctantly doled out in three pennies and a threepenny bit.

'A railway.'

'I'm not playing any more,' said May.

'No, look.' Bryant pointed to a narrow-gauge track that cut across the lawn.

'Ahem.' The detectives looked around. The skeletal servant coughed discreetly into his fist. 'I am Alberman, the butler,' he announced. 'If you'd care to follow me.' Alberman had dark, deep-set eyes, a thin bony nose and matching legs: a heron crossed with an Anglepoise lamp.

The detectives followed him into the house. The central steps led directly into the great hall, which was monochromatically tiled, symmetrical, balustraded and orchestrated to amaze new arrivals, even if the walls were blighted with patches of damp. To either side of this great chamber were the wings, and endless wide doors.

Alberman commanded them to wait with a wave of his hand. He did not take instruction but merely required the detectives to obey, having pegged them as inferiors. Monty had already wandered off. A country weekend had more arcane rules than a game of cricket, one being that the guests were graded into distinct categories: landowning gentry, esteemed regulars, respectable country folk, clergy, tenants and, at the very bottom of the social order, Londoners. These two giggling young twerps were not only from the Smoke but were clearly employed in some kind of public service. Neither of them was suitably dressed for the country. The taller one was wearing brown city shoes with wide blue trousers, and the short one looked as if he had stolen his wardrobe from Flanagan and Allen.

Alberman resolved to ensure that they were given the draughtiest rooms, the lumpiest beds and the longest walks to the dining room.

10

STAY AWHILE

In the black-and-white-tiled hall, on a baroquely carved table of gilt inset with a great slab of blood-coloured marble, all the accepted invitations for the weekend had been neatly arranged in rows so that there would be no embarrassment over forgotten names.

'You two are the only ones not down here,' Monty confided. 'It's frightfully un-PLU to turn up without a written reply to an invitation.'

'PLU?' whispered Bryant.

' "People Like Us",' said May. 'Don't you read the supplements?'

They were surrounded by the kind of sculptures that made their presence felt by the amount of room they took up, rather than impressing with any artistic merit. On every side paintings rose to the ceiling, conjuring the gloomy claustrophobia of a chapel. The air smelled of polish, candle wax and mildewed corners, much like any provincial church.

'I'll do the explaining,' said Monty. 'Try to blend in.' He diverted off to the reception room in search of alcohol.

Bryant, with the deference of an East End ragamuffin doffing his cap in a cathedral, duly trotted behind the butler and tried not to look like a trespassing peasant. He hated being reduced to the status of a tradesman so easily, but was powerless to avoid the pernicious grip of his upbringing.

May, on the other hand, was bouncing along, checking out the portraits and tapestries, running his hand over the banisters and stopping with mouth agape before the main hall's stained-glass windows, a melange of British myths that included King Arthur, Guinevere, Herne the Hunter with his bow drawn and, rather more oddly, the martyrdom of St Edmund, pinned to a tree with arrows. He was shamelessly fascinated by everything he saw, and kept nudging his partner.

'That looks like a real Gainsborough, and that's an early Joshua Reynolds,' Bryant whispered back, amazed. 'If I had a Stanley knife and a rubber band I could get one up my jumper.'

'Art cannot be evaluated by what it would fetch up Petticoat Lane,' May replied.

'I bet these are copies anyway,' said Bryant. 'The originals will be stashed away somewhere. The owners of this pile would never be able to afford the insurance.'

'What makes you say that?'

Bryant sniffed the air. 'It reeks of rising damp in here. Take a look around. There's dry rot in those skirting boards, the carpets are threadbare, the ceilings need replastering and I think you'll find these are mouse droppings.' He kicked at what looked like black grains of rice with the toe of his shoe.

'So why are the owners hosting a weekend?'

'Because they need something in return. That's how they work. You wait and see. Stay close, we mustn't lose Lurch.' Together they climbed the central staircase.

'Where is everybody?' May asked the butler. 'Is this what normally happens?'

'This way, sir,' said Alberman, ignoring his question.

'You're to have the Willow and Larch Rooms – they are adjoining suites.'

As they continued up, the staircase became darker and narrower. 'Hey, where are you sticking us?' May peered over the banisters at the floors above. 'We'll be in the attic in a minute.'

'I am sure you have many questions about the house.' Alberman led them along a slender corridor with creaking, tilted floorboards and set about opening the second-to-last bedroom door.

'How old is this place?' asked May.

'Tavistock Hall was completed in 1831 and is a three-storeyed mansion of six bays arranged around a central pediment,' Alberman recited in a condescending tone reserved for his standard speech to guests. 'The design is Neo-Classical Palladian with Gothic Revival additions and some unfortunate Victorian amendments. The grounds were based around designs first created by Capability Brown for Heveningham Hall in Suffolk, and the great fireplace in the drawing room is from the school of Robert Adam. The wainscoting was later embellished with foliate motifs inspired by the Renaissance revival, and the abstract ornamentation is characteristic of the Aesthetic Movement. Further information concerning the architecture and decoration may be obtained in the library.' He pronounced this last word with four syllables and a rolled R, *li-ber-rar-y*. 'The other guests have already arrived. Your bags will be brought up imminently. Cocktails are at seven thirty and dinner is served at eight o'clock sharp. Please respect the hot water.'

Without bothering to make any eye contact with them he turned and walked away.

'Creepy butler, that's a good start,' said Bryant, stepping into his room. 'There should be a suit of armour holding an axe somewhere. Blimey, it's freezing in here.' He rubbed his hands together briskly. 'I bet it's just the same in summer.'

'Thick walls,' May replied, following him in. 'Let me have a nose at yours first, see who's got the best one. No four-poster? Horrible bedspread. Fancy toiletries – lav but no bathroom.'

'It's probably at the end of the hallway, along with the respectable hot water.'

'My grandmother used to have a bed like this.' May tried to bounce on it but the mattress did not give. 'Feels like it's stuffed with horsehair, or possibly a horse. If Queen Elizabeth slept here she wouldn't have got much kip. You wouldn't shag anyone on this in case they put their back out.'

'Do you have to be quite so vulgar?' Bryant complained.

'Oh please,' said May, 'why do working-class people always get so prissy around the upper crust? Haven't you heard? We're going to be classless soon. Look at this place.'

'You're right,' said Bryant, 'it's only the wallpaper that's holding it up. The old school tie doesn't work any more.'

'What do you mean?'

'Well, if all these old houses are collapsing you'd think the lords would muck in together and save them. Yet look at Monty, selling out his pal for the public good.'

'Except you don't believe Monty any more than I do. There's something odd about this entire set-up.'

Bryant was thinking ahead. 'I should make contact with Fruity Metcalf and call Gladys at the unit as soon as possible. We need more background information.' He looked up at the stained, bowed ceiling. 'Come on, let's have a gander at your room.'

They scooted around to Willow and compared it to Larch. 'Great view,' said May, 'misty meadows and the call of the curlew.'

Bryant intoned:

> 'The curfew tolls the knell of parting day,
> The lowing herd wind slowly o'er the lea . . .'

'I'm not playing the game any more, I can't do poems,' said May. 'Besides, you've had all my change.'

'Fair enough. I don't like Thomas Gray much anyway. Too drippy.'

May pulled off his jacket and tossed it on the bed. 'Who do you think Monty's meeting? Hey, maybe we'll get to go cow shooting or grouse riding or something.'

'You do realize that this is my idea of hell, don't you?' Bryant ran a thumb along the dust on the windowsill. 'There are trees all over the place and you can't even see another house. There's nothing but scenery. A weekend filled with stiff upper lips, out-dated theatrical games and slaughtering anything that moves.'

'We are supposed to be working. Anyway, look upon it as an education. I imagine the grandest place you've ever been in before this is Waterloo Station.'

'Actually, my granddad was in the Royal Naval Hospital at Greenwich and we went to visit him,' Bryant replied, check-ing the cupboards for anything interesting. 'That was pretty grand.'

'What did he have, scurvy?'

'No, he caught something insanitary off a belly dancer in Port Said. Where are the owners of this gaff?'

'I think we're about to find out in approximately' – May checked his watch – 'twenty minutes.'

Manifesting himself in the open doorway, the antediluvian valet deposited their bags with a thump, and for a moment looked as if he might fall down with them. He had removed his topcoat to reveal a shabby green frock-jacket and a striped knitted scarf. It looked as if he had been softened over many years with a ball-peen hammer, as one might tenderize a steak, until there were no firm lines left about him at all. 'Begging your pardon, sir, I'll be on this floor tonight if you need anything. My duty cubicle is at the end of the corridor. If it looks like I'm asleep, just give me a tap. I'm Parchment.'

'Of course you are,' said May, making a show of digging

into his pocket for change, but Mr Parchment had turned away before he could be tipped. 'Wow, he's got to be like a hundred and eleven years old.' He watched the bent-backed skivvy hobble off into the gloom. 'If this was the 1920s I'd have had a servant.'

'If this was the 1920s I'd have been one,' Bryant replied. 'I think you're supposed to leave a tip in the room when you leave on Sunday. I read something about it in *Country Life*.'

'I'm not sure he's going to make it through until then. Do you think his name's really Parchment?'

'It's traditional for the master to give his servants new names in country houses. It aids memory and indicates ownership.' Bryant halted for a minute and looked about. 'Does this whole thing feel like some kind of weird practical joke to you? I keep expecting to see Christopher Lee outside the window. Are we being set up? Where's Monty disappeared to?'

'You have a very suspicious mind, Arthur.'

'Of course I have, I'm a copper. I see a cute child playing with a ball and wonder if he's stolen it. We'd better find our witness. Come on, let's get togged up.'

Bryant returned to his room to unpack. He was alarmed to find the contents of his trunk rather more haphazard than he had hoped for. The one pair of black trousers he could find clearly belonged to a circus clown, and his evening shirt only had a front. There was a selection of bow ties, one of which rotated. The toecaps of his shoes were clean, but the backs were filthy. That didn't matter so much; it was more important to look normal going into a room than leaving it. Changing, he improvised as best as he could, then slicked down the remains of his hair and checked himself in the mirror above his handbasin. 'Not exactly Cliff Richard,' he told his reflection, 'but it'll have to do.'

A few minutes later, May knocked on Larch.

Bryant opened the door and took a step back. 'My word, you scrub up well. I would never have recognized you.'

May was wearing a double-breasted evening jacket with black silk lapels and a black bow tie, his hair thickened and combed with a fringe. 'One has to make an effort,' he said. 'I see you didn't.'

Bryant's clothes looked as if they had been tossed on to him from a distance. Nothing fitted properly. His pinstriped blazer and grey Oxford bags had possibly last seen duty in a touring production of *Hay Fever*, or at the Windmill Theatre, where he might have passed as a low comic between nude tableaux. A pair of wide, striped braces had pulled his trousers halfway up his chest, and a partially unravelled polka-dotted bow tie had become marooned around the side of his neck.

'I can't get this blooming thing to stay done up.'

'Come here.' May tackled the bow. '*Right over left, left over right, fold it back and pull it tight.* There. My dad was in an orchestra. I used to have to tie his bow tie for him every night. Let's go downstairs and see what we're up against.'

They started to walk. May raised his hand and stopped Bryant. 'What is that?'

'What's what?'

'That clicking noise.'

'I don't hear anything.' Bryant continued on.

Takata-takata-takata.

May halted him and looked down. 'It sounds like you're wearing tap shoes.'

Bryant stopped and raised one foot. 'I am,' he said apologetically.

'They're not going to be much good if we need to creep about this place in silence. We're undercover, remember?'

'Sorry, they came from the actors' wardrobe bag.'

'Tap shoes on a stakeout,' said May. 'Incredible.' He headed towards the stairs. 'From now on we can't afford to let Monty out of our sight.'

II

HAPPY TOGETHER

DS Gladys Forthright had managed to locate Tavistock Hall in one of Bryant's old map books.

Beneath the etching of the grand mansion and its hunting grounds was a dense history cataloguing family scandals and misfortunes, but the narrative ended in 1902 when the book had been published, so she called the Daily Telegraph Information Service. They rang her back with their latest data, and she telexed East Canterbury Police Station with a request for confirmation.

The news she received was not what she had been expecting: army manoeuvres were about to close the roads and isolate the area for much of the weekend. Apparently there had been a bit of a cock-up at headquarters.

Gladys wasn't sure why she was so suspicious, but she decided not to keep Roger Trapp in the picture. It was better he didn't discover that in their final job for the unit his detectives were possibly about to walk into some kind of ambush.

'Why the hell haven't they called in?' Trapp stalked to the window, held his elbow behind his back and peered down into Bow Street. 'Somewhere in this teeming metropolis my detectives have waltzed off with the only man who can put Sir Charles Chamberlain behind bars. This is Kasavian's doing. He's got it in for me. I've never trusted him. What kind of a name is Horatio anyway? He's struck a deal with them just to try and wind me up.'

It seems like he's succeeded, thought Gladys Forthright as she watched her boss through hooded, knowing eyes. She had outlived four unit heads in as many years, and this one was neither use nor ornament. The former bookkeeper had been placed in charge because he could produce what was called for in the department so long as it was put to him in basic English and very slowly. Unfortunately he didn't understand the first thing about his detectives.

'If there's a problem, I'm sure they'll find a phone box,' she said, threading a new carbon into her Remington typewriter. 'John warned me that Mr Hatton-Jones wouldn't be dissuaded from his weekend plans. They can't simply tie him up. They'll have to stay close by and use this friend of yours—'

'Fruity's a damned good chap considering he has only half the requisite number of limbs,' said Trapp. 'As honest as the day is long and utterly trustworthy. He'll report everything back to me. I have to wonder, does this fellow Hatton-Jones really need protection?' Roger scratched at his dry scalp, producing another unseasonal snowfall. 'Chamberlain may have played fast and loose with the rules but he's hardly going to have his old pal done in, is he? He's a knight of the realm, for heaven's sake! The pair of them went to Oxford together. It's a waste of manpower, having both of our men acting as chaperones. He's a CPS witness, not some Soho spiv.'

'Mr Kasavian told me that Hatton-Jones planned this weekend over a month ago,' said Forthright, aligning her paper in the typewriter. 'He wants John and Arthur to get more information out of him. They're hoping to spread the net wider and find out who else accepted bribes from Chamberlain.'

'So they've assumed his guilt before a trial? That's nice, isn't it? And they've taken my only two coppers to do it. Do something useful, darling, and fetch me some tea, would you? I might as well have a cuppa before I head off.'

'I thought we'd be staying at the unit this weekend, so that if they called we could help them out,' said Gladys.

To Trapp, this idea was genuinely amazing. If banks and pubs could close at three he could certainly knock off at six. 'Do you honestly think I've nothing better to do than wait around here? You're not to stay here either, do you understand? Nobody in this unit is going to help them.'

Gladys set aside her report with a sigh and went to the kettle. While she waited for it to boil she reapplied fierce scarlet lipstick. She had no telephone at home, so she would have to spend the next forty-eight hours at Bow Street without letting Trapp know. Luckily her ex-husband had agreed to take little Janice for the weekend. *You're going to owe me one for this, boys,* she thought, pouring Trapp's tea.

The dinner gong made Bryant jump.

He stood beside May on the landing of the central staircase, looking down at the acre of tiling in the hall. There were now several pairs of crusted galoshes by the front door. 'I haven't got any wellingtons – have you? I didn't think it would be muddy.'

'We'll have to borrow some.'

'I brought this with me.' Bryant pulled a booklet from his back pocket. '*The Pocket Guide to Country House Etiquette.* It's bloody complicated. Before the First World War there were at least four servants for every member of the household. Get this: head butler, under-butler, valet, housekeeper, ladies' maid, kitchen maids, still-room maids, between maids, footmen, scullery and laundry maids, odd men, hall boy, gardener, gamekeeper, groom and cook. That's not counting all the villagers who came to help out. Were the people who lived here paralysed or something? Did they have to be carried about in palanquins and spoon-fed?'

May looked up at the stained-glass windows and the dazzling colours they cast. 'The upkeep must have been incredible. No wonder the habit died out. What does it say about weekend parties?'

'You're supposed to call them "Saturdays-to-Mondays". You arrive either at five p.m. on Friday or on Saturday lunchtime, never in between. If you do turn up at another time you have to take a cold tray for dinner.' Bryant read from the booklet as he trailed May down the stairs. 'The host comes out into the front hall to shake hands with everyone. You're asked if you would like to "freshen up", meaning make yourself presentable, then you go to the library to be introduced to the other guests. None of that has happened to us. All the rooms have names, which you're expected to memorize.'

'There's a guide to them in your room,' replied May. 'In this house they're all flowers on the ground floor, trees upstairs.'

'Apparently some guests change into lounge jackets after dinner. That's two changes of clothing in one evening.' Bryant looked down at his trousers. 'My theatre trunk seems to contain costumes for *Miss Hook of Holland* and *Chu Chin Chow*. There's a magician's suit, but I dread to think what's in the pockets.'

'The room guide says you have to tip the people who bring you trays and make your bed, and inform the butler if you wish to rise late. There was something about how much each person gets at the end of the stay. A ten-bob note between us should do it.'

'What if we get it wrong?'

'What do you care, you're never going to see them again,' said May dismissively. 'Anyway, a police officer must outrank at least one or two of them. What about Trapp's gardener pal, Fruity Metcalf? Where is he?'

'Out in the gatehouse, I think. We'll have to find an excuse to slip away. Do you know if butlers still iron the newspapers?'

'I thought that was a myth.'

'It stops you from getting ink all over your hands.' Bryant swallowed nervously. 'I wonder what else they do – break in new shoes for you, pre-chew your food? Oh God, I bet there are going to be games. Do you know how to play cards?'

'Not a clue. Draughts and chess, that's about it. You?'

'Snap and Happy Families. We're buggered.' He fiddled with his bow tie, attempting to loosen it. 'We're going to be sussed at the first hurdle.'

'That thing looks as if it's choking you.' May eased the knot for him. 'Try not to be so uptight. It's 1969, not 1935.'

'It's been a long time since I had to do something practical in the field.'

'You weren't freaked out when you had to chase a killer through the Palace Theatre.* Come on, let's find Monty.'

The gong was a call for aperitifs in Iris, an immense blue-painted reception room with white wainscoting, Indian carpets, Chinese lacquered cupboards and a blue marble fireplace upon which stood an ormolu clock, ticking between caryatids and bulbous aquamarine vases. Overhead a Waterford glass chandelier gleamed dully. The air smelled of damp and disuse, like a room in the back of a museum where uninteresting pots were kept.

May entered the room and quickly headed towards a maid in a white apron and black miniskirt. As she handed out Martinis, Bryant realized that they were the last to arrive. A group of guests lurked near the drinks table as if protecting themselves from predators. The men were mostly in black, the women in pastel gowns, and yet it wasn't like any house party that featured in Bryant's booklet. There was an uneasy

---

* As recounted in *Full Dark House*

artificiality about the gathering, as if a group of strangers had been forced into slightly too modern versions of traditional country weekend attire.

Monty came storming over. 'Where have you two been?' he hissed. 'You'd better stay close so I can keep an eye on you.'

He's got that the wrong way around, May thought, already growing ill-humoured. He looked over at his partner, whose discomfort was manifesting itself in a trickle of sweat descending from his brow. Bryant tried to pull a handkerchief from his jacket pocket, but it was attached to a string of world flags.

'And who's he come as?' Monty asked, pointing at Bryant. 'Bertie Wooster?'

Bryant stuffed the flags away. 'The coat belongs to the Great Flambini.'

'Why are you wearing argyle socks?'

'I thought they were the right thing.'

'On a golf course, you imbecile, but not here, and not with your trousers halfway up your shins.'

'It's not my fault,' said Bryant. 'The chap playing Charles Condomine was shorter than me.'

'Who the hell is Charles Condomine?'

'He's in *Blithe Spirit.* These are his strides.'

'Do you have any idea what he's blathering on about?' Monty asked May.

'My colleague borrowed some theatrical clothing for the weekend,' May explained.

Monty aimed a sigh at the ceiling. 'If you embarrass me any further, I'll have you put back on the beat.'

'We're already going to be back on the beat after this,' muttered Bryant.

'Just make the introductions and we'll take care of the rest,' May assured him.

'All right, but if you do have to speak try not to have opinions. I don't want either of you noticed.'

Monty walked away, abandoning them. The detectives stood some distance off from the other guests. A West Indian man with a spectacular Afro stopped to appraise them. He wore a purple dinner jacket and a canary-yellow satin shirt, a case of one outsider attracted to others in a similar position. 'I don't know you,' he said, pointing between them. 'You must be new recruits. I'm Slade Wilson.'

May reached forward and gripped Wilson's hand in a firm, strong shake. 'Jack March,' he said smoothly, turning to his partner. 'And this is—'

Bryant had forgotten who he was supposed to be. Caught unprepared, he looked as though his eyes were about to pop out. 'Arthur,' he said in a small, strangled voice.

Wilson nodded encouragement. 'Arthur . . . ?'

'Arthur – Askey.'

'Oh.' Wilson looked puzzled. 'You mean like the comedian.'

'Yes,' Bryant managed. 'We're not related. I'm a cousin.'

Wilson glossed over the potentially awkward moment with the ease of a man who knew that the art of cocktails was the etiquette of whoring. 'I'm Mr Burke's interior conceptualist,' he explained, pointing a finger around the room. 'His artistic designer. He's hired me to get rid of all this hideous dreariness.' He got blank looks. 'Donald Burke? He's about to become the new owner of Tavistock Hall.'

'I didn't know it was being sold,' said May.

'Oh, they've been planning it for months. The old lady and her son are still here, of course. *They've nowhere else to go,*' he whispered. 'I can't wait to get my hands on these rooms. Who owns a library any more? The coming colours for the seventies are prune, sage, sepia and *bois de rose.*'

'So you're a decorator,' said Bryant.

'At the prices I charge, I'm a conceptualist,' Wilson replied. He was about to be flippant again but something in Bryant's eyes drew out an honest response. 'Look, I admire the old elegance, but it's simply too expensive to restore. It would cost a fortune to recreate the original mouldings and finishes, so I'll cover them in veneers and give Mr Burke what he wants.'

'What *does* he want?'

Something about Bryant's earnestness made Wilson drop his camp pose and answer honestly. 'Something soulless and fashionable, I imagine. Perhaps one day in the future another owner will take down the coverings and restore everything that's been left underneath.' His gaze flicked around the room. 'At least I won't have been responsible for destroying what was here. Why are *you* here?'

'We're businessmen,' said Bryant. 'We're on business.'

'What kind of business?'

'Nothing special, just . . . business. Businessy things.'

Hatton-Jones appeared beside them with a bottle of champagne. 'I had to go to the kitchen to find this,' he said, hastily cutting across the conversation. He regarded Wilson with suspicion. 'What are you up to?'

'I was explaining how I'm going to remodel this draughty old mausoleum.'

'Donald is opening a business institute, not a nightclub for poofs,' said Monty. 'If you're hoping to get money out of Burke, I suggest you go with classical simplicity, so none of your nig-nog colours. It's all right, he knows I'm joking, don't you, Slade?'

Bryant was about to protest at Hatton-Jones's language when May stood on his toe as a warning.

Wilson leaned towards Bryant in confidence. 'Apparently Mr Burke won't be dining with us. Strangers make him uncomfortable. Can you imagine? The thing is, Mr Askey – may I call you Arthur? We are going to be spending the weekend in close proximity, after all – he trusts *nobody*. I suppose he's so rich, he assumes everyone's after something. But then of course everyone here *is* after something. They're all waiting for him to put in an appearance. I've been watching their greedy little eyes search the room as if they're expecting a papal audience.'

Hatton-Jones wandered off with his bottle, and their corner of the library fell awkwardly silent. Wilson turned around and found an unsmiling woman standing behind him with her grey hair pinned up in an alarming pompadour and bone-white hands clasped together. She wore a high-necked grey woollen dress with a cameo on a chain that added an extra touch of Victoriana, as if she was awaiting discovery in some ancient album of family photographs. An air of disappointment hung over her like a funeral veil.

'Lady Banks-Marion,' said Wilson, clearly unnerved. 'How lovely to—'

'I am looking for my son,' she said in a hard clear voice that was used to giving instructions.

'I haven't seen him yet,' said Wilson. 'Perhaps I could—'

'When you do, kindly tell him to come and find me.' She gave Bryant and May a brief chilly evaluation and moved swiftly away.

'Beatrice, the lady of the house,' Wilson explained. 'Not one for small talk. Best to keep out of her way. She can turn you to stone with that stare.'

Bryant watched her cut through the gathering like a tall-masted ship avoiding pack ice.

'If the house is being sold why is she still here?' asked May. 'Doesn't she find it upsetting?'

'That's the point,' Wilson confided. 'She can't do anything or go anywhere until the cash is in the bank. None of us can.'

'Slade, we have new faces, how lovely.' A short, full-figured woman joined them and outstretched her hand. She had bobbed auburn hair and a perfectly round face, scrubbed of make-up and as healthily complected as the milkmaid in Vermeer's painting. There are artfully shapeless dresses, but hers was of navy-blue wool and not one of them. 'I'm Donald's wife, Norma. Have you been filling the heads of these nice young men with stories about my husband?'

'I've been looking forward to meeting Mr Burke,' said May. 'He sounds like he has grand plans for the house.'

'That's kind of you to say so, Mr—'

'March. Jack March, and this is' – he glared at Bryant – 'Arthur Askey.'

She inclined her head gracefully towards Bryant, making him fall a little in love. Her eyes were small, bright and kindly. 'We really shouldn't make excuses for Donald. He's being the most frightful bore about this weekend. He says he didn't know so many others were invited, and he hates meeting new people. Slade and I persuaded him to come down to Kent and sign the papers.'

'Donald hasn't even seen the property he's buying, except in photographs,' Wilson explained.

'And now he says he won't come and mingle until he's sorted out some kind of legal matter. He's probably buying another company; he usually is.' She gave a merry little laugh. 'All I see are great stacks of paperwork piling up everywhere, making my countertops untidy. It's all gobbledygook to me. I tell him, go and be a captain of industry if you must, just leave me in the kitchen, that's my territory. A wife's place and all that. I'm not much of a women's libber.' Her gaiety faded. 'He works terribly hard. I think stress needs to find a way out, don't you? He's not himself these days. Perhaps the new project will help us both. I still can't believe that this wonderful old house is going to be ours after the weekend.'

'When do you think Toby will finalize the sale?' Wilson asked her.

'Toby Stafford is Donald's lawyer,' Norma explained politely. 'You'll have to ask him about that, I'm afraid. I think there's a plan afoot to get everything signed by tomorrow. Toby's down here with us, but he doesn't tell me anything. They think I won't understand. I just thank the stars I found Slade.' She patted the designer's arm. 'I wouldn't be able to cope with choosing all the furnishings alone. Everyone told me, if you want something covered up and prettified it has to be Slade Wilson. Now, let's see, who else haven't you met?' She scanned the chattering group. 'Ah, you really must be introduced to the lord of the manor. Harry – please do come and say hello.'

A paunchy, balding middle-aged man sporting shoulder-length blond hair tied back with a leather braid came loping over. He raised a hand in greeting. 'Welcome to Tavistock Hall, peace to you both. Jack and Arthur, yes? Monty tells me you're working for him. Harry Banks-Marion.'

He was the only member of the gathering not in some form of dinner dress. Instead he had chosen a blue Nehru jacket draped in large wooden beads, with a polo-neck kaftan of pale orange lace, a silver Indian necklace, bracelets, green flared trousers and moccasins. He had a tattoo of Jimi Hendrix on the back of his right hand, and was followed by a small piglet. The dainty little creature was pink with reddish blotches, and wore a sparkling diamanté necklace. She had perfectly round blue button eyes, and looked up at them with her snout twitching wetly, as if waiting to be introduced.

'*Lord* Banks-Marion,' Wilson corrected.

Harry looked embarrassed. 'Well, technically yes. Harry Charleworth LeStrange Kinroth Banks-Marion, Lord Banks-Marion if you like. "Woofy" to my old schoolfriends. I do think the hereditary peerage is worth preserving. Its principle creates a sense of innate commitment to the welfare of the nation. Although I understand that the times are rather against us. And this little lady is Malacrida.' He reached down and patted the piglet's head. 'Don't worry, she's very intelligent and house-trained.'

'Your father would be turning in his grave if he knew you were selling the house,' Norma admonished gently. 'I think your mother is looking for you.'

'She always is,' sighed Harry, accepting a fresh glass from

a waitress. 'You of all people should be happy about the sale, Norma. Slade, *you* know what the overheads have done to us. Anyway, the ashram will be somewhere to come at the weekends with all your friends. You're going to love it.'

'Donald is going to transform Tavistock Hall,' Norma explained. 'We'll live here, but he's going to turn half of it into a business training institute.'

'Doing what exactly?' Bryant asked.

'To be honest I have absolutely no idea. He did try to explain but I'm afraid he rather lost me. My husband is originally from Chicago and is therefore fascinated by any building more than a hundred years old.' She laughed lightly. 'He loves the sheer *unnecessariness* of it all. Did you know, there's a lake with a Grecian folly, and an Italian maze?'

Malacrida suddenly trotted away across the room, and Lord Banks-Marion gave a raucous shout of glee, running after her. Bryant began to suspect that he had been smoking something stronger than tobacco.

Wilson moved gracefully on. Nobody stayed with them for more than a briefly allotted period, and the conversation remained bubble-light. Bryant wondered if this habit was also mentioned in his country guide.

Lord Banks-Marion's place was taken by an expensively suited, heavy-bellied man with a pocket chain looping across his waistcoat. Everything about him seemed designed to project an aura of stability and trust, but the effect was undermined by his brown wig, which was absurdly obvious, being too large, too dry and too ill matched to his greying sideburns.

He shook hands with everyone. 'Toby Stafford. I seem to be going around apologizing for my client.' He jovially offered his cigarettes to the others before tapping one out for himself. 'I told Donald that one five-minute appearance would save me an hour of explanation.'

'Is there some kind of problem with Mr Burke?' asked May.

'He has been diagnosed with a – well, perhaps *phobia* is

too strong a word. I understand he has become uncomfortable in crowds.'

'We're hardly a crowd,' May pointed out. 'There are only a few of us.'

'But the others – outside the house,' said Stafford mysteriously. 'I think Norma did marvellously getting him this far. She told him it would be rude not to meet the owners of the property he's intending to purchase.'

'Has anyone seen him at all this weekend?' Bryant asked.

'I believe several of the guests have spent time with him.' Stafford blew smoke over their heads. 'And I imagine the reverend has already attempted to make his presence known.' There was disapproval in his voice. 'The rest of us will just have to wait our turn. Mr Burke is in the driving seat here, although I suppose you've noticed that already. We are merely poor satellites circling his very wealthy moon.'

'What's the form for the weekend?' asked May. 'Nobody's told us what we're expected to do.'

'I'm afraid I can't help you there,' said Stafford. 'I'm staying down in the village. I prefer to keep my clients at arm's length. I have an appointment with Donald tomorrow morning, just to go over the final paperwork, then as soon as his signature is on the deeds I'm heading back to London. And I imagine he'll be out of here like a shot, leaving his wife and Mr Wilson to share decorating tips. It'll be interesting to see if Vanessa Harrow leaves with him.'

'Who's she?' May scanned the room.

'Miss Harrow hasn't turned up yet, but I understand she's planning to attend.' Stafford glanced back at Norma Burke to make sure she was out of earshot. 'She's Donald's mistress. I think it's extraordinarily civilized to allow her along. Or foolish.'

'So Mrs Burke knows about her?'

'She'd have to be very stupid not to have noticed. It's been in all the society pages.'

'But whatever happens this weekend the house will be signed over, won't it?'

'Indubitably.' Stafford smiled as he reached over to a bronze ashtray and ground out his cigarette stub. 'After all, it's in the interests of everyone in this house. We're going to be one big happy family, for the weekend at least.'

'Do you think we have to stay with Monty?' May wondered after Stafford had taken his leave. 'Couldn't we just clear out to the nearest inn and collect him on Sunday afternoon? I can't imagine any of this lot are going to try and nobble him. For a start, Monty seems to know them all.'

'Maybe that's what he's worried about,' Bryant replied, looking around. 'That it'll be someone he never suspected.'

12

A HOUSE IS NOT A HOME

Alberman gave another theatrical cough and announced a move to Lavender, the dining room, a vast half-panelled plasterwork hall lined with diagrammatic paintings of horses. Here, a new set of complications arose involving place settings and empty chairs. Bryant stared down at a polished chestnut dining table covered in a bewildering array of silverware.

'Golly, look at this lot,' he marvelled. 'It'd fetch a few bob down Petticoat Lane.'

'Perhaps you could think a little bigger than nicking the cutlery,' suggested May.

Bryant nudged him. 'What, go for the cruet?'

May took a deep breath and studied the guests they had yet to meet. He counted six settings on either side, but there was an unoccupied chair beside Norma Burke. The two remaining seats were next to each other; they had no place cards and had presumably been laid out for him and Bryant. Bryant lowered himself on to a chair that creaked ominously, then realized that everyone else was waiting for the ladies to be seated. He smartly rose again just as the ladies sat.

As the conversation began in earnest he was reminded of the

Veneering dinner party in *Our Mutual Friend*. In Dickens's novel the guests were latently dependent on their benefactor, but in this case the benefactor had not deigned to join them. It was all very odd.

Studying the portraits in the dining room, Bryant recognized the common features of Tavistock Hall's Hanoverian and Victorian residents, extending up to and including Harry Banks-Marion. All had such protruding eyes, ruddy cheeks and weak chins that generations of artists had clearly reached a mutual understanding and abandoned any attempt to ameliorate the family's hereditary appearance. Instead their patrons had been arranged in Corinthian poses, at sunset, surrounded with spaniels, hidden among baskets of flowers or inside voluminous folds of material. It might have worked if the paintings had not been placed together in a row. Organized in a timeline to the present day the descendants rapidly became caricatures, looking like increasingly distorted funhouse mirrors.

At the end of the row of portraits were Beatrice, Lady Banks-Marion, placed before a rose-draped pergola at sunset in an attempt to soften her, and Harry, painted sitting on a kitchen chair in the style of Augustus John, in an attempt to harden him. Beyond them was only a melancholy blank space, suggesting that the evolutionary line had turned into a cul-de-sac.

As Bryant looked around at the assembled diners, a distant alarm bell sounded in the back of his brain. He felt as if he was being presented with the first clues to a puzzle that had yet to reveal itself, but this feeling was displaced by the arrival of the waiters and the horror of brown Windsor soup. As the ladling-out began, the dining room succumbed to the atmosphere of a municipal care home.

At the last minute, one more guest swayed in. The table collectively turned to look and fell silent. They saw an impossibly perfect blonde with coral lipstick, black eyeliner, gold hoop earrings and lemon-yellow high heels. She wore a very short, low-cut lavender and rose net gown, and looked like one of those

European starlets who went by a single name. She was also drunk. The temperature and tension torqued sharply. Eyeballs swivelled back to the only person who had not moved – Norma Burke.

'I'm sorry I'm late,' said Vanessa Harrow, offering a sunny if unfocused smile. 'The only cab I could find had an ugly driver so I held out for one a little more hansom. Ha ha.'

There was a small deathly silence before the conversation renewed itself. Miss Harrow seemed unfazed and swayed about the room looking for somewhere to park herself.

Arthur Bryant found himself seated beside a nondescript cardigan-clad woman who ignored his only stab at conversation and opposite a young, intense-looking vicar with whom he knew better than to attempt one.

May was having an easier time of it, as the stunning late arrival had pulled up her own chair and wedged herself in next to him, throwing out the table's carefully planned order. For some unearthly reason she seemed to find May's every utterance shriekingly hilarious. Bryant was mystified by the easy charm that made his partner so magnetic to half-cut women. He wondered if they would have to keep the same table-places all weekend, in which case he imagined the hours dragging past as if mired in treacle.

Serving the dinner on fine bone china did not make it more attractive. In the jellified soup, gristly chunks of beef surfaced like stewed wads of chewing gum. The starter was followed by a choice of haddock lacquered in burned cheese or fatty slices of peppered beef lying in a pool of crimson gore, each paired with a selection of overcooked, carminative vegetables.

Bryant prodded the beef with his fork and leaned over to his partner. 'This bull isn't dead, it's just hurt. Any decent vet could get it back on its feet. And why would anyone cover fish in cheese unless they had something to hide? It's all stone cold.'

'I imagine it's a fair walk from the kitchen,' May replied. 'Haven't you noticed? We're being served last.'

Five minutes later Bryant tapped his partner on the arm with a fork again. He was growing bored and petulant. 'I want to go home.'

'Talk to your neighbour,' said May. 'Make an effort.'

Bryant looked down at the cardigan-woman's plate, which was empty except for a small puddle of spinach. 'Not hungry?'

She shot him a withering look. 'I'm a vegetarian.'

Of all the responses that flashed through his mind, the best would probably have been a silent nod and not, 'So was Hitler.'

He added hastily, 'I mean there were lots of other vegetarians too, Pythagoras, Voltaire, Tolstoy . . .' When he looked back, she had turned away.

For dessert there was Black Forest gateau or spotted dick, coated with a poultice of rubbery custard. The room grew colder than the meal. Only the wine remained ruby and robust. Bryant caught slivers of conversation and found his thoughts drifting to crime novels he had read. Bodies in libraries, detectives in turmoil, accusations, theories and a surprise culprit. Could that happen here? It seemed as if all the key ingredients had been assembled. But which of the guests would be marked for death? Who would be prepared to kill?

The problem, he decided, was the crevasse that separated fiction from fact. Most crimes were sad and sordid affairs. Nothing unusual happened in country houses, or if it did it was kept hidden from public gaze.

At nine the group adjourned to Lupin, the library, for brandies poured from cut-crystal decanters arranged in ascending order of age, bearing silver tags around their necks like foundlings. Six immense bookcases stood against walls of willow-green damask, matched in silks that hung in graceful folds above a jade velvet sofa and an array of wingback armchairs. The carpet was a bronze-tinted Aubusson, its colours picked out in a leather folding screen. Armed with a candle taper, Parchment put in a brief reappearance, perhaps to assure the assembled guests that he had not passed away.

Bryant opened the French windows and went out to the patio, its herringbone brickwork blotched green and white from the roosting starlings that rattled and crackled in over-head crevices. The autumn clouds were pink and blue, crows calling in the dying light. Rabbits lolloped through the grass. Something in the bushes shrieked in pain, as if it was being torn apart. The trees were black against the sky.

He thought back over all he had heard and seen in Tavis-tock Hall so far, and the strange sense of foreboding settled over him once more. There were tiny signs – fractures in con-versation, odd looks, unaired grievances – but no suspicions he could really put his finger on.

Digging through the secret pockets of the magician's jacket for his pipe, he resigned himself to the less palatable conclu-sion that there would be no excitement this weekend. He looked up to the first-floor windows and counted them until he reached the master suite where Donald Burke and his wife had presumably taken up residence. Each of the corner rooms had a tall door leading on to the covered balcony.

Just then the Burkes' door opened and a stout figure with long grey hair emerged, one hand on the paunch of a grey satin waistcoat, the other holding a cigar. His face was hid-den by the shadow of the immense wisteria that had entwined itself around the balcony supports. He leaned against the railing smoking, his head inclined towards the darkening fields. He was wearing white gloves that stood out against the twilight.

Donald Burke was finally putting in an appearance.

A distant boom made the bricks tremble beneath Bryant's feet and signalled the start of the army's war games.

13

WITH A LITTLE HELP FROM MY FRIENDS

May stepped out on to the patio, joining his partner. 'What are you looking at?'

'I just saw Donald Burke on the balcony.'

'Is he coming down to join us?'

'I don't think so. Would you?'

'I'm putting on a brave face,' said May, lighting a Park Drive. 'You, poor chap, couldn't look more bored if you were dead. Perhaps you should switch places with me tomorrow.'

'It wouldn't make any difference,' said Bryant with a sigh. 'People react to me as if they'd just found a spider in the bath.'

'Did you have the spotted dick?'

'Certainly not,' said Bryant, 'I'm constipated enough as it is. Maybe you're right, though. I should swap the grumpy old bag next to me for the girl who's laughing at all your lame jokes.'

'Oh, you mean the delectable Vanessa Harrow. She's a nightclub singer. She drank gin with her dinner. Alberman clearly wasn't pleased. She's quite the most delightfully mercenary creature I've ever met. Her antennae extended any time somebody mentioned money. I rather like her honesty.'

'You rather like all girls regardless of whether they turn out to be charming, venal or insane,' Bryant reminded him. 'Gladys calls you the Leicester Square Lothario. Monty's making it pretty obvious that he doesn't care for your companion.'

'No, I think he cares for her too much. She's avoiding him.'

'Really? I missed that. I wonder why she was invited?'

'You're joking, aren't you?' May tried to read his partner's face but it was, as ever, a masterpiece of misinformation. 'Look at her, Arthur! She's young and gorgeous. She knows she's gorgeous and uses it of course, but she doesn't yet appreciate the fleeting power of youth. For now, though, she'd be invited to a funeral just to brighten up the service.'

'Thank you. Wise words from the Carnaby Street Casanova.' Bryant cleared his throat in a disapproving manner. 'Our mystery millionaire isn't showing much interest in her. He looked like he was thinking something over, as if he wanted to come down but something stopped him.'

'Well, Monty's starting to get agitated.'

They peered back into the library, Lupin. Hatton-Jones was by the fireplace smoking furiously and staring at the French windows as if thinking of making a break for it. Bryant studied him thoughtfully, trying to follow the undercurrents running through this odd gathering of guests. It was an alien experience, being among people with hidden agendas. When his own family and friends held a party it usually involved a piano and a knees-up in a pub, drinking after hours, old songs, old arguments, a fight and a few tears, the air cleared, friendships reaffirmed, and somewhere a kiss. It was messy, foolish, natural.

This was altogether more predatory and troubling.

The moon had risen in an ink-fresh sky. It cast a milky glow across the patio that faded off into indigo. The lawn shone. There were calls from the trees beckoning the night. Everyone drifted outside to have a look.

'What a pity Donald's missing this, he's probably forgotten

the time,' said the mellifluous Vanessa, appearing beside May and taking his arm with a natural carelessness that he found delightful. 'It must be an easy thing to do in such a lovely place. I forget things all the time. I'm as silly as a sheep.'

'We know, dear,' Norma Burke added. 'Perhaps I should go and check on him, seeing as he's my husband.'

'Everyone knows why Vanessa's here: to be with Donald,' Slade Wilson confided to May as Norma Burke and Vanessa Harrow went back inside. 'Norma seems to have accepted it.'

'Perhaps she has no say in the matter,' said May.

'Perhaps she relishes the opportunity of insulting her rival all weekend,' replied Wilson. 'Lord Byron said that a mistress can never be a friend. When you agree, you're lovers, and when it's over, you're enemies.'

'Ah, there you are,' cried Monty, slapping Wilson on the back. 'Can't you find some coon music to cheer the place up?'

Wilson shot Bryant a look of secret complicity. *Don't say anything.* 'I'm afraid Lord Banks-Marion has commandeered the record player.'

His lordship had put on a Pink Floyd album that sounded like someone playing an organ at the bottom of a well. He proceeded to fishtail around the patio in time to the music, waving his hands over everyone before delving into a suspicious-looking tobacco tin. When his eyes alighted upon the detectives he beckoned them conspiratorially.

'Come and meet Sir Winston,' he said, holding a finger to his lips. 'Mummy doesn't like me going out during get-togethers but the weather may not hold up and it would be a shame not to give him a run. Follow me.'

He fairly tripped down the lawn, followed by the prancing pig Malacrida, and then dived behind a hedge.

'Is he potty?' asked Bryant as they headed after him.

'The upper class gets away with calling it eccentric,' said May. They rounded the corner and found themselves before a complete miniature railway station named Tavistock Halt.

At its only platform stood an apple-green steam locomotive with brass trims and a single enclosed carriage.

'I had Alberman fire up the old chap for us, just in case,' Harry explained, heading for the driver's seat. Malacrida ran ahead of him, bustling into her usual spot next to him. 'I thought you'd be interested. Sir Winston was built in 1927, modelled on the Green Goddess at Hythe, although of course that's a 381-mm gauge, and we couldn't really compete. I was going to upgrade to a Krupps with a two-tone horn but they're German-made and Mummy wouldn't let me. All aboard.'

The detectives seated themselves behind Harry, who squeezed the release handle, opened the cylinder valve, blew the forward whistle in two short blasts and took off the horizontal brakes, moving the train smoothly out.

Sir Winston set off with a satisfying chug, past the flowerbeds towards the lake and its boathouse.

'My grandfather had it built,' his lordship called back. 'We all loved riding Sir Winston. We used to let the tenants' children come and wave to us. Grandfather was going to put in other stations but – well, the war and everything.'

'How long has Tavistock Hall been in your family's hands?' asked May through the billowing steam.

'Oh, we've always been here. The present building's only about a hundred and fifty years old but it shares its foundations with the earlier hall. Tradition has always held us back. Even the staff uniforms never changed. When I was a boy they still wore dinner livery of navy-blue tailcoats, breeches, white stockings and waistcoats. Keep your head in here, we're going past some holly bushes.' Branches scraped at the engine as it chuntered past. 'The pater owned land from here to the coast and treated his tenants well. There were scandals, of course – there always are in the great houses of England – but the old man was adored. It was automatically assumed that I would continue the line. You never get to make decisions for yourself. Duty, and so on.'

The miniature train steamed around the edge of the illuminated lake, scattering ducks to the treeline. As it passed the tiny
mock-Gothic boathouse the puffs of cotton-wool smoke that
pulsed from the engine's chimney completed the nostalgic scene.

'Lovely, isn't it?' Harry shouted. 'I'm sorry to see it go in a
way. Grand country houses like Tavistock Hall were built on
the availability of cheap servants. The Great War collapsed the
domestic labour market and most of our land was sold off to
pay bills. Let's pull in here for a second.'

He tugged on the brake, leaving the engine to idle, and turned
to face them, leaning on the back of his red leather seat. 'I feel I
can talk to you. You seem different from the others somehow.'

'I think we can agree on that,' said Bryant.

'I know what you're probably thinking, that I'm the bad
son foolishly frittering away his legacy, but you know what
my father and grandfather did back there?' He pointed up to
the shadowed house. 'They held dinners for twenty in the
Lavender Room, complete with their dogs and cats and monkeys and mistresses. They had seven indoor servants and four
outdoor ones, including one whose sole duty was to clean
their hunting kit. Their women redecorated constantly. They
dyed the doves in different colours and held baroque masked
balls in the Venetian style. They invited the Astors and the
Mitfords, Wallis Simpson and Cecil Beaton, who once came
disguised as a field of rabbits. They held costume balls and
dressed as Beau Brummel and Lady Caroline Lamb, and shot
so many partridges that the estate had to be restocked with
imported fowl. And when the villagers complained about the
rents or the enclosed common land, they raised the levies to
pay for more grand parties.'

Harry seemed intent on confirming Bryant's worst fears
about the aristocracy, but there was something boyish and
doomed about his honesty. He stroked Malacrida's head
absently and rearranged her necklace. 'We're quite useless, you
see. We're flightless birds. We were never bred for survival, and

when the waterhole shrank we intermarried until half the family had to be locked away. We could manage to feed and clothe ourselves so long as we were within reach of a bell-pull, but that's about all. Most of our servants were given the names of their predecessors so that we wouldn't have to remember who they were, and they all had to be shorter than my grandfather, who did not wish anyone to stand above him. Father would come down and tap the barometer, pat his dogs, eat his breakfast and shoot his grouse, and if the guests bored him, which they always did, he would head off to the village pub and not return until everyone had left. His kind were hanging on to their estates by the skin of their teeth until one by one . . .' He gave a deep and melancholy sigh. 'Let's head back.'

The train completed its circuit, chugging steadily towards the moonlit hall once more.

Nobody appeared to have noticed their absence except the lawyer.

'I suppose Lord Banks-Marion was telling you his side of the story,' said Toby Stafford as they re-entered Lupin. He steered them across the room, keen not to be overheard. 'Did he tell you that after his father died he set off on a voyage of self-discovery?'

'No,' said May. 'Where to?'

'Where do you think? India, of course. Along the way he discovered marijuana and LSD. Came back from Goa with a couple of fashionable accessories, an annoying flower-child girlfriend and a maharishi. I don't suppose you saw the ashram he's set up in the walled garden – the train doesn't go through there. Take a walk around the back of the house tomorrow morning. You won't be able to miss it. He says it's a peace camp. It's a shanty town, litter and filth everywhere, a reeking dosshouse of camouflage tents for every finger-bell-waving pot-smoking cloudhead in the county. No wonder his pet pig feels at home there.'

Bryant was surprised by Stafford's strength of opinion. That was their main advantage, he realized. As outsiders they were here only to listen.

'So the ashram will have to go when Mr Burke takes over the hall,' May assumed.

'I'm afraid those are the sort of details nobody has worked out,' said Stafford, lighting a cigar. 'Mr Burke has so many interests around the world that his attention hasn't been concentrated on Tavistock Hall. He left it to his wife to sort out, and she can't manage her own domestic arrangements, let alone take care of a place like this. I imagine she's in sole charge of cushions and curtains, which is why she has Slade Wilson in tow. The owners of Tavistock Hall once owned most of Crowshott, and still have the right to grant leases to several of the village tenancies. The property situation is a legal minefield. The tenants are worried about Donald Burke buying the place. For reasons that nobody seems to remember, their current leases are tied to the estate only while there's a member of the Banks-Marion family in possession of the title, so you can imagine how much bad feeling there is. Some of them took out an injunction to try and stop the sale, but while they were still arguing about the terms a buyer was found. Now I have to deal with the mess.'

'What's Lord Banks-Marion's take on it?'

'He's in two minds, naturally. His childhood memories are all here, but he can't afford to keep the hall. He's trying to persuade Norma to let him and his wastrel pals stay on, at least until it's been rebuilt.'

'What do you know about Mr Burke's plans for an institute?' asked Bryant.

'It will use experts to train a new generation of company directors. All very exclusive,' Stafford explained. 'Of course, houses like this usually only become boys' schools, golf clubs or asylums. I believe the fixtures and fittings are remaining with the property, assuming Mr Wilson doesn't chuck them all out. As soon as it's been refurbished Lord Banks-Marion and his merry troubadours can dance off over the hills with their flutes and tambourines, not to mention a decent wad of cash.'

'So Mr Burke is purely here to sign the papers? Is that why he won't come out of his room?'

'He's passing through on his way from Chicago to Paris, and according to Vanessa he asked her to join him on the trip. Did she give anything away over dinner?'

'No,' said May, 'the conversation was very casual.'

When Hatton-Jones realized that the lawyer was confiding in his minders he grew agitated and came beetling over to listen in. 'Oh, *Vanessa*,' he said, 'poor girl, she's so sublimely dim, she can't see that her sugar daddy will ditch her the moment she becomes demanding. I heard he got her the job singing at a Mayfair club that's little more than a knocking shop. She's a bit of posh he picked up on his travels not long after he married poor old Norma. I suppose his wife is making the best of a bad situation by befriending her.'

'Mr Burke's the reason why *you're* here, isn't he?' asked Stafford in a tone that was graceful enough for Monty not to notice the rebuke.

'Well, yes. I'm rather hoping he'll make time to see me.'

'Why, do you have a business proposition?'

Monty accepted a Park Drive from May. 'Who doesn't these days? Look at us: nearly a quarter of a century out of the war and the country still doesn't have a pot to piss in. The one thing you can say about Americans is that they certainly know how to make money. We sit around in underfunded research units inventing things, and they show us how to turn our ideas into hard cash. They roll up their sleeves and put in the hours while we close the banks down on the Glorious Twelfth so that the managers can go grouse-shooting.' He lit his cigarette and exhaled. 'There's a reason why America's most famous play is *Death of a Salesman*. It touches a national nerve. Selling and self-sufficiency are in their blood. I have a proposition that may haul me out of debt if I act fast enough, so naturally I'm looking to get my snout in the trough before everything here goes to the dogs.'

Once again Bryant was startled by Monty's ebullience. He did not seem to care about the impression he made on others. It was time to start collecting Farthingshaw's information, but he wasn't sure how to go about it. 'Do you think it will?' he asked. 'Go to the dogs, I mean?'

'Oh, I can see the writing on the wall. Even you must have noticed that Swinging London is fast losing its swing. Harold Wilson is all played out – the PM's "white heat of technology" speech did nothing for the nation, and the Tories are waiting in the wings.'

'I thought Edward Heath didn't have a chance of winning the next election.'

Monty took a drag and waved the smoke away. 'He's seen as wet and awkward, and the "confirmed bachelor" thing bothers the husbands, but he's certainly the housewives' choice. If he places well in the Sydney yacht race this Christmas he'll get the male voters too.'

'Really?' Bryant was surprised. 'You think they'd be swung by something like a boat race?'

Hatton-Jones leaned in close and confidential. 'Tell me, what do you think we really want from our leaders? I'll give you a clue: it's not intellect. We want fervour and decisiveness, that's all. A sign that a captain is at the helm. And this time it's literally what we're going to get. I think he's going to seize the moment.' He drained his brandy glass, but had nowhere to set it down.

'And you are too,' Bryant suggested.

'Abso-bloody-lutely. So you see why I had to insist on attending this weekend. On Monday morning I'm about to shoot down my best chance of a future in the building industry because my oldest friend, a man whom I've known most of my life, is dragging us into disrepute. I dare say he'll try and take me down with him, but I've a back-up plan. The only problem is that it's going to need a hefty injection of cash. Which is why I need to leave with Burke's signature on my paperwork by Sunday evening.'

'What if you don't?'

Monty didn't answer. He didn't need to.

'How well do you know Mr Burke?' asked May, catching his partner's eye.

'Very well and hardly at all,' Monty muttered, the brandy thickening his tongue. 'I've read all his interviews and I've spoken to him a few times, but I haven't yet met him face-to-face. Men like Burke have to protect themselves from dishonourable opportunists.' He said this with no sense of irony. 'To get hold of him you have to go through his staff. When I heard that Vanessa was going to be here as well, I thought there might be another way.'

'So you're planning to effect an introduction through her?'

'It's my best chance. There's no point in trying Norma. She hasn't the faintest idea about her husband's affairs, business or otherwise.'

'But Slade said she knew all about—'

'Vanessa? Slade's just a glorified window dresser, hardly on the inside track. Norma has one priority: taking care of her husband. She's here to make sure he gets what he wants this weekend. She likes to keep him happy.'

'If you don't mind my asking,' said Stafford, 'what exactly are you trying to sell Mr Burke?'

'My dear chap, I'm doing the same as everybody else, enjoying the hospitality of our hosts and hoping to save my bacon at the same time.'

Bryant wandered off down the garden and lit his pipe. He looked back at the patio where Monty stood beneath the wisteria vines firing his opinions at May. From time to time the others drifted over to his partner. Men joked and confided;

women smiled and flirted. The most extraordinary thing was that John seemed entirely unaware of his power. When people spoke to Bryant, it was usually to ask where May was.

He puffed at his pipe and looked around at the misted landscape. The countryside was still a novelty to him. Manicured emerald gardens were hedged by profusions of wild flowers in artful disarray, petals of saffron, crimson and blue. A grey slate path led down to another ornamental lake, at the centre of which was a small island topped with a white Grecian folly.

Bryant's eyesight was poor in the half-light. He could see the water rippling, and large white birds of some kind. There was also the motionless figure of a man, standing near the bamboo flambeaux that marked the lake's edge.

He really needed to find Fruity Metcalf's gatehouse before it got too late.

Tavistock Hall appeared to have receded into the turquoise night. The interior was ablaze with golden lights, the present and the past folded together. As a child he had passed an afternoon traipsing around a grand house with other day trippers, and the experience had left him cold. Most disappointing of all was the library, which had nothing readable left in it. At least now he had a chance to study this peculiar world from the other side of the velvet ropes. It seemed likely that he would be able to observe the guests in peace without anyone trying to start a conversation.

'Hello, I don't think we've been properly introduced,' said the vicar, popping out from behind a bush and offering his hand. He had a large wooden cross inset with Navajo turquoise around his neck, and had changed into a fawn sweater tucked into maroon elephant-cord bell-bottoms. His blond hair was fashionably long. It should have made him appear fresh. The decade was awash with Anglican vicars striving to be culturally relevant to the young. But there was an unhealthy waxiness to his pallor, so that he looked like someone who hung around the *Top of the Pops* studio waiting for underage girls.

'What were you doing in there?' asked Bryant.

'Um, a particularly fine example of *shrubby umbellifera*,' he replied, flicking a leaf from his sleeve. 'Such lovely gardens. Actually I was escaping from Mr Wilson. He's most determined to be friendly, but I can't say I approve of his type.' He smiled suddenly, revealing a neat palisade of perfect white teeth. 'The Reverend Trevor Patethric. Everyone calls me Trev. Trev the Rev. Lady Banks-Marion always puts on such a marvellous weekend here.'

'I'm Arthur – Askey,' said Bryant uncomfortably. He watched as the vicar dusted petals from his jacket, his smile serenely smug.

'I say, have you met the new owner yet?'

'Why, has he come down?' Bryant asked.

'It seems so. By all accounts he's a pretty switched-on chap.' Patethric pointed off to the left, where Norma Burke was standing beneath a clematis-covered pergola at the end of the lawn, talking to a man with long grey hair in a grey business suit and white gloves. 'I'm not sure he would welcome smokers.' He gave Bryant's pipe a pointed glance.

Bryant puffed long and hard. 'Old Sailor's Navy Rough-Cut,' he said. 'It's more aromatic than a ciggie.'

'Perhaps, but I think you'll find it's not terribly healthy.' The vicar gave a somewhat theatrical cough. 'I'm hoping to talk to Mr Burke about the church. We badly need a new belfry, and several of the tapestries have to be replaced.'

'So you're after a handout too.'

'I wouldn't put it so crudely, Mr Askey. After all, I'm acting on the Lord's behalf.' He looked up at Tavistock Hall with satisfaction. 'This house has been very good to us over the years. My predecessors have always been most grateful, but it's time to step up and be more generous. A benefactor would, of course, have a private chapel named after him.' The vicar's eyes were illuminated by the thought.

'I thought vanity was a sin. Isn't that what you're encouraging?'

'Many of our parishioners are decent, upstanding members of the community,' said Patethric. 'We can hardly expect them to worship in impoverished circumstances.'

'I'm surprised to hear you say that,' said Bryant. ' "Do not lay up for yourselves treasures on earth, where moth and rust destroy and where thieves break in and steal, but lay up for yourselves treasures in heaven. For where your treasure is, there your heart will be also." Matthew 6:19.'

The vicar was momentarily lost for words. 'We're working to save souls. The Devil is waiting to take those who slacken in their devotions.'

'I admire your dedication,' Bryant admitted, 'but you can't use religion as a threat.'

'Some of my older parishioners are hoarding fortunes when they could be helping the church.' The reverend cheerfully slapped him on the shoulder, startling a wood pigeon in the trees above them. 'I'll be conducting Sunday morning service at St Stephen's and this house always attends along with its guests. I presume I'll see you there.'

'Don't presume,' Bryant warned. 'I'm a practising atheist.'

Patethric's smile slipped a little. 'You cannot practise something you don't believe in.'

'Have you never met a politician? Atheism is simply the process of accepting responsibility.'

The reverend wagged a finger. 'I'm going to have to disagree with you.'

'When?'

'Religion is history, Mr Askey.'

'Yes, it's history without any facts.'

'Surely you don't want to take the risk of not believing in Him?'

'Trust me, I'd be taking a bigger risk if I did.'

'But God is merciful.'

'Then he must be a different God from the one who killed over fifty thousand men just for looking into the Ark – 1 Samuel 6:19.'

'You can't imagine we poor mortals could make a world this complex without divine intervention?'

'On the contrary,' said Bryant cheerfully. 'I find it hard to imagine anything simpler than Darwinian selection, which seems the most natural thing in the world. It's certainly easier to swallow than a creation myth involving a vengeful cloud-based deity manipulating worshippers with the promise of undeliverable rewards and unprovoked threats of damnation, quoting a contradictory guidebook filled with violent cruelties reserved for non-believers.'

The poor reverend had not encountered so many blasphemous opinions in a single sentence before, and froze out his companion with an impossibly reasonable smile. 'Well, it has been most invigorating talking to you, Mr Askey.'

'And you too, Mr Pathetic.'

'Patethric,' said the reverend irritably. 'It's Cornish. I'll pray for you.'

'And I'll think for you.'

The vicar managed to spot someone across the lawn and was gone.

Well, it's not the vicar, thought Bryant, and then realized, *Oh God, I'm eliminating suspects and there hasn't even been a crime.*

14

PAPERBACK WRITER

The weekend was under way, and the house obligingly glowed for its guests. Alone once more, Bryant moved a little closer to the pergola and listened.

Norma Burke and her husband seemed to be disagreeing about something, arguing in that constrained way people did when they knew they could be observed. Unfortunately, beneath the shade of the clematis vines and at this distance, it was impossible to discern the problem. It was probably something trivial. Arguments always seemed more interesting from the outside. He only heard Norma's reasoned replies.

'You must stay away from her . . . But it was your idea in the first place . . . They know you're not well, so it won't come as a shock . . .'

It was no use. He could not get close enough to hear them properly. Instead, he decided to slip away and find the gatehouse.

At the end of the sunken lawns, beyond a tall yew hedge, a small brick building topped with a miniature version of the hall's mansard roof stood to one side of the slate path. It looked like a tiny French chateau, but this too was in dire need of repair.

Bryant ran lightly over the grass and stopped in front of it. There was no bell so he knocked. The front door swung open and a low, square fellow in a grubby knitted cap stuck his head out. He was so weathered and solid that he might have been carved from a block of teak. Grey mutton-chop whiskers sprouted from his face like a particularly virulent form of lichen.

'Brigadier Metcalf,' said Bryant. 'Arthur Bryant. My partner's up at the house.'

'Call me Fruity, sir, all my friends do.' He shook Bryant's hand with his left fingers. His empty right sleeve had been ironed flat and was pinned to his tweed jacket. Years of military service had ensured that even his casual clothes were parade-ground smart, although one shoe was mismatched, with a specially enlarged rubber heel. He hobbled forward and gave Bryant the once-over, noting his peculiar attire. 'Is that what they're wearing in London now? I don't get up there much.'

'I had to borrow some clothes. Have you located Monty?'

'Yes, I'll be keeping an eye on his comings and goings, sir. I was just watching the house from the lake.'

'Good. Anything to report yet?'

'No, sir. You'd better get back up there before they miss you. I'll meet up with you in a little while if you like. We can go for a pint. Just come and knock on my door.'

Bryant went back to the bar and refilled his glass. Monty was wrestling with another bottle of second-rate champagne. The evening felt more relaxed now. Even Lord Banks-Marion had forsaken Pink Floyd for the easy-listening pleasures of Burt Bacharach.

'A bit harsh on the vicar, weren't you? Most of the reverend's parishioners are old. He provides them with comfort.'

He looked up and found a woman watching him with amusement while she waited for her Martini to be shaken. She had been seated to his left during dinner, wrapped in her loosely knitted cardigan, and had rebuffed his clumsy attempt at conversation. Now she had changed into a midnight-blue dress and had released her auburn hair, so that it tumbled about a pair of huge lime plastic earrings. The transformation was startling.

'Oh, you overheard that,' Bryant said, smiling.

'It's what we writers do, darling. We're as nosy as policemen. Look, we may have got off on the wrong foot at dinner, so let's try again. I'm Pamela Claxon.'

'Arthur Askey,' said Bryant, thrusting a hand at her. He tried to remove the curse from his pseudonym by emphasizing the second syllable.

She shook his hand vigorously. 'Didn't you have a moustache earlier?'

Hell, Bryant thought, *I wonder where it went.* 'Yes, I shaved it off.'

'Why?'

'Impetuosity.'

'Goodness. I had you pegged as one of Harry's dreary business colleagues, but they would never have bashed poor old Trev the Rev like that.' She watched as the polo-necked vicar looked around hopefully for someone else to befriend. 'He rubs me up the wrong way too. He tries to be groovy and insists on accompanying the choir on his guitar. Last Sunday he had the parishioners' children building the walls of Jericho out of old hi-fi boxes, then encouraged them to kick them all down, something they took to with too much enthusiasm. The sexton got a kick in the shin when he tried to separate them.'

'Is that why you're here, because you live locally?'

She took stock of the plump young man standing before her in an outfit intended for golf, or possibly quoits. 'You aren't really a businessman, are you? And I don't believe for a second that your name's Arthur Askey.'

'It's true that I'm here in a more official capacity,' Bryant confided.

Pamela's eyes burned with victory. 'I knew it! This is about Donald Burke buying the hall, isn't it, and this mysterious business institute of his. The deal doesn't feel kosher to me. He's laundering money or something equally nefarious.'

The penny dropped. Bryant pointed. 'You're Pamela Claxon, the crime writer.'

'Oh dear, recognition.' She grimaced but was clearly pleased. 'Don't worry, I'm not going to ask if you've read anything of mine.'

'But I have,' Bryant replied. 'All of the Inspector Trench books, in fact, from *A Killer's Eyes* to *Hands of the Strangler*. I must ask you, is it really possible to murder someone with their own hair?'

'Robert Browning thought so.' She sounded relieved. 'That's not usually the first question mystery writers get asked.'

'What's the usual one?'

' "Have I heard of you?" It requires a certain level of clairvoyance to come up with an answer to that.'

Bryant laughed. 'And what's the worst thing people say?'

' "I really enjoyed your first book." ' You smile but you want to stab them with a fountain pen. You're right, by the way, I live nearby and knew Harry's father.' She lowered her voice. 'The family was on its uppers long before Donald Burke stepped in, you know. Burke's got absolute pots of money. He'll be good for this place.'

'So you think it's a wise move, selling the house?'

She bit the olive from her Martini and moved him away from the other guests. 'Tavistock Hall is full of history that could easily be lost for ever. I'm pleased they've found someone who'll stave off the wrecking ball. Even so, Harry and Beatrice are selling the house with all the furnishings included. I think they're mad. There's a Stubbs in the hall, did you notice? And a lot of Pre-Raphaelites in the bedrooms, not that they're worth much these days. The pair of them are anxious to get Burke's signature on the papers this weekend.

That's why they're being such generous hosts. Normally you'd be lucky to find any booze here at all. Beatrice doesn't drink and Harry is a dope fiend.'

'It seems everyone has an agenda,' said Bryant. 'What's yours?'

'Truthfully? I'd quite like Burke to finance a book about the hall and its scandalous inhabitants. Something he could leave out as a coffee-table book at his institute. The old lord couldn't sanction such a thing because they were his relatives, but Burke has no connection with the property. Why are *you* here?'

Bryant was a terrible liar with a tendency towards unnecessary elaboration, so he avoided the question. 'Let's see how the rest of the weekend goes first,' he said. 'I'm rather out of my depth in a place like this. I'm not the hunting, shooting and fishing type.'

'Don't worry about that, neither is Harry,' Pamela assured him. 'He doesn't approve of hurting animals. But you'll be hard pushed to avoid the parlour games. Tell you what, let's team up. Keep an eye out for me and I'll keep one out for you.'

'Ah, there you are, Pamela,' said Trev the Rev, looming over them. 'Might I have a word?'

As she was drawn aside by the vicar she cast a knowing glance back at Bryant, who found himself secretly delighted to find an ally.

He wandered outside, where Donald Burke's wife was standing alone in the shadows beneath the wisteria. She had her back turned and a handkerchief in one hand, as if she had been crying.

'Where's our mystery man?' asked May, joining his partner. 'I was hoping to introduce myself.'

'He's elusive, I'll say that for him,' said Bryant. 'I think he upset her. Did you get a look at his hands?'

'No, why?'

'He's wearing white cotton gloves.'

'Gloves in September?'

'We're in the countryside. I guess it gets cold at night.'

'But *white* ones?'

'Maybe his wife packed the wrong pair. It's suggestive, don't you think?'

'Of what?'

'I thought this assignment would be more straightforward,' Bryant muttered. 'I'm surprised Monty didn't race out there to collar him. What's he really after, do you think?'

'Who, Monty? Maybe he's in debt. I can't get a straight answer out of him. He just says there has to be a deal this weekend.' May watched the reflections in the window, checking that no one else was close. 'I don't suppose there's any great secret about what Monty wants; he's after a guarantor, so that he can provide himself with a safety net when this business with Chamberlain turns ugly. And maybe he really does want to do the right thing. What? You're shaking your head.'

'I don't know, John, he seems a rather unlikely crusader. Doesn't the old school tie overrule morality?'

'With respect, Arthur, I think the East End chip on your shoulder is kicking in. On Monday morning Monty is going to stand up in court and betray his oldest friend. That takes a lot of courage. I know he's an idiot and a racist but let's give him the benefit of the doubt about Chamberlain for now and remember why we're here. An East End family died under rubble. We have to get Monty to that court. Chamberlain must be made to pay for what he did.'

Bryant looked around. Monty was standing by himself on the patio, looking out at the gardens, pensively drinking and smoking. 'Has it occurred to you that he might be playing us both for fools? I wonder what he's thinking right now.' He led his partner back inside the house.

Monty Hatton-Jones was thinking about money, how to get it, hold it and spend it. Money was really the only thing that interested him any more.

He breathed in deeply and walked about under the eaves. The evening was chilling down and becoming damp. He could smell grass, lavender, cows. He heard a bongo drum being slapped somewhere inside the walled garden, and another noise: something that sounded like two heavy stones being rubbed together.

A sprinkling of dust sifted down and settled on his shoulders. Puzzled, he looked up and saw a spiky-haired gryphon peering at him.

The gryphon had been carved in Bristol in 1823, and was nearly three feet high, made of granite. Monty might have had time to think that this mythical creature, half lion, half eagle, was the king of both land and air. Or he might simply have noticed that it was leaning further and further out until suddenly it had slipped over the balustrade and was travelling down towards him at great speed.

They heard the crash inside the house.

May was the first to come running out. He found Monty lying face down on the herringbone patio, crimson blossoms opening below his white shirt collar. The gryphon lay in three neat pieces as if it had been prepared for carving: legs, winged body and head. A drop of blood fell from its stone beak on to the brickwork, as if it had fed and was now done with the world.

15

I HEARD IT THROUGH THE GRAPEVINE

Monty lay immobile. May knelt, checked for vital signs and turned him over. 'Is there a doctor anywhere nearby?' he called. 'He's still breathing.'

'Dr Walgrave lives in the old cottage at the end of the lane,' said Pamela Claxon. 'I could cycle over.'

'I think he's OK. It looks like a surface wound. He must have turned his body in time. It caught him on the shoulder, barely touching his head.' May opened Monty's collar and examined his clavicle. The skin was torn off in a two-inch patch and the surrounding flesh was already starting to swell up and bruise, but the bone was intact. The gargoyle had landed a glancing blow.

While May stayed with the victim Bryant ran into the hall and up the stairs, taking them two at a time. At the end of the second floor was a steep wooden staircase leading to the servants' floor and, beyond that, the roof. Reaching the top staircase, he pushed open the unbolted panel above his head and emerged on to a narrow parapet that ran around the sloping tiles.

Up here the wind was fierce and buffeted him. He immediately saw where the gryphon had been displaced. There had been six of them, equally set along the main façade of the house. They were cemented in place, but two were fractured at their bases and one was now missing. He pushed against the other severed statue, but even with one hand planted against each of the creature's wings he could barely shift it. There wasn't enough room to get leverage, and there was no way it could have fallen by itself. He realized that the only way to topple it would be by raising his feet against the roof behind and pushing hard with the full width of his back.

In the damp mulch behind the spot where the gryphon had stood was a clear footprint – a man's shoe, not large, a zigzag pattern on the sole. Bryant hunted around and found the end of a cigarette, a tipped Embassy Filter. Someone had waited for Monty to appear. Bryant pocketed the dog-end and rose.

He ran back downstairs and found that the women had moved Monty inside, and were laying him on a couch. A cold flannel had been compressed on his wound to staunch the blood flow.

Monty tried to sit up when he saw Bryant, but winced in pain and fell back. Pamela removed his shirt while the cook, Mrs Bessel, who told everyone she had driven an ambulance during the war, unrolled a crepe bandage around his shoulder.

'It's only broken the skin,' she said, 'but it's badly swollen. There could be a hairline fracture. We've had bigger accidents in the kitchen. Hot oil, cleavers.' She held up her thumbnail. 'A corkscrew went under there only last week. He'll live.'

'How are you feeling?' Bryant asked. 'You're lucky to be alive.'

'No thanks to you,' Monty gasped, pulling himself on to one elbow with a wince of pain.

'I suppose you want to get back to London as soon as possible now.' Bryant turned to the others, who were keeping their distance, unsure of their roles in the drama. 'Could you leave us for a moment? We may need to remove his clothes.'

'Don't worry, I'll make it to the courtroom by Monday,' said Monty once the room had cleared. He seemed pretty sprightly for someone who had just been brained. 'A few inches over and that damned gargoyle would have split my skull in half. I can't stay here. It wasn't an accident. Somebody just tried to kill me. Why haven't you caught them?'

'Did you hear or see anything?'

'Yes, I heard a grinding sound. Like a granite gryphon being pushed over a parapet on top of some poor sod, which is what it bloody was. It's a good job I looked up when I did.'

'Please, think carefully. Take me through it.'

'I stepped outside for some air. I heard something above me and looked up. I saw what I thought for a second was a great bird taking off from the parapet. I moved my head to get a better look and then I realized the gargoyle was moving. I saw a pair of hands pushing at it, a man's hands.'

'Are you sure?'

'I can tell a man's hands from a woman's, damn it! Next thing, the creature was falling from the balustrade and hurtling down at me. I moved, not really thinking about the direction, and then I was flat on my back with a terrible pain in my shoulder. The gryphon was in pieces all around me, and I couldn't raise my head. Someone wants to stop me from testifying. Have you tried contacting Chamberlain?'

'We can't do that,' May explained, 'not without jeopardizing the case.'

'I have an idea,' said Bryant. 'When the doctor gets here I'll tell the others that your injuries are more serious than they are, and that you're confined to your room and can't have visitors. We'll deliver your meals until it's time for you to leave, but nobody else comes in or out. It's the only way to keep you safe.'

'So now you want to place me under house arrest as well. No, forget it.' Monty lowered himself back down on the couch. 'It can't be that hard to find out who tried to kill me. Good God, there aren't that many of us staying here.'

'Who did you mention your visit to?' Bryant asked. 'It was supposed to be a secret.'

'It doesn't matter, does it? You two goons were meant to look after me.' Monty lay back, closed his eyes and thought for a minute. 'I think I told someone at the club, and Harry obviously.'

'I need the names of everyone you told.' He handed Monty his pad and pencil. 'The doctor's on his way. Try to stay still.'

'I need a large brandy,' Monty moaned, 'I'm in shock. Make it a triple.'

Bryant pulled his partner aside. 'I've been dying to find out what's making his bag so heavy. Why don't I pop upstairs to his room while he's out of action and have a quick look around?'

May seized Bryant's arm. 'No, Arthur, you cannot go nosing through his belongings. He's a private citizen, not a suspect. He has rights. He could have been killed. We've only got one job to do this weekend, and that's keep an eye on him.'

Bryant was not to be mollified. 'It's no good. I have to see for myself. Cover for me. Don't let him move around.'

Ignoring May's protests, he slipped out into the hall and made his way to the central staircase. He was about to head upstairs when Alberman appeared on the landing.

'Can I be of assistance, sir?' he asked.

'I was just admiring your skirting board,' Bryant lied.

'I should be happy to give you a tour of the hall tomorrow morning after breakfast,' he said, remaining in position.

'I thought I'd just get something from my room.'

'Elsie is turning down the beds, sir. I'll inform you as soon as she's finished her present duties.'

'There's been an accident.'

'So I understand. The doctor is being summoned.'

Alberman was not to be shifted. Perhaps it was merely country house etiquette, but Bryant couldn't shake the feeling that their movements were being carefully controlled. As he walked back along the corridor to the library, he became increasingly indignant. *I'm an undercover police officer,* he thought, *I have every right to investigate.* Perhaps there was another way upstairs.

He stopped a waitress with a tray of empty glasses heading for the kitchen. 'Can I get to the first floor without using the central staircase?'

'You could go through the servants' quarters and up the rear stairs,' she replied, 'but the guests aren't allowed—'

'Oh, don't worry, I've cleared it with Lord Banks-Marion.' He attempted what he hoped was a winning smile. 'Which way?'

The waitress pointed to a door that opened into the back of the house.

Bryant tried the handle and stepped inside. Suddenly the fine wallpapers and paints ended, leaving walls of rough grey plaster, bare wooden floors and the lingering smell of cabbage. This was how the serving staff answered calls and made sure that the breakfast trays they sometimes delivered to the bedrooms arrived hot. From the staircase at the rear they were able to reach other parts of the house without bumping into their employers.

The servants' stairs proved ill lit and confusing. Parts had been closed off. When he finally emerged on the first floor, he found Monty's room at the far end of the passage. The door wasn't locked, so he slipped inside.

He had no idea what he was looking for. The bedroom chest of drawers contained some neatly ironed shirts, a scarf and tie, a manicure set, hairbrushes and a cardboard A2 folder. Bryant began unwinding the cord that bound it.

Downstairs in Lupin, Monty was restless, and May was running out of ways to keep him in the room. 'What about

Vanessa Harrow?' he asked as Monty stretched his bandaged collarbone, testing it.

'Let me tell you something about her.' He winced, sliding the webbing back into place. 'Vanessa may put on an evening gown to go to work at night but she is not a nightclub chanteuse. Whatever she does these days to make so many old men happy doesn't involve singing "Blue Moon" until four in the morning. I need a smoke.' He patted down his pockets, looking for his cigar cutter.

'Are you saying that Burke put her to work as a call girl?'

Monty mutely shrugged.

'Why would he do such a thing?'

'Why do rich men enjoy humiliating beautiful women? Because they can.' He looked inside his lounge jacket. 'Dammit, I had the thing earlier.'

'Perhaps you left it in the dining room,' said May. 'I'll get it.'

'No, it's in my DJ. We'll continue the conversation when I come back.' With that he rose with a cry of pain and hobbled off towards the stairs.

May ran outside and stood beneath Monty's window. He could not see whether Bryant was still inside, so he stood on a patio bench. The top of his partner's head briefly appeared and vanished again.

Knowing that Arthur's investigative technique involved plastering his prints everywhere and throwing everything on to the floor, he could hardly bear to carry on watching.

Bryant sat down on the corner of the bed and opened the folder. Pages of monthly statements cascaded out and landed around his feet. Other sheets contained notes on monthly running costs. He dug out a packet of aniseed balls and began to read.

This was what Monty was going to show Donald Burke? A prospectus for a new company? Disappointed, he turned over more papers: invoices, projections, evaluations, boring lists of typed figures.

From this angle he could see under the chest of drawers. At first he mistook the grey metal container for a cash box, but it was longer and flatter. He tried sliding it out with his foot but it was surprisingly heavy, so he got down on his knees and dragged it. When he tipped the thing no sound came from inside. He shook it and tried raising the lid, but it was wedged shut. Rising with the box in both hands he felt something fall out of his trouser pocket and heard aniseed balls rattle all over the floorboards.

Then he heard footsteps outside.

A bed, a chest, a chair – there was nowhere to hide and no time to think. He had scattered Monty's belongings everywhere. Dropping to the floor he tried to slide under the bed and realized that there was no room. The maid had stacked folded piles of curtains beneath it.

He dropped between the bed and the window. His idea – as much as he had put any thought into it at all – was to borrow the box for a few minutes and find a way of opening it, then return it before Monty noticed its absence. He could see that the window was half raised. Outside was the wrought-iron covered balcony entwined with wisteria branches.

The bedroom door opened wide.

'What the bloody sodding hell!'

Monty's polished brogues passed him, then stopped dead before the mess. His shoes crunched down on aniseed balls. Then they turned and headed towards the toilet.

Bryant extricated himself with difficulty from the side of the bed, grabbed the box and climbed through the window on to the balcony just as Monty returned.

There was a good chance that he could not be seen from the far side of the railings, behind the wisteria branches. With the box weighing heavily in his hands he clambered over and lowered himself in among the leaves.

Unfortunately, as soon as he had done so the box began to slip out of his hands, and Bryant watched in horror as it slowly dropped. Squeezing his eyes shut, he waited for the smash, but none came.

Monty re-entered the bedroom and was now going through the chest of drawers. Bryant peered through dusty, dead flowers, fighting his hay fever, praying that Monty would not look under the chest of drawers and see that the box was missing.

Monty saw that the box was missing.

His eyes bulged from their sockets as he felt around on the floor, cursing the ache in his damaged shoulder. He stormed about the room, tearing back the coverlet and batting the curtains, squeaking with pain all the time.

Bryant looked down. The box had fallen into a cleft between the wisteria branches about three feet below his left foot. He raised himself and peered over the railing once more. Monty swore spectacularly and stormed from the room. This time he took the key and locked the door from the outside.

Bryant tried to shift his position in the tree, stretching downward to reach the box, but he felt the wisteria branches crackle and shift. A spray of dried blossoms tumbled down on to the patio below. As he could not climb lower he tried to reach the box once more, but it was too heavy to lift with his fingertips.

There was a bang as a branch came away and fell below.

A panicked wood pigeon flew into his face and he swung backwards like a trapeze artist, neatly turning upside down and slithering to a stop so that he was hanging on to the vines by his shoes. One of his trouser braces was caught around a branch. The remains of a bird's nest fell past him.

There was another lurch downwards as more pieces of vine cracked. His braces stretched and made a peculiar noise. He felt himself sliding lower. At least now he was able to grasp the box, which had sustained a large dent in one side. Unfortunately the lid was sealed tighter than ever.

He realized that the back-strap of his braces was now

caught on a stump. He didn't fancy unbuttoning them and ricocheting headfirst to the patio without his trousers.

Peering through the leaves he could see that the French windows were open, but he needed May to come outside again. He wondered if he could impersonate a wood pigeon's call.

This, he decided, *is a very undignified start to a weekend at a country house.*

16

REACH OUT I'LL BE THERE

While the others topped up their drinks before retiring, drifting between Lupin and Snowdrop (the library and the billiard room), John May seated himself in a wing-backed chair and made a list in his notebook.

> Monty Hatton-Jones
> Lord Banks-Marion
> Lady Banks-Marion
> Donald Burke
> Norma Burke
> Vanessa Harrow
> Slade Wilson
> Pamela Claxon
> Reverend Trevor Patethric
> Toby Stafford

Ten not including himself, his partner or the staff, or their informant Fruity Metcalf, whom he had yet to meet. *Arthur's right,* he thought, *we have the cast of a murder mystery right in this house. The businessman, the lord and lady, the millionaire, the wife, the singer, the designer, the novelist, the vicar and the lawyer. And nine of them share a single reason for being here. They all want something from Donald Burke. But could any of them be a potential assassin?* He bounced his pencil on the pad, thinking. In the room beyond, Vanessa Harrow was laughing softly with the interior designer. On the stereogram Sandie Shaw was singing 'Always Something There to Remind Me'.

May rose and went back out into the hall. At the open front door the butler, Alberman, was taking in a package from Parchment.

He slipped behind a grandfather clock and listened. 'It's for Mr Burke,' the valet explained. 'He left it in his car. He's most anxious—'

'You can leave it with me.' Alberman held out his hand. 'I'll make sure that he gets it.'

May heard the front door close and risked peering around the edge of the clock. Alberman was setting down the black leather case on the hall stand.

'Alberman, where the devil are you?' Lord Banks-Marion called from the billiard room. 'Why don't you ever come when I need you?'

May tiptoed out as the butler obeyed his master's call.

The box lay on the hall stand with its lid closed. It looked like a cutlery case, rectangular and flat, but was embossed with italicized initials, *DB*, in gold. Checking that the coast was clear, he flicked open the catch and peered inside.

On a red velvet pad lay six pairs of pristine white cotton gloves, identical, thumbs upwards, neatly pinned in place. He quickly closed the box and headed out of the front door, leaving it ajar.

It was a warm night. The air was filled with mayflies. A full moon illuminated the drive of cypress trees. As he walked around the house, he looked in at the glowing rooms. The guests could have been arranged to form perfect tableaux, illustrations of wealth and privilege from an earlier time.

As he stepped across the herringbone brick, May considered the gap between these images and their reality. The guests of Tavistock Hall might appear carefree, but he was starting to see how desperate they were. From the snippets of urgent conversation he had overheard, it was clear that most of them needed financial support to make it into the approaching decade. Drawing a deep breath, he took in the countryside's crisp night air.

At the rear of the house he was hit on the head with a stick. When he looked up, he found his partner hanging upside down from a tree.

'What on earth are you doing up there?' he called.

'I'm just having a rest, what do you think?' Bryant stage-whispered. 'I was trying to reach something.' He rotated slowly, dangling like a bat in a cave. 'Can you get me down?'

'I don't know. Hang on.' May climbed up a piece of trellis and reached out a hand. 'Can you untangle your braces?'

'No, they're sort of knotted.'

'Then you'll have to undo them and let go. You just have to trust me.'

Bryant popped the buttons and let go.

May made a grab for him but the falling weight was too much. His partner was swung into a rhododendron bush with a crash, like a portly acrobat who had lost his rhythm.

'I found something in Monty's room,' Bryant said, crawling out on all fours and spitting leaves. He had clumps of wisteria stuck down his shirt, bits of wood and petals all over his jacket and a piece of nest in one ear. The right knee of his trousers was torn open. He dropped the metal box on to the lawn with a thud. Luckily there was nobody around to hear them.

'What is it?'

'I have no idea. I can't get the lid open. It weighs a bloody ton.'

'What are you going to do with it?' asked May. 'It's all bashed up. We can't return it to his room in this state.'

'Fair enough.' Bryant brought the heel of his tap shoe down on the lid and tried to break it open.

'Are you sure you're up to field work?' asked May. 'It's safer being a back-room boy.'

The lid was jammed tight. 'I have to find somewhere to hide this until I can get into it. For God's sake, hold it for me.'

'I'll put it in your room.' May took the box. Bryant held his trousers up with one hand and brushed himself down with the other. 'At least I made contact with Fruity Metcalf. There's something very strange going on around here.'

'Stranger than you falling out of a tree – how?'

'I'll tell you when I've a bit more to go on. Go back to the house and cover for me, will you? You might have to calm Monty down a bit. Punch him in the neck.' He stuck out his tongue and removed a piece of branch. 'I don't know how James Bond manages it.'

Fruity Metcalf stumped to the door of his gatehouse, wiped his mouth on his working sleeve and answered the knock. 'Mr Bryant. I was just having some supper. Want some? I shot it myself. Where have you been?'

'Sorry about that, Fruity, I got stuck in a tree,' Bryant explained. 'You don't have a spare belt I could borrow?'

'I've got a piece of string.'

'That'll do.'

Metcalf held open the door. The inside of the gatehouse was chaotically furnished with items left over from the main house, but warm and cosy. 'I saw Hatton-Jones outside. What was all the ruckus?'

'He was attacked by a gryphon,' said Bryant. 'He's swearing at everyone so I think he's all right.'

'That fellow's been up to something all evening.'

'How do you know?' Bryant asked, accepting a length of baling twine from Metcalf and threading it through his belt loops.

'I saw him over by the herb garden, looking back at the house and counting the first-floor windows. He seemed to be searching for a particular room. I thought you were more worried about somebody going after him, not the other way around.'

'I am,' said Bryant. 'Did you have any luck digging up dirt on him?'

'I made some notes.' Metcalf checked his watch. 'Come on, I'll buy you a swift pint at the Goat and Compasses.'

'Won't they be shut by now?'

'They keep their own hours.' He ushered Bryant out of the door so he could lock up.

'Is this your regular haunt?' asked Bryant as they walked.

'One of them. Sometimes I go over to the Red Lion at Knotsworth. I've an old comrade-at-arms there, and the beer's cheaper.' Metcalf had a severe rolling gait that made him move like a sailor on a storm-tossed sea. 'Lost my leg below the left knee,' he explained. 'Landmine. Got a prosthetic fitted at Roehampton, but it chafes. In a funny way the loss always balanced me out, what with the right arm gone. Now I tend to rock about. I still get around all right though. I can manage the gardens. It'd take a bit more than this to slow me down.'

The pair headed out of a side gate in the garden and down a winding lane that cut deeply between the fields. The twisted, dense patchwork of the land showed through in rectangles of brown and olive green, stitched by the anthracite thread of roads. Their route was lit by the faint amber aurora still glowing on the horizon. The air smelled of honeysuckle, cut grass and cow dung.

'Unusual name,' said Bryant, studying the sign above the inn that showed a goat standing upright in leather thigh boots with a masonic compass in one raised hoof.

'It's a corruption of "God Encompasses",' Fruity explained as they ducked beneath a low warped beam. The half-timbered structure had weathered several centuries but seemed unlikely to manage many more; its red-tiled roof sagged alarmingly and even its entrance was leaning so heavily that a new door had been shaved down to accommodate its posture.

Inside, the barman stood slowly drying a dimple mug with a tea towel, making Bryant feel as if he had stepped into a Hammer film.

Fruity eased himself against the bar. 'It's early seventeenth century, so they tell me. The only pub in Crowshott.'

'What's the village like?'

'Nothing to write home about. Twenty houses, most of the residents bad-tempered and over seventy.'

Bryant cast a critical eye over the beer pumps. 'Do they know that Lord Banks-Marion and his mother are planning to sell the property?'

'Yes, and they're very upset.' They ordered pints of opaque mahogany-coloured bitter in mugs as the barman rang one of several last bells for the sake of propriety. 'Her ladyship and her son have to stay out of the village now.'

'What have you got on Monty?'

Metcalf checked his notes. 'I put out a few calls to old friends in Fleet Street. They didn't come up with much,' he said as they seated themselves. Apart from the barman there were only two other occupants, old farmers as shrunken and wizened as windfall apples. Metcalf scraped a match along its box and lit the stump of a roll-up. 'Hatton-Jones's company posted a bad year. If Chamberlain goes down Monty's business will collapse. Past relations between them were fine by all accounts.'

'Monty's story that he's acting as a witness for the prosecution on an anti-corruption ticket feels false,' said Bryant thoughtfully. 'I can't imagine he's out for anyone but himself.'

Metcalf drank the head off his beer. 'Maybe you've misjudged him.'

'What about his personal life?'

'Last year Monty's wife caught him having an affair so he kicked her out of their Mayfair flat. She tried to take him to court but didn't get anywhere. He's a notorious philanderer, but the lawyer dug up some past rumour of an indiscretion on her side and the judge ruled in favour of him, so she got nothing. Why is he here?'

Bryant took a slug of his bitter and grimaced. 'He's after some lolly. Reckons he's got a proposition for Donald Burke, but Burke only came down here to sign the papers and be with his mistress. He's staying well out of everyone else's way for now. I can't say I blame him. What do you know about this proposed business institute?'

'I've no head for business,' Metcalf admitted. 'The war killed any ambition I once had. You see someone die in front of you and making money no longer matters. They've promised to see me all right here, so I'll stay on. What is it they say? The crows always ride out the storm better than the pilot. What happens up at that old house has no effect on me.' He glanced towards his empty right sleeve. 'Nothing affects me any more.'

'What about this weekend?' Bryant asked. 'How was it planned?'

'Burke was the first to be invited.' Metcalf wiped froth from his whiskers. 'The whole thing was arranged for him. Harry and his mother have spent their last shilling on the event. Harry wants permission to keep his ashram in the grounds and stay on.'

'Why, though? Surely he'll have enough money to go wherever he likes.'

'Don't you believe it,' said the barman, who had a broad old Kentish accent and had apparently been listening to every word of their conversation. 'This feller they got coming to buy the hall is being charged well over the odds from what I heard, but his lordship spends every penny that trickles through his fingers. He paid some madwoman from London five hundred pounds to cleanse the building's aura, if you please. She went up there, read some incantations, waved a few magic sticks around and sprinkled salt everywhere. Londoners!' He barked alarmingly. 'His lordship had trouble finding anyone who was interested in taking the place off his hands. Tavistock Hall needs half a million spent on it to become proper habitable again. His lordship's run up bills for miles around. I supply his spirits but I haven't been paid for three months, and the butcher's worse off. And that's not the half of it. There's many folk here who'd like to do him harm. Move over.'

'Top us up first.' Metcalf indicated his empty pint to the landlord.

They moved in front of the crackling fire with full glasses, the young detective, the crippled old soldier and the bored barman. Cinders ascended from the hearth and burst from the pub's chimney pot as if trying to alert constabularies of the licensing infringement.

Some time later, Arthur and Fruity heaved themselves out of the Goat & Compasses and crossed the pub forecourt. As Metcalf turned the corner, something flew past his right ear. He touched his hand to his woollen cap and turned around. Two gumbooted young men were leaning against a dry-stone wall, dimly outlined against the night sky. 'Garn, clear off!' shouted one. 'Go back up to the hall and stay out of our village!'

The other stooped for a rock and hurled it. Bryant pushed Metcalf out of the way. It cracked against the wall of the car park. He was about to head over to the lads and threaten them with arrest when he realized that doing so would ruin his cover. He had no idea who they might know, so he reluctantly carried on walking. 'I presume they're tenants?' he asked.

'The natives are restless,' Metcalf replied. 'They're losing their homes. Let's get out of here.' They headed off up the moonlit lane as further stones clattered behind them. 'The whole village is up for sale now,' he said, 'but nobody in Crowshott can afford to buy their own place. If you're looking for a reason why somebody might get hurt, that's it.'

17

TWIST AND SHOUT

Bryant left Fruity Metcalf at the gatehouse and went back into Tavistock Hall, where he found that most of the guests had drifted off to bed. Ever alert to movements in the house, Alberman appeared from the gloom to inform him that Lord Banks-Marion had headed down the garden to his ashram. Bryant cocked his ear and heard the twangling of poorly played sitars emanating from what appeared to be a Mongolian yurt. He smelled cigars, perfume and incense.

As he passed the door of the library he saw that May was sharing an immense overstuffed sofa with Vanessa Harrow. Leaning in, he beckoned. 'John, I mean Jack, could I possibly tear you away for a moment?'

'What do you want?' whispered May, stepping outside the door. 'I was getting on well there.'

'What makes your hormones override your common sense?' asked Bryant, amazed. 'You do realize she's a millionaire's mistress? He could pay to have your legs broken.'

'It was all very innocent,' said May. 'She was offering to take me around the delphiniums.'

'I imagine that at this time of the night they're past their best, as indeed are you. How many whiskies have you had? Technically speaking we're still on duty.'

'Relax,' said May, holding up the decanter, 'I've been doing some research. Let's find somewhere quiet.'

Slipping into Lavender, they found that the dining room had been cleared and the tables polished and separated. They located a pair of whisky tumblers and dragged two badly stuffed armchairs from the corner where they had been hiding a section of damp, rotted wallpaper.

'Monty seems to have survived his ordeal intact,' said May. 'He's furious about his room. You could have left it tidy. I've got Alberman and Parchment patrolling past his bedroom door, just to make sure that nothing else happens to him. You were right by the way: the old lord didn't like his servants to have difficult names. Parchment's real name is Prabhakar. You don't think the gargoyle could have accidentally come loose, do you?'

'Not a chance,' said Bryant. 'That thing weighed a ton. Nothing would have blown it over. Someone had been up there, though. What about the rest of the guests, what are they about? This designer fellow, Slade Wilson, do you have any idea where he fits in?'

'I think he's just another butterfly attracted by the colour of money,' said May, pouring drinks. 'Burke's lawyer, Toby Stafford, is going to be managing the day-to-day finances of the new business institute. He's staying over at the Red Lion in Knotsworth.'

'So he wasn't invited to stay at the hall?'

'He was but chose not to. He's not keen about having to socialize with Harry, given that the negotiations are still ongoing.'

'I got the impression that the deal had been finalized.'

'For the property, yes, but they're arguing over the inclusion of all the fittings. The wording on the initial document wasn't clear. You may have noticed some fine paintings on the staircase. Lady Banks-Marion wants to get some of them excluded. Harry, in his eagerness to sell the house, signed them away.'

Bryant sipped his whisky, thinking. 'I'm more interested in Donald Burke. Why would Norma allow her husband's mistress under the same roof, do you think?'

'Yes, it's a bit of a puzzler, isn't it? I'm told the wife's fiercely loyal. Of course she stays in the background and leaves the finances to him, but she'd have to be very dense not to realize that Vanessa Harrow is being kept by him. Apparently it's been all over the scandal rags. Burke's considerably older and used to getting his own way.'

'A regular captain of industry, then.'

'According to Harry, Burke simply announced that he would attend with his mistress. Perhaps he wasn't expecting the wife to trot along.'

'That would explain the tension in the room. I don't care much for whisky. Are there any beers?' Bryant managed to reach a bottle and an opener without leaving his armchair. 'What about the novelist, Hooter?'

'Claxon. I think she's an ally of Mrs Burke's. Her books are in the library and I saw Norma Burke reading one of them.'

'Yes, I've ploughed through them too. As for the vicar . . .'

'I suppose there's always a vicar.' May examined his cut-crystal glass. 'It's a country house tradition, isn't it? He has the local parish at the bottom of the hill, St Stephen's. He's after money, too. As soon as everyone heard that Burke was visiting for the weekend I imagine they appeared like flies on a dunghill.'

Bryant took a swig of beer. 'Do you think any of Harry's guests could actually have been hired to attack Monty?'

'It seems far-fetched. And if there's a rotten apple, I have no clues so far,' said May. 'Harry's father was the fourteenth in his line, a true Edwardian and greatly admired. He had high hopes for his son. Harry went soft in the head. His mother blames the Beatles. He was kicked out of Charterhouse and Sandhurst, then dropped out of his social engagements calendar in order to launch some kind of manifesto for world peace that involved him running around naked in body paint waving sparklers. He ended up in a Calcutta hospital suffering from an overdose of LSD. Meanwhile, the hall was falling apart. The ceiling in the master bedroom caved in and one of the bathrooms subsided, taking half the plumbing with it. Most of the staff walked out. The old man's lifetime addiction to claret and laudanum finally got the better of him and he was carted off to St Stephen's churchyard. Who do you think presided over his remains?'

'Let me guess, the Vicar of Stiffkey himself, the good Reverend Trevor?'

'Right, and that's when Harry persuaded his grieving mother to sell the pile. The big surprise is that Donald Burke isn't planning to boot him off the property. Americans always have an exaggerated respect for the English aristocracy. I can't imagine why. He probably thinks Harry is charmingly unconventional.'

'Maybe he senses a fellow eccentric,' said Bryant.

'Do you have any idea why Burke would send for six pairs of white cotton gloves?' May explained what he'd seen.

'Not a clue. You know how men get when they become rich. Nobody denies them anything.'

'According to Norma he wanted to buy the place sight unseen – sent the wife and lawyer over to check it out. The plan is to hack away the damp and dry rot, put in new plumbing and remove the most damaged walls, but there's a row going on about what should be saved from the historic interior, which is why Wilson is here, to fight in Burke's corner against the conservationists.'

'You managed to gather quite a bit of intel while I was downing pints with Fruity,' said Bryant, impressed. 'Do *you* think someone tried to kill Monty?'

'It's hard to tell,' said May. 'I'd like him to stay with the group as much as possible, but he has a habit of slipping away.'

'Then let's take a walk through the house, just to make

sure that he's safe where he is,' said Bryant. 'Come with me. I'd better take off my tap shoes. I don't think creeping around after dark is encouraged. Alberman's already got his beady eye on me.'

'I wanted him guarding Monty, but the family keeps putting him on the main staircase.'

Tavistock Hall had bedded down for the night. Somewhere a hot-water pipe clonked. In the first-floor passageway the edge of a tapestry flapped, and dried leaves fluttered in an amphora. Even the floorboards were stretching out and ticking back into place.

Removing their shoes, the pair headed for the stairs and made their way up in the gloom, past a dozen grim portraits of ancestors. The wind had risen and was moaning faintly through the warped frames of the lead-light windows. A few lights showed under bedroom doors. Most of the hall bulbs had been removed, presumably to save money. A threadbare runner lay over the polished planks of the corridor, which creaked like a ship's cabin as they walked across them.

'I told Monty to keep his door locked tonight,' said May. 'Just in case.'

Bryant pulled a crumpled page from his jacket and used his lighter to illuminate some pencil lines. 'I think he and I have had the same thought,' he said. 'We both counted the number of windows from outside.'

'Why?'

'Because the bedroom doors don't match up. I traced a plan of the house from a book in the library earlier. This can't be correct. The right-hand corridor has four doors, the left five. Each room has three windows, two in the bedroom, one in the loo, which would make 27 windows in total, right? Alberman told me all the bedrooms are identical in size. But there are 28 windows, arranged in two sets of 14.'

'How old is that plan?'

'Mid 1920s.'

'There you are. The house has probably been altered a lot since then.'

'There have clearly been some cosmetic changes but I can't see anything structural. It's odd, though. There's supposed to be another door.' Bryant ran his hand over the wood panelling. On one side of the corridor two of the bedroom doors were more widely spaced. 'The panels look original to me, but there's definitely a space behind here. Feel.' He put his hand to the spot where the joints joined and could feel the draught that caused the tapestry to stir.

'Why do you always have to make a mystery out of everything?' asked May. 'Someone's done a surreptitious bit of DIY, OK? It was probably—'

A door creaked behind them. The Reverend Patethric stuck his head out. 'Oh, it's you, Mr Askey. I thought I heard something. These old houses—'

'Just off to say my prayers, Reverend,' said Bryant hastily. 'I'll say one for you.' As the door shut, he turned to May. 'Why is he staying here? Doesn't that strike you as odd?'

They made their way further along the corridor. 'That's Burke's room at the end,' said May. 'He and his wife have the corner suite but there's no extra window in the end wall.'

'But that's for a different reason,' Bryant pointed out. 'One of the earlier manor houses on this site was erected during the reign of William III, so it was probably bricked up. The window tax lasted for more than a century and a half, so I guess when the house was rebuilt it kept to the revised number of windows.'

'You've been down in the library, haven't you.'

'Part of the job.'

'You didn't nick anything?'

'Not this time, no.'

They stopped before the door and listened. No sound came from within, but a shadow passed in the strip of yellow light beneath the door.

'Nothing going on here. Let's see if we can spot anything from the outside,' Bryant whispered.

Heading downstairs, they stepped out on to the back patio and walked across the lawn, looking up at the house to where the balcony ran past the bedrooms on the first floor. Outside the end suite they watched as the figure with long grey hair stepped out on to the balcony, pacing back and forth. He left a trail of cigar smoke behind him. A transistor radio was faintly playing an old Beatles song: 'Twist And Shout'.

'It's funny,' whispered Bryant, 'Trev the Rev told me that Burke hated other people smoking.'

Burke suddenly threw his cigar from the balcony and began dancing.

'What on earth is he doing?' asked May.

'The twist, I think,' said Bryant.

Norma Burke came to the window in a pale blue quilted nightdress. 'Come back inside, Donald,' she said, her voice carrying on the clear night air. 'Before somebody sees you. I told you not to drink so much.'

'I'm going in,' said May. 'You're watching the wrong one. It's not Burke who's at risk, it's Monty.'

Bryant remained on the lawn to watch the peculiar spectacle of the twisting millionaire.

18

SUSPICIOUS MINDS

'Where the hell have you been?' Monty demanded of Bryant. He dragged the pair aside just as May was forking kidneys on to a plate. 'Somebody violated my room last night.'

'Oh dear. Was anything taken?'

Monty's mouth opened and shut again.

The three of them were the first ones down to breakfast on Saturday morning, which had been laid out in Primrose, the south-facing breakfast room. A dozen silver tureens set along the sideboard offered a substantial start to the day. Monty was bandaged under his shirt, as stiff and lopsided as the Hunchback of Notre-Dame.

'I told you I was being stalked. At first I assumed that the maid had left the window open and my papers had got all blown about, but it appears to have been the work of an idiot. All my documents had been taken out of my bag and simply strewn around. They're trying to put the wind up me.'

Bryant wasn't really interested in Monty's complaints. His concentration had been monopolized by the buffet. 'Why would anyone do that?'

'It's an act of industrial espionage. And there's this.' Monty opened his hand and revealed a loop of silver thread. 'It must have come from someone's sleeve.'

'Slade Wilson was wearing a jacket with a silver trim last night,' said Bryant, keen to shift the blame. 'Why would he search your belongings?'

'It's obvious,' Monty replied. 'I'm a witness for the prosecution. He was looking for my trial notes.'

'Do you have them with you?'

'Of course I do! I'm rehearsing with them over the weekend.'

'You don't think Wilson was recruited by Sir Charles Chamberlain?'

'You're the copper, you tell me.' Monty poked him in the chest with a fat finger. 'Find out what he's up to. If anything happens to me, you and your pal are finished.'

'Is there anything you haven't told us?' asked Bryant, wary that the older man could have him removed from the unit if he complained to Farthingshaw.

'Certainly not.' Not a muscle twitched as he stared Bryant in the eye. 'If it wasn't espionage it must have been those filthy hippies, looking for money to buy drugs. They'd fumbled through my clothes and my balcony had bits of branch all over it.'

Bryant found himself quite enjoying Monty's discomfort. 'But why would they only target your room?'

'Because I'd left the window open and there's a vine outside. They must have climbed up.' Monty blanched. 'Or it could have been someone sending me a warning not to appear at Monday's trial, someone I'd never suspect.' His eyes swivelled madly. 'That bloody vicar.'

'The *vicar*?'

'Well, clearly he's not a *real* vicar, he's bogus. Nobody can look that cheerful all the time. You have to find out. Question him on bell-ringing or something.'

'I think you should be the one to do that,' said Bryant, looking at Monty's hunched shoulder.

'You're making jokes at a time like this? I tell you I saw him lurking in the passageway when I went to the bathroom.'

'Did he say anything?'

'Nothing much, but he was still hanging around outside his door a few minutes later, when I came back.'

'It's not a very effective way of silencing you, is it?' May made a move towards the sausages but was beaten to them by Bryant, who had piled his plate with kedgeree, eggs, mushrooms, beans, bacon, toast, butter and marmalade.

'You two aren't taking this very seriously, are you?' Monty hissed. 'It could be "The Adventure of the Speckled Band" all over again.'

'I think that was rather an outré death even by Conan Doyle's standards.' Bryant waved him aside with a sausage. 'I mean, how could Grimesby Roylott be sure that the snake was going to bite his victim?' It was typical that Bryant would remember the name of the villain in a Sherlock Holmes story but not his own alias.

'Look here, up until now I've been very patient with the pair of you, but I want some proper protection. Since you got here all you've done is stuff your faces and drink vintage wines.'

'We've had some excellent brandies too,' Bryant pointed out. 'Funny, he didn't want us around before, did he, John?'

'I seem to recall he told us to buzz off,' May agreed.

'Before we can protect you we have to understand where the danger lies.'

'And what have you identified?' Monty demanded to know.

'As far as I can tell there are a number of high risk factors, not the least of which' – Bryant paused to check his watch just as a loud explosion rattled the windows – 'is that one.'

'What the hell was that?' Monty cried, looking up in alarm as the chandelier swayed above them.

Bryant held up a folded rectangle of paper. 'Alberman brought me a telegram. It's from our unit. There's a French major general visiting the local barracks to take part in a military exercise; that noise we heard last night was the starting cannon. Owing to an administrative cock-up they marked this area down as enemy territory. Army HQ mistakenly thought Tavistock Hall was empty, so they closed the road. It doesn't look like anybody's going to be leaving the house for a while. It's possible that somebody here knew you would be trapped.'

Monty looked horrified. 'What do you mean, trapped?'

'There's only one road connecting Crowshott to Knotsworth, and it's going to be shut for the next twenty-four hours,' Bryant explained. 'Normally that wouldn't be much of an inconvenience to anyone around here, but nobody told the army that the Banks-Marions were hosting a weekend party. You weren't the only one lured by the thought of pitching a business opportunity to an American millionaire. Any of the other guests could have found out that you were staying for the weekend and decided it would be the perfect opportunity to get rid of you. Then there's Harry.' Bryant bit the end off a mustard-smeared sausage and chewed thoughtfully.

'What about him?' croaked Monty, growing visibly weaker.

'He's a loose cannon if ever there was one. We need to know who he's talked to and what he's said. And the hippies – we have no idea who's staying in that ashram. They could be criminals. Finally there are the good villagers of Crowshott, some of whom are about to lose their homes because of the Banks-Marions and Mr Burke.'

'Then surely they're all more at risk than I am,' said Monty, looking almost relieved.

'That would be the obvious assumption,' Bryant answered, 'but we should think a little more deviously than that. How much would you say Sir Charles Chamberlain stands to lose if he's found guilty?'

Monty considered the question for a moment. 'He has clients all over the world. There are governments keen on hiring him for major rebuilding projects.'

'And the only thing that stands between his fortune and total ruin may be you. Wouldn't it be worth putting some real effort into discrediting you, and coming up with the kind of elaborate plan you wouldn't see coming?'

'You're saying Burke is a decoy, a trick to lure me here?'

'Possibly,' said Bryant. 'I can't think on an empty stomach. Will you excuse me? My sausages are getting cold.'

'Did anybody else hear that extraordinary bang?' asked Norma Burke, entering the breakfast salon. She was dressed in full English county attire, tweed skirt, tartan cardigan, hair tied back, lace-up shoes. 'It gave me quite a fright.'

'The army,' Monty replied, too worried about himself to make an effort towards civility.

'I was wondering if I could have a word with your husband,' said May, seizing the opportunity.

'You'll have to get a move on,' Norma warned. 'He said something about going into the village this morning. He has a breakfast meeting with his lawyer. He insisted on walking. Do you think it's safe for him out there?'

'It should be so long as he keeps his wits about him,' May replied. 'I imagine it would be easier to dodge a Chieftain tank on foot.' Casting a longing glance at his heaped plate, he realized what he would have to do. 'Perhaps I should go and keep an eye on him, just to make sure. We can't have anyone getting flattened.'

'Good idea,' said Bryant. 'I'll guard your breakfast.'

Norma poured herself a coffee. 'What brings you here, Mr Askey?' she asked.

For a moment Bryant forgot his alias and looked around, but he recovered fast. 'Mr March and I are working with Monty on a number of business ventures. He wangled us an invite for the weekend.'

She stirred her coffee thoughtfully. 'So you're petitioning my husband too? How disappointing.'

'I didn't know he would be here,' he replied truthfully.

Her eyebrows rose. 'That rather makes you unique in this crowd. Word of Donald's largesse has a habit of getting around. He was never like this before his breakdown.'

'I wasn't aware he had been ill.'

'It's hardly a topic one raises over the dinner table, Mr—'

'Please, call me Arthur.'

'My husband had been overworked for a number of years. Of course, we weren't always wealthy. People forget how hard times were after the war.'

'But your fortunes changed.'

'Yes, and good fortune brought new friends.' She lifted the lid of a tureen and peered inside. 'But it made him suspicious of everyone. My husband has a penchant for investing in new ventures, but he avoids anyone who looks like they might have something dubious to sell.'

'Like Mr Hatton-Jones.'

Norma dabbed at her hair absently. 'I'm afraid so. He keeps asking Miss Harrow if she'll introduce him to Donald. I can't think why.'

Bryant decided to remain silent.

Harry came in from the garden and checked the tureens. 'Are the kidneys still warm? According to the papers the weather's due to turn nasty,' he said merrily. 'I think we should play some games. I love games.' He helped himself to some porridge and stood examining the ladle. After a moment he pulled something black and hairy out of it. Bryant was horrified to realize that it was his moustache.

Harry didn't seem bothered by his discovery, and merely flicked it into a saucer. 'I say, did anyone hear that boom? I saw an army tank charging across the bottom of the field just now, followed by a load of chaps with bushes on their heads. I think they were armed with bayonets. They don't normally come this close. They've ruined the croquet lawn. The reverend was in the lane on his bicycle, pedalling hell for leather. It looked as if he was going to the village. The soldiers were right in his path. I hope they're not using real bullets. Some-body could get killed.'

Pamela Claxon appeared in the doorway. 'Am I the last one down?'

'No, and of course Wilson hasn't put in an appearance yet.' Monty forked scrambled egg into his face. 'You know how wogs have trouble getting up in the mornings.'

Bryant laid down his cutlery. 'How would you know, exactly?'

'Oh, we had a couple of 'em in our platoon, perfectly decent chaps but they nodded off whenever the sun came out. It's in their nature.'

'Did it ever occur to you that Mr Wilson might find the way you speak to him offensive?' Bryant asked. The other guests fell silent and listened to the argument.

'I treat him exactly the same way I treat everyone else,' Monty insisted. 'He's knows I'm only joking.'

'Don't you think it's demeaning to refer to him by what you presumptuously take to be the characteristics of his race?'

Monty looked shocked. 'Not at all. People don't complain about *The Black and White Minstrel Show*, do they?'

'Actually they do,' said Pamela.

'Well, when I next talk to my little coloured friend I'll ask him if he minds the odd joke, shall I?' asked Monty angrily.

'I would never allow my detective to say things like that,' Pamela muttered.

'Ah yes, the Trench fellow,' said Monty dismissively.

'*Inspector* Trench.'

'He sounds like someone from the gas board. You know, Inspect a Trench.'

'He's very popular,' Pamela bristled.

'I dare say,' Monty agreed. 'There must be many servants who enjoy reading that sort of stuff.'

'Good morning,' said Wilson, wandering in wearing a bus-red dressing gown. 'Was that thunder just now?'

'Good morning, Mr Wilson,' said Bryant. 'Monty here wants to ask you something.'

Another explosion shook the room, delicately rattling the chandelier. A plume of plaster dust settled over the kedgeree.

'Gosh, I hope the pile doesn't fall down before Donald moves in,' said Harry, studying the ceiling with concern.

'If it does I imagine my husband will want his money back,' replied Norma, dusting off her shoulder.

Wilson looked puzzled. The smile faded from his lips. 'Monty, what was it you wanted to ask me?'

Monty's perpetually marbled complexion finally paled. From this point on, the weekend took a turn for the worse.

19

THE GIRL WITH THE SUN IN HER HAIR

The military manoeuvres had not scared off the wildlife: the grey morning fog had dissipated far enough to reveal curlews in a field and a pair of large glossy crows standing like bookends on a low stone wall. There was also something furry and crimson lying disembowelled in the road. May blew into his cupped hands and carried on walking. He had brought nothing suitable for tramping muddy lanes. His shoes looked as if they belonged in Jermyn Street, not the Kent countryside, so he had been forced to borrow some rather outsized wellingtons.

As the mist rolled back a little further he caught a glimpse of Donald Burke's stocky figure striding around the next bend. The millionaire had donned a tweed overcoat and hat, but was instantly recognizable from the grey hair over his collar and his wide-legged gait. For an older man he moved with tremendous speed and purpose. Although May tried to close the gap between them he was soon out of breath.

The road meandered through the fields like a river, winding deeply within tall, dense hedgerows of hawthorn and bramble. There were no turn-offs, so Burke could have only one destination in mind: Crowshott. Halfway along the lane the hedge was torn apart where a tank had crashed through it and ploughed mud from its tracks across to the next field.

By the time the road opened out into the village there was no sign of Burke. He had simply turned a corner and vanished.

May was brought up short. A lichen-pocked stone cross stood on the green beside a duck pond. Against the window of a grocery store leaned a butcher's bike, its wicker basket filled with paper packages. A grey-uniformed nanny passed by with a perambulator. In the distance he could hear the whine of a milk float, its metal bottle-cages rattling. There was no one else to be seen. The road led in two directions only: one went on to Knotsworth; the other headed back to the hall.

For all of last night's talk about the country's changing social order, here it felt as if nothing had altered in over a century. Kent was still the sempiternal garden of England, yeasty with beer and hop pickers, its hedgerows plump with blackberries, its villages becalmed the year round except for two weeks in August when holidaymakers passed through on their way to the coast. The first motorway south had opened now, which meant there were even fewer visitors passing through.

If Donald Burke was meeting his lawyer it seemed likely that he would head for the Red Lion in Knotsworth, where Stafford was staying, but Norma had said 'the village', which surely suggested Crowshott.

May entered Crowshott's only telephone box and called Directory Enquiries, who gave him the number for the Red Lion. The landlord told him that Mr Stafford had gone out early, but he could try the Goat & Compasses, as they also did breakfasts, so he headed over there.

Just as Bryant had found him the night before, the barman was slowly polishing glasses behind the counter. 'G'morning, sir,' he said, 'are you here for breakfast?'

'Is there anyone else in the dining room?' May asked.

'Just one. Through there. Mind your head.' He pointed the way through a narrow arched door marked 'Duck or Grouse'.

Vanessa Harrow sat alone by a lead-light window with her elbows on the table, one hand clasping the other. Against the smeared glass, with the pale sunlight shining through a haze of smoke, there was something leonine about her. She was wearing an amber slash-neck top, a heavy rope of yellow plastic beads and a scent, Chanel No. 5, rather exotic for a country pub. He tried not to find her entrancing.

She looked up as he approached. 'Hello, Jack. You escaped as well.' She pointed to the empty chair opposite with her cigarette.

'I'm not interrupting anything?' May looked around for any sign that Donald Burke had been in the room. A bright yellow overcoat and matching beret hung on a stand but there was nothing else.

'No, I was just – I thought it would be nice to get away for a few minutes. The tea and toast are fresh. I didn't feel like facing another veiled inquisition from our fellow guests this morning.'

'I'm not very good at table talk either.' May helped himself to a cup.

'I thought you did all right last night.'

May laughed. 'I might have been better in the 1920s, when the old order was still in place around here. At least I would have known what was expected of me.'

'You mean servants laying out your clothes and that sort of thing? Instead of Harry dancing about to his sitar music and everyone asking impertinent questions about sex?'

'Were they? I missed that part somehow.' He helped himself to toast.

'My relationship with Donald seems to intrigue them, but they don't quite know what to do about it. I suppose in the old days I'd have simply been snubbed.' She stubbed out her cigarette. 'One senses that the traditional country house rulebook is being torn up. And a good thing too, I suppose.'

'Why do you say that?' May asked.

'Darling, haven't you seen the way they anatomize me, the painted strumpet from Mayfair? As if they occupy the moral high ground. They're all so desperately keen for me to reveal the blots in my copybook, just so it'll give them something to talk about back in London. You and your colleague don't seem so judgemental. You're out of place down here.'

'Arthur says the days of the grand weekend are over,' said May. 'He thinks all these old mansions will be soon knocked down or sold off for flats.'

'I imagine he's right. Who can afford them now? I mean, except for Americans. Perhaps they'll be our saviours.'

'Speaking of whom, you haven't seen Mr Burke here, have you? His wife said he was coming to the village for breakfast.' He tried to sound casual.

'I haven't seen anyone else.' She glanced towards the kitchen. 'You can ask the waitress.'

'You weren't meeting him yourself?'

'Now why would I do that?' Her wide, innocent eyes defied him to disbelieve her.

'I thought you were close friends.'

The question went unanswered. Vanessa looked away to the window.

'I'm twenty-four, Jack. Three years ago, my father died. They said it was a heart attack, but it was the war that killed him. He couldn't make sense of the world any more. When I was a little girl I wanted to be a nurse and bring out the best in people, but somehow I ended up working in a nightclub, where I only see the worst of them.' She drew out a fresh Consulate and lit it. 'My poor father. He walked down the street looking at others of my age, the way they dressed and behaved, and couldn't understand what the war had been for. I tried to explain to him: this is *exactly* what you fought for, so that people could be as free as this. It wasn't the kind of freedom he had imagined.'

'I'm sorry about your father,' said May. 'I think many people feel the way he did.'

'Donald Burke found me my job. He's been kind to me.' She looked him straight in the eye. 'Shall I tell you the absolute truth, Mr March? I know they all think we're having an affair, but we're not. Donald was told about me by Toby Stafford, and called to offer me employment. He and Norma don't have children, and Donald's only a little younger than my father was when he died. He suggested we might occasionally go to a party together – is that so terrible? But so far he's been too busy to take me out. He's clever and rich and successful, and he's a Republican so of course all the English socialists loathe him. But his taxes pay for their mistakes.'

'Lord Banks-Marion certainly seems happy about selling the hall to him,' May pointed out.

'Harry's family were old high Tories, but he ceased to be part of the establishment after he refused to struggle on with the ancestral pile.' Vanessa tapped her cigarette with a crimson nail. 'The sale is an act of betrayal. He was thrown out of his father's club over it. You do realize that this isn't just a jolly weekend in the country, I suppose?'

'What do you mean?' asked May.

'There are two factions: Donald's loyal and desperate supporters, and those who hope to persuade Harry to refuse the offer and reclaim his birthright. They'd rather see Tavistock Hall turned into a filthy old hippy retreat than go to an American who'll lovingly restore it.'

May buttered himself some toast. 'So who's who?'

'Lady Banks-Marion wants to keep the house, even though there's no money left for the restoration.'

'What about selling the fixtures and fittings?'

'I imagine that was one option, which was removed when Harry threw them in to sweeten the deal.'

'Who else?'

'The Claxon woman is as thick as thieves with Norma Burke,

but I heard she has the ear of someone who works closely with our prime minister-in-waiting, Mr Heath, although nobody seems to know why. I imagine they would prefer to see the hall remain in English hands. On the other side there's Slade Wilson, who's highly thought of in certain London circles and not quite as silly as you'd think. He wants Donald to buy the hall, as does Toby Stafford. Then there's your pal Monty, who seems eager to collar Donald about some project of his own.' Vanessa studied him with fresh interest. 'You listen but you don't say much, do you? Anyone would think you were taking notes.'

'Do you think I should?'

She reached forward and pressed a forefinger against his shirt. 'You don't fool anyone, Jack. I know all about you.' She continued to study him for a moment, then sat back. 'You're not a friend of Monty's. I've seen the way he looks at the pair of you, as if he can't wait to give you the slip. You're his minders.'

'I've disturbed you for long enough,' May said, checking his watch and rising. 'I'd better be getting back.'

'Fine,' said Vanessa with a mischievous smile. 'Keep your secrets, but I'm on your case, Mr March, so you'd better watch out.'

As May passed the barman, still seemingly at work on the same glass, he asked, 'Have there been any other gentlemen in for breakfast this morning?'

'No, sir,' he answered. 'You could try the Red Lion. But you can't drive down the lane today. The army has closed it off, third time this year. It plays havoc with our deliveries.'

As he left the inn, the Reverend Patethric shot past the end of the road on his bicycle, pedalling fast. A line of heavy grey cloud had formed along the horizon like a distant Atlantic wave. The wind had risen, and cawing crows were riding the branches with feathers a-flutter as if they were at sea.

Slipping back into the village's only telephone box, he counted out some more coins and rang Gladys Forthright at the unit. To reach her he had to dial 'O' for the operator and push button A when she answered.

She sounded tired. 'Good morning, John. I thought you'd call. I sent Arthur a telegram about the army closing the road. How is it going down there?'

'Someone took a whack at Monty last night, but he's all right. Arthur seems to think that something worse is going to happen unless we can stop it. He says he can intuit confrontations from overheard conversations and body language. Personally, I think it's a load of rubbish. He's started getting interested in crackpot sciences lately.'

He heard the pages of a notebook being turned. 'I've got some background checks for you. Do you have a pencil?'

'I'll remember. If we do have a fifth columnist in our midst I need all the help you can give me.'

'Well, it's not Harry Banks-Marion,' said Gladys. 'He's the real thing. In fact, they all are as far as I can tell. There's nothing hidden up anyone's sleeves. Harry's father was Edward, Lord Banks-Marion; the mother is—'

'I've met her. Beatrice. She must have been quite a society beauty in her day. Rather severe and tragic now.'

'She had her portrait painted by John Singer Sargent. It's in the National Portrait Gallery now. Harry's technically the sole heir to Tavistock Hall. Just before his son went off to India the father planned to change his will and leave the house to the nation, until he found out that it wouldn't exempt the family from taxation. What's that awful noise?'

May placed a finger in his ear and squinted out through the glass. 'There's a tractor in the field behind that appears to be spraying mud in every direction. Does Harry have any enemies?'

'I've only turned up one: Major Julius Tilden, an old friend of his father's. He lives in Crowshott's only other grand house and tried to block the sale. He's one of the fellows involved in the army game that's keeping you at the house this weekend.'

'I don't suppose you've had any luck calling them off?'

'I've not been able to reach anyone. They're all on field phones. I tried getting someone from the village to go over there, but they're not about to run across a field full of troops carrying live ammunition. Even the Canterbury constabulary told me to keep everyone away.'

'Fair enough. What else have you got?'

'The vicar, Trevor Patethric. He's not without his secrets. Great things had been expected of him at Balliol but he was sent down. You'd probably like to know why and I'd love to help you, but it's Saturday and no one is answering their telephones. Whatever he did was enough to have him packed off to a small Kentish parish instead of taking up a position high in the Church. Slade Wilson redecorated Chatsworth, or possibly Chequers, depending on whom I spoke to. His designs didn't go down well – too modern, apparently – but he's at the top of everyone's commissioning list. Famous for creating parties at country houses, everyone got up as characters from *Tales of Hoffman* with the local villagers dressed as sheep and goats, that sort of thing. Born to Jamaican diplomats and a confirmed bachelor, with all that *that* implies. Got himself into a bit of a situation with an earl's son some years ago and it ruined his social standing. Ever since then he's been trying to climb back up the ladder.'

'I guess he sees Tavistock Hall as his key to success,' said May. 'Anything else?'

'Hang on a sec.' He heard boots clomp off and return. 'I knew you'd want to know about Donald Burke so I went to the newspaper files on Newman Street first thing and pulled everything they had on him. He's a self-made man, born early in the century – I don't have an exact date – and raised in Chicago by an English mother and an American father. He made some wise investments in art, real estate and inventions – he patented those soap-dispenser things they have in public bathrooms – and he never seems to put a foot wrong. Very well liked and highly thought of. He used to be a keen sailor. I found some photographs of him and his wife in the files. Rather handsome, taken on board his yacht somewhere on the south coast.'

'So, no hint of any scandal or misdeed?'

'I've only been looking for a short while but so far there's nothing. I mean, *nothing*. He's square-jawed and true blue, but he does have a couple of weaknesses. He works alone and keeps his cards close to his chest. I'm told he keeps an inner "trust circle", and only those who have proven they can be relied upon are admitted. Everyone else is kept at a distance. I spoke to a former employee who says that since his breakdown he's become more suspicious of everyone and harder to work with, although his instinct for good investments is as sound as ever.'

'That fits with what I've been told.' Something hit the window of the telephone box. He peered out at the tractor, which seemed to be deliberately hurling earth at him.

'He gives his employees explicit instructions not to speak unless they're spoken to first,' Gladys continued. 'He refuses to attend shareholder meetings and won't have his picture taken, although I found a few pictures in the files snapped covertly by newspaper photographers.'

'What about his wife?'

'Nothing much. She's supportive but stays away from his business affairs. She's on record as being anti women's lib, believes a wife should be a good cook and keep a nice house and that's about it. She's a grocer's daughter from Nottingham. I can't find out anything about how they met. That part doesn't ring true.'

'Why not?'

'The wife of a high-flyer like Burke? There should be something more, shouldn't there?'

'Perhaps her background was less than wholesome, so he scrubbed her past from the papers.'

'Which brings me to Vanessa Harrow,' said Gladys, checking her notes. 'A bit fast by all accounts. The gossip columnists love her and she clearly plays up to them, the archetypal dumb blonde.'

'That's not what I'm getting from her at all,' said May.

'Then it's a ruse to keep men where she wants them,' said Forthright.

'How do you know that?'

'We've all done it, John. You probably want to know if she's sleeping with Donald Burke.'

'She says she's never been out with him.'

'I could run a check on her account when the banks open and find out if she deposits money from him.'

'Forget it, we don't have that long.'

'She's been photographed leaving his Mayfair flat, but I'm still waiting for several journalists to call me back with more details.'

'Keep at it, Gladys. If anything important comes up, leave a message with Fruity Metcalf. He has a telephone in his cottage.'

'I've got the number.'

'Anything else on the novelist?'

'I haven't had time to check yet, although I do have one of her murder mysteries. It wasn't very good. I guessed who did it.'

'That just leaves Monty himself. I don't suppose you thought of—'

'I did, as it happens. You say he and Sir Charles Chamberlain were great friends?'

'So he tells me.'

'It might have been the case once, but they had a falling out. You remember Jimmy the Weasel?'

'From the Bethnal Green mob?'

'The very same. He's got a mate in Barings Bank who reckons Chamberlain and Hatton-Jones fought over a woman, a certain blonde nightclub singer.'

'You don't mean—'

'The very same. It seems that while they were arguing about her, Burke stole her away.'

'So now Monty's down here in the embarrassing position of trying to strike a deal with Burke in front of his former mistress. It makes me wonder what else I'm missing.'

'One other thing. Monty's company isn't doing well. He has a lot of angry creditors chasing him.'

'That's very helpful, Gladys. Keep on the case, would you?'

'If you speak to Roger, don't tell him I'm helping you. He gave me specific instructions not to aid you in any way. And be careful.'

'Why?'

'Burke has friends in the military. Maybe he knew the army would be conducting manoeuvres this weekend. He could have brought everyone together for a purpose. He could even be the one who wants to prevent Hatton-Jones from testifying.'

'Gladys, I assure you this is all about keeping Monty safe. Maybe I should have insisted on him staying in London after all. I'd better be off before they miss me back at the house.'

'One last thing, John,' said Gladys. 'Keep an eye on Mr Bryant for me? You know how he tends to hurl himself into situations.'

'Don't worry, I'll make sure he doesn't come to harm. Do me a favour, will you? I don't know when I'll be able to get through to you again. Check around and see if we have any-one else in the area. If Arthur's intuition proves right, we may need some extra help here.'

'I'll do my best, but it's Saturday morning. You know how hard it is to get hold of anyone.'

Gladys rang off and May headed back into the hedgerows, keeping an eye out for rifle fire. As he turned back into the lane he disturbed a huddle of rooks, busy pecking the eyes out of a rabbit.

20

PURPLE HAZE

The clouds had blackened and were dipping down, blossoming like ink being released into water.

The girl was wearing a string of plastic orchids, purple silk harem pants, body paint and a beatific smile, even though it was starting to rain. She swayed to the sound of the sitar, her eyes closed, wrists raised in what she imagined was a *nautch* pose, but her braided blond hair presented her as anything but Indian. Her finger-bells chimed in time to the music.

Harry might have called it an ashram, but this collection of half-collapsed tents and packing crates, piled on to the churned-up lawn of the walled garden, was as far from the idea of a spiritual hermitage as one could imagine. A dozen hippies, mostly young girls, sat and slept among emptied shopping bags and backpacks. A naked three-year-old squatted on a plastic potty crying while her mother remained cross-legged, sketching a tree and smoking from a bong. Another girl was arguing with a young man in a fringed suede jacket and a huge Afro. Next to them a boy with long lank hair was standing on one leg with his eyes closed, humming, his half-naked painted body motionless in the marijuana haze.

The garden faced a nearby barn, past which Fruity Metcalf was dragging a sack of hedge trimmings. The air around the encampment was heady with incense, but it could not mask the stench of unemptied toilet buckets. In the distance a volley of shots was fired, releasing a cloud of blackbirds.

As well as being a policeman, Arthur Bryant considered himself a social scientist. Part of him was fascinated by the re-emergence of tribal patterns in the new world order, and part was merely suspicious of a bunch of layabouts sitting in their own ordure talking rubbish. He wondered if they followed their leader, or if he was led by them.

'Welcome, Mr Askey!' cried Lord Banks-Marion, capering before him, followed by the necklace-adorned piglet Malacrida, who was fastidiously picking her way through the litter. 'You're the only one of Mr Burke's esteemed guests to come and visit our peace camp.'

'Mr Burke's guests?' Bryant repeated. 'I thought they were yours.'

'No, no! I am no longer the lord of the manor. In a few hours' time Tavistock Hall will belong to him, every woodworm-riddled, dry-rotted, deathwatch-beetle-filled plank of it. He sees a part of historic old England; I see an albatross around my neck.'

'That isn't how your father saw it.'

'Daddy was forever harping on about our duty to the tenants and complaining that we couldn't afford to heat the library.' He brushed a lock of blond hair from his purple-tinted granny glasses. 'We have a nonsensical addiction to bricks and mortar. We should be looking inwards to the improvement of the spirit, not outwards to the laying of damp courses and the cleaning of gutters. The temple of peace is in the mind.'

Harry stopped dancing about and bent over in a coughing fit. He spat, waited, coughed again, then stood up. For a moment he seemed to forget where he was, suddenly less like a spiritual being than a middle-aged man in a state of confusion.

'So you're going to stay on here?' asked Bryant. 'What will you do when Mr Burke's business institute moves in? Won't they want you off the land?'

'We're going to convert them with the power of love,' said Harry, seemingly in all seriousness.

'Ah, I see.'

'Do you though.' He looked up at the lowering sky and felt the rain on his hand. He dug into his kaftan, found a roach, inserted it into a clip and lit it, coughing again. 'I say let the businessmen come and take over. This is the last weekend party that Tavistock Hall will ever see. The lights are going out in the country houses, and we shall not see them lit again. The hall deserves to go to Mr Burke. This millstone around our necks is an opportunity for him.'

Bryant stared at his host with new understanding. Lord Banks-Marion may have been befuddled by dope but his thinking made a certain nihilistic sense. It seemed that nobody was quite who he expected them to be.

The rain was falling hard as May arrived back at Tavistock Hall.

He re-entered the vestibule and left his borrowed gumboots in the rack, then took a stroll through the silent house. In one of the drawing rooms Pamela Claxon and Vanessa Harrow were playing cards. The Reverend and Lady Banks-Marion were taking coffee, and Slade Wilson was reading a magazine. The guests sat like becalmed passengers on an ocean liner, vaguely waiting to dock in a distant port but unable to do anything for themselves.

Bryant and Hatton-Jones were coming down the main staircase. 'He's like the Scarlet bloody Pimpernel,' fumed Monty. 'Have you seen Donald go by here?'

'No,' May replied. 'I followed him to the village but lost him.

He was supposed to be meeting his lawyer. I presume they're
going over the papers before bringing them here to be signed.'

'Well, did you speak to Stafford?'

'He was out. I left a message. I assume you want to pitch
your business proposition to Burke? Why not wait until he's
got the business of the day over and done with?'

'Because it'll be too bloody late then,' said Hatton-Jones.
'He'll be off like a shot. He's avoiding us all. If he didn't want
to talk to anyone why didn't he just arrange to see his lawyer
somewhere else?'

Norma overheard them and came out into the hall. 'If
you're looking for my husband, he's back. I saw him a minute
ago. He told me he was going to look for something in
Lupin – I think that's the library. He was after a book, one of
Pamela's, something about vanishing coffins.'

'Finally,' said Monty rudely, pushing free of the detectives.
Bryant looked along the corridor and saw someone retreating
around a corner. He set off to follow closely behind Monty.

May stayed behind with Norma Burke. 'That man doesn't
give up easily, does he?' she said, watching Monty race off. 'I
don't think he'll have much luck. My husband is very good at
avoiding people he doesn't want to see, especially ones as desperate as that poor fellow.'

'You can't come with me,' Hatton-Jones hissed. 'This is private business!'

'And you're our witness,' Bryant reminded him, catching up.

'Mr Burke,' called Monty. The millionaire stood with his
back to them in the doorway of the library, backlit by the
French windows, one white-gloved hand resting on the
lintel.

'Mr Burke, I wonder if I could have five minutes with
you—'

But Burke stepped inside the room and shut the door in his
face.

'He probably didn't hear,' said Bryant encouragingly. He arrived before the closed door and pushed down the handle. The door swung wide.

The room was empty. There was no sound in the library except for the faint tinkling of the chandelier, which was swinging slightly in its ceiling rose.

'What the hell—?' Monty turned on his heel, looking about the shelf-lined room. 'Where did he go?'

Bryant crossed to the French windows and pushed open one side. Metcalf was still on the lawn, awkwardly filling a burlap sack with hedge trimmings, oblivious to the sifting rain. 'Fruity,' he called, 'where did Mr Burke go?'

'I haven't seen him,' said Metcalf. 'He didn't come past me.'

'He must have stepped out of these windows a moment ago,' replied Bryant. 'Are you sure?' But Metcalf had already turned away and was limping off to empty his sack.

'I'm afraid I didn't see anyone come out either,' said Pamela Claxon, heading across the dry part of the patio with her cigarette holder high in one hand. 'Who are you looking for?'

'Mr Burke,' said Bryant distractedly. 'He was in here a moment ago. He couldn't have just disappeared.'

Inside the library, Monty was frenziedly searching the wall sections and bookcases. 'Perhaps there's a secret passage or something. Don't these old houses have them?'

'In films, yes.' Bryant pulled out several books and found that among the volumes on animal husbandry there were a number of rare crime novels. He tried to stop his concentration from being diverted. 'It has to be a trick of some kind.'

'There must be something, a lever or button. Maybe there's a door hidden behind one of these panels.' Monty dropped to his knees and tried pulling loose part of the skirting board.

They spent the next fifteen minutes testing the walls, but the room was lined with solid brick all the way around.

Bryant stared up at the chandelier and frowned. 'We both saw him come in, didn't we? That thing moved slightly.'

What bothered him more than the disappearance itself was the reason behind it. Why would anyone feel the need to stage such a ridiculous hoax?

On the floor lay a luridly coloured paperback. Bryant picked it up. *The Three Coffins* by Pamela Claxon.

'Isn't this the one he came to get?' he asked. He turned the volume over and read the jacket copy: ' "The weekend guests at a country house find themselves witnesses to murder . . ." '

21

POINT OF NO RETURN

The fine weather was now just a memory. The countryside had lost its colours, gone into mourning for the end of summer. The bruised clouds blurred the tips of the trees as they grew heavy and dropped. The air became fresher and colder as it filled with the sound of pattering rain. A crow flew high, its wings rising and falling, but it got nowhere.

The gardener shifted himself to find some cover and the ashram's inhabitants, wrapped in plastic sheets, climbed inside their tents. Someone forgot the baby, and only brought it in when it began to scream.

The lunch gong had to compete with distant shelling and the rumble of the approaching storm. The apprehensive guests had begun to assemble in Lavender, where the weekend luncheons were to be laid out. A buffet of cold salmon and beef, much of it left over from the night before, had been placed on a long table, but it felt too early to eat. The illusion of a fine old country house going about its rituals oblivious to the outside world was offset by signs of furtive stage management; decorative blankets thrown over threadbare armchairs, a television set unplugged and disgraced in a corner, some folding chairs stacked behind a door.

The thunder that rattled the windows was impossible to distinguish from army gunfire, and the collective mood became jumpier. Toby Stafford arrived and headed directly to the Rose Room, where official business was traditionally conducted. A desk, pens and extra chairs had been provided for him. Everyone was waiting for Donald Burke to appear for the completion of the sale, but the longer he stayed away from the group the more keenly his disdain for them all was felt. Could he, they all wondered, be having second thoughts at this late stage?

In the drawing room, Hawthorn, the maid was laying out board games, cards and dressing-up props to fill what threatened to be a long wet afternoon. There was no radio except for a single portable transistor in the kitchen, and the only phone sat on its own little table in the hall. The house was a ship marooned in a green Sargasso sea.

Bryant stood at the window in Lavender trying to see if he could spot any soldiers in the fields, but the rain was now falling in dense curtains, obscuring the view. He noticed that Monty was keeping away from the eaves, perhaps wary of being landed on by another mythical beast. He was peering out of the doors smoking nervously.

May joined his partner at the window with a stick of celery in one hand. 'This is like the Phoney War, waiting for another assault on Monty.'

'Either something *will* happen or *is* happening or *has* happened but I have no idea what,' Bryant agreed. 'And the waiting is going to get worse because, oh joy, there are going to be games this afternoon. That television in the corner's got a blown valve. I'll have to miss *Juke Box Jury*.'

'It finished a couple of years ago,' said May. 'Don't try to pretend you know what's in the charts.'

'I do know. What kind of fool do you think I am?'

'I don't think you're a fool, I just—'

'No, that's the name of a song in the Top Twenty.'

'Arthur, don't you think you could handle this weekend alone? It doesn't take two of us to keep an eye on him.'

'Where did this come from suddenly?' asked Bryant suspiciously.

Seeing that Vanessa was nearby, May lowered his voice. 'It's just that a friend of mine is throwing a big party in Chelsea tonight. Couldn't I just tiptoe away, maybe ask Vanessa if she cares to join me?'

'Nice try, mush, but if I'm going to be stuck here having a lousy time you are too,' said Bryant. 'Suppose somebody has a go at Monty and you're not around?'

'No one's going to have a go at him,' May sighed. 'That gryphon came loose by itself.'

'I found a footprint and a cigarette.'

'When were you going to tell me?'

'When I remembered. They could have been there since the last time someone went up to clean the gutters.'

'Nobody's been snooping in Monty's room except you. You probably resettled that stray thread from downstairs. You always manage to transfer your dinner around.'

Bryant blew the fluff off a Fruit Gum and offered it to his partner. 'There are too many things that don't make sense here. Norma Burke said her husband wouldn't join the gathering until he had sorted out his business with Toby Stafford, but Stafford just told me he waited all morning for Burke to show up at a café in Knotsworth. He's starting to think that Burke has changed his mind about the purchase. I explained that we saw him briefly this morning, but that he quite literally vanished.'

'Has anyone spoken to him today, apart from his wife?'

'I don't know. Let's find out.' Bryant turned from the window. 'Did anyone speak to Mr Burke this morning?' he called.

Slade Wilson raised a carrot. 'I had a short meeting with him in the drawing room – what's it called? Hawthorn.'

'What about?' Bryant asked.

'Just a few ideas for the new colour scheme. I was thinking aubergine; he was more on the page of prune. We agreed the redecoration budget.'

'Anyone else?'

'Ah, actually I had a brief word with him about the church roof,' said Trevor Patethric. 'He has very kindly offered to help us in our hour of need.'

'He did?' Norma Burke looked sceptical. 'I do find that surprising, considering he's not set foot in a church in years. Did my husband pledge money to anyone else? You perhaps, Vanessa?'

Bryant looked around. The temperature in the room dropped. 'No, Norma,' Vanessa replied. 'I have my own savings. I didn't have to marry anyone to make myself financially secure.'

'I'm surprised the Church survives in this day and age,' said Wilson testily. 'All that ridiculous gold drag.'

'Ecclesiastical vestments, Mr Wilson,' snapped Patethric. 'I suppose you'd know a lot about dressing up. The scandal of your balls has reached even our modest parish.'

The temperature fell a little further. The very air felt electric. Bryant sensed the clenched features around him and wondered who would break first.

'Talk of scandals invariably involves the Church, I find,' replied Wilson coolly. 'All that wealth, the valuable land, the ecclesiastical silver, and still you snatch money from penniless old ladies.'

'The silver belongs to the people,' said Patethric.

'But it doesn't, though, does it? Not really. Any more than the fine old masters dotting these walls belong to the people.'

Thunder rolled over the meadows and a fresh squall of rain hit the windows.

'Unfortunately my son decided to include the Gainsborough, the Stubbs and the Reynolds with the house,' said Lady Banks-Marion. 'We could have sold them at auction, but now it's too late.'

Harry opened a tobacco tin and began rolling, something he did whenever he was agitated. 'Perhaps you should have taken more interest in the sale, Mummy. The furniture could have been sent off to auction years ago but you weren't interested.'

'Somebody had to take over the daily running of the house,' Lady Banks-Marion bit back. 'I was left here while you went off to India and—'

'This is not a conversation to be held in public, Mother,' cried Harry, hurt.

'You should have gone to jail for what you did.'

'I refuse to listen to this.' Harry placed a hand over one ear. 'I must go and talk to my peace collective. It's not fair that you won't allow them in the house.'

'Those girls out there in your ashram look about sixteen,' Pamela Claxon agreed. 'I know where the law stands on this; I write crime novels.'

'I rather like your novels,' said Harry.

'He means he likes the covers,' said his mother. 'My son is not literate. Although of course your books are not literature.'

Moments later everybody was arguing at once. The detectives could only stand back and watch in confusion.

'You think you could have got more for the ugly little Pre-Raphaelites in the bedrooms?' Harry asked his mother. 'Most of them are less valuable than the frames they're in. What about the Chippendale dining-room set? Why not tear up the carpets and sell the parquet as well?'

Lady Banks-Marion turned to May, something most people did sooner or later. 'There were no other takers for the hall, Mr March,' she said. 'Harry agreed the deal with Mr Burke's lawyer and threw in everything but the family silver, and now we can't back out. Really, I cannot sit here listening to this nonsense any longer.' She set down her napkin and rose to leave.

'Can we not prevail upon you to stay?' begged the reverend.

'Look out, Trev's after your daubs,' warned Wilson. 'Ask

him what happened to the ones that used to hang in St Stephen's. Perhaps we should all go home.'

'I'm afraid none of you can go,' said Bryant, finally starting to enjoy himself. 'Not while there's a risk of someone being hit by a stray bullet. The army isn't going to reopen the road until tomorrow morning.'

Something thumped against the bottom of the French windows. Everyone stopped talking and looked about. Harry's necklaced piglet was bumping the glass with her snout.

'Malacrida!' he cried. 'You poor thing.' He went to the window and opened the latch to let her in.

'I've told you, I do not want *swine* in the house,' said Lady Banks-Marion.

'Don't let her hear, she's very sensitive,' replied Harry, reaching down to pat her on the head. Malacrida's blank button eyes remained fastened on him as she was stroked. She seemed to be smiling more happily than ever.

Bryant caught a look of puzzlement on Harry's face as he rose. Harry raised his right hand and examined it, then slowly turned it to the others.

His palm was glistening and crimson with blood.

22

BITS AND PIECES

For a moment nobody moved.

'Everybody stay where you are,' said Bryant, raising his hand to them as the piglet left bloody trotter prints across the rug. Somebody gave a small scream.

'Now look here,' said the reverend in a voice he reserved for keeping children off the backs of pews, 'who are you to tell us what to do?'

'I'm a police officer,' Bryant said, 'and this is my colleague Mr May. We're detectives.'

'I *knew* it,' said Pamela Claxon. 'You only have to look at the size of their feet. What are those, elevens?'

'You might have picked a better name than Arthur Askey,' Wilson told Bryant, offended.

'Let me go with her,' said Harry. 'Malacrida knows me. Pigs are very sensitive. It might be nothing. Perhaps somebody in the ashram has had an accident.'

'All right,' said May, 'get her to take you to where she was.'

'That may not be so easy,' Harry admitted. 'She tends to search for rotten food.'

Bryant stayed behind, watching over Monty while May

and Harry followed the piglet out through the French windows. Malacrida led the way across the patio and on to the lawn, moving with fast, dainty steps. When May looked back he saw everyone crowded at the windows, peering out.

Malacrida veered off suddenly and pranced into a flowerbed. She stopped abruptly and began digging. May examined the ground around her but there was nothing to see except wet grass and shrubbery. 'It's the lavender bush,' said Harry. 'She likes lavender. Malacrida! Naughty girl!' He scampered after the little piglet but she was off again, heading for a hole in the hedge.

Fruity Metcalf must have been following the commotion because he appeared still chewing a mouthful of his own lunch and clumped after them. 'You can go around just here, gentlemen.' He led the way to a larger opening in the greenery.

At the far end of a short muddy field was a creosoted wooden barn, its door wedged half open. Harry slowed apprehensively and removed his spectacles, wiping the rain from them. 'No, I don't think I care to go in there.'

'Why not?' asked May.

'It's the pump for the septic tank.'

'What's that noise?' May cautiously moved to the doorway. He fell back as an enormous raven burst out of the shadows with a shriek and flapped its way off into the rowans.

The barn was dark and smelled strongly of chemicals. A motor was running but sounded as if it might stall at any moment.

'There's a light switch on the wall to your left,' Harry called out.

May felt for it and turned it on.

Ahead was a rectangular box some twelve feet long with various pipes running into it. The angled sides were anodized steel and stained a reddish-brown. The air was acrid with the meaty stench of manure, rotting vegetables and solvents.

May looked up and saw a rickety wooden walkway above

them, running the length of the barn. It was reached by two primitive wooden staircases. One section of the walkway's pine railing appeared to have been freshly split. The pieces hung down over the machine, which was grinding in an off-kilter fashion, a series of irregular thumps suggesting that something large was caught up in it.

Metcalf headed for a large red plastic button under the machine and was about to hit it when May stopped him. 'I may want to take fingerprints from that. It's better if you leave before the ground gets too messed up.'

Pulling down his shirt sleeve, he carefully pushed the button and let the rotor slow down. The whine ceased and an oppressive silence filled the shed.

'It shouldn't have been running,' called Harry, still refusing to enter. 'It's self-starting. When something is fed into it the pressure on the blades kicks on the motor.'

'What *is* it?' asked May, peering into the shadowed patches beneath the contraption and covering his nose. His expensive patent-leather shoes had been swallowed by squelching mud.

'The treatment plant for the house,' said Metcalf. 'It's not supposed to be exposed like that. There should be a plastic mesh cover on the top.'

'Why is it open at all?'

'You'll have to ask his lordship.' Metcalf gave a quick backward glance and scuttled out, clearly anxious not to be involved.

'Lord Banks-Marion, I need your help. Would you step inside for a moment?' May asked. His lordship had changed colour, so that his face now matched his pale green kaftan. 'Why is this device operating without a guard?'

'The original ventilation lid rusted through some years ago so I put plastic mesh over the top,' Harry explained sheepishly. 'It was only meant to be a temporary measure. It must have fallen off. There are an awful lot of things to do around here.'

To see over the side of the machine May had to stand on

tiptoe. At the bottom of the macerator was a layer of thick brownish-grey scum. The chemical smell was eye-stinging. The plant's contents, which looked rather like a heavy country stew, were steaming in the cool air.

May squinted up at the walkway again. He began to feel uncomfortably hot. 'Surely nobody could be so stupid as to . . .' he began. 'How does it work?'

'Oh Lord,' cried Harry, covering his nose and mouth. 'I can't.'

'Please, we need you.'

'The original house was self-sustaining,' he explained. 'We grew our own vegetables and slaughtered our own animals. I tried to make the kitchens vegetarian but Mother wouldn't have it. There was always a cesspit here. It was the perfect spot because there's a large drainage field behind.'

'How does it work?'

'Waste is discharged into the tank and treated with bacterial acid. Anything organic can be fed into it and turned into slurry. The resulting methane is released through a pipe at the back of the barn. I tried to keep it all as far away from the house as possible. I added a pair of rotary blades to remove solids and increase the tank's efficiency. That's why you could hear the engine.'

Harry peered over the edge of the machine and was energetically sick.

'That's evidence!' cried May, horrified. He shoved Harry back outside.

When Bryant arrived he found his lordship bending over with his hands on his knees, fighting for breath. 'In there,' he said, spitting out and pointing behind him.

The detectives unscrewed the trap beneath the rotary blade and examined the solid waste that had been caught before it could reach the storage tank.

A human arm slid out in the muck and rolled over, its fingers open, crablike. On the fourth finger of its left hand was a gold wedding ring. It was followed by several ribs and part of a leg with a moon-pale kneecap still attached by its pink tendons. Several other identifiable items could be seen in the trap above the liquefied remains.

'I need some gloves and a hose,' May said. 'Arthur, could you have a look around?'

Bryant found all the equipment they needed stacked against the side wall of the barn. A few blasts of water revealed the non-organic materials in the sludge: a watch, a chunk of shoe, part of a man's tie. May knelt beside the emptied slurry and used a stick to extricate something else from the effluvium – a strip of skin with grey hair and an ear attached, and the remains of a white glove.

'Please don't tell me that's who I think it is,' said Bryant.

'The man everybody came to see,' replied May.

'Well, they can see him now. He's all over the place. How long does this contraption take to dissolve organic material?'

Harry appeared distracted. He forced himself to think. 'Usually around twelve hours, but I had the tank relined so that I could add hydrochloric acid to speed up the process.'

'Why would you do that?'

'Solids were still building up in the tank. I was trying to reduce the number of times we needed to have it cleaned out. Trouble is, it makes the air in here unbreathable.'

'So if someone was overcome by the fumes and fell in from up there, how long would it be before their organic remains were reduced?'

'The rotary blades would already render them into small pieces. It depends on weight and size but I don't suppose there would be much left after about four hours.'

May looked at his watch. 'It's after two o'clock now.' He looked back at the doorway and tried not to think of the anxious faces behind the windows. 'What on earth are we going to tell them?'

'The first thing we have to do is seal off this area and put a call out to a forensics unit,' said Bryant. 'Given that the army's playing silly buggers all around us they may have to be choppered in.'

They emerged from the stifling barn with relief. 'It makes no sense,' said May. 'What was he doing anywhere near the septic tank?'

'One has to assume he didn't know what was in there. Let's not jump to any conclusions just yet,' Bryant warned. 'We need a positive identification. I'm afraid it's going to mean asking Mrs Burke to examine the remains.'

'We don't have the authority to handle this, Arthur. Shouldn't we phone it in to Canterbury first?'

'We can't afford to waste any time.' Bryant breathed out and looked up at the thunderous sky. 'Whatever's left of him will break down fast.'

He ran across to Metcalf's gatehouse and found the door open. An old Bakelite telephone sat on a window ledge, but when he raised the receiver the line merely buzzed and crackled. Dialling 999 made no difference. As he replaced the handset, clouds darkened the room.

As the detectives headed back to the main hall, a bloated crow strutted past them on the grass, turning to caw. Everything had assumed a sinister significance. The anxious guests stood motionless, waiting at the windows.

'Do you want to tell them or shall I?' asked May.

23

LET IT BLEED

'There's been a . . .' May looked at his partner, unsure of what to say.

'An incident,' said Bryant.

'Mrs Burke, we need you to come with us. I'm afraid it won't be a very pleasant experience.'

Norma's eyes widened. She looked to the others for help.

'Norma, do you want me to come with you?' asked Pamela Claxon, rising from her chair.

'I think it better that she comes alone,' said May.

Growing more alarmed by the moment, Norma Burke followed them out of the house. They walked in silence, down through the field and around the hedge to the barn. In the distance, the boom of a large gun shocked starlings into the sky. Mrs Burke reached out for May's arm as she slipped on the muddy grass.

Inside the barn, Harry had found some hand-held battery-operated lights, and had set them around the macerator. Laid out on an unfolded piece of oilskin were the tie, the watch, the remains of a white shirt, a piece of grey waistcoat, the torn-up Oxford toecap shoe and some pieces of white glove.

'Oh.' Norma looked from one item to the next and took a step back to steady herself. Nobody needed to ask if she recognized them.

'There's some other . . . material . . .' May said gently. 'I wonder if we could persuade you to take a look.'

'It's all right,' she said. 'I need to see.'

He brought her slowly back to the edge of the oilskin sheet and opened the second bundle, revealing the left arm and the hand with its wedding ring, and the torn ear. As she examined the remains he took a torch and held it over each of the chunks of flesh in turn.

Harry ran another torch beam over the side of the macerator. 'There are some more pieces,' he called back. Shockingly white fragments of bone protruded upwards from between the blades. More grey hairs caked the sides of the trough. Mrs Burke looked away and covered her face. May thought she might fall, but she recovered sufficiently to return to the items on the oilcloth.

'Give me a minute,' she asked.

May waited. Norma leaned in closer to examine the hand with its wedding ring. 'He never removed this,' she said quietly, 'not once during the entire time of our marriage. On the inside you'll find an inscription – *cor fidele* – faithful heart. See the little scar on his wrist? When he was twenty-one he decided to tattoo himself with his girlfriend's name, but they broke up, so he cut it out with a penknife.'

Bryant thought of the arms Monty had seen pushing against the gargoyle on the roof. Was it conceivable that he had been attacked by Donald Burke? If he knew that to be the case, Monty would be a suspect.

'What on earth could have happened?' Mrs Burke asked.

'When did you last see your husband?'

'I suppose it was just before lunchtime. I really don't keep track of his whereabouts. I told you, he was going to Knotsworth to meet Toby Stafford.'

'It seems Mr Burke returned without seeing his lawyer and came out to the barn.' Bryant pointed up at the broken railing in the walkway. 'He must have fallen in from up there.'

'Why would he have deliberately walked into a place like this?'

'We have no answers yet,' Bryant admitted. 'It seems out of character. Maybe he was just having a look around and wondered what was in here.'

Norma headed to the wooden walkway and started to climb up.

'I don't think you should do that, Mrs Burke,' said May.

'I want to see.' She stood at the top of the stairs, so unsteady that she had to grab one of the wooden posts to keep herself from falling.

May climbed the stairs. 'Please, come down. We don't know how safe it is, or why the railing should have broken just in that spot.'

'Perhaps he was leaning on it,' she said, taking his hand.

'This is no accident, Mrs Burke,' said Bryant. 'I think somebody pushed him.'

She looked back at him and her face crumpled. 'Oh, Donald.'

'We'd better take you back to the house for a while.' May took her arm and led her back down. 'We'll try to find out what happened here.'

'Can I at least have the wedding ring?'

'I'm afraid it will have to stay where it is for a while.'

It seemed a cruel thing to do, but he had no choice. After they had taken her back to the house the detectives returned to the barn and climbed the steps to the walkway. When Bryant bent close, he found that the split in the pine railing smelled fresh. He touched his forefinger to the wood. 'The sap's still wet. It was partly sawn through. I could see the saw-marks from down there. The tool must be around here somewhere. It all seems rather amateurish.'

'Or opportunistic. You might have avoided telling her that her husband was murdered,' said May.

Bryant shrugged. 'She would have found out sooner or later. It had to be somebody Burke knew well. Not many people would agree to come to a darkened barn smelling of sewage. He must have had a good reason for being here.'

'Vanessa Harrow.'

'Hard to imagine but I suppose it's not impossible,' said Bryant. 'You had breakfast with her, but she got back before you.'

'I dawdled. The lawyer, Toby Stafford, he's not staying at the house.'

'A possibility. Or someone we haven't met. I mean, Burke's hardly been hanging out with the rest of us, has he? Perhaps he knows someone else in the neighbourhood.'

'So he gets a call telling him to meet not at the house but in the *barn*? And when he does so he's lured up on to the walkway and pushed through the barrier? No, Arthur, it's all wrong.'

'Then come up with another scenario,' said Bryant, passing him a Fruit Polo. 'This'll stop you thinking about the smell. What are we going to do with those?' He pointed at the crushed grey body parts laid out on the sheet.

'Cover them for the forensic team,' said May, waving away flies. 'We'll have to call them from the main house.'

'What's that?' asked Bryant, heading over to a large piece of hooked equipment hung with pulleys and weights, and suspended from the rafters on thick ropes. 'Looks to me like a block and tackle. I suppose it's there to remove anything that gets stuck in the rotor. Look, there's a counterbalanced pulley that can move it over the chopper.'

'So if it can be used to pull things out, can it also be used to lower something in?' asked May. 'That would make the job much easier. Then you just saw through the railing to fake a fall.'

'I've been thinking,' said Bryant. 'What if somebody *instructed* Burke?'

'What do you mean?'

'What if they said, "Go to the barn, climb the walkway and look down into the macerator," and gave him a reason for being here against his will? They could have hidden something here, something they knew he'd want to get back. And then when he tried to reach for it, *boom*, he fell through the railing.'

'A bit elaborate, isn't it? And hardly guaranteed to work. Why not just conk him on the head—'

'That's it, even better,' said Bryant enthusiastically. 'They send him a note: "Meet me somewhere no one will see, be at the barn in an hour." Burke pushes open the door and peers in, *bang*, a whack across the back of the bonce, he's hooked on to the block and tackle and raised up – a child could do it – to be chucked into the macerator. The railing's sawn through so it looks like he's gone upstairs and fallen in, and the assailant leaves with the machine still running, chewing him to bits, job done.'

'Footprints out,' said May.

They left to check the ground outside, but the mud was far too churned up to reveal anything. They returned to the patio and stamped clay from their shoes. 'So no boot marks,' said Bryant. 'And most of the body chopped up into pieces the size of a stock cube. A perfect murder, just not the one we were expecting. Now what?'

'Well, I think we have at least ten culprits to choose from,' said May, nodding back at the house. 'It doesn't look as if we'll have to play murder games this afternoon. We have a real one to investigate. And I'm afraid the consequences could be much nastier.'

24

BORN UNDER A BAD SIGN

For over a century the British public followed the trials of meticulous, manipulative murderers like John George Haigh, Florence Maybrick, George Joseph Smith and William Palmer. Pathologists and barristers like Bernard Spilsbury and Edward Marshall Hall became stars in their own right. We will never know how many murderers were ingenious enough to evade capture. However, the nation was at the centre of two world wars that robbed death of all dignity and grandeur, and so the age of the clever killer soon came to an end.

Bryant replaced the book and took down another.

The Victorian obsession with poison and being poisoned came from its ease of availability. Arsenic was everywhere, in paint and cosmetics, dresses and wallpaper. It was cheap and readily available, and half an ounce could kill fifty people. Victorian gardens were filled with poisons. The seeds of the wisteria vine (Wisteria floribunda) contain high levels of wisterin and are lethally toxic.

This book too, he replaced. His eye was caught by another slim volume: *Australian Postal History & Social Philately*. He thought about nicking it.

'What are you doing?' called May from the hall, where he was trying the telephone.

'I'm, er, investigating the library,' said Bryant, stepping back to admire the shelves. 'There are dozens of books here about murder. Somebody here collects them.'

'You're reading books while I'm trying to get hold of a forensics team?' May dialled a third time and held the receiver away from his ear as the same series of squeaks and crackles ensued. 'It sounds like a duck eating crisps.'

'I bet it's the MOD,' said Bryant, examining the spine of a volume on Dr Crippen. 'The army intelligence corps could be using some kind of signal jammer.'

'More likely engineers making repairs. Or if we're being melodramatic, someone could have tampered with the line to the house.'

'No, if that were the case it would simply be dead.'

'Didn't you say Fruity's line wasn't working either? Someone knows we can't just drive out of here, and now we can't call anyone, either.'

'But one of us can still walk to the village.' Bryant reluctantly left the bookshelves and wandered out into the hall. 'The other can find out where everyone was when Mr Burke did a *tour jeté* into the bone-grinding machine. There's so much information to process. And yet I feel the first faint stirrings of apophenia.'

'I don't know what that is,' May admitted.

'The experience of seeing patterns in seemingly meaningless data.' He held out his fist. 'Paper, scissors, rock. Loser goes to the village.'

'There has to be a more professional method than this,' May complained. 'Besides, I always lose.' He feinted twice with his fist and opened his palm flat. Bryant had formed scissors. 'Damn. Best out of seven? Who do you think killed him? I mean, assuming you don't think he was suicidal and jumped in.'

'They all need Burke.' Bryant's paper covered May's rock. 'Maybe they're in it together. Who stands to gain the most?'

'That's the problem,' said May. 'If someone's killed the goose that lays the golden eggs, they all miss out. Slade Wilson won't get his commission, the vicar won't get his roof, Lady Banks-Marion is stuck with the house, Lord Banks-Marion will lose his ashram, the novelist doesn't get her book, Vanessa Harrow loses her benefactor, Toby Stafford loses his client.' May's scissors were blunted by Bryant's rock. 'Did we say best out of seven? Make it thirteen.'

'Tell you what, I'll cut you a deal,' said Bryant magnanimously. 'I'm no good at getting the right answers to questions. I'm an academic. You do the suspects. I'll try to reach the village without getting my ears blown off by any passing shells. Make sure nobody leaves, and see who's got an alibi.'

Together they peered around the door of Lavender. The guests now had the desperate appearance of citizens awaiting relief in a besieged town.

'Look at them all with their greedy little faces still plastered against the glass,' Bryant whispered. 'I honestly don't think it could be any of them. They haven't the stomach for murder. It's more likely that Burke was rolled for his wallet by a couple of hippies from his lordship's ashram.'

'A robbery gone wrong?' May attempted to wipe mud from his shoes with a filched dinner napkin. 'You think Burke felt a bit frisky and followed one of the nymphets into the barn hoping for a roll in the hay? In his white gloves? Then got over-excited and toppled into the mulcher? This isn't one of Pamela Claxon's murder mysteries, although heaven knows it could pass as one. You'd better see if you can get help before things get out of hand.'

Bryant was indignant. 'We've as much chance of uncovering

the truth as anybody else. The plods from Canterbury are more used to investigating who dug up the daffodils in the council flowerbed. We *know* murder. We're Londoners.'

With that, he donned a pair of enormous galoshes from the set arranged by the door, took the largest umbrella from the elephant-foot stand in the hall and, looking decidedly Christopher Robin-ish, set off for Crowshott.

'What's going on?' Toby Stafford demanded to know as May re-entered. 'Is there someone coming to sort this out?'

In the corner of the room, Norma Burke's usually immaculate coiffure had lost its formality. She was being poured teak-coloured tea while the others stood around awaiting instruction. Like actors without scripts, their air of helplessness was palpable. At their centre Lady Banks-Marion sat silent and frozen, her hands folded in her lap.

'It appears that Mr Burke has been murdered,' said May. 'His remains have been positively identified. There will probably be other – pieces of evidence, but we have to wait for help to reach us from Canterbury.'

'Oh dear Lord, what on earth could possibly have happened to the poor fellow?' asked Reverend Patethric with such forlorn empathy that May wanted to punch him.

'Mr Burke fell into the macerator that treats raw sewage from the house.'

'That's preposterous,' Stafford said. 'You're saying it minced him into pig food and none of us heard a thing?'

'I didn't say that,' said May, suddenly aware of his inexperience and youthfulness in a room mostly filled with his superiors. 'He may not have had time to cry out. Perhaps he couldn't be heard above the noise of the machinery. We're hoping that somebody might have seen him entering the barn.'

'But we were all in here,' said Vanessa. 'Weren't we?'

'Hold on, some came down to lunch later than others,' said Pamela. 'Can any of us say we saw everyone else?'

'We're not the only ones here, what about the staff?' asked Wilson. 'They're in and out all the time. And those hippies living in the walled garden?'

'I need each of you to write down your movements for me,' said May. 'Add any details you can think of. Did you look at the clock as you entered the room? Did you happen to glance out of the window? Did you see anyone outside?' He spoke to Alberman, who went to fetch paper and pencils. 'The more exact you can be, the easier it will be for me to eliminate you.'

After Alberman had returned and the pencils were distributed, along with a fistful of blank postcards, everyone found a seat and settled down to writing. May looked about the room. He felt as if he was holding an English class.

'Mr May, perhaps I might have a word with you,' said Lady Banks-Marion, rising and leading the way to the hall, not waiting for him to follow.

She stood beside the grandfather clock, grand and imperious, and waited while he closed the dining-room door. 'Tell me, do you have any experience with something like this?'

'A certain amount, your ladyship,' said May. 'My colleague has gone to the village to get help from a local team.'

'What are you even doing here?' she asked, honestly puzzled. 'You can't possibly be friends of my son's. Why is this weekend party being attended by two uninvited policemen?'

'We're escorting Mr Hatton-Jones.'

Lady Beatrice looked as if her worst concerns had just been confirmed. 'I knew that man was up to no good. Is he under arrest?'

'No, he's testifying for the prosecution in a criminal case. We're here to keep him safe.'

'From whom?'

'I'm afraid I'm not at liberty to say, your ladyship.' He could hardly tell her that he had no idea where the danger might be coming from.

'Very well.' Lady Beatrice had been taught never to reveal

her emotions. Her sangfroid was such a daunting reminder of the hall's past that she seemed more and more like the last of a lost species. 'If we were all in that room together at roughly the same time, how could somebody have murdered Mr Burke? Have you spoken to my son's layabout friends? I'm quite sure some of them have criminal records.'

'We'll talk to everybody in due course,' said May. 'First I need to ascertain everyone's movements. I'm afraid nobody can leave the house until we've completed some enquiries.'

'We all loathed him,' she said, almost to herself. 'One hates to speak ill of the dead, but there it is.'

'Mr Burke? Why?' asked May.

'Oh.' She waved the thought aside. 'Because he wants what we have, but hasn't earned the right to it. He didn't want anything to do with us. People like Mr Burke live for the acquisition of things, not people. He simply couldn't be bothered with anyone unless they were useful. This house is not some kind of relic to be collected into a portfolio, it is a part of England's history. You can't just buy it. You have to be born into it. I should never have agreed to sign over Tavistock Hall to him.'

'It seems to me that you had no other choice.'

She opened the glass face of the grandfather clock and absently corrected the minute hand. 'Tell me, Mr May, why do you think Donald Burke was so desperate to get his hands on Tavistock Hall? He was purchasing a background for himself. A man like that, without breeding or class, thinking he could simply snap up good stock and fit himself in as if it were a new overcoat.'

This, felt May, was more than a little disingenuous. 'Yet you still agreed the sale,' he pointed out.

'The property had passed to Harry, and he was adamant. I had no say in the matter.'

'What will happen to the hall now?'

'I dare say it will have to find its way back on to the

market,' she said. 'I cannot afford to have it repaired. One understands that London is awash with wealthy buyers these days. I suppose I shall end up living in a poky little flat in Knightsbridge.' She turned to him, faltering. 'I thought I saw someone this morning – but I don't . . .'

'Please,' said May, 'if you can help us in any way—'

She glanced back at the door. 'Vanessa Harrow. I'm *sure* I saw her going down towards the barn just before luncheon. I remember wondering what she was up to. Check her shoes if you don't believe me. She tracked mud into Lavender when she returned.' She gave a sudden wry smile. 'I suppose you know we have a ghost?'

'No, nobody's mentioned that.'

'The fourth lord. If an unforeseen calamity befalls the ancestral home he's supposed to appear at the top of the main staircase just before taking bloody revenge. I'd say buying the hall and kicking us out would be enough to bring him back, wouldn't you?'

'The event was hardly unforeseen,' replied May. 'Besides, it's your home once more, now that Mr Burke is dead. Unless Mr Stafford can find a way to honour his client's wishes.'

'I hadn't thought of that,' said Lady Banks-Marion.

'Right now, your ladyship, I'm more concerned with finding out why he died just a few minutes before he was due to sign the ownership papers.'

'A coincidence, surely.'

'Does it feel like one to you, your ladyship?'

She rested her hand on her embonpoint, alarmed. 'You're right. How naïve of me. Can you do something? I mean, before anyone else arrives. We cannot have a scandal.'

'The fact remains that a man is dead,' said May. 'I'll do what I can.'

He took his leave and was heading up the hall when Monty Hatton-Jones grabbed his arm. 'What if the murderer thought it was me?' he asked anxiously. 'Donald and I looked rather alike. He was older, obviously, and had greyer hair. And was a terrible dresser. His suits looked as if they'd been purchased from Woolworths. What if this assassin realizes his mistake and comes after me again? Look at me, I'm still bandaged up from his last attempt. You're supposed to be protecting me. You're not doing a very good job, are you?'

'You're still alive,' said May, pulling his arm free.

'You don't understand what you're dealing with,' Monty called after him. 'This has all been carefully planned. The house is cut off. The road is closed. The phones aren't working. I'm a sitting duck. If I don't make it to that courtroom on Monday the trial will collapse and it'll be on both your heads. Chamberlain has the weight of the establishment behind him.'

'But don't you?' asked May. 'Oh, I suppose he outranks you.' Part of him was happy to see Monty disconcerted and less cocksure.

As most of the guests were still filling out their postcards, conferring with one another and working as intently as pupils in an examination, May decided to risk his shoes once more and head off down the garden to the ashram. The tents looked sad and sodden in the rain, more like a refugee camp than a spiritual hermitage.

One of the girls emerged from her tent as he arrived and raised her hand in a twin-fingered greeting of peace. The others were barely visible under piles of Afghan coats and Indian blankets.

'I'm Melanie. I saw you at the barn earlier.' She wore a purple silk kaftan covered in chains of plastic marigolds. There were daisies woven through her hair and large red cold sores on her lips. She smiled sleepily at him and beckoned him inside. 'Please, come in, you're getting wet.'

She seated herself before him in a maelstrom of discarded clothes, food packets and blankets. The rain suddenly increased in force, drumming so loudly on the nylon roof that he could hardly hear her. She produced a ragged little joint and tried to light it. 'You have such a kind face. Can you play a musical instrument?'

'The recorder,' said May. 'I only got as far as "Come into the garden, Maud". It was meant to calm me down.'

'Did it work?' Melanie dragged hopelessly at the joint.

'Only after I broke it. Did you see anyone enter or leave the barn?'

She drew on the joint, held her breath for an age, then coughed out smoke, wiping her eyes. 'Which?'

'I don't know – enter.'

'Yes.'

'Who was it?'

'Where?'

'By the barn.'

'I've forgotten the question.'

May sighed. 'We're not on the same planet, are we?'

'I really have no idea.' She took another puff.

Exasperated, he pulled her to her feet, opened the flap of the tent and dragged her outside, pointing to the barn behind them. 'Did you see anyone going into *that* building over there this morning?'

'I thought I told you,' said Melanie, frowning. 'A chick, one of the guests, long blond hair.'

'Did she go in or come out?'

'Well, one state would suggest the other, wouldn't it? If you go up towards the clouds you have to come down again. That's physics. If you work for the Man and take his bread you turn into a pig. Cause and effect. "When I get to the bottom I go back to the top of the slide." "Helter Skelter", man.'

May looked about in exasperation. 'Is there anyone else I can talk to?'

She grabbed his hand. 'Wait, let me think. Both. She went in, then came out.'

'At what time?'

'Seven minutes past twelve.'

'How could you know that?'

'Watch.'

May waited. Nothing happened. 'What?' he asked finally.

'*Watch.*' Melanie held up her left hand and showed him her wristwatch. 'Then the machine started up.'

'Didn't you think that was odd?'

'Everything is odd, don't you think?' She offered him a toke but the joint was dead. 'It's odd that we don't just fly off the face of the earth and tumble away into space. We're glittering specks of light surrounded by unfathomable darkness. Doesn't that give you goose-pimples?'

'Melanie, somebody was killed in that barn this morning.'

'Who?'

'A rich old man with long grey hair and white gloves and a scar on his left wrist.'

'He should have checked his horoscope. It's just one less capitalist pig.'

'You can't think like that,' said May. 'You have to care about people.'

'I don't see why. Nobody really cares.' Her sweet smile faded a little and she gripped his hand more tightly. 'I think Harry loves his pig more than he loves me. Nobody cares if I live or die. He'll be remembered, that old man. I wish someone would remember me.'

Then she turned and fled back inside her tent, leaving May standing in the rain. *She's lost,* he thought. *Perhaps they all are. Arthur could be right after all.*

25

DO YOU WANT TO KNOW A SECRET?

Arthur Bryant ducked behind an elm tree just as a mortar bomb landed in the next field and threw clods of black earth into the sky. The air pulsed, stinging his ears. A burning mole landed at his feet.

Half a dozen soldiers in French uniforms dashed past with their rifles raised, vaulting over the hedgerows and across the road, only to vanish as quickly as they had appeared. A few moments later the birds returned to the tops of the trees and everything was as it had been except that there was now a ragged crater of mud in the pasture.

'Hi – wait for me, sir!' Fruity Metcalf appeared behind him, puffing and weaving from side to side, his good left arm pumping back and forth. 'It's not safe out here until they've finished chasing each other about. Twice a year this happens.'

He clumsily tried to light a Woodbine as he was walking. Bryant lit the cigarette for him and returned it, although the rain threatened to put it out. 'First somebody tries to flatten Monty,' he said. 'Then they kill the millionaire.'

'Why would anyone do it? I thought they were all here to see him.'

'Exactly my thought, Fruity.'

'Is Monty all right?'

'A possible hairline fracture in his collarbone but he seems to have taken it in his stride.' He slowed down to allow Metcalf to catch up.

'Several of those old stone things are cracked, and the sewage plant is downright dangerous. The whole house is falling apart. I should have checked. I let you down, Mr Bryant.'

'Monty told too many people he was coming here,' said Bryant. 'If we leave the house now we'll lose our only chance of catching the culprit. All I can do is make sure he's not left alone.' He hopped over a puddle, only to land in another.

'But if it's one of them—'

'A dilemma, I agree. Is it possible for anyone to sneak in from outside?'

'I suppose so,' said Metcalf. 'The main gates are bolted but it's easy to enter through the orchard or the servants' gate. There's only a low wall around that part of the property.'

'Do you have any theories about Donald Burke? If you can think of anything that would help . . .'

'Anyone with a secret is always open to blackmail.' Metcalf examined the glowing end of his cigarette. 'Perhaps it was Mr Burke who was doing the blackmailing. He could have arranged to meet someone in the barn. It's the last place anyone would have expected him to go.'

'What did you make of him?' Bryant asked.

'Oh, I didn't get to meet him,' Metcalf answered. 'I stay well out of the house and its affairs. The old lady and her son are always fighting. I hear them from the gatehouse. As for the rest – well, they don't venture outside much. I've been keeping a close eye on your friend, though.'

'Did you see him go anywhere near the barn?'

'No, sir. Didn't see Mr Burke for that matter. Lady Banks-Marion wanted me to rake up the leaves at the front of the house.'

'But he must have come up the lane from Crowshott. You didn't see him arrive?'

'No, but I was back and forth quite a bit. And I was more concerned with being able to see Mr Hatton-Jones through the windows.'

'Why is there a walkway in the barn above that ridiculous machine?'

'I believe his lordship put it there so he could clear blockages in the blades. It's too risky to lean over the sides of the chopper.' Metcalf scratched at his old woollen hat, thinking. 'Not being rude, sir, but perhaps it's time for a local team to take over?'

'No offence taken,' Bryant sighed.

They arrived in Crowshott, making their way past the stone cross dedicated to the fallen of the Great War, and headed around the rain-stippled duck pond into the little village high street. Bryant pushed open the door to the public bar of the Goat & Compasses and stamped out the rain on the flag-stones. As usual, the barman was standing behind the counter cleaning the same dimple mug. 'Af'noon, gentlemen.'

Metcalf nodded. 'Afternoon.'

'Do you have a police constable stationed here?' Bryant asked.

'No, there's one who comes over from Little Pethering on his bicycle some days.' The barman pointed up the lane. 'The last time I saw him was about eighteen months ago, after someone threw a meat pie at the verger. It was one of the parishioners, old Mrs Davenport. She wasn't happy with his grave-tidying. They managed to keep it out of the papers. Apart from that, there's only PC Stanley Wermold, but he's still off with his feet. They've been playin' him up something chronic.'

'Where's the nearest criminal investigation unit?'

The barman laughed. 'Won't be finding one of them anywhere between here and Canterbury, or even Hastings.

They're a rough lot down there, squaddies mostly, not that I've ever been. We've only got Stanley and he's not working at the moment. He's here.'

'Where?' asked Bryant.

The barman pointed around the corner to a spot beside the fireplace. A corpulent elderly man in half of a policeman's uniform lay across an armchair snoring lightly. 'He's celebrating his retirement. Six pints of cider, four large whiskies. He'll be out for the rest of the day.'

'When does he retire?' Bryant asked.

The landlord checked the calendar. 'Nineteen seventy-four.'

'Do you have a telephone we can use?'

'No.'

'We need to get hold of somebody in authority,' said Metcalf.

'And you can after tomorrow lunchtime, when the road is open again,' the barman replied. 'The phone box there is free for 999 calls. You newcomers are always in such a rush. I've heard about that there "Swinging London" and all, and I can tell you, there's nothing like that going on down here. You can't wear miniskirts and kinky boots standing in a field. All those layabouts in military jackets. The Beatles want putting in uniform.' The paradox of the argument escaped him.

'Ah yes, the Beatles,' Bryant agreed. 'Who knows how much damage those soothing lyrical harmonies could do to youthful minds. Come on, Fruity, the phone box. I hope you've got lots of change.'

When Sir Giles Gilbert Scott designed the red telephone box he had not imagined it covered in graffiti and filled with cards advertising buxom blondes in leather corsets. Tendrils of decadence were already spreading out from Swinging London, it seemed, reaching down into the pristine dells of Kent. Bryant left Fruity outside, waited for the pips, shovelled in coins and quickly outlined the morning's events to Gladys Forthright.

'Can't you get Monty out of there?' she asked. 'Roger will go crackers when he finds out what's happened.'

'Then it's your job to make sure he doesn't,' Bryant warned. 'We've lost our only advantage; they know we're police officers now. Worse than that, Monty told others about his plans, so it's possible that one of the guests is an imposter and killed Burke by mistake, thinking it was him.'

'That means he's still in danger.'

'He'd be in just as much danger if he tried to leave, Gladys. He'd never make it on foot. Vehicles have to take the only road out, and it sounds as if it passes right through the centre of the battlefield. Have you managed to get hold of anyone in charge of the manoeuvres?'

'No luck so far. It's a secure military exercise. The whole point is to ensure that there's no contact with the outside world. Do you want me to see if I can get someone in to you?'

'You'll need to track down a team in Canterbury, assuming they work on Saturdays.' Bryant thought for a minute. If he was being honest, he hated the idea of bringing in an outsider and losing the case to them. 'I'll call you again when I get a chance.'

He hung up and fell in beside Metcalf. 'Let's look in at the church while we're here, and do a little checking behind the good reverend's back.'

St Stephen's had a Gothic perpendicular spire and an ancient, uneven cemetery with plenty of leaning tombs covered in crows. Over one of its fallen headstones a mangy dog sacrilegiously squatted, its haunches trembling. For a building dedicated to the joyful worship of the Lord, it had the punitive, melancholy atmosphere of a prison.

Leaving Fruity to finish a fag under a tree, Bryant pushed open the church door and entered. He had never felt comfortable in the houses of God, associating them with gruelling rites of childhood: saying farewell to dead grandfathers and the observance of distant, obscure ceremonies involving hushed prayers, peculiarly phrased bible passages, muffled tears and shamed repentance. However, the north and south transepts boasted fine stained-glass scenes, of Adam and Eve and the Tree of Knowledge, and King Arthur and Sir Lancelot. The air smelled of burned candles, lavender polish and damp wood. A collection box featured prominently. Bryant gave it a rattle. It sounded empty.

'There's only me and the woman who comes to do the flowers, sir,' said the verger, appearing from the shadows just as Bryant was about to wander off down the nave.

'What happened here?' Bryant called back, his voice muted by the thick walls. 'Where are all the wall hangings?' He pointed to the lighter panels on the walls, and the rectangles free of dust where tapestries had once hung. The church had been stripped of all adornment.

'Everything's been sold off,' said the verger. 'There's not much of a congregation left.'

'Did the diocese agree to it?'

'I don't know, sir. I suppose the reverend had to pay the bills somehow.'

'I don't care how broke he is, it shouldn't look like this,' said Bryant. 'When did it happen?'

'In the spring, sir.'

Bryant had seen parishes in London's East End which had been bombed and looted, and they looked healthier. 'Can you take me to the sacristy?'

The verger mumbled a complaint, but led Bryant away. They were gone for a few minutes. When the detective re-emerged, he was dusting himself down.

'This gets more interesting by the minute,' he told Fruity. 'Our vicar isn't quite what he seems.'

'He steals,' said a wavering high voice from the rear of the church. An old woman in a tattered brown coat and knitted tea-cosy hat finished praying and unfurled herself from her pew to regard the detective. She pointed at the wall. 'The vicar. I've seen him do it. He takes things when he thinks nobody's looking.'

'What does he do with the things he takes?' Bryant asked.

'Don't listen to her, she's always in here, she's crazy,' said the verger.

'He takes them away in his car, a sports car, red, the chariot of the Devil.' She crossed herself and scurried away before the verger could lash out.

'Wait, where does he take them?' Bryant called after her, but the door swung shut behind her.

Bryant ran out into the churchyard. The parishioner was making her way between the gravestones, dislodging crows. 'The Devil is here,' she cried. 'The Crowshott Grym will come for him.' With a squawk of alarm she trotted around the corner buttress and was gone.

'Well, that was a rather Shakespearian exit,' said Bryant, amused. 'What was she talking about?'

'Just a local superstition, sir,' said the verger, following him out. 'The Crowshott Grym is a mythical beast. I wouldn't worry about it. Every village in these parts has a few folk tales attached. We still have plenty of old Victorians living around here.'

In the distance a barrage of gunfire sounded like thunder.

'And what's Crowshott's folk tale?'

The verger shook his head dismissively. 'A variation on all the others. The Devil takes the form of a creeping black beast that lives in the trees near Tavistock Hall. It was set there to guard the house. They say that if the hall should fall, the beast will come down from the darkness within the branches and bare its long fangs, and will tear out the throat of anyone who sees it. It's just a children's story.'

'I'd hate to hear the adult version,' said Bryant.

'Nothing changes here,' said the verger. 'The past is the present. The more you Londoners try to change the world, the less it affects us. People are people and beasts are beasts.'

Something that sounded like a baby in distress cried out in the bushes behind them. Bryant shivered and pulled his jacket a little tighter. He waved Fruity over. 'Let's get back before anything else happens.'

'You can't keep us all here against our wills,' warned Pamela Claxon. 'Even Inspector Trench wouldn't do that.' The guests had moved to the more comfortable surroundings of the reception room, Iris, but there was no disguising the fact that they were prisoners.

John May sorted through the alibi postcards and felt none the wiser. The narratives were vague and randomly ordered. Out in the hall he heard Bryant coming in. His partner appeared in the doorway looking windswept.

'I hope you got on better than I did,' he said, shucking off his coat. 'It looks like we'll have to manage by ourselves for a while. Are those the testimonies? Let me have a shufti.' He flicked through the cards. 'What did you ask them to do, write essays? This is no good. Let me have a go.' With a sigh, May stepped aside.

Bryant strode into the middle of the room to address the group. 'All right, you lot, let's keep it simple. Who left the house this morning?'

Vanessa Harrow and Toby Stafford raised their hands. 'I went to the village for breakfast, as Mr March knows,' said Harrow. 'Sorry, he's May, not March, isn't he? And Mr Stafford was waiting for Donald.'

'Miss Harrow, you were seen near the barn,' Bryant pointed out.

'It couldn't have been me.' She blew her nose. 'Poor Mr Burke, what an awful end.'

'Inspector Trench would work this out by a simple process of elimination,' said Claxon.

'I seem to remember that in one of your novels the victim was hit by a meteorite,' Wilson reminded her. 'Your inspector isn't real, darling. He'd probably come up with the kind of theories you mystery writers always favour, death by poisoned pots of marmalade, trained monkeys and electrical cables hidden in bedsprings.'

Claxon was dismissive. 'Inspector Trench uses his intuitive skills. I can't bear Hercule Poirot, always judging people by their looks. He even complains about the shape of their heads. And Miss Marple's worse. She never thinks the killer is a stray burglar. It's always a duchess or a tycoon. And this ghastly obsession with ways of egress; she's forever enumerating paths, roads, doors and windows. Why would any cop worth his salt let the nosy old cow into a crime scene? All she does is gossip about shifty-looking foreigners in the village.'

'Last month in California five people were butchered by members of a cult for no reason that makes a shred of sense,' Wilson reminded her. 'There were no poisoned trifles or rifles hanging out of windows on bits of string there, were there?'

'You have to admit the situation we're in does feel like something from one of Miss Claxon's murder mysteries,' said the reverend.

'And it will require the same approach to its investigation,' said Claxon with determination. 'A murder mystery is a construct that relies on anagnorisis, the sudden revelation that reveals the true situation.'

'So it's like cheating,' said Wilson.

'No, it's technique. We mystery writers use many other devices: red herrings, unreliable narrators, deus ex machina, peripeteia – that's reversal of fortune. Then there's Chekhov's gun, in which a minor character is revealed to be of major importance.'

'But it isn't how real life works, Pamela,' Wilson reasoned. 'Only a madman would do something like this.'

'Except that none of us is mad,' said Claxon. 'Are we?'

'Miss Claxon, he – or she – may show no outer symptoms,' said May. 'You know what they're saying about Charles

Manson? He doesn't wake up each morning thinking he's crazy. He wakes up each morning thinking *you're* crazy.'

'I thought you two were supposed to be police detectives,' said Claxon. 'Can't you do something?'

'Then it's time to play the truth game,' said May, looking at his partner. But Bryant didn't reply. He was too lost in admiration for Pamela Claxon.

26

YOU'RE NO GOOD

'Very well, let's get this over and done with,' said Lady Banks-Marion.

She sat in the centre of the room, steely and calm in a straight-backed chair, beside her son. Harry was sitting cross-legged on the floor with his beloved piglet. Malacrida had been rinsed of bloodstains and was still smiling, but now there was something ghastly about that permanently upturned mouth.

'Could somebody ask Alberman to join us?' said May.

'What, the butler did it?' Monty snorted down his nose unpleasantly. 'The butler *never* does it.'

'I'll go,' said the reverend.

While they waited, May turned to the group. 'As this is an official police interrogation you are required to answer as you would in a court of law.' He wasn't sure about that, but it sounded good and was worth a try. 'When I collected the details of everyone's whereabouts I found I had ten cards instead of nine. This was the extra one.' He held it up so they could all see the card that read: 'They are all guilty'.

He let that sink in for a moment. 'Note it says "they", not

"we". It was written by somebody who knows you all and considers themselves innocent. Hard to imagine the killer writing it. So who did?'

He let them discuss the question with each other for a minute.

'Next.' He displayed a pair of white gloves. 'Yesterday morning Donald Burke had six pairs of these taken up to him. What for?'

'I can answer that,' said Norma Burke, glancing at the others. 'He couldn't bear the thought of touching anyone. He had a phobia about germs. He didn't like to speak about it and neither did I. It made him look weak. He'd left his glove case in the car.'

'Then – forgive me, Mrs Burke – if he had a fear of disease what made him enter a sewage treatment plant?' asked May. 'Did he see Miss Harrow go in ahead of him?'

The singer shot May a look of betrayal. 'So now I'm a siren who lures men to their doom in cesspits? What kind of a girl do you think I am? I didn't go anywhere near there.'

'That's odd,' said May, 'because one of Lord Banks-Marion's ashram pals, a girl called Melanie, says she saw you enter just before lunchtime. She gave us a description that only fits you. Were you there, Miss Harrow? Truthfully?'

'I thought I saw Donald in the garden, so I may have passed close to the ashram. But I didn't go inside the barn, I swear.'

'Why should anyone believe you?' said Monty. 'You're nothing but a common tart.'

The room exploded into uproar. Even the vicar said something colourful.

'She'll tell you she's a nightclub singer,' Monty shouted, 'but this is who she really is.' Removing his wallet from his jacket, he unfolded a photograph and held it up between his thumb and forefinger. It showed a heavy-set girl in a split-sided skirt and heavy eye make-up standing in a Merseyside backstreet. 'Her real name is Brenda Miles. She once spent a month in jail for soliciting. She had to work hard to get rid of those extra pounds, and her Liverpool accent.'

'It wasn't how it looks.' Vanessa's face crumpled. 'Why would you have that? Why?'

'To remind you of your place, which is not here among decent people.' Monty turned to the others. 'Her meal ticket didn't want anything more to do with her so she came back to me, didn't you? I was down near the barn before lunch, quietly having a smoke. She came and found me. And this time I turned her down. Well, you're out of a job now, so I imagine that next week you'll be under the arches at Piccadilly Circus with the other girls.'

'It wouldn't be the first time a whore has slept under these rafters,' said Lady Banks-Marion unhelpfully. May was about to step in, but Bryant held him back.

Vanessa looked younger somehow, and frightened. 'I didn't want to be here. I had nowhere else to go. I thought Mr Burke would be kind. I'm not his – I don't belong to him. I never went to bed with him. I never even got to meet him.'

There was another pause while everyone digested this latest confession.

'So you lied about going out with Mr Burke in London?' asked Bryant.

'I heard his name mentioned at the club, that's all. I was in financial trouble and Toby got me the job there—'

'It's true that I wrote to Mr Burke, asking him to employ Vanessa,' said Stafford. 'There's nothing wrong with that.'

Monty would not be placated. 'Admit it, Brenda, you slept with the owner.'

'No, Monty, I only slept with you,' she said lifelessly, 'and that was a dreadful mistake. Donald called me and was kind. He gave me advice, and that's all he ever gave me.'

She looked over at Norma, who nodded imperceptibly, as if she had known all along. 'He told me to stop relying on men of bad character. He meant you, Monty. That's why he was avoiding you. He'd heard enough about you not to trust you.' She turned to each of them. 'You can call me indecent, but you're the indecent ones. You did this between you, behaving so hypocritically. You created this whole poisonous situation.'

'I'm afraid something else has come to light,' said May, studying the assembly. 'Your ladyship, perhaps you'd repeat your allegation?'

'I am being blackmailed.' Lady Banks-Marion sounded as if she scarcely believed it herself. Everyone stared at her blankly. She held up the letter that had been under her hands. 'This is an amendment to the purchase contract for Tavistock Hall stating that the house is to be sold with all its existing furniture, fixtures and fittings – a clause I'm convinced my son was coerced into inserting without my approval. A short while ago Mr Stafford told me that he will not rescind it.'

'I'm afraid my hands are now tied,' said Stafford, his briefcase propped against the leg of his chair.

'You could remove it,' said Lady Banks-Marion. 'You could act like an honourable man. But instead you imply . . .'

'What did he imply to you, your ladyship?' asked May.

'My son – my son . . .' She faltered, her confidence evaporating.

'Your son enjoys the company of very young ladies,' said May. 'In fact, the girl he married in India—'

A ripple of shock passed around the room.

'Riya was given to me when she was fourteen,' said Harry, jutting his chins defiantly. 'She had been in the paid service of various uncles since the age of nine. I rescued her from that life and paid for her education.'

'You also married her in an illegal ceremony,' said Beatrice angrily. 'You exchanged her prison for one of a different kind. Did you never consider that our name would be dragged through the mud?'

'Wait, you have a *wife*?' said Pamela Claxon, catching on later than everyone else.

'In India, Pamela,' Wilson explained as if talking to someone who was profoundly deaf.

'Your son made no secret of his proclivities,' said Stafford sanguinely. 'I have my own reputation to protect.'

'What reputation? You're a lawyer,' Beatrice spat back.

'Did you imply that Lord Banks-Marion would be exposed unless the revised contract was allowed to stand?' May asked Stafford. 'If you did, it makes you a blackmailer.'

'I merely told him that any contest to the sale could result in bad publicity,' muttered Stafford. 'It has nothing to do with the matter at hand.'

'Actually it does,' said Bryant, stepping in. 'It gives Lady Banks-Marion and her son a motive for getting rid of Mr Burke. Presumably they assumed that without him there could be no sale.'

'That is an outrageous suggestion,' cried Beatrice. 'Mr Stafford has manipulated us from the start.'

'I'm sorry, Lady Banks-Marion,' said Norma distractedly. 'I didn't know about this. Toby, perhaps it's best if you withdraw from the negotiations.'

'Before we proceed any further,' said May, 'does anyone else have anything to confess?'

'I'm afraid I saw Vanessa too,' said Slade Wilson, raising a timid hand. 'Sorry, Vanessa, I saw you coming back from the barn.'

'What time was this?' May asked.

'It must have been right before lunch, at around a quarter to one. She stopped on the patio to clean some of the mud off her shoes.'

'All right – I did go there,' Vanessa burst out suddenly.

'Then why did you lie?'

The guests collectively held their breath. For a moment all

that could be heard was the rain at the windows, until a distant boom pulsed the panes.

'I know you won't believe me,' she said. 'I found a note in my bedroom from Donald. It asked me to meet him in the barn at noon.'

Claxon rolled her eyes in disbelief.

'Do you have the note now?' asked Bryant.

'No, I don't know what happened to it. I'm not lying to you this time, I swear.'

'What happened when you got there?'

Vanessa appeared increasingly panicked. 'I heard some kind of machinery running. I had no idea what it was. I looked in through the door but couldn't see Donald. I didn't want to stay there because it was noisy and smelly and I was wearing my luncheon dress. So I left. That's all that happened.'

'You're lying,' said Monty. 'You followed him out there, and found him on the walkway. Men like Burke are always fascinated by machinery. He went up to take a better look. You followed him up there and he said he wasn't going to pay for your little Mayfair flat any more. And in your anger you shoved him. You're a harlot and a murderess.'

'No, it's not true.' Vanessa seemed determined not to cry. She carefully rose to her feet. 'I don't care which of you did it because whoever wrote that note was right; you're all bad people. Whatever happens from this point on is your fault.' She walked unsteadily towards the door. The guests watched her go in damning silence. May wanted to stop her, but decided to allow her a dignified exit. There was, after all, nowhere she could go.

'I think you've said enough, Monty,' warned Bryant. 'Unfortunately there is something else we have to discuss.' He held out his right hand. The others craned their necks to see what was in it. 'I found these on the way back from the village, lying on the pathway near the patio. They are the exact match of one I found among the reverend's things at St Stephen's.'

In his palm were a pair of needles, glistening and sinister, wrapped in a handkerchief. 'When I entered the church I noticed that the walls were bare and the silver plate was missing from the sacristy. I talked to the verger, and he allowed me to search the room. How long have you been a heroin addict, Reverend?'

Trevor Patethric dropped his head in his hands.

'Reverend?' May tried. 'Help us to clear the air.'

'You have no idea what it's like,' he murmured in a voice so low they could barely hear him.

'Perhaps you could tell us.'

'I was working with youth groups, trying to help them. To do that I had to know what they were going through. I needed to understand.'

'And you got a little too close,' said Bryant. 'You caught their habits. And you sold the fittings from the church to pay for drugs.'

'A few trivial pieces of plate and some inferior hangings, nothing of use to the community. *They* needed them and then *I* needed them. I tried to find the money that would help them. I couldn't talk to anyone. Obviously, the diocese was no help, and there are no organizations to aid us with something like this. In London, perhaps, but not here in the countryside. The pleas I made to the bishop fell on deaf ears . . .'

' "They are all guilty",' May reiterated, looking at the slip once more. 'What interested me was not so much the wording on the card, but how it found its way to me. The only people who hear and see everything are the staff, and they have no voice. Mr Alberman, perhaps you could explain why you wrote this card and slipped it in with the others?'

27

ALL ALONG THE WATCHTOWER

No change of expression crossed the butler's face. He sat impassive, waiting for the detectives to finish speaking. Rainwater dripped steadily through a damp patch in the corner of the ceiling, hitting the floorboards like the ticking of a clock.

'*They,*' said May. 'Written by an outsider. The guests were informed that we were officers, but not you. How did you know who we were? And if you had something to say, why not come to us and say it?'

'How could I?' Alberman replied. 'I am supposed to see nothing; I am supposed to hear nothing. My opinion does not and should not count.'

'Then why write it?'

'Because of him.' Alberman pointed at the Reverend Pate-thric. 'I am a God-fearing man, sir. My father was a butler, and so was my grandfather. We asked no questions. We attended church on Sunday evenings, after our duties in the great house were finished. We had one afternoon off a week and we always did as we were told.'

He nodded gravely towards Lady Banks-Marion. 'My employer is a fine lady, one of the last. But she is surrounded by those who mean her harm. This vicar told us we were wrong, that our image of God was outdated and should go. He denies almost every Christian doctrine and joins his friends from the ashram, performing lewd acts and taking drugs in his own churchyard. And Lord Banks-Marion, with his messages of peace and love, dances about in his garden full of concubines, playing the fool while this house collapses about his ears.'

'Who else, Mr Alberman?' asked May. 'Who else is guilty?'

Bryant looked about the room. There was a sense that the gathering was collectively pressing itself into the back of its chairs, like air passengers braced for further turbulence.

Alberman studied each of them in turn, unable to conceal his disgust. 'All of these people are only here to prey upon my lady's good nature.'

'How do you know?'

'Look at them. The writer of bad mysteries, the legal parasite, the pederast artist, they come here to complain about the house and the food and the staff, but they eat and drink and lie to her ladyship's face because they are nothing more than leeches. They came to beg money from Mr Burke and now he is dead.' He stabbed his finger at them. 'My lady is from Olympus and you are all from the gutter. You should be grateful she opens her doors to you, every one.'

As if in response, rain-laden wind smacked at the windows like a spiteful child.

'Well, that was quite a speech,' said Pamela Claxon, applauding cheerfully. 'I'm jolly glad you told us what you really think, Alberman. I have a feeling Inspector Trench would have quite a lot to say about the poor quality of the staff service at Tavistock Hall.'

The butler ignored her, addressing only his employer. 'I'm sorry, your ladyship. I had no right to speak out of turn. I have disgraced myself. I have broken the first rule of my profession, for which I can only offer a profuse apology.'

'I'm glad you spoke your mind, Alberman,' she said softly.
'So you knew we were policemen?' asked May.
'Of course. Servants know everything. You talk. We listen.
Ladies, gentlemen, if you will excuse me.' He rose, dipped his
head and slipped silently from the room.
The meeting broke up shortly after.

Nobody was leaving, not while tanks rumbled near the
lane and shells splintered the trees at the end of the meadow.
Even the starlings and blackbirds had finally fled from the
roof. A heavy grey vapour, part mist, part military, was drifting across the fields and gardens, removing the contours from
the clipped hedges. A partially denuded topiary of a rearing
horse now loomed out of the mist like a funerary sculpture.
The house now felt like a ghost ship, lost and rudderless.

Bryant took his pipe outside and waited under the eaves for
his partner to join him. 'I thought that cleared the air a bit,'
he said.

'If by *cleared the air* you mean poisonous accusations and
enough admissions of sin to keep a clergyman busy for a
month, yes, I suppose so,' said May. 'What now?'

'I honestly don't know.' Bryant released a curl of perfumed
smoke into the wet air. 'I'm not equipped for this. These
people – it's like looking at a series of funhouse mirrors. No
one is who they appear to be.'

As he drew on his pipe, a florin-sized raindrop fell from
above and put it out with a sizzle. It felt like an omen. 'Do me
a favour and stay close to Monty, would you? His injury isn't
serious and he's talking about getting out. Now that he has
no reason to stay he'll either make a dash for it or remain at
risk here. Either way, we need to keep a careful eye on him.'

'We could call Gladys again,' said May. 'She can keep trying to get hold of someone.'

'It means we'll lose the case if she does,' said Bryant. 'We
didn't just fail to protect our source, we somehow allowed a
murder to take place on the premises. Sir Charles Chamberlain's

defence attorneys will argue that Monty can't appear as a material witness because he's technically under suspicion of murder in a separate investigation.'

'But that's ridiculous.'

'I can't think of a better way to get crucial evidence discounted, can you? It goes without saying that the effect on us will be disastrous. The unit is already close to being disbanded. Roger Trapp will never be able to keep it going after this.'

'Arthur, what you're suggesting is unthinkable. We can't simply hide a murder.'

'Therein lies the paradox,' said Bryant, with a crafty little tilt to his head that suggested he had an alternative route planned in his head. 'But there *is* a way out of the problem.'

'I've a feeling I'm not going to like this.'

'We close the investigation ourselves and get Monty back to London alive and in one piece by Monday morning.'

'How do you propose to do that?'

'I don't, *you* will. You're our secret weapon, John. I'm the ideas man. You know how to talk to people. I always put my foot in it, but you have the gift of the gab. You can worm the truth out of everyone. Look at what we've already uncovered: a call girl, a blackmailer and a drug addict, not to mention Lord Banks-Marion's exposure as a seducer of underage girls. I have no idea where to head next in a case like this, but it's right up your street, all this *talking* to people about their feelings. Heaven knows I've tried but *Homo sapiens* are a closed book to me. I don't understand their emotions. You can do it, but we have to be ready for the fallout.'

'What do you mean?'

Bryant stared out into the garden, where Fruity was cheerfully bagging leaves, oblivious to the rain. 'If the case is solved, everything will fall apart. The house sale will be withdrawn and the scandal will kill what's left of this house and its family. But if *we* handle it rather than the Canterbury CID, we may be able to limit the damage.'

'I don't understand you,' May admitted. 'Why do you care about what happens to any of them? I thought you hated them all.'

'I don't hate anyone,' Bryant replied, 'but I abhor their boringly predictable weaknesses. Monty was right: when they heard that a millionaire would be in attendance this weekend they turned up at the trough right on cue. Unfortunately Burke was the one who ended up in it.' He picked up a twig and scraped out the bowl of his pipe. 'So, as we have nothing left to lose, are you and I in agreement?'

'I suppose when you put it like that we have no choice. We'll just have to give it our best shot.'

'If anybody asks I'll hold the party line, that no one from outside can get here until tomorrow. You and I will need to make sure that they don't. We'll keep Stafford here where we can watch him. I suppose the vicar is expected to hold services tomorrow. You'd better make sure that Alberman and Miss Harrow don't do anything rash. I didn't like that exit line of hers about whatever happens next being our fault.'

'Oh God, you're right.'

May sprinted back inside the house and ran upstairs to the first floor. The door to Vanessa Harrow's room was locked. He knocked, then hammered on the panels with his palm. No sound came from within.

Parchment was slumped on the bench of his wooden alcove at the end of the corridor. He was leaning against the wall of the planked box and looked dead. In his hands were knitting needles and three-quarters of a hideous striped scarf.

'Mr Parchment?' May gave him an experimental shake.

The old man sat up with a start, his eyes wide. 'Is there another fire?'

'No. Are you all right?'

The old man looked down at his scarf and needles. 'Sorry sir, sometimes I knit and think. Sometimes I just knit.' He set aside the knitting and turned up his hearing aid. 'Can I help you with something?'

'Do you have a set of room keys?' May asked loudly.

Parchment fumbled in his desk drawer and handed over a set to him. 'I ask the guests not to lock their bedrooms,' he said, still coming round. 'They have a habit of taking souvenirs. We lost a set of taps once.'

May ran back to the bedroom door and unlocked it.

Vanessa Harrow was lying on her bed asleep, but when May shook her she did not awaken. A small brown bottle lay beside her on the coverlet. He picked it up and read the label: 'Nembutal'.

A partially drunk bottle of Gordon's gin stood on the bedside table, along with a half-filled water glass. He thought, *Get her awake, make her throw up, walk her around,* but first he held a hand over her mouth and nose.

That was when he realized she was no longer breathing.

28

ALBATROSS

Lieutenant Coultas wiped his clouded spectacles and searched the rainswept field.

There was no part of him that was not soaked. A handful of sodden, shell-shocked sheep cowered by a shattered hayrick. Great clods of earth had been torn from the pasture all around them, leaving loamy craters across the landscape. Several hawthorn bushes had been blasted apart and a roll of barbed wire had been unspooled across a ha-ha. One could be forgiven for thinking that the Germans had finally invaded this corner of Kent.

Captain Debney had been crouching under a maple tree when Coultas found him. Debney pretended he was doing something important with a pair of secateurs and a field telephone. 'Can you warn the farmer that his fences have been knocked down, Coultas?' he said, going on the offensive. 'I suppose the French understand that we're not actually meant to engage in combat?' He picked up his field glasses and trained them on the terrified livestock. 'It's not a good idea to frighten sheep, you know,' he said ruminatively. 'They tense up and it spoils the meat. You can't eat clenched lamb. Has anyone reached the objective?'

'No sir, but some lads took a wrong turn and shelled the safari park at Dimmington. They damaged a wall – nobody hurt, but a few of the animals got out. There's an ostrich running around here somewhere. I'm trying to find out what else they've lost. The keepers are very upset. They're doing an inventory.'

'I hope nothing rare has gone missing. You know what the French are like. If they come across something exotic they'll try to eat it. You'd better send off the usual letter of apology. Use the one we sent to the old people's home.'

'And we've had some intelligence that there are people in the old hall, sir,' Coultas added. 'They've been seen in one of the nearby meadows.'

Debney put his glasses down. 'Hell's bells, how did that happen? You're telling me we have civilians in the middle of a battlefield, surrounded by men using live ammunition?'

'That's about the size of it, sir. We tried to contact them but their line is out of order.'

'The local exchange is probably getting comms interference from us. You'd better send someone over in a jeep and get them out.' Debney rose and cracked his knees.

'I suppose we could do that, sir,' said Coultas hesitantly. 'But they may not like being moved out. If push comes to shove they could kick up a frightful stink. It would be easier to inform the battalions to stay below this point here and keep out of range.' He tapped the boundary line of the field on his carefully refolded Ordnance Survey map. 'If we make sure that the road between Knotsworth and Crowshott stays free of fire they'll be able to come and go in safety.'

'So we don't tell them?' said Debney. 'I say, that's a bit underhand. I suppose we can't allow a bunch of civvies to bugger up an exercise as important as this, eh? Just make sure that nobody gets blown to bits. We don't want a repeat of what happened in Richmond Park. Ducks all over the place. I sincerely hope I never have to pull another goat out of a pond.'

'We'll keep a watch on the hall, sir, don't worry,' Coultas promised. 'If we see anyone else heading across the fields I'll put out a ceasefire order.'

'Jolly good,' said Debney, only half listening. 'The menu for tonight's Hands Across the Water dinner has already gone up the Swanee. We had terrible trouble getting hold of courgettes and now I hear there's no custard available. I don't want anything else going wrong. These are international war games. We can't afford to have anyone hurt.'

Lady Banks-Marion wandered from room to room, lightly touching the silver-framed photographs and the backs of armchairs, trailing the tips of her fingers across the polished surfaces of gate-legged tables, recalling histories in everything. Here was the gigantic brass peacock from which Harry had fallen and split his lip as a three-year-old. There was the portrait of Ellen Terry given to her mother by the great actress herself. Each room had a hundred stories to tell, but now it felt as if these memories were bleaching away in the cruel glare of the modern world.

She headed back towards the library where Norma Burke sat at the window watching the incessant autumnal rain.

'This is the only room where I can find peace now,' she said, seating herself and leaning her head back against her armchair's lace antimacassar. 'I feel like a spirit preparing to vanish with the sale of the house.' Water patterns dashed down the walls of green silk damask. The fat leather spines of books surrounded her, weighing down the house with their remembrances.

Norma Burke was a good listener. She had learned to remain silent and respectful around her husband. Settled in a nearby armchair with a shawl around her shoulders, she brought calm to the room, and being practical by nature very little panicked her. Rather, she sought practical solutions.

'I do not understand what happened to this family,' Beatrice continued.

221

'What was the house like when you first came here?' asked Norma.

'Everyone always wants to know that,' said Beatrice wearily. 'When people ask about the past, it's a sure sign that the present is disappointing. Our parties never lasted more than forty-eight hours, but there were so very many of them.' Her ladyship clasped one bony hand in the other, as if holding herself together. 'My husband would invite dignitaries from the Foreign Office, and I had the Duchess of Portland to talk to. There were always too many people trying to be clever. Brightly burning flames that never lasted. The furniture fifty years out of date, the tricks in the kitchen to make the food go further, so much *hospitality* on show. The hunts and the shooting parties, and musical evenings, too much forced gaiety and far too much dressing up. Chinese lanterns in the garden, electroliers in the gathering rooms – the lights could be seen for miles. The villagers removed their hats. Deference and respect. All gone. This is the last weekend we shall ever hold, which I suppose makes it memorable.'

'I'll remember it as the one at which my husband was killed,' replied Norma quietly.

'Oh my child, I'm so sorry.' Beatrice reached over and clasped her arm. 'One becomes so isolated in a place like this, only thinking of oneself. Your poor husband. You must be utterly distraught.'

'Not as much as I thought,' Norma replied, gently removing her hand. 'Donald left long ago. We hadn't been close for a number of years. There was always too much work to be done. But I shall miss him. People never really understand what couples do for each other.'

'My husband left us nothing except this old house and his debts.' Beatrice looked up at the damp patches on the ceiling. 'It was his life. A home, a garden, a horse, a wife: that was the preferred order. I don't need to tell you how much of a disappointment his son was to him. A weak, silly, easily led child. This is an age that tests such people and exposes their flaws to the light.'

'I had no idea that Toby Stafford had sent you a letter,' said Norma. 'I would have stopped it had I known.' She poured them both tea from the silver service that had been laid out on the walnut-inlaid table before them. 'Men have had too much power for too long. Look at the mess they make of things. I feel sorry for Vanessa – if a girl has to make a living for herself, it makes sense to take money from foolish men. One can hardly condemn her for that. You and I should decide what to do.'

'I think I'm ready to leave now,' said Beatrice. 'There's nothing left for me here. But without your husband buying the hall, I don't know what will happen to us.'

'I shall keep his promise,' Norma assured her. 'The sale of Tavistock Hall will go ahead, but only if that's what you truly want. It can become a business centre in accordance with my late husband's wishes, and you will be finally free of the place.'

'Then I suppose we must put our faith in those two peculiar young policemen.' Beatrice rose and went to the window. The damp was bad for her bones. The wet afternoon fog still clung to the hedgerows, obscuring the outer world. 'This has always been an unfortunate house. I remember the night the Marchioness of Abbingdon fell over her Pekinese. She went headlong down the stairs and broke her neck. Two years later one of the maids was violently assaulted in her bed. They never caught the fellow who did it, although we all knew who he was. We were so adept at hushing up scandals. How appropriate that there should be one final humiliation in store for us. I would dearly love to leave first thing in the morning, before anything else terrible happens.'

'I feel sorry for you,' said Norma, and instantly regretted it.

The matriarch's eyes were as clear and penetrating as polar ice. They looked through and far beyond her. 'You have nothing to feel sorry for, Mrs Burke,' she said crisply. 'The

Banks-Marions of Tavistock Hall have always known how to take care of themselves. I will accept your offer because it is time to do so and because it suits my purpose. Without the money to save it, the house is nothing but a burden. You may keep it all, the linens, the silverware, the china, the tapestries. And all of the paintings except for the Stubbs, the Gainsborough and the Reynolds, providing you have them reframed. The Pre-Raphaelites are vulgar and virtually unsaleable. I have no further need for them, and I have no further interest in the subject.'

If Norma had felt any pity for the old lady, it was most tested in that moment.

29

PEOPLE ARE STRANGE

Beset by obscuring gloom inside and out, Tavistock Hall had become a creaking mansion of shadows and secrets.

The mangled remains of the corpse lay hidden in a corner of the barn, covered with a tarpaulin, and Vanessa Harrow rested in her room, guarded by Dr Walgrave. The bright-eyed, egg-bald physician had been hoping for a sunny afternoon of cricket. Instead he had been visited by the cook, Mrs Bessel, and asked to attend at the hall. Not knowing what to expect, he had arrived with his usual satchel of palliatives and had found himself with an unconscious woman on his hands.

'She's lucky to be alive,' he said, closing his bag. 'I dare say your colleague here must have thought she was dead. Her breathing and pulse were extremely suppressed. I'm sure these young people do it to seek attention. I expect she made the common mistake of taking too many tablets, which made her vomit. It's harder than you'd think to get the amount right. Most of them came back up before they'd had a chance to reach the gut and dissolve.'

'Can we at least talk to her?' asked Bryant, trying to peer around Vanessa Harrow's bedroom door.

'No you cannot, young man, she's asleep now and will be for some considerable time, probably until tomorrow morning,' said Dr Walgrave. 'Do you have any idea what made her do it?'

'If she needs a counsellor I'll arrange for her to speak to the appropriate service,' said Bryant, who had little time for officious doctors.

'As you wish.' Walgrave saw that he would get nothing from the detective, and turned to May, whom he found more amenable. 'I suspect the gentleman, Mr Hatton-Jones, has a fractured clavicle. I warned him that he'll need an X-ray and some orthopaedic treatment when he returns to London.'

'I'll make sure that he gets everything he needs,' May assured him.

'At least Mrs Bessel did a good job of bandaging him up. I must say, there's always something happening up at this house.'

'Why, have you been asked to attend here for other reasons?'

'Those girls,' said Walgrave, lowering his voice, 'living in tents without sanitation. I've had to treat several of them for diseases of a delicate nature. And there's a small child not being properly looked after. I'll be writing all this up in a report. I should talk to Lady Banks-Marion. I suppose I don't have to send it.'

Do the upper classes get special treatment from everyone? thought Bryant. *Even doctors?* 'Do you have any advice?' he asked.

'Yes, don't spend the weekend with people you don't like,' replied Dr Walgrave. 'To whom should I send my bill?'

'You don't get to send anyone a bill, you're helping the police,' Bryant snapped. 'And you can put that bag down, because you're not going anywhere just yet.'

'But the road gets flooded here, Mr Bryant, and I'm on foot. I really can't stay here any longer. My wife gets most upset if I'm late back.'

'We need to go inside Miss Harrow's room for a minute.'

'But I told you, she's sleeping.'

'We won't disturb her. There's something I need to clear up with you.'

'Very well.' He followed the detectives into the bedroom.

'You say Miss Harrow didn't keep down the pills she took,' Bryant said in a low voice.

'That's right,' Walgrave agreed, 'I found four of them whole in the sink.'

Bryant looked at the undisturbed patient. 'If they weren't dissolved, why is she sleeping so heavily now? She didn't take a powdered sleeping draught?'

'No, they were regular tablets. The bottle was lying on the coverlet. It has her name typed on it and the prescription is printed on the label, one a night for two weeks only.' Walgrave felt he had been kept here long enough, and looked at the detective with ill-concealed impatience. 'I assume two or three had time to dissolve in her stomach, which is why she's sleeping so soundly now.'

'But wouldn't they have all dissolved at the same time?' asked May.

'She drank some gin – I can smell it. Then there's the half-drunk glass of water.' He indicated the tumbler on the bedside table. 'I imagine she used either the gin or the water to wash the tablets down.'

Bryant pointed back at the table. 'Look at the glass. There's sediment in the bottom of it.'

Puzzled, Dr Walgrave reached out for the water tumbler.

'No, don't touch it.' Bryant took out his handkerchief, raised the glass to the light and studied the thin trickle of white powder on its side. 'There were two types of sleeping medication. One from the Nembutal pill bottle, which has a prescription in her name typed on the side. And another, in solution, already in the glass. She wasn't trying to kill herself at all. She had a slug of gin and took a heavy dose of sleeping tablets but they were only five milligrams, and as they were the last ones in the bottle she was presumably familiar with their effects.'

Dr Walgrave did not like anyone else trespassing into his area of expertise. 'This is pure surmise on your part.'

'Then let's surmise a little further.' He turned to May. 'Miss Harrow finally goes to meet the man who has been so kind to her, but doesn't see him. A little later she hears about his death, then everyone launches accusations at her. She goes to her room in a state of tension and misery. She just wants to be away from everyone and sleep for a while. She takes four five-milligram sleeping pills, washing them down with some of the water. But she coughs up the tablets in the bathroom and it's the *sleeping draught* dissolved in the water that has put her to sleep. And the only thing that saved her life is not drinking the full glass.'

'Really, that sounds rather far-fetched,' said Walgrave.

'Then test the water,' said Bryant. 'See if the sediment matches this brand.' He showed Walgrave the triangular sliver of shiny blue paper he had spotted in the waste-paper basket. 'Somebody tore open packets of powdered sleeping draught and added them to her water glass. I suppose it's possible they may not have considered that she would use it to wash her own tablets down. But the combined effect of the tablets and the powder could easily have caused her death.'

'They very nearly did,' said Walgrave. 'Who would have done such a thing?'

'That's what we intend to find out,' said John May.

They finally let Dr Walgrave go home, and stood by the front-door steps, beyond the reach of the falling rain, breathing in the cool damp air.

'One death and two near-fatalities.' Bryant unwrapped a tube of Fruit Gums and offered them to his partner. 'We're in the middle of a war zone, figuratively and literally. At least they've stopped shelling the fields for a while.' He listened, hearing rain in the trees.

'It's impossible to do anything more while we're marooned

here,' said May. 'Lord Banks-Marion doesn't even have a telex or a decent working phone line. How are we going to get any concrete evidence? Everyone's defences are up. They're all so bloody *English*, all sarcasm and fish-eye stares when you question them.'

'Now you're starting to sound like me,' said Bryant. 'We're not wanted here. Even innocent people are unnerved by police; you know that. The guests may not realize it, but they're giving themselves away, offering up clues even though they don't know it.' Bryant took the tiny triangle of blue paper from his pocket and turned it over in his fingers.

'Wait, you have clues?'

He twirled the paper. 'Oh, more than one.'

'Do you want to tell me about them?'

'Not yet.'

'If you wait much longer there may not be anyone left to tell.'

'You must have noticed that there are alliances here as well as enmities. Which means there are those who are willing to supply alibis. I've been struck by a number of inconsistencies.'

'You'll be struck by something else if you don't start sharing them with me.'

'I need to understand a little more. I think we should talk to the staff.'

May reluctantly followed his partner to the basement to speak with the hall's invisible occupants.

'You'll have to be quick,' said Mrs Bessel, the cook, who, Bryant could not help noticing, had flour above, below and inside her nose. 'I didn't get the afternoon baking out. Once I'd have served fresh eclairs, fig and walnut loaf, maids of honour, cheese and pimento sandwiches and queen cakes. We don't have the staff or the budget for that sort of thing any more. There used to be twenty of us here, now there's just six. It's absurd to think you can run a house this size with what we've got.'

'What *have* you got?' asked Bryant, sniffing the air. The room smelled of rising dough, vanilla and fried butter.

'A butler, me, the housekeeper, a part-time parlourmaid, a valet and the groundsman. What's more Mr Parchment is older than God's boots and the groundsman isn't allowed inside the house.'

'Have you always been in service?' Bryant's hand crept towards a piece of plum cake and was slapped away.

'My mother and grandmother, and her mother too,' said Mrs Bessel proudly. 'That was back when they used to run two servants' tables, top and second, with its own rules and dinner times just like them upstairs.'

'Did you meet Mr Burke?' asked May.

'The cook doesn't meet guests.' It was clear that Mrs Bessel considered the very idea to be absurd. 'We was told he would only eat salads and have meals in his room, that's all. And cherry huffkins, if you please, which I haven't made since I don't know when. We used to flavour them with hops around here, and leave a little thumbprint in the top of each one, proper traditional.'

Mrs Janverley was the housekeeper, crimson-handed, baggy and burnished by years spent in lightless laundry rooms. She looked as if she had never heard a joke in her life. Seated in her room behind the kitchen, she glanced up from her linens book and removed her glasses. 'Yes, I heard about the unfortunate accident,' she told them. 'Not the first in this house.'

'How often do the sewage men come out to the barn?' asked Bryant.

'They're here once a fortnight to empty the septic tank,' Mrs Janverley explained. 'The mechanism has to be hosed out and its blades are changed once a year. There's also a fortnightly maintenance check. That's the groundsman's job.'

'You mean Mr Metcalf?'

'That's right, although of course it's difficult for him to get about. He can't do stairs. I'm given to understand that Mr Burke fell from the walkway. Is that correct?'

'Perhaps,' said Bryant. 'He could have been lowered in just as easily. Can you think of any reason why Mr Burke might have gone out to the barn?'

'There is no reason to visit it at all, less'n you have to empty it,' said Mrs Janverley firmly. 'The smell alone would keep anyone away.'

Elsie the parlourmaid agreed with a sour little moue. 'It's a horrible smelly place, proper nasty. I wouldn't go down there, not with my nerves.'

'She's on edge,' said Mrs Janverley. 'We all are.'

'Elsie, were you taking care of Mr Burke's room?' May asked.

'Only tidying up and making the bed, not laundry,' she explained. 'The guests used to arrive with their own maids but those days are long gone. Mr Parchment's on call for all their other needs, if you can manage to wake him up. He stays in his night booth on the first floor.'

'How often does Lady Banks-Marion host weekend parties?'

'Hardly ever now, at least not since I've been here. This is my last maid's job. When they close the house up I'm going to my sister's place in America.'

'You don't like working for Lady Banks-Marion?'

Elsie pulled a face that was even less flattering than the last. 'Oh no, she acts like King Edward's still on the throne, and she pays the same wages an' all.'

Next they went upstairs and spoke to Parchment, who was knitting in his nook. The valet's night booth was a cross between a stationery cupboard and a ship's berth, its comforts arranged with military precision. Bryant had seen similar slatted wooden compartments at pensioners' barracks. They were designed to remind old soldiers of their days in service.

'I understand you're in charge of laying the tables and keeping the bedrooms and their guests comfortable,' said May.

'The world's changed, hasn't it?' Parchment replied, setting down a partially finished scarf and turning up his hearing aid. 'The old order's gone, sir. There are no country squires any more. The prime minister says we're all equal now. Look at the Beatles, all of them millionaires and they're from Liverpool!'

Bryant caught his partner's eye.

'There's no work left for me,' Parchment said tiredly. 'When the last war broke out most of the country house owners around here couldn't wait to sell up to the Ministries of Defence and Education. Soldiers and schoolkids did what the bombs couldn't; they smashed up everything they could lay their hands on.' The speech, probably one of the longest he had made in thirty years, looked as if it had worn him out. 'Knole House is the only other big manor house around here, sir, over in Sevenoaks. One of the biggest in the country, that is.'

Bryant had heard of it. Virginia Woolf had set her novel *Orlando* there. 'Could you get a job at Knole?'

'I'd like to,' said Parchment. 'It's a calendar house. Three hundred and sixty-five rooms, fifty-two staircases, twelve entrances and seven courtyards. I don't suppose they need anyone like me.'

'Do you like working for the family?' Bryant asked.

'I like Lady Banks-Marion, she's a decent sort. She has rules that can't be broken. But her son is soft in the head. He still makes fun of me. I told him, I'm Ernest Prabhakar; it's an old Indian name. My mother was Indian, see.'

'What will you do, then?' asked Bryant.

'Me? I'll get myself a cheap little flat near one of the big London hotels. My references are good. They still do silver service at Claridge's, Simpson's and the like, and the money's better. I'm not young and I like my sleep in the afternoons, but I've still got my knees and most of my eyesight. I can manage dinner and supper sittings until all hours.'

'Did you meet Mr Burke?'

'I saw him but I didn't talk to him. It's not my place.'

'Do you talk to any of the guests?'

'Only Mr Wilson. He needed some help with the measurements for the bedroom but I wasn't about to stand on a chair.'

'So none of the servants were allowed to talk to Mr Burke?'

'Nobody except Mr Alberman, sir. He'd be the only one who could do that.'

They went to check on the butler.

Alberman could shed no further light on the deceased houseguest. He continued to pack his suitcase as he spoke. 'Mrs Burke took care of him,' he explained. 'It was my impression that his health was poor.'

'What made you think that?'

'He walked slowly, and she had to guide him. I thought perhaps he had gout. I heard cross words between them.'

'Why would he want to buy a house this size if his health was failing?'

'It is not my position to ask questions about the guests of my employers,' Alberman replied. 'My job is to ensure the smooth running of the household, not to hold views.'

'You certainly held views a short while ago,' May pointed out.

'That needed saying, sir.' He placed a perfectly folded shirt into his case and lovingly smoothed out the material, adding a set of whalebone brushes. He had very few belongings to pack. 'I had been intending to hand in my notice for several months,' he replied to Bryant's unasked question. 'It was only out of respect for Lady Banks-Marion that I held off. But the time has come to leave.'

'Surely you can't desert her in her hour of need? You can't leave tonight anyway,' May warned. 'The road is closed until tomorrow.'

'I have lived in this house for the past twenty-seven years,' said Alberman, drawing himself up. 'There are arrangements to make before I go. Staying one more night will be no hardship.'

As they came out of Alberman's room and headed downstairs, they passed Harry Banks-Marion and his smiling piglet on the grand staircase. For a heavy man, he tripped down the steps with balloon-lightness.

'I wanted to ask you,' said Bryant. 'How did you come to know Donald Burke?'

'We were introduced through Toby Stafford,' Harry replied. 'Toby and his wife were staying in Crowshott in the spring. They were passing through Kent looking at properties, and I nearly ran him over.'

'Was he all right?' asked May.

'Oh yes, just got splashed with mud. There are no pavements, you see, and I was doing a toad.'

'I'm sorry?'

'Toad of Toad Hall. Driving a bit too fast. But we got talking, and I mentioned the problems I was having with the house. Toby explained that he was looking for a property where he could open his client's business centre, and one thing led to another.'

'Was your mother in the car with you?' asked Bryant.

'What? No, she was at home.'

'And Mr Burke rang you?'

'The very next day.'

'Well, that was extremely revealing,' said Bryant as they continued on down the staircase and out of the house.

'You think so?' asked May.

'Oh, very. Didn't you?'

'Not really, no. Did I miss something?'

'Probably.' The familiar glint of mischief appeared in Bryant's eye. 'Perhaps I shouldn't tell you. It will be interesting to hear your observations later. We can compare notes.'

'I'm not sure I have any notes.' May was put out. They had always shared their information in the past.

'I need to break open the box I stole from Monty's room,' said Bryant. 'Interesting that he hasn't mentioned it. What did you do with it?'

'Ah,' said May. 'I was going to tell you about that. I left it in the library, under one of the armchairs, but it seems to have disappeared.'

'What do you mean? Where could it have gone?'

'I'm not entirely sure. It's possible that Monty may have searched the house and taken it back.'

'Well, we don't have time to find it now. You have to come back to the village with me,' said Bryant, 'somebody there must know something. Shopkeepers. We should be able to catch them before they close. You need to come with me in case I miss anything. You know what I'm like.'

'All right, but I'll tell Fruity to keep a close eye on the place and make sure nobody else gets in.'

A few minutes later they set off for the village of Crow-shott, watched by a shell-shocked parliament of rooks.

30

WALKING IN THE RAIN

In London, the rain had yet to arrive and ruin the afternoon.

Gladys Forthright checked the telex memo she had been keeping in her pocket. 'The prosecution has confirmed that if Monty doesn't appear on Monday they'll have no case,' she said, handing Roger Trapp the offending note.

'All right, Gladys, I can read.' Trapp snatched the sheet from her. He should have been at a cricket match in Regent's Park and was most put out that Gladys had insisted on meeting up with him.

They were seated in a garishly painted Camden Town coffee bar called My People Were Fair and Had Sky in Their Hair. Until last year it had been called Eddie's and had sold pie and mash, but since the name change their counters were filled with pineapple upside-down cake and espressos, catering for the in-crowd.

'I guess this tape recording Hatton-Jones made of Chamberlain's bribery attempt isn't enough to convict him,' she said.

'No, but it's a back-up,' said Trapp, scanning the page. 'The main thing is that we know the Hackney development collapsed because of Chamberlain's faulty designs. Surely there's enough evidence to secure a conviction?'

'Too many rogue elements in the production chain, apparently.' Gladys pointed a crimson nail lower down the message. 'It's in there somewhere. The defence is going to put up an argument saying that the land was subject to subsidence and should never have been chosen as a public housing site. Smoke and mirrors. They'll say they can't guarantee that Chamberlain's company is directly responsible for the fault.'

'But what about his conversation with the planners, the recording, the bribery, the failure to tender?'

'Unless there are names directly mentioned on the tape it'll be circumstantial at best. They need a direct witness.'

Trapp lowered a spoon into his cappuccino with dismay. 'I hate these things,' he complained. 'Why do they put chocolatey stuff on the foam?'

'You could have had a latte or an espresso.'

'I don't want to have to remember ten names for a cup of coffee. You don't have ten names for tea. Anyway, we've got a direct witness, haven't we? Monty's not going to back down or anything.'

'No, but . . .' She wondered how much to tell him. There was already a vein like a fireman's hose throbbing at Trapp's temple.

'Out with it, for God's sake.'

'The situation has become more complicated,' she ventured. 'Shall I order you a cup of tea instead?'

'What do you mean? Bryant and May are in a country house in the middle of nowhere. How much trouble can they possibly get into?'

You'd be surprised, thought Gladys as she beckoned a waitress. 'There's been an unexplained death.'

'What do you mean: "unexplained"?'

'Well, an accident or a murder.' After the waitress had set

down a plain froth-free coffee before her boss, Gladys described the situation to the best of her understanding.

Trapp was appalled. 'Are you telling me that Hatton-Jones could be a suspect?'

'John thinks not, because he has a solid alibi. He tells me Monty was having lunch with the others at the time,' said Gladys.

'So there's no problem.'

'There will be when Canterbury get hold of it. Monty knew the deceased; he was a fellow guest at the site of his murder. They'll move to disbar his testimony.'

'And how do you come to know about this?' asked Trapp suspiciously. 'Bryant and May are keeping this under their hats, aren't they? They haven't informed the local constabulary.'

'Mr Bryant's fear is that if outsiders become involved they'll detain Hatton-Jones, and he won't be able to deliver his testimony on Monday morning. Even if they don't, his eligibility as a witness will come under question.'

'Well, that's just *great*.' Trapp glared at the young coffee drinkers around him with hatred and frustration. The Peculiar Crimes Unit had a history of inheriting easily frightened department heads operating beyond the limits of their expertise, a practice that had begun at its inception and which would continue long into its future. 'Of course, a local force won't care about any other ongoing investigations. In fact, they'd probably relish the chance to screw everything else up for us. They all hate this unit, you know. Those detectives of yours get the pick of the cases.'

'Well, they've got one now,' said Gladys.

'Then you'd better pray that they solve it fast,' warned Trapp. 'It's going to be the last case they ever get their hands on.'

'Bloody hate the lot of 'em,' said Major Julius Tilden, who clearly did not believe in holding back, even to complete strangers. He owned the second grandest house in Crowshott but preferred to potter about in its whitewashed stable cottage behind the Goat & Compasses. 'Once they had the run of the land around here. Now they've ended up without a pot to piss in, if you'll pardon my French.'

The major was leaning on his gate with an umbrella raised in one hand and pruning shears in the other. Undeterred by the weather, he had been torturing his roses to within an inch of their lives when the detectives came past and introduced themselves.

'I went to Eton with the old lord,' Tilden continued, happy to have someone to talk to. 'An appalling human being, although he took out his fair share of the Hun in his time, unlike the conchie son. The grounds were opened to the public for a while, you know, but some of his wife's jewellery went missing so he closed them again. It wasn't the first time things vanished from that house. We all assumed it was a member of the public, but then rumours started flying around about the son needing money. You know he went off on the hippy trail, seeking some kind of spiritual enlightenment?'

'So we heard,' said John May.

'He was paying a fortune to a friend of the Maharishi Mahesh Yogi, that ridiculous guru chap the Beatles all went to stay with. These mullahs and mystagogues were wandering about collecting followers as easily as holy men in nineteenth-century Russia.'

'I take it you don't believe in that sort of thing,' said May, picking up the major's cuttings for him.

'To the people of Kent, transcendental meditation is something you do on the loo.'

'And to you?'

'I can reach a higher plane of consciousness simply by nodding off in an armchair.' The major snapped his shears shut. 'I say, ramrod back, I bet you've a good seat. Do you want to come riding one morning? I've a middleweight bay hunter that should suit you.'

'I'm afraid I don't ride,' said May. 'Did the police become involved? About the robberies, I mean?'

The major reached over and snipped the top off a perfectly healthy nasturtium. 'Good heavens no. The house always dealt with its own problems. Getting the police involved would have been quite unthinkable.'

'What happened to the house during the war?' Bryant asked, studying the obsessively manicured garden with distaste. What was the point of living in the country if you didn't let it grow wild about you?

'They didn't want any more soldiers billeted there,' the major explained. 'One can hardly blame them, what with all the damage they did to so many fine houses – so they turned the state room into a dormitory for a reputable boarding school. But there was more trouble. Harry was only young but even back then he couldn't be trusted around girls.'

'How do you feel about the hall being sold?'

'It'll be disastrous for most of the older residents. They still have tied tenancies. Tempers get very heated at the village hall.'

They thanked the major and left him murdering some marigolds.

In an ironmonger's shop in the high street they spoke to a man the customers called Young Albert, although he had to be at least sixty. His clipped moustache matched his brown overalls, and his hands were calloused and deformed from decades of using ratchets and saws. He stood before a hundred tiny wooden drawers containing screws, bolts, nails and washers. The shop smelled of brown paper, oil, sawdust and metal filings.

'We never see them down in the village,' he confirmed. 'The boys take groceries up on their bikes. The vicar came in once or twice. Asked me if I wanted to buy some silver plate, wouldn't tell me where he got it. Needs a haircut, that fellow. And that crime-writer woman, Claxon, she came in yesterday.'

'What did she buy?' asked May.

'Nothing. She wanted to know about the sewage treatment plant up at the hall, how it all worked. I asked her if there was something wrong with it and she said no, it was research for a murder mystery she was working on. She asked me if it could grind up a body, if you please.'

'Did she indeed?' Bryant gave May another one of his over-emphatic looks.

'I told her that some probably could, but only if the corpse was fed in directly from above so that it couldn't clog the blades. I know about that sort of thing. I was in the Home Guard. We drew up plans for what to do in the event of an invasion. Anyway, she decided it was too far-fetched and settled for rat poison instead. Writers are a funny lot. I read one of her Inspector Trench novels once. This chap dissolved his nagging wife in an acid bath. It was very enjoyable.'

They found Edie Markham further along the high street. She was a heavily upholstered lady with a helmet of tight curls who sold eggs and butter while dispensing nuggets of advice. She was quick to add her tuppenceworth. 'It's a nice place to live. We have everything we need here. There's a community hall and a very good library with no smut. We even had an amateur dramatics society until they staged a Harold Pinter and put people off. There aren't so many little ones now, though, like there were during the war. Evacuees. They did some thieving around the shops, and then there was some bigger trouble. One of the girls was sent home.'

'Why?' asked May, 'what happened?'

'Nobody in the village really knew, but there were stories about Lord Banks-Marion – well, he wasn't the lord then. He's what we call a toucher. His father wanted him put away. We thought he'd be sent to Broadhampton.'

'If there was criminal activity why didn't the police get involved?'

'The Chief Inspector was an old friend of the family. He used to go up there after church for a glass of sherry, and things mysteriously sorted themselves out.' She girded herself and leaned in closer. 'There've been more recent scandals too. It's said Lord Banks-Marion makes dirty films up there. It's none of our business, of course. We always saw all the family at the summer ball and the Christmas fayre. They used to put on a lovely spread.'

'What will happen if the hall changes hands?'

'I imagine we'll all be kicked out of our cottages, unless the new owner has an accident and dies. We don't want anything to change. You're in London, where everything's different all the time. Topless dresses and Perspex coffee tables won't catch on down here.'

'How do you know I'm from London?' May asked.

Edie stifled a laugh. 'You're dressed how a townie thinks he should dress in the country. Begging your pardon, you think we're your poor cousins, but that's how we see you: rich in wealth and poor in health.'

'We're not even rich,' said Bryant indignantly as they walked back to Tavistock Hall, umbrellas locked against the squalling rain. 'I can't help being from the Smoke. My most distant relative only lived three streets away. Nobody around us was evacuated in the war.'

'Why not?'

'Our parents were more scared of woods and animals than bombs. A squirrel got into our house once and everyone had hysterics. The closest we ever got to the countryside was a Sunday afternoon walk on Hampstead Heath, and even then we always got home before dark, just in case we got lost. It's funny when you consider I was quite happy wandering around the Whitechapel boozers at midnight.'

The war games had started up again. From somewhere in the distance came the popping of rapid gunfire. Suddenly the hedge parted and several panicked sheep shot across the road. Bryant kept a wary distance.

'So what *did* you do as a nipper?' asked May.

'When I was ten I spent all my time in the British Museum, trying to translate the Rosetta Stone. I couldn't imagine life outside London, where people were surrounded by mud and had to get up at five o'clock to milk the owls.' Bryant gave an involuntary shudder. 'All this getting to know your neighbours malarkey isn't natural. I come from a city where it's a badge of honour to still not know who lives next door ten years after they've moved in. It's too dark and too quiet here. I'm quite glad of the odd explosion. It reminds me of London.'

'You don't think Vanessa Harrow killed the old man and then tried to commit suicide out of guilt, do you?'

'It's a theory.' Bryant dug out his Lorenzo Spitfire and made a valiant attempt to light it while May held his umbrella. 'He arranges to meet her in a place where they won't be overheard, for the purpose of breaking off the affair she says they never had. She attacks him in the heat of the moment, and is then filled with remorse and shame.'

'You sound as if you don't believe it,' said May.

'I don't.'

'Why not?'

'Appetite,' Bryant replied. 'She still attended luncheon and ate like a horse. You wouldn't, would you, not after doing something like that?'

'It does seem rather unlikely.'

'And then we have Miss Claxon, asking how to dispose of a body.' He paused to take a long, pleasurable puff on his pipe.

'If you were really going to kill someone would you get advice on it first?' asked May. 'Besides, what would her motive be?'

'Unrequited love,' replied Bryant glibly. 'She's knocking on and she probably doesn't get many suitors with legs that thick.'

'You've never been very good with women, have you?' May suggested.

'Don't get me wrong: I think she's perfectly charming. I'm trying to see her with a copper's eye.'

'And that's how the police decide guilt, is it? Her legs are a bit thick so she doesn't have suitors, therefore she's a murderess. Heaven help you.'

'I told you, people aren't my strong point,' Bryant replied, twirling his umbrella dangerously.

'Then it's time you worked on your social skills,' said May. 'You can take over the questioning when we get back. Just try not to antagonize everyone.'

'How else are we going to get results if we don't?' Bryant asked, not unreasonably.

'You know what I'm saying,' said May. 'I just don't want to see anyone else throw spaghetti over you.'

'Oh, that was ages ago. The bishop has probably forgotten all about it.' At the next bend in the lane they found that the road was now flooded. A wide, dark pool ran between the hedgerows. 'Cripey, how deep is that, do you think?'

They found a length of branch, climbed around the side and lowered it into the water. It came out wet to a depth of almost two feet. 'This section of the road is below the level of the surrounding fields,' said May. 'Let's hope the rain stops soon, or nobody's going to be able to reach us at all.'

The crows turned their heads to watch as the pair headed back to the hall.

31

DAZED AND CONFUSED

The detectives were heading along the first-floor corridor when they were once more grabbed by Monty, popping out of his room. The tourniquet of bandages now extended to his neck, leaving him with an alarmingly crimson head.

'How could you just go off and leave me like that?' he demanded to know. 'It's too late for Burke; I'm the one who needs protecting!'

Bryant pushed his way past Monty into his bedroom and began opening drawers. 'All right, where's the box?' he asked. 'You took it back, didn't you?'

'What box?' Monty had a lousy poker face.

'The grey metal one, flat, heavy, lock on the front.' He looked under the bed. 'You had it in your luggage. I decided to take care of it for you.'

'It was you who searched my room?' cried Monty, outraged. 'It has nothing to do with you. Your only job is to get me to the Law Courts on Monday.'

'Since the murder attempt on you and Mr Burke's death, everything is to do with us,' said Bryant. 'If you don't tell me

I'll search the room again. I think I'll start by cutting the linings out of all your clothes.'

'No, don't,' Monty pleaded. 'You made enough of a mess last time. You're supposed to be a detective. Don't you have a system rather than chucking everything on the floor?'

'Where is it, then?'

'Under my pillow,' sighed Monty.

Bryant pulled the pillows from the bed and dragged the box out. 'Do you have a key?'

'In the top drawer of the chest over there.'

He fitted it into the lock and thumped the battered lid until it popped open. Inside was a pocked grey lump of stone.

'No wonder it was so heavy. What is it?' asked May.

'Unless you've been given clearance to view all the evidence in the case against Chamberlain, it has nothing to do with either of you.' Monty folded his arms with finality.

'For God's sake, Monty, do you want us to help you or not?' cried May.

'Oh all right.' He leaned closer. 'If you must know, it's a piece of concrete.'

'I can see that. Why are you carrying it around?'

'To prevent tampering,' Monty explained. 'It's part of my evidence for Monday. It's a sample of the resinated material Sir Charles was using in his buildings. I didn't trust his lawyers to make a case for it, so I got one of my men to locate a sample from the Hackney housing project.'

'That's industrial espionage, Monty,' said May, 'and it's been through your mitts so it's potentially contaminated evidence. You won't be able to get it seen in court.'

'I can damn well try.'

Bryant closed the lid of the box and set it down on the chest of drawers. 'I don't understand you. Why is it so important to take Chamberlain down?'

'Why?' Monty seemed amazed by the question. 'After all I've told you about him?'

'You're still not telling us the full story. You came here to raise capital from Donald Burke.'

'That's right. He sent me a letter saying he was interested.'

'What was the deal?'

'My testimony will destroy Charlie's credibility in court. The scandal will wipe him out. I'm doing the right thing, but it's also an opportunity.'

The truth dawned on May. 'You're raising the money to take over Chamberlain's company.'

'Obviously I was going to keep my name out of the deal. But it's academic now, seeing as Burke is dead and I've lost my backer.'

'Monty, you are a piece of work,' said May angrily.

Monty shifted his shoulder and grimaced in pain. His face was redder than ever. 'Burke and I could have made a fortune together. I just needed a little extra capital to ease my cash flow, no more than thirty thousand. He would have got me back on my feet and given me a way out. It was a safe deal for him.'

'You obviously enjoy doing deals,' said May, 'so I'll do a deal with you. Appear in the witness box on Monday morning, give an honest testimony so that the law can decide Chamberlain's culpability, and we won't press charges.'

'For what?' Monty was indignant. 'I did nothing wrong!'

'You had an undeclared motive for prejudicing the case.'

Bryant poked him in the chest. 'We need each other, Monty. If we don't close the case, you don't get to testify.'

A ravine had opened in the rainclouds, revealing blue sky. The sun was setting behind the emerald palisade of cypress trees. As in the days of trench warfare, birdsong had returned in the brief absence of gunfire. It appeared to be the perfect Kentish evening, pink with mist and fresh with the scent of wet grass.

Bryant looked upon it with a jaundiced eye. There was mud everywhere, the cows stank and were all these trees really necessary? As a child he had been terrified of the bare, sickly elm in his street with a branch that scraped at his bedroom window like a witch's hand and sent him under the blankets. And now here he was, surrounded by them. Instead of homely, chirruping sparrows there were huge black birds, omens of misfortune that hopped towards the house as if preparing to invade it. He had read somewhere that the collective noun for ravens was an unkindness. If that's what they were, it suited them perfectly.

It was no good, he decided. He was a Londoner. He belonged indoors.

John May, as usual, seemed to fit in perfectly well. In the city he was brisk and decisive. Here he was chatty and apt to linger. Even his clothes appeared to have lost their starch. Where Bryant was brittle and uncomfortable, May was supple and relaxed. He fell naturally into male conversation and luxuriated in the company of women. These displays of social ease only made Arthur edgier. To counteract the effect he stepped back inside the reception room, Iris, and went to work.

Pamela Claxon stood beside a gigantic Qing dynasty vase, smoking with her right elbow in her left hand, lost in thought. She jumped when Bryant came up behind her, almost knocking the vase from its pedestal.

'I'm sorry, I didn't mean to startle you,' said Bryant, who had intended exactly that.

'Given the likelihood of one of us being a murderer and that we're not allowed to leave the house tonight, I'd appreciate it if you didn't creep about like a strangler.' She blew smoke in his face.

'That's one thing he hasn't done,' said Bryant.

'What?'

'Strangled anyone. Although he seems to be working his way through a repertoire of elimination attempts. But why Vanessa Harrow? What did she know that could place her at risk?'

'You do realize how absurd our situation is, I suppose?'

248

said Claxon. 'If I put this in one of my crime novels nobody would believe a word of it.'

'Stranger things happen,' Bryant countered. 'John Reginald Christie was a respectable community officer and a serial killer who managed to get an innocent neighbour hanged for his crimes. And at the Savoy Hotel an Egyptian prince called Ali Fahmy was shot to death by his wife, who got off and then faked a pregnancy to try and cheat his will. Real lives often play out like melodramas, especially in the East End, where I come from. Lords and ladies commit murders too. They just stand a better chance of getting away with it.'

'But nobody really knew Donald Burke, did they? He was just a visiting guest. So why would anyone kill him?'

'He was more than a guest, Miss Claxon. Everyone in this entire village needed something from him.'

'Then why don't you have any leads?'

Bryant pulled a notepad and pencil from his jacket. 'I made a list of all the people I've met here,' he said. 'Please.' He showed her to the armchair opposite. 'One person is dead and two have been attacked, so we can rule out those names.'

'Inspector Trench wouldn't,' said the novelist. Her large eyes were accentuated by accretions of black mascara. 'That fellow Monty could have faked an accident to shift suspicion from himself.'

'How? He was hit by a falling gryphon.'

'He might have tied a length of fine fishing wire around the gargoyle and pulled it, taking care to manoeuvre himself so that he only suffered minor injuries.'

'He fractured his collarbone, Miss Claxon. Apart from the sheer unlikelihood of such an act, we'd have found the fishing line, wouldn't we?'

'Not if he'd quickly detached it and hidden it in his clothing.'

'He's not a character from a John Dickson Carr novel,' said Bryant. 'In real life people don't go around staging elaborate murders. What would be the point? He came here to try and massage a deal out of Burke, not kill him via some ludicrous Heath Robinson contraption. They'd never even met.'

'That's a bigger stumbling block, I admit,' said Claxon. 'I'm used to reviewing problems in their more abstract form. But without premeditation it could be anyone. A drunken tramp hopping over the outside wall.'

Bryant decided that he was growing to like the novelist. 'Motive, Miss Claxon,' he reprimanded her.

She lit another cigarette from the end of the last one. 'All right, who else do you have on that list?'

Bryant checked his notes. 'Discounting the indoor staff, who lead entirely separate lives from the members of the household and their guests, I've met eleven potential suspects here.'

'You mean including me.'

'Of course. Of these eleven, two live in the grounds but not at the house, and have minimal contact with the residents. Those two are the groundsman, who never comes inside and is barely equipped to walk, let alone commit murder, and ditzy Melanie, Lord Banks-Marion's girlfriend, who lives in the ashram smoking dope with an assortment of comatose friends, none of whom is allowed inside Tavistock Hall.'

'What about class war?' Pamela suggested. 'We know how hippies feel about the gentry.'

'Then that would make Lady Banks-Marion and Harry the most obvious targets, wouldn't it?'

'Hippies require no motive, or at least not one that makes sense.' She took a drag and blasted smoke everywhere. 'Look at what just happened to Roman Polanski's poor wife. Flower power might have been well intentioned but it backed a large part of an entire generation into a cultural dead end. What if the same breakdown of order is happening here? Who knows what strange ideas go through the minds of those spaced-out twerps sitting in the mud? They could have started a cult and be planning to massacre all of us in our beds.'

'Would your Inspector Trench discount them?' Bryant asked.

'Probably, because he prefers a satisfying motive.'

'Then we shall as well.'

'That's not very scientific.'

'Let's play it your way for a moment. If it's a proper country house murder it needs to follow country house rules.' Rising to his theme, he counted off on his fingers. 'Of the other suspects, there's the vicar, whom we now know to be a drug addict. Diminished responsibility? Mania? A misguided attempt to obtain money?'

'What about Slade Wilson? He may seem very nice but he was quick to throw suspicion on poor Vanessa. He needs the commission for the house and was hired by Mrs Burke, so why would he jeopardize his position by killing her husband? What would he have to gain? Now, if Inspector Trench—'

'Can you not drag in imaginary policemen?' asked Bryant. 'It's hard enough sorting out the real characters without having to deal with literary conceits.'

'What about Lord Banks-Marion, or even his mother?' she suggested. 'What if they changed their minds about the sale and could think of no other way out?'

'Setting aside the fact that they're at war with one another, why would they attack Monty and Miss Harrow? It makes no sense. And can you honestly imagine someone like Lady Banks-Marion lowering a body into a grinder?'

'Frankly, yes,' replied Pamela. 'I've met more members of the aristocracy than you. They lack empathy except when it comes to guns and horses.'

'Which brings us to Mrs Burke,' sighed Bryant. 'Embittered over her husband's unfaithfulness, she decides to take matters into her own hands . . .'

'. . . and in doing so, destroys the source of finance that allows her to live a life of ease.' She wafted the thought aside along with her cigarette smoke. 'She admitted she knows nothing about her husband's business. OK, she might have a valid reason for attacking Miss Harrow, but that chap you arrived with, Monty? Why clobber him with a gargoyle?'

'Then that just leaves you,' said Bryant. 'But I can't think of a single reason why you would want to kill Burke unless it was for research, which seems a bit drastic. And you asked the local ironmonger about committing a murder, something I can't imagine you doing if you were really planning one.'

'You get around, don't you?' said Pamela, impressed.

'So what do you think?' He watched her intently as he closed his pad. 'We're out of suspects unless you count Toby Stafford, who has just lost his biggest client and therefore his motive, or the butler, who has never done it in any mystery I've ever read.'

'You obviously missed my novel *Trench's Last Case*,' Pamela pointed out, 'in which the butler Bellows stabs his master with a sharpened dessert spoon before lobbing it into the chandelier.'

'And they say that the detective story is the recreation of noble minds,' said Bryant.

'It can't be Claxon,' he decided as he walked in the night-garden with May. As the clouds closed in once more, the sky grew darker than the surrounding treeline. 'Not that I ever really thought it was her. Writers can take out their murderous frustrations on the page.'

'Could this have something to do with the permissive society?' May wondered. His cigarette and Bryant's pipe left contrails of smoke in the ominously still evening air. 'I mean, the moors murders raised the possibility of a link between moral permissiveness and violent crime, didn't they? Could we be looking at entirely motiveless murders?'

'If we weren't in this location I'd be inclined to agree,' said Bryant. 'But why here? Why this weekend? Could you honestly think of a worse time to go after someone, in a house full of incredibly nosy guests?'

'If it was about acting before Burke signed the papers on the hall, the killer had no choice. They had no way of knowing that Toby Stafford was controlling Harry and the sale.'

'Why do you say that?'

'Because if they did they would have known that the result would be the same whether Burke was dead or alive. It would have removed the purpose of killing him.' May raised his hand and felt the first fat drops of rain falling once more. There was a distant sound like an immense, slow rock fall. 'Monty, Burke and Vanessa. Come up with the next one in the sequence.'

'Fishing line,' said Bryant. 'Pamela suggested that Monty staged his own accident. She's enjoying all this.'

'If we turn up in her next book I'm suing her. Let's get inside. I think there's a storm coming.'

Bryant fell in beside him. 'Good idea. We've left our witness alone for too long. Fruity can only watch the place from the outside. We need to be in there with them.'

'Then why *don't* we take Monty back to London tonight?' asked May. 'The cars are all still here. We could get him out of harm's way and turn the others over to Canterbury CID. If they try to haul us back we'll put the CPS on to them.'

'That's a point. Where are all the vehicles?' Bryant swivelled around. 'Did Alberman put them away?'

They headed around to the front of the house and the empty forecourt. The sky had sealed itself again, and the rain was returning in earnest. In the lane beyond a solitary street lamp had come on, lighting the silvered pathway that meandered through the meadows. When they reached the garage beside the east wing they found its heavy wooden doors padlocked. Bryant peered through a crack in the planks. The cars were all lined up inside.

He hopped through the long grass to Metcalf's cottage. 'Fruity,' he called, knocking, 'where is the garage key?'

Metcalf appeared from the side of the gatehouse in his ratty woollen cap, immense wellingtons and a wartime greatcoat, the empty right sleeve neatly fastened by a large gold safety pin. For a man with only two limbs he managed to scuttle about with considerable speed. Reaching past Bryant, he spat out chewing tobacco. 'Hang on a minute, sir, I'll get it.'

Bryant followed him into the little kitchen and waited while he checked a drawer. 'That's odd. It's gone. I always keep it in here.'

'Do you have a spare?'

'No, sir. I locked the garage doors last night because of the soldiers in the area. The hall has had trouble with them before. And the car keys have gone as well. I put them all in a tobacco tin, right here.'

'Do you always leave the front door of the gatehouse open?'

'It only has a latch. There's no reason to put a lock on it, sir. No one comes down here.'

'Where were you just now?'

'Clearing the leaves on the drive. The work has to go on, sir. There are always chores to do in a house this size. I wanted to get finished before the storm.'

'Could somebody have come into the gatehouse while you were out?' asked May.

'They'd have to know what they were looking for.' He turned to Bryant. 'What's going on? You're a copper, you must have some idea.'

'I'm more of an academic,' Bryant admitted. 'John and I belong to a specialist unit. In London we have resources to call upon. Is there any way we can get into the garage?'

'I've got a crowbar somewhere, but his lordship won't be very happy if I damage the door.'

'We'll vouch for you,' said May. 'Where is it?'

They went to look. May took the tool from the woodshed and slipped it beneath the wooden bolt that ran across the garage door. Under his full weight the wood splintered and the padlock came loose. He swung open the doors.

'What's the matter?' Bryant asked, trying to see over his partner's shoulder.

They stepped inside and walked about, examining the vehicles, peering into the interiors and dropping to the floor to see beneath them. May walked to the rear of the garage, tried one of the car boots and found it unlocked.

'Six cars, and every single tyre has been slashed, even the spares,' he said. 'It would have taken time and determination to do this. We need to get everyone out of the house right now.'

'Think, John,' said Bryant. 'That's what whoever did this wants us to do. We've revealed our true identities. The longer we stay here, the more chance we have of catching them.' He turned to the groundskeeper. 'Fruity, can you make the house safer?'

Fruity scratched so hard at his woollen cap that Bryant was afraid lice were leaping for safety. 'I could chain the main gates shut, and perhaps someone could keep all the doors and windows bolted, but that's not up to me. If you want you can put Monty in my gatehouse. I could make up a bed for him.'

'No, if anything happens to him it's my responsibility,' said Bryant. 'I'll contain the problem in the main house but we can't turn it into a prison. We need access. John, I'll be back in a few minutes.'

'Where are you going?' asked May.

'To the ashram,' Bryant replied. 'To see if they really are a cult.'

32

HIPPY HIPPY SHAKE

War Is Not Healthy For Children and Other Living Things
Make Love Not War
Keep on Truckin'
Woodstock – 3 Days of Peace & Music
Power to the People

The damp dayglo posters were peeling from the walls of the Mongolian yurt. 'It was amazing, man, I went – I was there just a month ago and I still can't believe it. Tomorrow night we're going to land on the moon.'

'They landed on the moon in July,' Bryant pointed out.

'Oh, cool. Then maybe next year it'll be, like, Neptune. We're going to spread love and joy to other planets.'

The pale, lank-haired young man in the Indian headband touched his Woodstock poster with immense tenderness. He said his name was Donovan, and ill advisedly employed American slang with an Oxbridge accent. 'You had to be there, man. The bands, the people – so many people. The whole thing was a gas. I dug it all, the mud, the rain, the music, the hassles. What a summer! What a time to be alive! The greatest rock festival of all time, and men walking on the friggin' *moon*!'

'And Charles Manson,' said Bryant. Donovan was sitting cross-legged on the earth floor, something Bryant was not about to do in his string-tied Noël Coward trousers, so he stood awkwardly in the mire.

'Come on, man, do you see a poster saying "Death to Pigs" here? We're for peace, not violence. Did you see *Easy Rider*? It's the establishment that wants us dead, not the other way around.'

Further back in the tent somebody overheard Donovan and began picking out 'The Ballad Of Easy Rider' by the Byrds.

'How did you get to Woodstock, Mr Donovan?' Bryant asked. 'That's in America somewhere, isn't it?'

'My folks paid. They're breadheads, they can afford it. Here.' He handed his joint to Bryant.

'I'm on duty, and I'd be breaking the law, just as you are.'

'Laws don't mean anything. What's illegal one year is legal the next. You have to look at the bigger picture, man.' He cupped his hand and blew into it, opening his fingers. 'Poof, there go your laws, all blown away.'

'Did you go with Lord Banks-Marion to India too?'

'Of course. I'd follow him anywhere.'

'You know that's what members of cults say, don't you? They swear blind allegiance to their leader.'

'No, no.' Donovan shook his blond locks vigorously. 'You don't understand – it isn't like that. We're a collective.'

'But he's the one who lets you stay here.'

'No, the planet belongs to all of us. Mother Earth gives all her children permission. Although Harry gives us pocket money.'

'Did Lord Banks-Marion really marry an Indian girl?'

'Well, they held a symbolic ceremony with all these orange flowers. We told him it wasn't legal,' Donovan admitted. 'Some of the locals threatened to, like, kill him. My father's in the Foreign Office. He pulled some strings and got Harry out. Please, come and sit.'

Bryant looked about for somewhere dry and clean to perch. Finally he opted for a stack of dog-eared back issues of the *International Times*. He sat with a wince of pain. In all this damp his hip had started to throb.

Donovan noticed how awkwardly Bryant was balancing himself. 'What's the matter?' he asked.

'I think I'm getting arthritis,' Bryant replied, rubbing his leg.

'Bummer. You're too young.'

'My doctor said it can hit at any age. There's nothing I can take for it.'

'That's not true, man.' Donovan withdrew a hand-rolled tube from an Old Holborn tobacco tin and lit it, passing it across. 'Try this.'

'What is it?' Bryant suspiciously sniffed the air.

'Sinsemilla. Seedless Mary Jane. It's medicinal. A cure for the symptoms of arthritis, except the Man doesn't want you to know.'

'Medicinal?' Bryant squinted doubtfully at the reefer.

'Sure, man. Ask any doctor. It's been used to ease arthritis since, like 2800 BC.'

'Really?' Bryant took a tentative puff and coughed.

'You have to hold it down,' Donovan warned. 'My father looked into the Indian girl's case. Harry thought he could help her by getting her out of the country. He was trying to do a good thing, but the marriage was disallowed 'cause it wasn't registered. They were trying to make it all about paperwork, not love. So he had to leave her behind. And I know what you're thinking. It wasn't about sex, man. Harry just gets a bad rap because he's a freedom lover.'

'What about the girls here?' asked Bryant, his voice rising an octave as he exhaled. 'My partner met a lady called Melanie. What about her? Is she free to leave?'

'Of course, what do you think this is, a prison? She doesn't want to leave. She doesn't have anywhere to go. Her folks kicked her out. Her old man beat her up. She came here because she's in love with Harry. She's following her heart. The world doesn't understand . . .'

'The world has laws to protect girls from being exploited by unscrupulous older men. Who's in charge of this camp?'

Donovan shook out his hair. 'It's not a camp, man, and no one is in charge. We don't believe in hierarchies. Harry's made some mistakes but the stories about him aren't true.'

Bryant took another puff, managing not to cough. 'Let me put it another way. Do you know who comes and goes here?'

'New members have to be voted in by everyone.' Donovan pointed back to various bodies buried in sleeping bags. 'There are seven of us plus the kid and that number hasn't changed in months.'

'Then it should be easy to get names and addresses from you all.'

'We're here to be free, not to be hassled by conventions.'

'But Harry gives you money. Do you grow your own food? Where do you get your clothes? What about medicine? Education? Or do you just rely on your benefactor to keep supplying everything?'

'I knew you wouldn't understand,' said Donovan.

'I'm really trying to,' said Bryant with conviction. He took another drag on the joint, not realizing that he was supposed to return it. 'I can't name a single utopian society that has ever worked. I want to comprehend how your vision of the future operates without a patron at the top of it.'

'That's because you work for the Man,' Donovan insisted.

'But you could still drop out if you really wanted to. Don't be a part of the system unless you can change it. Look around you. The moon and stars don't belong to anyone; the trees are free.'

'Actually the trees belong to Lord Banks-Marion and I imagine the Americans have claimed the moon as their own,' said the detective, 'but I take your point. Part of me rather likes the idea of dropping out.' He sat back and studied the rainbow-striped roof of the yurt. 'I couldn't, though.'

Donovan sucked at the end of the joint and pinched it out. 'Why not?'

'It goes against everything I was taught. Work hard, keep your head down, do what you're told. Your father was in the Foreign Office. Mine was a street photographer who ran bets on the side. He ended his days sitting by the window drinking, barely able to move from his chair. He hated me being a copper.'

'Then you don't owe your old man anything.'

'Don't I? Shouldn't I ask myself why he was like he was?' Bryant struggled upright. 'It's been interesting talking to you, Donovan. I must go now. I feel quite squiffy.'

As he staggered back into the house, the enormity of what he had done began to prey upon his mind. 'John,' he called, pulling his partner into the great hall, 'I've been bad. I'm a bad person.'

'What's the matter?' asked May. 'Have you been smoking dope?'

Bryant leaned against a bust of the Duke of Marlborough. 'I lied. We could get out of here. We could find a way through the road at night, after manoeuvres have finished. We could get the Canterbury constabulary to take over, but I don't want them to. If they do, we're finished. We'll never get another chance.'

'You don't think we can solve the case.'

'I don't know.' He swayed against the statue. 'I thought it would be more – what do you call one of those cases that opens and shuts?'

'An open-and-shut case.'

'That's it. I thought it would be one of those. But it's more complicated.'

'You can't back down now, Arthur,' warned May. 'I'm in this with you.'

'Then you'll hold the line with me?'

'I already said I would.'

'Oh, stout chap, not that I ever doubted you. "Our doubts are traitors and make us lose the good we oft might win by fearing to attempt." Have you eaten? I could eat a horse, or at least the parts of the horse that, er, can be eaten.'

'Are you sure you're all right?'

Bryant brushed himself down and stood erect. 'Ask me again on Monday morning.' He slapped May on the back and tacked towards the dining room, Lavender.

The housebound guests had finished eating and had gathered in the library once more, but now the mood was sombre and awkward. Nobody wanted to be there. Pamela and Norma slapped playing cards on the table between them. Vanessa sleepily tried to concentrate on a book. Wilson paced about nervously, worrying at a fingernail. Lady Banks-Marion had her eyes closed and looked pained, as if she was having a bad dream.

Harry took it upon himself to apologize to the gathering. 'I'm frightfully sorry about the way the weekend has turned out,' he announced, as if it was merely a matter of bad weather having halted the shooting. 'I believe we're waiting for Canterbury Constabulary to get here. Meanwhile, the police want us to stay put.'

Before anyone could respond, Monty appeared in the doorway in his dressing gown. 'I don't know about anyone else but I need a bloody huge drink.' He headed smoothly to the bar, as if guided by rails. 'I was just talking to the groundsman. What's this about the cars being vandalized?'

'It's true, I'm afraid,' said May, secretly cursing Fruity. 'Someone's slashed all the tyres.'

'What's going on?' asked Wilson. 'Are we under attack?'

'It seems that way, Mr Wilson. We appear to be living in a scenario from one of Miss Claxon's novels.'

'If that were true we'd have guessed the identity of the killer long before now,' said Wilson tartly.

'I've been going through my husband's belongings, looking for anything that might help us,' Norma Burke announced. 'I knew Donald would be spending time with his lawyer, so I planned to work on a scrapbook of his achievements while I was here, just for something to do.' As if realizing that the admission sounded pathetic, she hurried on. 'I don't know if it will help but I have a folder of photographs and press articles you can look at.'

Bryant tottered into the room. He had mustard smeared down his shirt front, but seemed in better shape for having consumed a few calories. 'May I see?' he asked, seizing upon the folder with interest.

He laid it out on a side table and went through the contents. Donald Burke appeared outgoing and intense in early snapshots. In one press photograph he was shaking hands with the Lord Mayor of London as Norma beamed by his side. In another he stood raising a glass at a banquet, next to a portly elder statesman who, Bryant realized with a shock, was Winston Churchill. In the final pages of the unfinished scrapbook were blurred stills of Burke several years later, overweight and fending off the press, his head down, refusing eye contact. It seemed that as his businesses became ever more successful his own dissatisfaction increased.

'Couldn't we walk to the village now that the army exercises have finished for the night?' asked Pamela Claxon.

'Assuming we can get across the flooded roads, what good would it do?' Bryant responded hastily. 'It's too late to reach anybody. Our unit doesn't have a switchboard and tomorrow's Sunday, so nothing's open.'

'Then we'll just have to make the best of things,' said Lady Banks-Marion, placing a small silk cushion behind her back. 'Perhaps a rubber of bridge?'

The lights went out. The dark was oppressive and total. Vanessa gave a yelp of surprise.

May rose to his feet. 'Arthur, stay here with Monty. Where is your fuse box?'

'It's behind the kitchen, in the basement,' said Harry. 'I'll do it, I know this house in the dark.'

He and May made their way along the corridor leading to the rear of the hall. Here, all ornamentation ended as they crossed into an old flagstone passage. Water could be heard dripping around and above them. In darkness the house settled into its surroundings, reasserting itself, as if seeking to remind the guests who was really in charge.

'Hang on.' Harry reached into a cupboard and found a metal torch. 'It often happens when we get heavy rain. The wiring needs replacing.'

On the wall of an alcove where the boots and umbrellas were stored hung a grey steel cabinet. Harry opened it and checked inside, examining the orderly ceramic blocks with lengths of copper wire running through them. None of them looked burned or blackened. 'That's odd. It's not the fuses.'

'Is there a generator?'

'No,' said Harry. 'It never worked properly so I took it out. We switched to the mains supply when they ran new cables over from Crowshott. I couldn't see that we'd need the old generator any more, what with the upkeep . . .'

'Then there must be a break in the cable,' said May. 'How does the line get to the house?'

'It runs under the fence at the end of the property and comes into the ground floor behind Snowdrop.'

'I'm sorry – you have to remind me.'

'The billiard room. Do you think someone could have found a way in and cut it? How would we know?'

'We'll be able to see part of the line that runs from the house to the street junction box.'

They headed back to the library just as Alberman arrived with lamps and bundles of candles. 'Alberman, can you make sure every corridor and room has a light of some kind?' asked May. 'And perhaps you would confine the staff to their rooms for now, just so we can keep track of everyone.'

Alberman hesitated, not used to taking orders from outsiders. 'You had better do as he says,' Lady Banks-Marion decided as she accepted a lamp. The candles were set about the room, lending it a sepulchral air.

'I think someone should walk to the village and see if the power's out everywhere or if there are any phones working,' said Pamela. 'It's half past nine. There may still be someone about.'

'Good idea,' Bryant agreed. 'I'll go.' He turned to May. 'John, can you stay here and look after everyone?'

'We don't need "looking after", Mr Whatever-your-name-is,' said Lady Banks-Marion. 'We simply need to know when the professionals are arriving to tell us what exactly is going on.'

'I'm sorry you don't consider us professional,' said Bryant, buttoning up his raincoat and accepting a torch from Harry. 'I hope that in the next few hours we may earn your trust. If we fail now, the consequences are unthinkable.'

'What do you mean?'

'There's more at stake than you realize or care about, your ladyship. The investigation will end in Kent, but its consequences will be felt in Hackney.'

Leaving the huddled guests in considerable puzzlement, Bryant turned up his collar and headed out into the drizzle.

33

PRETTY WOMAN

As the only street light in the lane had gone out, Bryant was forced to light a torch. Even in the rain he heard nightjars and song thrushes sheltering in the hedgerows, but no sound of any vehicle reached his ears. He had started to detest the countryside by day, but walking through it at night proved truly unsettling. The wind buffeted his back. He could see the tops of the trees moving against the clouds. Something in the next field emitted a terrified shriek, bringing him to a halt. There was a frenzied scuffling in the long grass right beside him that made him leap back.

He thought of a film he had seen a few years earlier, *Night of the Demon*, and imagined a great dark creature clawing its way through the woods towards him.

'I will never smoke that stuff again,' he promised aloud. He dug an Aztec bar from his pocket and devoured it as the rain tipped down his neck.

The street lamps in Crowshott village glowed brightly, but there was no one about. The shops were shuttered and the only house light was the one illuminating the swinging sign above the Goat & Compasses. Bryant paused beneath it, bashed the rain from his hat and entered.

He half expected everyone to stop talking. A pair of old farmers were hunched over the great fireplace, where several partridges now hung inside the chimney breast. Two younger men in waistcoats and gumboots were playing darts. A glamorously painted woman sat at the bar nursing a large gin. The barman was, as always, slowly cleaning a glass. A clock ticked as if marking off the end of life.

'I need to make a call.' He dug into his jacket for his PCU card and showed it to the barman.

'This is an entry ticket for Walthamstow Greyhound Stadium,' said the barman, handing it back to him.

'Oh. Sorry. Here.' He found his PCU identification and held it high, uncomfortably aware that it did not look as official as a CID badge.

The barman carried on wiping his glass. 'There's a pay phone down the road.'

'What's that, then?' Bryant pointed at the heavy black Bakelite phone lurking in the shadows of the bar counter.

'We had it disconnected. The line is crossed with old Mrs Trubshaw up the road. Try placing a bet and all you hear is her, on about her bowels. Best to stick to the phone box. It's always the same when the army's playing silly buggers. Operation Britannia, my arse. A right bunch of layabouts. Half of them are hiding in the bushes smoking that there dope. The brave ones all died in the war.'

Bryant had had quite enough of the devious ways of country folk. 'Oh for God's sake,' he snapped. 'Let me at that damned phone or I'll have you closed down for breaking the licensing laws and running a bar that smells of disinfectant block and cow manure.'

The barman grudgingly unlocked the counter flap and raised it in silence. Bryant rang Gladys Forthright at Bow Street.

'Arthur, I've been trying to reach you for hours,' she began. 'The line to the hall is down. Is everything all right?'

He turned away from the barman. 'The power's gone out

and all the cars have been sabotaged. Someone in the house means to stop Monty from testifying.'

'The forensics team won't get to you until tomorrow morning. There's a lot of localized flooding and more rain on the way. Do you want me to check with the Kent Electricity Board?'

'I'm certain someone's cut the cables. None of the other houses in the area are affected. There have been attacks on other guests. No one's panicked yet but it's only a matter of time.'

'Couldn't you bring Hatton-Jones back to town?'

'Even if we could get the tyres patched, someone has taken all the car keys.' He waited, listening. Gladys knew him too well. He could almost hear her thinking it through.

'If you bring him back, you won't be able to solve the case yourself.'

The barman was watching him with interest. He moved as far away from the counter as the cord would allow. 'It's more than that, Gladys. I can't trust the local squad. If it's left to them, Donald Burke's killer may never be found.'

'Arthur, you're not following procedure. You don't have enough seniority to get away with it. You could wreck the case against Chamberlain.'

'You think I don't know that?' said Bryant, upset. 'Our only chance is to end this before the Canterbury team moves in. If we can do that—'

'But how? This isn't what you're good at. God, I've worked with you long enough to know that you need your books, your history, your – I don't know how you do it, but it isn't by conducting interviews. It's why you never went into the Met, isn't it? You couldn't do what they do.'

That was the trouble with Gladys, he decided, she was far too smart to be stuck at the pay level of sergeant. 'Did you get anything else on Burke?'

'Just background. He was born in 1905 and married his wife in St John's Wood in 1936, when she was just seventeen.'

'So she's what, fifty now? And he was sixty-four.'

'Some years ago he collapsed from overwork and was ordered to rest. I couldn't find anything about it in the press, so you'll have to ask his wife. A journalist I spoke to said that when he recovered he was less friendly, distant, not one of the lads any more, only interested in making money. Still, he was certainly good at that. He made a killing on the stock market. His investors said it was as if he could read the future.'

'They call it an intimation of mortality, Gladys. It sharpens the mind no end. When did the press start putting around rumours that he was seeing Vanessa Harrow?'

'Six months ago, but there's no evidence that they were ever together, just gossip. He paid for her flat but they were never seen in public, no matter what the press tried to insinuate.'

'Was this out of respect for the wife, do you think?' Bryant wondered. 'Why didn't he get a divorce?'

'Perhaps she wouldn't grant him one. Where does Hatton-Jones fit in?'

'He indirectly introduced Vanessa to Burke. She needed a job and he gave her the number of Burke's lawyer, Toby Stafford.'

'Why did he do that?'

'The Mayfair nightclub is in Stafford's name. She got the job and Monty lost the girl, if indeed he ever really had her. So there could have been bad blood between Monty and Donald, except that Monty needed him. None of it provides an explanation for Burke's death.'

'What about physical evidence?' asked Gladys. 'There must be something.'

'Some inconclusive boot prints and a piece of sawn-through wood. It's unlikely we'll get dabs from the barn. All we have is a bag of chemically degraded flesh and some unreliable witness statements. We're not in control of the situation.'

'It sounds like all you can do is keep Monty safe until help arrives.'

'Yes and no. I've an inkling – something somebody said to me. A strange parallel . . .' His attention began to drift.

'Sorry, Mr Bryant, I'm not with you.'

'Gladys, I have to go.'

Bryant rang off and bought himself a pint of murky Kentish ale. 'How far is Knotsworth from here?' he asked the blonde woman sitting alone at the bar. She was a few years older than him and wore a long black woollen coat, but he could see that the lining was crimson silk, rather racy for the sticks. She was voluptuous in the best sense, rounded and full. Years later Bryant found it impossible to recall her without describing good red wines. As she crossed her legs he realized she was wearing high heels.

She turned her glass in her hand. 'About four miles. Too far to walk at this time of night. There are hardly any street lights. Why, are you staying at the Red Lion?'

'I need to visit someone there.'

'Leaving it rather late, aren't you? You're in the wilds of Kent, darling. We keep farmers' hours around here.'

'But you don't.'

'I don't have to get up and let the pigs out at dawn, thank God.' She turned to him with a bangled hand outstretched. 'I'm Celeste. I'm going that way. There's a back route over higher ground. I can give you a lift.'

'You've been drinking.'

'Darling, the most that can happen around here is that I'll run over a rabbit.'

'Then I accept your offer,' said Bryant.

Celeste picked up her keys from the bar counter and led the way to her car, ignoring the sarcastic remarks from the two young men playing darts.

'You're not from around here, are you?' she said, casting a glance at him.

'Bethnal Green originally.'

'I'm guessing that's somewhere in London.' Her Mini

269

Cooper sat beneath a solitary street lamp. As she unlocked the door he saw that it was bright yellow and had gaudy daisies and sunflowers painted on the roof. 'What's a nice boy like you doing in a dreary place like this?'

'I'm staying at Tavistock Hall.' Bryant gratefully climbed inside.

'Lucky you. One of his lordship's weekend parties? Up at the crack of ten to feast on devilled kidneys before heading off to slaughter something avian?'

'His lordship is a vegetarian.'

'I hear they're all mad up there. It's quite the talk of the village.' She untangled her coat and threw it on to the back seat. She was wearing a low-cut blue cocktail dress.

'I didn't mean to spoil your evening.'

'What do you mean?'

He indicated the dress and shoes.

'Oh, I wasn't going anywhere else. A woman has to feel attractive occasionally. Otherwise I'll follow this lot into wellingtons and knitted hats. All the women around here walk like farmers. But of course they gossip like fishwives.'

'And do you believe the gossip?'

'Darling, it's mostly ancient history.' She crunched the gears and they lurched away. Bryant reached over and turned on the headlights for her.

'What do they say about Tavistock Hall?'

'That the old lord was put in an asylum and the son is a drug addict who believes in free love. He talked his mother into selling the house to some reclusive millionaire.'

Not entirely inaccurate, he decided. 'Anything else I should know?'

'The Crowshott locals are convinced they're going to lose their tenancies. They were going to go up to the hall last week and confront his lordship, but they bottled out. They're old Tories, easily outraged. They love disparaging members of what my father used to call the Upper Ten Thousand, but you should see how quickly they turn back into peasants and doff their caps when the horses go by. During the war the National Union of Fascists had an office in Crowshott – no surprise there.'

'You're a mine of information, Celeste.'

'Have you met Edie Markham? She owns the village dairy. She adores Harry and Beatrice, although I can't imagine they've ever spoken to her. The furthest Edie has ever travelled is to Canterbury on a day out. She thinks London is a spiritual sewer. She saw a shocking play on telly and promptly offered her services to Mary Whitehouse. No wonder her husband is drunk all the time. She thinks I'm a harlot because I go to the pub by myself, but why shouldn't I? My husband is no longer with us.'

'I'm sorry, did he die?'

'He moved to Cardiff, which amounts to the same thing. I'm a forty-year-old divorcée, so I'm not quite past it. How old are you?'

'How old do you think?'

'Forty?'

Bryant shot her a horrified look. 'Certainly not, madam.'

'I guess London ages you.' The car bounced over a rabbit. 'Got one,' she laughed. 'Light me a fag, would you? They're in the glove compartment. Speaking of local history, do you know about the legend of the Crowshott Beast?'

'I heard it was a monstrous creature that guards the hall.'

'Well, there are a lot of different stories. The most common one is that it's a Grym.' The Mini's headlights illuminated the canopy of trees, so that they appeared to be racing through a green tunnel. 'It's a sort of cross between a huge wolf and a wild pig. In the Welsh Marches it's known as the Jack o' Kent, but there's many who think it originated here. The story goes that once it was an ordinary man who was tricked into helping the Devil build a bridge somewhere near Crowshott. After the stonework was finished, Satan said he would take the first living soul that crossed the bridge. Jack threw a bone across the bridge and his dog chased after the bone, forcing Satan to take the dog instead. He had been cheated, so in revenge he turned Jack into a creature that roams the fields at midnight. It roars twice as a warning, but if you hear it a third time you know it's right behind you, about to attack.'

'You do realize you're talking to someone who has never even seen a hedgehog?' Bryant peered out into the darkness. 'I can't sleep here. It's too dark and it sounds weird at night.'

'What do you mean, weird?'

'I keep hearing things in bushes.'

'You really are a city boy.' She laughed. 'Someone should have warned you. Kent is full of gruesome shades. Dead Man's Island lies opposite the Isle of Sheppey. It was used as a burial ground for convicts who died in floating prison hulks. You can still see coffins and bones sticking out of the mud. It's no wonder people believe in hauntings around here.'

'Look, I'm jumpy enough as it is,' said Bryant. 'We have a murderer in the house.' The moment the words were out he realized he had said too much. It was to be a defining feature of Bryant's entire working life, his inability to keep his mouth shut. 'You can't tell anyone,' he added, making matters worse.

'What do you mean, a murderer? My God, you *are* a police-man, aren't you?' Celeste's eyes were already large but widened further. 'I knew it as soon as I saw the size of your feet.'

'A detective, actually. I'm going to Knotsworth to conduct an interview.'

'A murder investigation, eh? It won't be the first one at the hall.'

'Yes, I heard about the servant girl.'

'No, they say old Lady Banks-Marion killed her husband, didn't you know? Slowly poisoned him with weedkiller until he went mad. No case was ever brought against her. I pay no mind to it myself. So who's been murdered? Not Lord Banks-Marion?'

Common sense finally kicked in. 'I'm not able to say anything else,' Bryant replied.

'I thought not. I suppose you know there are secret passages all over the house, dating back to the time of the Reformation?'

'That's not possible,' said Bryant. 'It was built more recently than that. Secret passages, a phantom beast – I feel like I'm in a Sherlock Holmes story.'

'That's because living in Kent is very much like being in the late nineteenth century. And of course it was full of writers producing dark tales. Woolf at Sissinghurst and Charleston, Dickens in Broadstairs, Chaucer and Marlowe and Conrad and Peake. It's changing now, though. Even the hop pickers don't come here like they used to. Soon the Garden of England will have vanished for ever, buried under little brick boxes.' She slid the car into the forecourt of the Red Lion, spraying gravel, then pulled up the handbrake and turned to him. 'Here you are. How are you going to get back?'

'I don't know.'

Celeste removed the keys and handed them over. 'Why don't you borrow the car? You can return it tomorrow. I only live around the corner. Everybody knows me. I don't mind helping the police with their inquiries. Do you have any idea how boring it gets here?' She gave him a mischievous smile. 'Besides, it'll give me an excuse to say hello to you again.'

Was that what I think it was? Bryant thought, entering the pub with a silly smile on his face. *Wonders will never cease.*

The luxuriantly moustached landlord of the Red Lion wasn't used to out-of-towners turning up after 10 p.m., especially ones wearing belts made of string, and looked at him as if he was a burglar.

'Could you get Mr Stafford on the dog and bone for me?' Bryant asked. 'The phone,' he added, remembering where he was.

'I'm not allowed to give out information about our guests,' the landlord replied.

'I'm sure it wouldn't breach the Official Secrets Act if you looked in your guest book and simply let me know if he's staying here.'

The landlord peered down his long nose and perused the pages. 'We *do* appear to have a guest under the name of Mr Stafford.'

'Thank you.' Bryant headed for the staircase.

'Wait, you can't go up there!' shouted the landlord, but Bryant had already taken the stairs.

34

I CAN'T EXPLAIN

'It's no use, I need some fresh air,' said Pamela Claxon, rising. When she opened one of the doors to the patio the candles in the library blew out, and Lupin was once more plunged into darkness.

'Alberman, can you keep those lit?' asked May. 'Can everyone answer to their name please? Lady Banks-Marion?'

'Yes.'

'Lord Banks-Marion?'

'Here, unfortunately.'

Trevor Patethric?'

No reply.

'Reverend?'

'I haven't seen him for a while,' said Lady Banks-Marion.

'Where could he have gone?'

'Home, I imagine,' she suggested. 'He's got his bicycle, and said something about needing to prepare for tomorrow's sermon.'

May decided to deal with the problem in due course.

'Miss Harrow.'

'That's me.'

'Mrs Burke?'

'Here.'

He could see Pamela Claxon outside, smoking. 'Slade Wilson?'

'Present.'

'Monty?'

There was no answer.

'He said his shoulder was hurting a few minutes ago,' said Norma Burke wearily. 'He wanted to get some tablets.'

'Lady Banks-Marion, may I bring the groundsman in to keep an eye on everyone while I check on Monty?' May asked.

'We do not allow the ground staff in the house,' the matriarch firmly reminded him.

'But surely under the circumstances?'

She sighed deeply. 'Very well, just this once.'

May went to the window and called Fruity Metcalf in from his post in the garden. 'Can you keep watch here for a few minutes?' he asked.

Metcalf looked down at the herringbone patio and hesitated. Anyone would have thought that he'd been asked to cross the River Styx.

'Just stay on watch until I get back, can you?'

'I'd be happier in the hall,' Metcalf called. 'I have muddy boots.' He might be a civilian now, but the military manner was clearly never far from the surface.

'Very well. Stay outside the front door. But don't leave. Did you see the vicar?'

'Yes, he was heading home on his bike. Tomorrow's Sunday. He'll be needing to—'

'Write his sermon, yes, I know.'

Back in Lupin, there was a new commotion.

'It's Pamela,' said Wilson. 'She's fainted.'

May found the others standing around her at the edge of the French windows. 'I'm fine,' Claxon said, accepting an arm and hauling herself up. 'I just felt a bit dizzy for a minute. Smoking too many of these damned things.' To the consternation of Lady Banks-Marion she flicked her cigarette out on to the grass.

They waited in the flickering darkness. May stepped on to the lawn and looked up at Monty's window. There were no lights on. Where else could Monty get tablets?

'Just – try to look after each other,' said May, feeling any semblance of control fast slipping away from him. 'I'll be back in a few minutes.' He went into the hall with his pocket torch. A flight of stone steps took him to the basement, which held the kitchen, the wine cellar, the china room, the butler's pantry, the silver safe and the still room, where drinks and jams were made.

He shone the torch around but found nothing. The ground-floor rooms were all empty so he headed up the great staircase to the first-floor bedrooms. When he reached Monty's room and pushed down the handle, the door would not open.

'Monty?' he called. 'Are you in there?' Pressing his ear to the wood, he could hear nothing inside.

May shone his torch along the carpet runner and then up the walls of the corridor. He sensed the figure rather than seeing it. There was a displacement of air and a darker form was caught in the edge of his beam. It started in surprise and immediately broke into a run.

'Hey!' May shouted, pounding along the corridor. The figure's movement was suggestive of a woman. It turned left at the end of the landing, running past bedrooms on the easterly side of the house.

May was fast and quickly closed the gap. He had familiarized himself with the layout of the house when he arrived, and knew that the next left turn ended in a solid wall with nowhere else to go.

Making a leap for the fleeing figure he slammed into a narrow side table, dashing a crystal bowl filled with red roses to the floor. The momentary delay was enough to allow for an escape. As May swung around the corner, he was startled to find the end corridor empty. There were no doors on either side, and only a tall panel of wood stood before him. At its centre was a painting of an incredibly plain woman on a horse.

He could see wet footprints leading from the water spilled by the smashed bowl, but they ended in mid-stride. Whoever he had been chasing had vanished. He returned to Monty's room and shouldered open the door.

He found Monty Hatton-Jones lying like an axed tree on the Egyptian rug beside his bed.

Toby Stafford was seated in an oval pool of light at the table, still working when Bryant knocked. 'I'm sorry to disturb you,' he said. 'May I come in?'

'Ah, Mr Askey. No, what was it – Bryant?' Stafford removed his spectacles and dropped them on to an immensely detailed floor plan of Tavistock Hall that covered the table-top. He was still in his pinstriped suit and tie, ever the lawyer. 'I wasn't expecting anyone at this time of night.'

'You're studying the house?' asked Bryant.

'I have to finish the job,' said Stafford wearily. 'Even with Mr Burke gone. There's an outstanding issue with the surveyor's report.'

'I wonder if I could ask you a few questions?'

'I suppose so. I must say I didn't buy the "Askey" thing. New at this game, are you? Please, make yourself comfortable.' He rubbed the bridge of his nose. 'It must be important for you to venture down here.'

'In the absence of being able to talk to Mr Burke, I thought you could shed some light for me. Are you still in his employ – I mean, technically?'

'Is this a formal interview?'

'No, just a chat.'

'Very well.' Stafford settled back in his chair. Rain pattered on the window behind him. 'He's still my client, in that

I continue to represent his interests until somebody tells me not to.'

'How long have you been handling his affairs?'

'For the past eighteen months or so. By the way, I'm not a blackmailer. Lady Banks-Marion misread my intentions—'

'Not interested right now, Toby. Why was Mr Burke's nightclub put in your name?'

If Stafford was surprised by the question he was careful not to show it. 'He thought I should invest in it, so that when it turned a profit and we came to sell it I could pass the shares to his wife.'

'Why did he want you to do that?'

Stafford donned his glasses and studied him with acuity. 'Mr Bryant. You're not married, are you?'

'No, sir.'

'In this country women don't have equal pay and their rights are still curtailed by government legislation, and that's the way the old boys' network would like to leave it. Donald Burke loved his wife very much and wanted to protect her, so for the past few years he's been putting those protections into place. She may have no interest in running his empire but she does not deserve to be discriminated against. Mr Burke was not an easy man to deal with, but I felt him to be an honest one.'

'Why?'

'In my profession you get a feeling for these things. He donated privately to charity; he treated his employees fairly and behaved responsibly. I don't need to tell you that in the City of London this is fairly unusual behaviour. We are no longer benevolent Victorians, setting up charitable societies for the improvement of the nation.'

'What's your connection to Mr Hatton-Jones?'

Stafford gave a rueful smile as he tapped out a Pall Mall and lit it. 'Our families knew one another. He wanted to find a job for Miss Harrow.'

'You didn't disapprove?'

279

'It was not my concern.'

'So you got her a job at the club. And that was where she met Mr Burke.'

'I assume so.'

'What do you mean?'

'It's not something we ever had cause to discuss.' Stafford sat back. 'I don't see your point, Mr Bryant.'

'I'm sorry if I'm being obtuse. If Mr Hatton-Jones lost his girlfriend to Mr Burke, it would give him a reason—'

'Ah, I see. A *crime passionnel*. I find that unlikely. Mr Burke's reclusiveness extended beyond the realm of business.'

'What do you mean?'

'I mean that not only could he not touch or be touched by other people, he was not bedding down with Miss Harrow. He held his wife in too much respect.'

'And how would you know such a thing?'

'Because he once confided in me frankly.'

'How frankly?'

Stafford folded away the house plans as he considered his answer. 'He explained that he could no longer bear the thought of intimacy on any level. I am given to understand that it was an after-effect of his . . .'

'His breakdown,' said Bryant. 'Do you have any corroboration for this, from his wife perhaps?'

'I saw Mr Burke's medical report. You're not the only one who's suspicious, Mr Bryant. When I hear that a man has been disposed of so effectively that he can only be identified by chunks of his flesh, I start to think that perhaps I've been had, and that man isn't dead after all.'

This is interesting, Bryant thought. The same idea had crossed his own mind. 'But why would Donald Burke fake his own death? His businesses were thriving, he was happily married, he had everything he could want.'

'I didn't say that I believe it to be true. As it turns out, Norma Burke was not the only person to identify her husband's remains.'

I am given to understand that Miss Claxon also viewed the body and identified the, ah, artefacts, while you were out of the house. In fact, I was the one who suggested she should do it.'

'I don't understand,' said Bryant. 'Why?'

'Because as you pointed out yourself, the chemicals in the tank are probably removing any possibility of future identification. I thought it was important to get a corroborating opinion.'

'You did the right thing,' Bryant admitted, wishing he had thought of it. 'Do you have any idea who killed him?'

'I have my own theory, as it happens,' said Stafford. 'I don't believe there is a murderer.'

'That's impossible. There would have to have been too many coincidences—'

Stafford pointed paired fingers at him. '*Exactly*, Mr Bryant. In a court of law, coincidence is the striking occurrence of two or more events at one time, apparently by mere chance. And that is precisely what we have here. I believe Donald Burke decided to take his own life, and could not have been thinking clearly or he would never have selected such a gruesome method. We know that he had been ill before. He had developed phobias and underwent bouts of depression. As for Mr Hatton-Jones, he unfortunately suffered an accident in a very old house that is falling apart. Alberman told me there have been more than a dozen mishaps over the last few years, so many in fact that the more superstitious villagers believe the house is jinxed when it is merely in need of repair.'

'And Miss Harrow?'

'She is highly strung and thinks emotionally, and accidentally overdosed herself.'

'But you trusted her enough to recommend her for a job with Mr Burke.'

'As a nightclub singer, Mr Bryant. It's hardly brain surgery. People make mistakes in tense situations.'

'Somebody cut the power to the house tonight, and damaged all the cars.'

'Forgive me: you're in the business of creating a narrative that fits these events, except that you cannot,' said Stafford. 'You've failed to explain anything – you said so yourself. Ask the servants about accidents, or if the power has ever failed in a rainstorm before, or even deaths. I think you'll reach the same conclusion pretty quickly.' He rose and opened the door. 'If you'll forgive me I really must get on. There are still surveyors' documents that need checking before I can process any paperwork on the house.'

'So the sale goes ahead.'

'I am given to understand that this is the wish of both parties. I'll see you at the house in the morning when our business can be concluded, barring any further unforeseen problems.'

As Bryant drove back from Knotsworth in Celeste's car, he thought about everything that Stafford had told him. For the first time he began to get a clearer picture of Burke's death, and he was sure it most certainly did not involve suicide.

Two scenarios presented themselves. Burke arranged to meet someone in the barn, overcoming his reluctance to do so because of the urgent necessity of the meeting. The person he went to see was either standing above him on the makeshift wooden walkway that Harry had constructed, or waiting for him on the ground. If they had been above, in the course of their conversation this other person had stepped forward and reached out to touch him. Burke had reacted violently, lurching back, and had gone through the railing. Not murder perhaps, but manslaughter. If they had met him on the ground, then Burke had been knocked down and attached to the block and tackle, and fed into the machine while unconscious but alive. Murder with extreme prejudice.

He arrived back at Tavistock Hall, crunching gears and spraying gravel across the lawn. The lights were still out. In the lamp-hung hall he stopped and listened, but heard nothing unusual. *What a mess,* he thought. *I only hope John's been able to keep the peace.*

35

TURN! TURN! TURN!

'It's just a bump,' said May. 'You'll live.'

'A bump? It's the size of a bloody duck's egg!' Monty had changed into a maroon silk dressing gown and would have looked like an extremely dissipated version of Noël Coward if he hadn't had a rivulet of blood running down the left side of his face. He gingerly touched the back of his head. 'I heard him come up behind me and turned just in time. A few seconds slower and he'd have cracked open my skull.'

'That's the second time you've been lucky.'

'If that's your idea of luck I'm never going to Aintree with you.'

'What did he hit you with?'

'Something so big that he had to swing it. It felt like a . . . you know, road menders have them.'

'A bucket of tar.'

'No – shovel.'

'Then he could only have caught you a glancing blow. Monty, you're indestructible.' May had searched the floor of Monty's bedroom and found no weapon of any kind. 'You'd better find somewhere to sit down,' he warned. 'You probably have concussion.'

'I'm getting a bit fed up with being . . .' He had to stop and think for a minute. 'Attacked.'

'I told you not to leave the room, didn't I?'

'It should be easy to work out who was . . .' The word evaded him for a moment. 'Missing?'

'I don't know. Half the candles were out.' May shrugged. 'I couldn't see everyone.'

'It's ridiculous, he couldn't have just vanished,' said Pamela Claxon, sticking her head around the bedroom door and raising a lantern. 'Where are these footprints?'

They went back to the end corridor. May shone the torch down at the floor. The boards were still wet from the smashed bowl, but the marks were barely readable now as prints.

'He must have passed right by you,' said Monty.

'Nobody got past me,' said May.

Claxon bent down and rubbed the water between her fingers. 'Rubbish, you weren't concentrating. Whoever it was must still be on this floor somewhere. The bedrooms are empty because the guests are downstairs. We'll have to search everywhere.'

'I've done it before,' said May. 'It doesn't make any difference. Monty, why did you come upstairs?'

'My collarbone was aching. I wanted to take . . .'

Claxon and May waited for him to finish. 'Poison?' Claxon suggested.

'Some aspirin, and then I decided to change.' He clutched his head. 'I feel – unusual.'

'Listen, old chap, you'd better take it easy for a while. We could probably fetch the doctor back if you like.'

'That quack? No thank you. Ooh.' He sat down very suddenly on the side table. 'I usually hear when anyone walks past. The floorboards creak. I keep hearing your partner clickety-clacking past like he's auditioning for a musical. Ever since you two circus clowns got here nothing has gone according to plan. When I get back to London I'm going to . . .' He lost the words again.

'Be more forgiving?' May suggested.

'Have you reduced to traffic wardens,' snapped Monty.

'Why don't we all go downstairs now?' Claxon suggested. Somewhere outside an owl hooted, making them jump.

Guiding the complaining businessman between them, they made their way back to the main staircase, reaching the hall to find Bryant just returned.

'Did I miss something?' Bryant asked. 'What's wrong with Monty?'

'Someone hit him on the head. Possibly with a shovel.'

Bryant's blue eyes widened. 'And he's still in one piece? Wow. You're lucky he only hit your brain. I assume he got away.'

Of course he bloody did,' cried Monty vehemently. 'You two couldn't catch a   what are those things with stripes?'

'A badger?' said Bryant.

'A zebra?' Claxon offered.

'A cold.' Monty stuck a finger in his ear and wiggled it. 'I mean, what was the point of winning the war? Are there any Germans here? Steady the Buffs.'

'I think we'd better get the doctor back,' said May.

'John, can I have a word with you?' Bryant asked, leading his partner aside to Hawthorn, the flickering drawing room behind the library. Alberman's dexterity with lamps suggested that the house was no stranger to blackouts. 'I talked to Toby Stafford. He put forward an interesting idea. What if Burke isn't dead?'

'What do you mean?'

'Suppose he set up this entire weekend to fool everyone into thinking he'd died?'

'Why would he do that? What would he gain from it?' He peered back at the doorway, where Monty was being led towards the library by the solicitous novelist.

'I suppose it would get him out of having to spend millions on Tavistock Hall. I saw Stafford poring over a floor plan of the house. Suppose there's subsidence or something?'

'He's buying it for a song, Arthur. It's being sold at below market value.'

'It's not just this place. The tenancies are tied to the property. In order to have them vacated he has to buy out over twenty leases and untangle rights on all sorts of land parcels. Suppose he knew that the land was going to drop in value. Say, if the government was planning to build a motorway through it?'

'So he tells no one, not even his own wife, plants a misleading note for Vanessa, then throws some of his belongings into the sewage treatment plant and somehow Norma still manages to positively identify his remains, including his own ear? Instead of pursuing the matter through legal means, something of which he's had considerable experience? I suppose Norma could have made a mistake under the circumstances, seeing how we put her under pressure to identify him because *you* wanted the matter resolved before anyone else could take over the investigation.'

Bryant was affronted. 'You're saying it's my fault?'

May shook his head. 'It just doesn't make any sense, Arthur. I've just thought of something simpler. Having fenced all the valuables from his church, our friend Trev the Rev realizes he's soon going to be under investigation by his diocese. In a state of panic he arranges to meet Burke to beg for a loan, and is turned down. As a desperate junkie facing the loss of his livelihood and a jail sentence he loses his temper, and bingo. Realizing to his total horror that he is now out of control, he strikes at anyone who crosses his path.'

'Not by lashing out at them,' said Bryant, 'but by climbing up to the roof and waiting for Monty to nip outside for a fag before pushing a gargoyle on top of him, which not only requires stamina but clairvoyance. And by the way, Trev the Rev has muscles like knots in bits of string. I don't think he'd have the strength to tip one over. I tried and could barely shift it. Let's not stop here, though. While you're at it, how about laying the blame on his lordship? Discovered *in flagrante delicto* with hippy chick Melanie, Harry slaughters Burke and prepares to feed him to his pet pig, until Monty threatens to give the game away and has to be retroactively bludgeoned with a mythical stone creature. What about Slade Wilson? Upset by Burke's choice of pastel paintwork and co-ordinating curtain material he despatches him, not with a nice piece of broderie anglaise lacework but by shoving him into a grinder that wouldn't be out of place in a slaughterhouse.'

'What do you want us to do then?' asked May, 'just sit around and wait for Monty to suffer another accident?'

'Hm.' Bryant rubbed his chin. '*Cunctando restituit rem.* It's a thought. I still think that leaving Monty with the others is the only way to protect him, and the best chance we have of drawing somebody out.'

'Arthur, if we don't get something by tomorrow at noon we lose everything.'

'You don't need to remind me.' Bryant threw his hands in the air. 'The problem is, I don't know what to do without my books.'

'Try some real police work for a change,' said May. 'And fast.'

Parchment staggered past the open door carrying a pile of bedspreads. 'I'm sorry, sir,' he said. 'There's a back staircase but I tend to miss the steps in the dark.'

'Parchment, is it true that the servants always used their own corridors and staircases?' asked Bryant. 'Celeste said something about the house having secret passages.'

'Who's Celeste?' said May. 'And secret passages? Really? That's just in books, isn't it?'

'No secret passages, sir,' Parchment confirmed, 'but the servants' corridor that runs from the kitchen to the floors above used to be bigger.' Looking as if he might collapse, Parchment set down the bedspreads with a wheeze of relief. 'It was so we could get the meals delivered hot without having to cross employers on the stairs. We stopped using all the parts when the house lost its staff.'

'So that's why the food arrives cold. What happened to its other branches?'

'That I don't know, sir. His lordship made a lot of repairs with plywood. He is not proficient in the craft of DIY.'

Bryant digested this. It seemed likely that someone still knew how to access the closed sections of the staircase. 'What time will people rise for breakfast tomorrow?'

'It's Sunday, sir,' said Parchment. 'A cold collation will be laid out early but the cooked trays aren't ready until eight.'

'Keep an eye open for anything unusual, would you?'

'You mean the ghost of the fourth lord?'

'Why, is he likely to put in an appearance?'

'Only in the event of sudden death or misfortune,' Parchment replied wearily.

'Have you ever seen him?'

'Yes sir, he wears his purple doublet and hose and a ruff, and he passes through the walls of the first-floor corridor. And he carries his head under his arm. He's partial to a chocolate biscuit. I'll be stationed in my night booth if you need me.'

They're all mad, Bryant decided. *We're not in a hall at all. We're in a lunatic asylum.*

36

A HARD DAY'S NIGHT

It had not, they decided, been a good night.

After escorting everyone to their rooms and making sure that they were locked in until morning, the detectives had slept in shifts. Bryant woke at dawn feeling unrested and nursing a powerful headache. He scratched at his hair, licks of which were standing upright like a brown egret's feathers, and looked out of the window.

It had been raining hard all night and the forecourt was now partially submerged. A hedge had subsided into the water, and an inedible-looking sheep was standing forlornly beside its waterlogged roots. The ashram was silent, soaked and still, its tents sagging and colourless, surrounded by a brown moat. The pale grey morning mist had been pummelled down by the rain, but remained drifting at the height of a man around the far edges of the lawn. Beside the window, a bough sprang up as a crow flapped away. Lightning flared in the distance. The landscape now owed less to Constable than Hieronymus Bosch.

Bryant completed his matutinal ablutions and contemplated his remaining outfits. *What's it to be?* he wondered, *Karl from*

'The Student Prince' *or Tony from* 'The Boy Friend'? He was assembling the least ostentatious items from both productions when there was a knock at the door.

'Arthur, are you awake?' May was more happily kitted out in his PCU livery of ribbed black roll-neck sweater and black trousers. Somehow he managed to make the uniform positively debonair. 'It's seven thirty. The forensics team is supposed to be here this morning, which presumably means before noon.'

'Four and a half hours. Not long enough,' said Bryant. 'Let's go.'

A quick roll call shouted through the bedroom doors produced exhausted responses from the remaining guests. Downstairs they found the breakfast room cold and deserted. In the hall Alberman was arguing with Mrs Janverley, the housekeeper.

'What's going on?' asked May.

'I can't find Parchment,' the housekeeper complained. 'I checked with Mrs Bessel and nobody has seen him.'

'That's odd. Could he have gone out to fetch something?'

'Only if I send him,' said Alberman, 'and I have not done so.'

'We saw him putting away bedspreads last night. Perhaps he's working in one of the upstairs rooms.'

'No, sir, I've just been up there. Today his duties consist of a little light cleaning in the basement, washing towels and so on. He's not very steady on his feet.'

The detectives headed downstairs, passing along a flagstone corridor lined with what appeared to be Victorian glass offices, timbered in the lower half. This was where the staff tradition-ally took their meals. Seated, they could eat in private. Standing, they would be able to see if someone had come downstairs.

'Back here,' said May. 'I passed it when we were trying to get the lights working.'

They stopped before a heavy oak door and pushed it open.

Inside, towels hung above a top-loading washing machine, but no one appeared to have been here since the previous day.

'What about his room?' asked Bryant. 'It's right under the eaves, isn't it?'

They climbed through the narrowing halls until they reached the smallest passageway of all. On one side the ceiling sloped to accommodate the angle of the roof. Each door had a worn brass slot above its handle, into which was inserted the name of the staff member.

May stopped before the door of Parchment's tiny room.

'Mr Parchment?' He rapped his knuckles on the panelling, then tried the handle. 'It's locked.'

He dropped to his knees and peered under the half-inch gap. 'I can't see anything. Maybe he's passed out.'

May nearly fractured his shoulder trying to break the door open.

'Let me do it,' said Bryant. He turned around and kicked upwards, so that the door handle snapped off and the door swung inwards.

'Where did you learn to do that?' asked May.

'Whitechapel,' said Bryant.

The room was immaculately tidy and completely empty.

'What about his night booth on our floor?'

Ernest Parchment was still seated on the narrow wooden bench that ran across his wooden booth. He was lying forward with his forehead down on the little built-in table.

'What is it?' asked Bryant warily. 'Heart failure?'

May tried to lift him. 'There's something sticking out of his head,' he said. He raised the valet by pulling on his shoulders. Parchment's head swung back. A knitting needle had been pushed so deeply through his right eye that only a few inches of it protruded. He had bled out over the bench. The immense striped scarf on which he had just finished working lay in his lap and was stained with blood, wet and pungent. Several balls of wool had unrolled around his feet like a spilt rainbow. Among them were various knitting needles in different sizes. May leaned the body back in its pew. He wanted to remove the offending needle and grant the valet some dignity, but knew he could not do so without compromising the evidence.

'No pulse,' he said. 'His body's still warm. Why kill an old man who plainly wasn't doing anyone harm?'

'This wasn't planned,' said Bryant, crouching low to study the valet's fallen materials. 'It was improvised. Can we at least put something over the poor fellow?'

They found a sheet and pinned it across the alcove. 'This must only just have happened,' said May. 'I didn't see anyone. Why is it we never see anyone?'

They tried the telephone in the hall but the line was still dead. 'It has to have been cut somewhere above ground,' said May.

If Alberman was shocked to hear about Parchment, he did his best not to show it. They followed the butler around the edge of the house and found that the power cables embedded at the far end of the patio had been cleanly severed. May crouched beside the bare copper ends. 'Someone's used wire-cutters. I can't fix this. We'll need an engineer.'

'I have a car with tyres that work,' said Bryant. 'I can go for help.'

May looked at the yellow Mini with sunflowers and daisies crudely painted across its roof. 'Where did you get that thing?'

'From a lady friend. I rather like it.'

May decided not to ask. He checked his Timex. 'If you go now, you should just be able to make it before the army starts firing again. But you may not be able to get back.'

'Four hours, John. There's still time.'

'No,' said May firmly. 'We had our chance and we blew it. We need outside help now.'

Bryant crunched the gears and lurched off in a shower of

gravel. May waited until the yellow Mini had disappeared behind the rain. As he turned, the butler passed across the hall.

'Does Mr Parchment have anyone we should notify?' asked May.

'I think there's a stepbrother in Kenya,' said Alberman. 'How did he die, sir?'

'He was killed with a knitting needle.'

'He knitted all the time. A lot of the older servants did. Could it have been an accident?'

'Not like any I've ever seen,' said May. 'It was probably the first sharp instrument that came to hand. But why him? It doesn't make sense. What could he have possibly known?' He slowly turned on the spot, thinking about the layout of the house. 'Get everyone into the reception room, including the staff. From now on nobody goes anywhere until the forensic team arrives.'

What have we done? May thought as he followed Alberman. *How did we allow such a simple assignment to turn into a disaster area? I should have forced Arthur to get help earlier. Even if we can still get Monty to testify in court, our careers are well and truly finished.*

'Mr May?' Pamela Claxon found him in the hall. 'Is it true that one of the servants has been killed?'

'We don't know what happened yet,' said May.

'I heard someone skewered him through the head, so it was hardly a typical knitting accident. What are we doing, hanging out here until he's picked us all off one by one, like in *Ten Little*—'

'No, we're waiting for a team to take over and secure the premises. The matter will be out of our hands then. You'll have to do whatever they tell you.'

Pamela had trouble lighting a cigarette. 'Inspector Trench would be able to solve the problem.'

'Then why don't you let him, Pamela?' May snapped.

'Bring him on, give him the evidence and get him to figure it out.'

'I can't,' she said. 'I can't bring him back any more.'

'Why not?'

She held out her hands. Her fingers were shaking. She reached inside her blouse and pulled out a silver ankh on a chain. 'He was wearing this around his neck.'

'Who was?'

'My hands – I started drinking again. I was dry for six years. My son – he fell off a roof. He was staying with some friends in the South of France. He told them he wished he could fly. They'd been experimenting with LSD. He never recovered. I haven't written a word since then. It's not true what they say; you can't drink and be a writer. Your synapses don't respond properly. You don't make the connections any more.' She wiped her eyes. 'You wanted another secret to come out? Inspector Trench is not coming back.'

'I'm sorry,' said May.

'Please, do something before anyone else gets killed,' she said. 'I have another confession to make. I know all about you and your partner. I did from the moment you arrived. I found you when I was researching an early Inspector Trench novel. You and Mr Bryant were investigating a death at the Palace Theatre. It was reported in the *Police Gazette*. You were written about as if you were heroes back then. You *must* be able to do something.'

'I can't,' said May. 'I can't work alone and Arthur – he's out of his depth here.'

'Then find a way for your partner to solve this,' said Claxon. 'You must hand him the key, even if it means . . .' She hesitated.

'What?' asked May.

She looked at him evenly, her eyes wide. 'Even if it means that the innocent are hurt.'

37

SOMETHING IN THE AIR

Arthur Bryant braked so sharply that he nearly hit his head on the windscreen. He studied the road ahead. The dip in the lane now mirrored the angry skies. Unfolding himself from the tiny Mini, he pulled down a broken branch and probed the expanse of water with it. There was no way across without flooding the engine. Even up here the rainfall had taken its toll on the road. High hedges rose on either side, with deeply ploughed fields beyond them. In the distance he heard the rapid rattle of gunfire recommence.

He backed up the Mini and parked it in a wider section of the road, then continued on foot. The flooding became more severe as the highway descended. The water table had risen and the fields were not taking the runoff away. Bryant's aunt had been flooded out when the Thames rose in Deptford, but it had never occurred to him that this kind of thing happened in the countryside.

When he reached Crowshott, he had an eerie sense of déjà vu. The rain had reduced itself to a saturating mist. The uniformed nanny was still pushing her pram, seemingly unfazed by the weather. A farmhand leaned against a wall watching him. The shops were all closed. The air smelled of wet leaves and turned-up earth, fresh and ancient.

He squelched to the phone box and checked his pockets for coins. 'There's been another death,' he told Gladys, sensing reproach in her silence. 'John and I can't deal with this. We've always had London's resources at hand, but there's nothing here that can help us. We've carried out interviews and done visual searches, but we have no equipment and nowhere near enough expertise. Hang on, the pips are going.' He inserted another shilling. 'Two deaths, three murder attempts involving a servant, a millionaire, a nightclub singer and Monty. It's so absurdly random.'

'You don't need any special equipment other than your own brains and instincts,' said Gladys finally. 'You're making excuses.'

'Pamela Claxon keeps telling me I should treat it like one of her mystery novels.'

'Why don't you? I assume the house has a library.'

'Yes, a very good one.'

'Does it have books about the family and the hall?'

'Yes, a great many.'

'Then go and do what you do best. Look through the books. You know how it always clears your mind. The unit isn't meant to function like a branch of the CID, Mr Bryant. We're supposed to make the connections that nobody else sees. John's keeping everyone safe, yes?'

'As best as he can. You know John; he takes everything so personally. As soon as we get clear of the house we'll lock Monty in a cell at Bow Street overnight. It's what I should have done at the start, then none of this—'

'Go to the library, Mr Bryant,' instructed Gladys.

He was trudging back to the car when a soldier with a mud-caked face and half a rowan bush on his head burst through the hedge. 'I say, are you up at the old hall?' asked Lieutenant

Coultas, out of breath. 'The Frenchies are giving us a run for our money. We all thought they'd be like the Italians last year, standing around complaining about the coffee and volunteering to be taken prisoner.'

'Why are you so near the house?' Bryant asked.

'Bit of a cock-up on logistics, I'm afraid. We're finishing at thirteen hundred hours, so you should be clear to leave then. Roads are a bit tricky, though. It usually takes a few hours for them to drain off. Should be passable by tomorrow at the latest.'

'Can you tell your sergeant major that we have a police investigation taking place at the hall and would rather not be shot at?'

'I'll see what I can do,' said the lieutenant, 'but it's awfully difficult finding anyone at the mo. The French are taking it all very personally. My superior officer got slapped in the face with a glove for being rude about Charles de Gaulle. Probably best to stay inside until after we've finished. Ta-ta!' He bounded off into the opposite hedge.

Tavistock Hall had a look of abandonment. Only smoke from the ashram's cooking pots betrayed any sign of life. Bryant let himself into the main house and went to the breakfast room, where Mrs Janverley was clearing the last of the cups.

'Where is everyone?' he asked.

'Your colleague is keeping them all together in Iris, sir,' she explained, pointing with a pastry fork. 'They're all very unhappy about poor Mr Parchment. Why would anybody want to hurt him? He never harmed a fly, except in the trenches, and that was only because he was doing his bit. I'm supposed to be in there with the others but I couldn't leave this mess.'

Of the group, only Vanessa Harrow looked well rested. Her hair was tied back and her cheeks were in bloom. She wore a dark blue sweater with a lemon chiffon scarf and seemed in happier spirits. 'I'm sorry to have alarmed everyone,' she told May. 'I only took the pills to make sure I'd get some sleep. I don't understand what could have happened.'

'The main thing is that you're well,' said May. 'No side effects?'

'I feel perfectly fine now. That poor old servant – what an awful thing to have happened. I feel so sorry for him.'

'It was murder, Miss Harrow.'

'Who would do such a thing?'

'The same person who added a sleeping draught to your water glass. You're lucky to be alive.'

'My God. The water was on the table when I went up to my room. I assumed Parchment had put it there for me.'

'Is there anything you haven't told us? Why would somebody want to silence you?'

'I have no idea. They were disgusting to me yesterday, pretty much all of them. I admit I was upset, but I just needed to rest. What will happen now?'

'The team from Canterbury will probably detain you all until they're happy that they have everything they need,' said Bryant. He left the others and walked out into the hall with his hands in the pockets of his absurdly baggy trousers, wondering whether to take Gladys's advice and go to the library.

He stopped in mid-stride and slowly walked backwards.

Something was different.

The stained-glass windows on the landing sent a diagonal stripe of crimson and blue across the opposite wall. The shadow of Herne the Hunter was sinisterly elongated so that it appeared to have been cast by someone standing at the window. The tip of the hunter's arrow could clearly be seen. It was the first thing he had noticed when he arrived on Friday evening.

But what had the arrow been pointing to? What was missing?

Mirror, painting, hall table – that was it; there had been a second picture there. It had disappeared. He headed back to Iris.

'Lady Banks-Marion, might I borrow you for a moment?'

She rose from a high chair without bending her back or using her hands, a skill that must have been taught to her in finishing school. When she saw the wall, her reaction was powerful and immediate.

'Do you know what's different?' Bryant asked.

'Of course I do. The boats have gone.'

'What boats?'

'Willem van de Velde the Younger's *Harbour Scene* is meant to be hanging there.'

'Is it valuable?'

'Extremely. Although not priceless.' When she saw the detective's blank look, she explained. 'It can be sold, Mr Bryant.'

'When did you last notice it?'

'One rarely notices the things in one's own house.' She thought for a minute. 'It was here first thing this morning, I'm sure of it, because of the way the light was coming in. You see how it looks as if there's an arrow pointing at it? Do you think Parchment saw someone take it? Could the person who stole this also have attacked him?'

'He was at his post in the corridor one floor up,' Bryant pointed out. 'It seems unlikely that the events are directly connected. Have you ever had thefts from the hall before?'

'Of course,' said Lady Banks-Marion impatiently. 'A house of this size always has trouble. It attracts undesirables. They get to know the parlourmaids and find ways to attend the parties. The villagers know this is our last weekend and are furious with us. I was half expecting them to try something like this.' She seemed more upset about the loss of the painting than the death of her loyal servant.

'Are you sure it wouldn't just have been moved for cleaning?'

'On a Sunday?' She looked at him as if he was an idiot. 'Cleaning is Mondays and Tuesdays. Well, don't just stand there, go and look for it.'

It seemed that the library would have to wait. Bryant conducted a less than systematic search of the hall, and when that yielded no results he checked the bedrooms before heading off for the basement. Near the fuse box he found a deep cupboard stacked with a pyramid of logs. Someone had stood on them recently, disturbing the pile.

At the back, the edge of an engraved frame met Bryant's fingertips. He pulled gently and found the picture, or rather what was left of it, because the painting itself had been inexpertly cut out with a sharp blade, leaving only the frame.

It can be rolled up and hidden, he thought. *Just how many crimes are taking place here?*

Having at least partially fulfilled Lady Banks-Marion's request, he went to the library and found himself a big armchair, a still-warm coffee pot and an ashtray. He needed to clear his head. Anthony Trollope had said that the habit of reading would last you until your death. He could have added that it was a tool to ignite the mind.

The great wall of leather-bound volumes faced him. Their immaculate spines suggested that most had never been read. Some recounted the history of the house and its owners, others pertained to the Kentish surroundings. To fully understand the tenants of Tavistock Hall would take years.

He had just two and a half hours.

Rising, he walked along the shelves, his fingertips brushing the dust jackets. The endless volumes of family history made for dry reading, and had clearly been produced with the cooperation of the estate, so were unlikely to contain anything detrimental or revealing. Animal husbandry, garden maintenance, guides to collecting art; after a few minutes he felt like giving up.

Away from the more illustrious volumes was a separate

case filled with old paperbacks. At least some of these appeared to have been handled. He found a first edition of Sherlock Holmes. Allowing the pages to fall open, he guiltily read from 'The Boscombe Valley Mystery'. Sometimes Conan Doyle could help where columns of statistical data failed.

His finger ran along a single line: 'There is nothing more deceptive than an obvious fact.'

What was the most obvious fact? Pulling his black notebook from his jacket, he dug out a pencil stub and made a careful entry.

He needed something else. In the other bookcase an elegantly embossed volume caught his eye: *The Treasures of the Wallace Collection*. His natural curiosity took hold of him.

The index revealed a name he had just heard. Willem van de Velde the Younger, Dutch marine painter buried in St James's Church, Piccadilly. And there it was, *Harbour Scene*, a not especially eye-catching painting that existed in several versions. As Lady Banks-Marion had stated, not priceless, but one that could be fenced if stolen.

There is nothing more deceptive than an obvious fact.

Heading back to the armchair, he poured himself a strong coffee and sat back, sipping with the cup perched between both hands.

The final weekend party.

Monty's accident.

Vanessa at the barn.

Burke's body in the macerator.

Parchment's brutal, slapdash death.

The barman in the Goat & Compasses: 'You newcomers are always in such a rush.'

Claxon telling him, 'If I put this in one of my crime novels nobody would believe a word of it.'

The white gloves.

The pig, Malacrida.

It was there at his fingertips, if he could only . . .

He went back to the beginning. It all started with Harry meeting Donald Burke. Norma explained that her husband was planning to buy the property without having seen it. He had no real interest in Tavistock Hall. He merely saw it as an investment opportunity. His friends admired his ability to read future trends. He wasn't interested in any of the guests. He was distrustful and wanted to be left alone. He knew four people: his wife, his mistress, his lawyer and, tangentially, Harry, who had been useful in securing the house below its real value.

Therefore, since he felt uncomfortable with strangers, he could only have been meeting one of those four in the barn. But Norma and Harry had been in the dining room and the lawyer had been stood up. So he *had* to have been seeing Vanessa Harrow.

Bryant set down his coffee cup and returned to Iris. Vanessa and Monty were sitting by the window. Vanessa caught Bryant's eye as he entered, as if she had sensed that he would come for her.

'It was you Donald Burke arranged to meet at the barn,' he said, a statement of fact. 'Yesterday, just before lunch. It could not have been anyone else but you, Miss Harrow.'

'I'd been to the village,' said Vanessa, fright showing in her eyes. 'I came back – didn't mean to – I never wanted . . .' The words died in her mouth.

'You never wanted what?'

'Nothing. I shouldn't have agreed to come here this weekend.'

'Why did you?'

'I – I – Please, leave me alone.' She rose suddenly and fled from the room.

'Vanessa,' called Monty, going after her.

'John, what am I missing?' Bryant asked his partner as they left. 'Why can't I get an outright admission from anyone?'

'Because you're chasing them around like a hound worrying foxes to death,' said May.

Bryant waved his hands helplessly. 'I can't understand what goes through these people's heads. If you asked me to find out whether Tavistock Hall was built on a confluence of ley lines I'd be able to figure out the answer, but all this . . . human emotion makes no sense to me.'

Outside the sky was thunderous once more. Penny-sized spots of rain had begun to clatter against the glass. 'There's no more time for abstract thinking,' said May. 'We have to be practical, and leave everything in a fit state so that it can be handed over. By the way, where's Fruity? He's supposed to be keeping watch for us.'

'I haven't seen him all morning.'

'Oh God, don't let there be another one.'

The rain began beating down so hard that they had to shout above it. 'It doesn't take both of us to look,' said May. 'You said you had clues. Do you know what's going on here or don't you? There's no time left to hold anything back.'

'I have most of the pieces, but the overall picture is – unfocused,' Bryant admitted helplessly.

'Then go back to the library and for God's sake find your focus,' said May. 'I'll try the gatehouse. I don't think we're in control of the situation any more.'

When he stepped out on to the lawn and looked back at the house, he saw only a monumental phantom, half lost in sweeping veils of rain.

38

STEP IN TIME

Bryant walked back into the hall from the library and passed by each of the other rooms: Snowdrop, Lavender, Rose, Iris, Hawthorn, Primrose, all decorated in pastels and perfectly tidy but badly laid out, with the English habit of pushing the furniture too far back towards the walls. On the first floor Parchment's upright body remained behind a sheet like a shop mannequin put into storage, while the undissolved parts of the first victim still lay in the barn outside.

He thought about the dissected Donald Burke and the bludgeoned Monty. The pair were roughly the same size, age and shape. It wasn't entirely unlikely that someone could mistake the two of them. Different scenarios replaced each other like pages in a flick-book. Burke turning up at the barn in place of Monty. The killer thinking Vanessa was a witness. Parchment placing the water glass on Vanessa's bedside table.

Once again, his thought processes had led him astray from what he had intended to do. As he was passing Primrose, the breakfast room, something caught his eye. There was a fresh black mark on the carpet in front of the fireplace. He entered and rubbed at the carpet with the toe of his shoe. The wrought-iron grate was covered in a new fall of soot.

There were no longer enough members of staff to keep the fireplaces lit. He noted that most of the ground-floor rooms had electric radiators. Someone had recently stood here.

Removing his pocket torch, he bent down and peered up the chimney. The flue was partially wedged open, but the beam could not light the brickwork above it. He needed to stand inside. Climbing over the grate and pushing himself into the chimney breast he rose and reached up, shoving back the flue. A shower of soot poured down over him.

Coughing, he felt around the edges of the brick. As he had suspected, there was a ledge just at the end of his fingertips. He gave a little hop, dislodging a fresh fall of soot. *I'm going to look a right Charlie if I'm wrong*, he thought, jumping again.

John May was walking around the gatehouse, trying to see in through the windows, but the gutters were overflowing and the ground underfoot was so slippery with mud and leaves that he had trouble getting close. From this distance he could not see into the rooms. He tried the front door but it was now wedged shut. The cottage was permanently shaded by the trees, and there were no lights on inside.

'Mr Metcalf?' The house was silent except for the patter of rain on its roof.

There was a small green wooden shed at the rear of the gatehouse. He was not expecting to find anything, but it was worth a try.

Inside it was too dark to see. He ran his torch beam over the tools that had been neatly arranged along one wall. Each item had a hook and fitted into a painted outline.

One large piece was missing: by the look of it, a sledgehammer.

An unpleasant feeling started to grow in his stomach. If

Parchment had seen something that had cost him his life, how much more likely was it that Fruity, employed by the unit as a double agent, had met his end? After all, he had been asked by Roger Trapp to report back on everyone.

May began searching the field behind the gatehouse with renewed energy. At the ashram he interrupted some kind of prayer meeting involving chanted responses, but no one was able to help him. Only Melanie and Donovan knew whom he was talking about.

The rain was falling harder now and his jacket was soaked. His shirt stuck to his back. Knowing how reluctant Metcalf was to go inside the house, he decided to walk the perimeter. He could hardly get any wetter.

There was no birdsong any more, only the whispering, suffocating rainfall. The rooftop of the hall was effervescent with water, its drainpipes inundated. It seemed as if the house might be sinking back into the loamy Kentish soil stone by stone.

Halfway around the wall he came to a break where an oak tree had been allowed to spread on wild scrubland. At its roots a hawthorn bush had grown between the trunk and some rocks. It was a melancholy corner, dark and foul-smelling, but what brought him to a halt were the shattered branches near the base.

He crouched and stared into the undergrowth, amazed that he hadn't noticed it before. The fallen leaves were saturated in blood. Partially hidden beneath them was a length of machine-tooled wood. Carefully reaching in, he dislodged the handle of the missing sledgehammer. Its iron head was draped in a skein of gore too thick to be washed off by the rain. The undergrowth bore marks of having been crushed. Leaves and broken branches were spattered with blood where a body had been dragged from the site. The raised rubber boot that had been attached to Fruity's artificial leg was lying on its side, torn and blood-soaked.

The trail ended as soon as he left the cover of the oak. Here soaked grass began, cut short and rain-flattened. The corpse could have been pulled in any direction.

He ran back to the house and into the hall, not stopping to remove his muddy boots. Pamela Claxon was on the stairs with a book in her hand.

'Shoes, Mr May,' she said, shocked.

'Have you seen Arthur?'

'He was either in Iris or Primrose, I can't remember which. You're treading in an awful lot of mud. Mrs Janverley will kill you.'

'Which one is Primrose?'

'The unheated one. Straight ahead on your left.'

He ran to the breakfast room and charged inside, only to find it empty. 'Arthur,' he called, 'where are you?'

'I'm stuck,' Bryant replied from somewhere inside the walls, his voice muffled. 'I think I've swallowed a mouse.'

May looked around and saw a pair of legs poking out beneath the chimney breast. 'What on earth are you doing in there?'

'Can you pull me out?'

He climbed in and tugged at Bryant's trousers. 'Try wriggling,' he suggested as soot fell all around them. Bryant came free and landed on his backside in a filthy cascade.

'Fruity Metcalf's had his head bashed in,' said May, spitting soot.

'Is he all right?' When Bryant blinked open his very white eyes he looked like one of the chimney sweeps from *Mary Poppins*.

'No, of course he's not all right, someone hit him with a sledgehammer and dragged his body away. We have to find him. Why were you stuck up a chimney?'

'To get this.' Bryant brandished a roll of filthy cloth tied with a piece of string. Together they stepped out of the fireplace. Bryant was completely black. The room looked like a bomb had gone off in it.

'What is it?' asked May.

Bryant coughed out something unpleasant, then dropped to the floor and tugged at the string on the roll. 'It's the missing painting. Primrose is the only room with an unlit fire. Behind the dampers in the chimneys of these old houses there's always a smoke shelf. That was where the thief put it.'

'Who?'

'Well, that's something I have to prove.'

'Can it wait? This is rather more important. I've got a murder weapon. Half-hidden inside some tree roots at the end of the property.'

'What about the body?'

'We need to conduct a proper search of the undergrowth. There's blood everywhere. I suppose he could have been buried, but I have a feeling our murderer has a nastier surprise up his – or her – sleeve. We'll have to get shovels.'

'That doesn't fit in with my hypothesis at all,' Bryant complained, ineffectually patting himself down. 'If it was a proper country house murder mystery it would be the guests who were bumped off, not the staff. The running order isn't right.'

'Wait, what hypothesis?' asked May, annoyed. 'You're supposed to be staying in touch with me. How can we work as a team if you keep holding stuff back?'

'It's just something that occurred to me a few minutes ago.' He blew into a white handkerchief, turning it black and leaving himself with a white nose. 'I may be wrong. I usually am. Not about that, though.'

He pointed at the canvas of Willem van de Velde the Younger's *Harbour Scene*, which had unrolled itself on the carpet. It showed so many unfurled sails against the sky that you could have been looking at a washing line.

'Not something I'd want on my wall, but I think I know who put it there.' Bryant sneezed revoltingly.

'Whatever is going on here?' asked Lady Banks-Marion

from the doorway. Once again she exhibited an annoying habit of talking only to May. 'This is really no time to play the fool.'

'We're not, your ladyship,' said May. 'My colleague has recovered your missing van de Velde.'

'I suppose I should thank him,' she said, 'but I'd rather you released my guests. And look at the mess you've made. We're all at the end of our tether. Why does he look like a minstrel?'

'I am here, you know.' Bryant coughed again, revealing a blackened tongue. 'If you'll bear with me for just a short while longer, your worshipfulness, I hope to have some answers for you.' He plonked himself down on the nearest chair and put his boots up on the one next to it.

'Not there, they're Hepplewhites!'

'I don't care whose they are, I'm knackered,' said Bryant.

'Arthur, we have to search for Fruity,' warned May.

'He'll have to hold on for a few minutes. If I can just find one last piece of the puzzle the rest will follow. And I think I know how to do it. Tell Alberman to assemble everybody in here.' He blew his nose again and made the mistake of looking in his handkerchief. 'Get him to bring me some old newspapers. And tea, lots of it. Cripey, I could get used to having servants.'

39

HAPPINESS IS A WARM GUN

It was, when everyone thought about it afterwards, an extremely bizarre gathering, a snippet from a forgotten British film, a page from a tattered paperback. Squeezed on to one rather fragile-looking sofa, looking as if they were waiting to see a dentist, were Slade Wilson, Vanessa Harrow and Toby Stafford. On chairs and in armchairs were Lord Banks-Marion, his mother, Monty Hatton-Jones, Norma Burke and Pamela Claxon. In addition to his neck bandage, Monty now had part of his head shaved and wore a pair of sticking plasters arranged in a cross, like a cartoon character who had suffered a mishap with an anvil.

May had handed the floor to his partner. Bryant had made a desultory attempt to wipe his face, but the result was more monstrous than before. He rose before them now, a lunatic lecturer in the physics of murder.

'Forgive me for handling this all backwards, but I think one solution leads to another,' he apologized. 'So I must start with the least important part, the stolen painting. When I heard it was missing I first suspected Reverend Patethric.' He paced before them excitedly. 'After all, he'd been a bit light-fingered around the church so it seemed reasonable to assume he'd know how to fence a painting. Even his parishioners had cottoned on to him.' He picked up one of the newspapers, rolled it and tied it in a knot, dropping it into the fireplace. 'Then I realized it couldn't be Trev the Rev.'

'Why not?' asked Wilson, raising a hand.

'The painting disappeared from its frame this morning. It's Sunday. The vicar was getting ready for the morning service at St Stephen's.'

'How do you know?' asked May.

'Because Mrs Bessel had a visit this morning from the lady who does the flowers at the church, and she saw the Reverend.' He knotted another newspaper and threw it into the grate. 'It had to be someone who was in the house between seven and nine. Sorry, it's a bit chilly in here.' Pulling out a box of matches, he struck one and touched its flame to the tangle of newspapers. 'It didn't seem a very female crime to me. I could be wrong, of course, but I thought the culprit might be someone who had dabbled in art and knew a little about marine paintings. I'm not saying an expert, but a person who lived in Greenwich, where the nation's biggest collection of maritime art is housed, someone who once worked in an auction house . . .' He turned to look into the fireplace, where the flames were flaring.

'All right!' Monty jumped up with his hands raised. 'Put out the fire! It's up the chimney!'

Bryant took the rolled painting from the sideboard and unfurled it. 'Would you like to explain why you stole it?'

Monty fell back into his chair, realizing he'd been had.

'For once in your life, Monty, tell the bloody truth,' warned May.

Hatton-Jones looked like someone who had just seen his true reflection in a mirror. 'I've been a fool,' he said. 'A middle-aged man chasing after a beautiful young woman.'

'An *overweight* middle-aged man,' added Pamela Claxon ungraciously.

'From the moment I set eyes on her I knew I was in terrible trouble.'

'Where was this?' asked May.

'At the Chelsea Drugstore on the King's Road.' Monty sat with his eyes downcast, keen to avoid Vanessa's gaze. 'I watched her dancing, so happy and carefree, as if she could do anything and go anywhere without having to think about it for a second. I was too old for all of that. My father made sure I started work the week after I left university. I was expected to be responsible and mature. But every business I tried my hand at failed, and the debts quickly mounted.'

'Oh, spare us the sob story, Raffles,' Claxon retorted before being cautioned by May.

'It was Toby Stafford who spoke to her first,' Monty continued. 'I knew him from Oxford, of course. The two of them started chatting, and he introduced me. But he did more than that. He made me out to be some kind of property millionaire. I saw her eyes light up, and realized she wasn't so innocent after all. But it didn't matter. Just to be in her presence was delightful.' He finally looked over at Vanessa, embarrassed. 'She soon found out the truth about me, though. Then she got the job at Donald Burke's club. She couldn't sing – she didn't have to. She could just stand there and people would applaud.'

'Did you know that Miss Harrow was going to be here this weekend?' Bryant asked.

'He couldn't have known,' said Harrow. 'I only decided to come at the last minute. That's why I was late for dinner on Friday.'

Monty looked shocked. 'Of course I didn't know. The entire weekend was arranged for Donald Burke, to make sure that he wouldn't back out of the deal. He was buying Tavistock Hall; he was the only one who mattered. The rest of us were just invited here as window dressing.'

Slade Wilson, who knew more about window dressing than most, looked highly displeased.

'When I heard that Lord Banks-Marion had sold him the house without even carrying out a full inventory on the paintings, I decided he wouldn't miss one.' Monty dropped his head into his hands.

'I had to include the paintings,' said Harry. 'I was scared that Burke might back out.'

The truth dawned on May. 'That's why you didn't want to leave, Monty. You couldn't take the picture any earlier in case we noticed it was missing. You thought that with everything else going on you could get away with it. You didn't reckon on my partner, Hawkeye.'

'And I wouldn't have noticed it without Herne the Hunter's help,' said Bryant, mystifying everyone.

'I thought I could sell the painting and pay off my debts, perhaps even win Vanessa back,' said Monty. 'If she only stayed with me for a few days it would be worth it.' He winced. 'I'm an absurdity.'

'Well, yes. You're not a murderer, though,' said Bryant.

'How can you be so sure?' Lady Banks-Marion asked.

'Because I have a few ideas about who is,' Bryant replied. ' "There is nothing more deceptive than an obvious fact." Sir Arthur Conan Doyle wrote that. You just need to ask yourself what the most obvious fact in this case is.'

'You know you told me to inform you when you were being unnecessarily mysterious and annoying?' said May. 'You're doing it right now.'

'With good reason, as I hope you'll soon see,' Bryant said.

'But we have to find Fruity. He could be lying injured somewhere—'

Bryant ignored him. 'Monty, you can make amends for your misdeed. If Lady Banks-Marion chooses not to press charges, we might see our way to overlooking the whole unfortunate incident with the painting.'

'Why would I do that?' asked the matriarch, arching an eyebrow.

'Because there's something that Monty doesn't know. Lady Banks-Marion, you knew your son had undervalued everything when he included the house contents in the sale, so you substituted copies of the paintings you wanted to keep, and not very good copies at that. I mentally compared Willem van de Velde the Younger's *Harbour Scene* with its facsimile in one of the books in the library. When you're copying a maritime scene it's a good idea to make sure you've matched the ships with the requisite number of masts. So perhaps, your ladyfulness, you can let him off the hook.'

Monty's face flooded with relief. 'I'll do anything you require.'

'We need to make sure that you testify at tomorrow's trial,' Bryant told him. 'But before that, we need to use you as bait.'

It felt a little like staking a rather portly goat out in a field for a dragon.

They sent Monty on to the driest part of the patio with a cigar and made him smoke the whole thing, first making sure that no one else could be seen on the same side of the house. As church bells rang in the distance, he stood self-consciously puffing away between the great stone urns that heralded the entrance to the gardens, attempting to look utterly unconcerned, trying not to consider the possibility that another stone gryphon might drop from the sky and flatten him.

The sky had once more dimmed to a dusk-like gloom, and the next downpour began. Autumn, the time when England decided to sandwich four seasons into each day, had arrived. Monty nervously strolled back and forth beyond the edge of the pelting rain, trying to pretend that he was just out there having a ponder.

'This is no good,' said May from behind the curtain in Lupin. 'Nobody's going to have a go at him under these conditions. It has to be when he's least expecting it.'

Sensing that they would start arguing again, Bryant had

released everyone from their incarceration together on the condition that they remained inside the house, but it was like herding cats. Only Pamela Claxon remained to watch Monty's performance.

'Can you go to the other end of the lawn?' Bryant asked. 'Alberman gave me these.' He produced a pair of bulky walkie-talkies and handed one to May. 'They're used by the beaters. Make sure you stay in my field of vision.'

May pocketed the handset and headed out across the grass. Monty lit another cigar and began strolling theatrically once more. He was shivering with cold and looked as miserable as a shot dog. May waited in the rain for twenty minutes.

Bryant watched them but was unable to stop himself from perusing a book, *A Popular History of British Seaweeds* by Reverend D. Landsborough. Empathy had never been his strong point.

May was about to give up when he saw one of Lord Banks-Marion's ashram acolytes wandering from the walled garden towards the spot where their decoy was pacing. Monty tried to shoo Donovan away with an elaborate set of hand signals, but the boy in the poncho and Indian beads was too stoned to notice.

'Hey, man,' he called, 'is that a Cuban cigar? Because Che Guevara is so cool.'

'You do know that he had a great many of his compatriots shot?' Monty pointed out.

The lad came closer, hopping up on to the patio. 'I just like his beret. I have his poster and everything.'

'Get away, you ridiculous little beanpole, you'll ruin everything.'

'What's your problem, dude? Hey, let me—' He reached for the cigar.

Something whizzed between them, causing a piece of brickwork to fly from the wall beside the library windows. Monty spun around and fell to his knees. Taking fright, the boy fell over his own feet and stumbled back to the safety of the yurt.

Bryant ran out on to the patio. Monty raised a hand to him in horror. 'I've been bloody shot!' he cried, displaying crimson fingers.

'It's only a bit of your ear,' said Bryant. 'Nobody needs lobes. It's just a nick. Get the housekeeper to bandage it. Then stay in the kitchen with the cook, away from all the windows.'

He looked about but May had already raced off in the direction from which the bullet had come. Moments later he was crashing about in the undergrowth, hunting the hunter.

40

VOODOO CHILD

'Where are they now?' asked Roger Trapp, passing a hand over his hair. 'Please tell me they're on their way back.' He was even more unhappy about being dragged into the unit on a Sunday morning, but Gladys Forthright had insisted on him coming into Bow Street. The bad weather was now hitting the metropolis. The streets around Covent Garden Market were inundated. At the weekends straw and cabbage leaves from the vegetable sellers got washed into the gutters and blocked them when it rained.

'Tavistock Hall is cut off,' Gladys explained. 'It rained all night and flooded the only road in.'

'You mean they can't get out and we can't reach them?'

'I've been in touch with the local constabulary. It usually subsides enough to let cars through after a few hours. The bad news is that they won't risk sending a team in at the moment.'

'Hell's bells, why not?'

'There was a violent protest march at Canterbury College last night and some students are staging a lock-in. Their team's still tied up dealing with it.'

'Isn't there anyone else in the area who works on a bloody Sunday?'

Gladys checked her telephone pad. 'There's another team at Deal, but I haven't been able to raise them.'

'Good God, this is a murder investigation at one of the great country houses of Britain, not a shoplifting incident at the Co-op,' Trapp complained. 'If the upper classes can't get protection what chance do the rest of us have?'

Gladys sensed that the indifference of the Canterbury team was partly annoyance that a pair of London-based detectives had already encroached upon their territory. One officer had told her: 'If they're already there, why the hell can't they handle it?'

Was it a good idea to tell Roger everything she knew? He would hear the details sooner or later. 'I'm afraid John and Arthur still haven't been able to make an arrest,' she admitted.

'My God, what an utter disaster. A simple babysitting job. I should have known.' Trapp fumed and paced. 'I should have made them stay home, here at the unit. At least they wouldn't have been able to do much damage.* Did you try the army? They're in the area, aren't they?'

'They won't lend us their helicopter. I got the official line, that their work is of international importance and takes precedence over local problems.'

Like every head of the PCU before and after him, Trapp's rage was so driven by frustration with his detectives that a prescription for sedatives should have come with the job. He wondered if Kasavian had set him up. The Home Office had an antipathy towards specialist units and was fond of using them to score political points.

Gladys did have one card left to play. A friend of Bryant's was staying in Knotsworth and could probably reach Tavistock

---

* Arthur Bryant would later manage to burn down the unit at Mornington Crescent just by 'staying home'.

Hall by bicycle. The phone line at the Red Lion was still working. She pulled down her telephone directory and looked up the number.

Maggie Armitage might have followed a different path had she not started dating a student of the late Aleister Crowley. As a boyfriend he had proven to be a bit of a non-starter but he showed her that atavistic shamanism, when used with an understanding of modern psychology, could sometimes ease the pain of troubled lives. Maggie embarked on an inordinate number of courses from dowsing to spirit revival. Her curiosity was unbounded, and her church was broad enough to encompass clairvoyance, biorhythmic feedback and harvest festivals.

She had met Arthur Bryant at the Wigmore Hall, where they were attending a talk entitled 'Whither Wicca?' by Dame Maude Hackshaw. He was young, she was younger and something might have come of that if they hadn't got into an argument about phrenology.

Maggie could have been a nurse or a psychologist but for her own empathy issues: she had far too much. (She cried watching the six o'clock news, and took home badly kept dogs until their outraged owners found her and snatched them back.) Instead she managed to find the most obscure way of helping others that did not involve making any money: white magic. A perpetual student, she was currently a Grand Order Grade II White Witch and had just joined the Coven of St James the Elder in Kentish Town, where much of her work currently involved feeding tramps.

It would have been easy to write her off as another kindly London eccentric but for her uncanny ability to find the truth in others. She was more often right than wrong in her estimations. Whether this was down to a genuinely attributable psychic ability or fortuitous guesswork was hard to say, but she had demonstrated her powers of foresight often enough that her neighbours were spooked by her, and consulted her before they caught aeroplanes or put up shelves.

When she received a phone call from Gladys Forthright, Maggie unthinkingly agreed to help.

'You haven't heard what I'm going to ask you yet,' said Gladys.

'Sorry, I thought you wondered what I was doing in Kent?'

'I was about to ask. What *are* you doing?'

'Where, dear?'

'In Kent.'

'Yes I am. Quite near Arthur, as it happens.'

'But you don't know where he is.'

'Isn't he at Crowshott?'

'Well, yes, he is.'

'There you are, you see. That's how I know.'

'But I didn't tell you.'

'Yes you did.'

'That was just then. I didn't tell you earlier.'

'Well somebody must have. You want me to look in on him.'

'Are you telling me?'

'No, I'm saying do you want me to look in on him.'

'Yes, if you're—'

'—in the area, I know.'

That was how conversations with Maggie tended to unfold. It could be quite confusing at times, and quickly had Gladys wondering whether she had been psychically coerced into calling her. But for once, as Maggie stood on the steps of Tavistock Hall in her sunshine-yellow mackintosh, matching plastic rain-hat and wellingtons, with her bicycle held upright in one hand and a bell-pull in the other, Bryant beat her by opening the door.

'You. How did you get here?' he asked rudely.

'I carried my bike over my head. It's nice to see you too, Arthur. You look like a panda. What on earth have you been doing?'

'Sorry, Maggie, we're having a disastrous weekend. It's turned into an Agatha Christie novel.'

'You mean short?'

'No, absurd. You have a knack for this sort of thing. Perhaps you can help.'

'I should cocoa. I've been up here before, chum.' She blew a scarlet curl from her eyes. 'I was hired to cleanse the house's aura. His lordship found me through my ad in *Time Out*. I just sprinkled some herbs about and sang madrigals. It paid for my spirit harmonium, and my bike.'

'Aren't you a bit young for Miss Marple?' asked Pamela Claxon, peering over Bryant's shoulder at the new visitor. 'Are we going to let everyone in now to have a poke about? Why don't we send for Hercule Poirot and Lord Peter Wimsey?'

'Aren't they fictional? Mr Bryant and I have worked together before,' Maggie explained.

'What, and you just happened to be passing? Jolly good piece of luck, wasn't it? Well, as all the normal laws governing chance seem to have been suspended, come on in, why not?' She took a drag on a Benson & Hedges Special Filter and jetted smoke over their heads.

'I don't think you have a say in this, Miss Claxon,' said Bryant, 'seeing as you're one of the suspects.'

'Are you Pamela Claxon?' asked Maggie, looking up at her in awe. 'The author of the Inspector Trench novels?'

'Yes I am,' said Claxon with unfeigned delight. 'Have you read them?'

'Yes. *Trench Steps In*, and *Trench Strikes Back*.'

'Did you enjoy them?'

'No, they were dreadful.'

'Then why did you read two?'

'I thought the first one might have been some kind of awful anomaly.'

'Then I hope you can do better than Inspector Trench, even dressed as a banana. He'd have sorted this mess out by now,' announced the irate author, blasting off in a backfire of blue smoke.

'Let me fill you in,' said Bryant, taking Maggie's arm and

walking her under the dripping, shadowed eaves where they would not be overheard.

'Death has spread his wings over this house.' She climbed on to the remains of a stone pedestal and looked up at the roof as if expecting to find some great dark creature crouching there.

'It has a human form, Maggie. Don't do this.'

'But I can feel a presence.' She touched the plastic ruby-coloured beads that looped around her neck.

'It's a crime scene, not a site of paranormal significance.'

'It's the birthplace of the Beast of Crowshott. I read about it in the local paper.'

'You mean the raven-duck-wolf-type-thing that stalks the fields at night?'

'Well, it's not a real beast, obviously.' Maggie jumped down from the wall and walked beside him. 'The idea came about because the villagers wanted to think badly of Tavistock Hall.'

'What do you mean?'

'The old lord's grandfather had a twin brother, Rowley, who was born with the same features but without a fully developed brain. He wasn't allowed to leave Tavistock Hall because he was a danger to himself, but one day he slipped away and walked into the village, to the old inn that stood where the Goat and Compasses now stands. Rowley had another distinguishing feature: a mark on the palm of his right hand. He demanded ale, and when the landlord saw his hand he refused to serve him.'

'Why?'

'Country superstition,' said Maggie. 'Rowley explained that he had allowed a thorn to enter his flesh and it had "turned sour" – gone septic, I imagine – until it was removed and cured with mercury. But the folk around here believed that Satan had a way of entering people through their skin in what was known as an "insert". A sliver of metal or human bone, a splinter or a thorn would be purified with a Satanic incantation, so that it could have a demon attached to it.'

'And it was introduced into the body to make the sufferer a disciple of Satan?'

'That's roughly the idea.'

Bryant nodded sagely. 'Interesting. Does your story have even the faintest trace of relevance?'

Maggie ignored him. 'The landlord decided that the boy was possessed, and his worst fears were confirmed when he heard Rowley speak, because he rambled and said he had ridden to the village with witches. To cut a long story short, they tied him to a tree and cut off the offending limb. Rowley bled to death. Everyone thought that the lord of the manor took it rather well, all things considered, and granted the landlord a pardon. He interred Rowley's body in the family graveyard at the end of the field, but for some reason the arm with the Satanic mark was buried separately nearer the house, and it was said that a hawthorn tree grew out of it.'

'There's a hawthorn just outside the window of the reception room,' said Bryant. 'Let me guess. From that tree came the Beast of Crowshott.'

'Creatures always seem to spring from the ground. One thinks of the Hydra's teeth. Of course it wasn't until later that anyone realized what had actually happened. Rowley's brother had arranged the whole thing with the landlord of the inn, to end the embarrassment of his witless brother once and for all. After the deed was done the landlord was found stabbed to death in a field. Ever since then it's been a tradition to employ a groundsman at Tavistock Hall with only one arm as a protection against the Devil.'

'Fruity wondered why he was given the job so easily,' said Bryant. 'We think he's been done in. So what was the moral?'

'Toffs are tricky,' said Maggie airily.

'We haven't located the remains of Fruity's body, but I suppose this means he's been disposed of in some manner that befits the legend. What does this beast do, by the way?'

'Oh, the usual thing, appears at midnight, roars three

times, eats you. Some of the more credulous villagers still won't come here after dark.'

'Well, thanks for cheering me up, Maggie. We already have thunderstorms, cut phone lines and a psychotic murderer roaming the premises. I knew there was something missing. All we need now is some kind of biblical plague, perhaps a rain of frogs. That would make it the perfect weekend.'

John May pushed his way through the undergrowth and found himself looking down at the spot from which the shooter must have fired. A pair of perfectly clear boot prints were indented in the mud, possibly a soldier's army boots, although he supposed they could have belonged to Pamela Claxon, who dressed in a somewhat masculine fashion and was fully prepared for the countryside. *Except it couldn't be her,* he realized, *because I saw her watching Monty stroll about.* He knew he wouldn't get any kind of a match on the prints without forensic equipment.

A search around the prints produced the single discharged brass cartridge. *The attacker didn't even bother to pick it up,* he thought. *I suppose it's possible one of those blithering idiots involved in the Anglo-French war games might have fired in the wrong direction and winged Monty by mistake.*

In the mud lay several cigarette ends, roll-ups with home-made filters made of cardboard. *Perhaps it's one of the hippies, although it hardly fits with their peace and love ethic. What would they gain by taking potshots at Monty? Their worlds are too far apart. Of course, Monty does look like their definition of the Man.*

He glanced across the field to the house. A single slat of sunlight had appeared through parted clouds and illuminated the façade so that it stood out against the flat green slope of the surrounding fields like a pop-up card. From this distance Tavistock Hall appeared so timeless and elegant that it was impossible to imagine the terminal collapse within. It was like the State of England, a carapace forged and hardened over centuries that hid the hushed disquiet of its inhabitants.

As he watched from the end of the lawn, Bryant appeared, accompanied by an elfin figure in a yellow mackintosh and gumboots, who marched with legs straight and arms thrown wide like a child avoiding puddles. As she came nearer he realized that only one woman could match Bryant's vivid description.

Extending a hand, he introduced himself. 'Hello, I'm John May, I work with Arthur.'

'Oh, I've heard so much about you, you poor man.' She smiled until her eyes vanished to crescents. 'I'm Lord Banks-Marion's witch. Your friend here was very kind to me once. Or at least he will be.'

'Was I? Will I be?' asked Bryant, confused.

'You must excuse me, I'm suffering from temporal displacement. A change in the weather. Maggie Armitage.' She shook May's hand with a rattle of her charm bracelet, then turned it over sharply. 'Goodness, what a long lifeline. Teeming with incident. Two accusations of murder, I see, but not until you're much older.'

May spoke over Maggie's head. 'Arthur, there was a bullet case where he was standing. He's not bothering to cover his tracks now.'

'You don't know it's a he,' said Maggie. 'Always leave the possibilities of gender open.'

May looked down and began to form a strong dislike of this strange flame-haired little woman. 'Arthur says you perform magic rituals,' said May.

'I take it you're a non-believer?'

'If you're talking about those *News of the World* articles featuring naked women dancing around bonfires in the woods, you're right, I'm not,' said May.

'Not a non-believer? Or not a believer? Let's see if I can change your mind,' said Maggie. 'Open your hand.'

As he did so, she held her fingers over his palm and a bright orange spark cracked between them.

'Ow!' May snatched his hand back and rubbed it. There was a blackened spot roughly in the shape of a star at the centre of his palm. 'What was that?'

'I don't know but it hurts like buggery, doesn't it? I learned how to do it but not what it's for. I can teach you if you like.'

'Can't you do something useful?' asked Bryant. 'Exorcize the dining room, summon Asmodeus to guard Monty?'

'I can't perform a ritual cleansing today.' Maggie sniffed the air. 'The air is too damp. An altered atmosphere can play havoc with the Seven Stewards of Heaven. White magic is a soothing balm to the soul but in bad weather it's like being on a roller coaster after eating a pork casserole. I could manage a general spell against the presence of evil. I'll need lavender, ginger, sandalwood and at least seven pounds of salt. And a rat, preferably a white one. I'm staying over at Maureen's in Knotsworth. She usually has the right equipment, but she's still in trouble with the villagers after influencing the outcome of the Easter pageant.'

'Why?' asked Bryant. 'What happened?'

'Jesus didn't come back and the Devil won.' She touched his lapel. 'Arthur, I tell you these things because you understand. You're not like your partner here. He is clearly the sun and you are the moon. You appreciate the power of the night.'

That was the last straw for May. With a roll of his eyes he beat a retreat to the house.

'We're running out of time, Maggie,' Bryant said. 'Is there any way you can help?'

'It's down to you, I'm afraid. You need to release your natural instincts. You're so bottled up inside. It's not just about your brain, it's about this.' She placed her hand over his heart. 'You have to read emotions, not just things. I saw some hippies; I think we should talk to them.'

'No, I've already tried that,' said Bryant, looking down

towards the musky mud-pit in the walled garden where the yurt and various teepees were erected.

'There's no use in me talking to the toffs, old sausage, I won't get anything out of them. Always start with the outsiders.' Maggie waved him away. 'Let me do this; you have no patience. I'll be back shortly.'

'But if they ask who you are—'

'They're not going to, are they?' said Maggie. 'They're hippies.'

She set off down the field towards the ashram, drawn by the scent of incense and the plangent twang of a sitar.

41

REVOLUTION

Maggie stepped beneath garlands of plastic marigolds and made her way to the Mongolian yurt. Several of the smaller tents had keeled over in the rain, so the largest yurt was now crowded with green nylon sleeping bags.

'Hello, I'm Maggie,' she said brightly, giving a peace sign. Ignoring the overpowering smell of patchouli and marijuana, she unbuttoned her rain slicker to reveal her Andy Warhol-inspired Mary Quant smock and cyclamen-coloured leggings.

Rising above the smoky, torpid atmosphere, a girl greeted her with the kind of hug an infant would give its mother. Clearly she recognized a kindred spirit in the white witch.

'Peace,' she said. 'I'm Melanie. Would you like some nettle tea?'

'I'd absolutely *love* some,' said Maggie, dropping down and sitting cross-legged on the floor. Melanie had the look of someone lost but hopeful of finding the way. There was such innocence in her eyes that a small sound of pity caught in Maggie's throat.

Melanie lit a primus stove and placed a tin pot on it. 'This is Donovan,' she said, pointing to an emaciated young man with Edwardian sideburns and skin so pale it could have bathed the tent in moon-glow. He raised a hand in greeting and went back to his book, a dog-eared copy of *Making of a Counter Culture: Reflections on the Technocratic Society and Its Youthful Opposition.* Somewhat incongruously, Donovan also seemed to have a stack of ancient girlie magazines with titles like *Mayfair, Fiesta* and *Razzle.*

'And that's Victoria,' Melanie added. Victoria was wearing an orange petticoat, a red cape, granny specs and a floppy purple felt Jimi Hendri hat. She also sat cross-legged, sketching on an A2 pad. She set down her pencil and grinned toothily. 'Hello there.'

'I thought I'd find Harry here,' said Maggie, looking around the sea of shaggy afghan coats, cooking pots, giant paper flowers, rubbish bags and assorted junk.

'He doesn't come down from the house when he has his wealthy guests staying,' said Melanie. 'He can't adjust his karma fast enough.'

'Well, he may have a point there,' said Maggie tactfully. 'Doesn't he let you go to the house?'

'His lordship doesn't want us in there, darling,' said Victoria, licking her thumb and smudging her pad. 'The last time we snuck in Donovan broke a pot. A hideous piece of chinoiserie, but apparently rather valuable. We can't get back on the road because we've got no bread. At least, not until Harry gets the money from the house.'

'What will you do then?'

'Maybe we'll head to Norfolk. Or Peru. Somewhere safe, before everything collapses.'

Maggie leaned forward with interest. 'Why, have you heard something? Is society going to collapse?'

'It'll just get incrementally greedier and more poisoned.' She considered her drawing from one angle, then another. 'The music is dying, the dream is over, youth power is over, one world is over. Last year, when all the riots happened, I thought everything would change. But we blew it. We should have lain down in front of the tanks.'

Maggie waited and watched while Melanie poured tea for them. 'Is Harry going to come with you?'

'His girlfriend is here and she's pregnant, so I bloody hope so.' Victoria gestured at Melanie. 'Although he's a Buddhist Catholic, so anything could happen.'

'Oh, congratulations,' said Maggie, although nobody looked very pleased. 'How long?'

'Five months,' said Melanie, gingerly touching her minuscule bump. 'I'd like us to get settled somewhere before winter comes, maybe find a squat in London.'

Maggie had an image of Melanie's child being delivered in a frost-covered tent and shivered inwardly. 'Yes, somewhere warm and safe would be a good idea.' She sipped her tea. They drank in silence, listening to the falling rain on the canvas roof.

'Why are you here?' asked Victoria.

'There's been some trouble at the house. The pigs are coming today, so you might want to put those away.' She nodded at Donovan's joint. 'Just for a while.'

'Oh, wow, thanks,' said Melanie gratefully. 'We can't afford to get into trouble, not now.'

Maggie studied them with concern. 'Will you please all be very careful? There could be someone dangerous out there. And the army's firing live rounds.'

'Teaching to kill instead of learning to love,' said Victoria. ' "O brave new world, that has such people in't." '

'You haven't seen anything strange going on, have you?' She looked from one drawn face to the next. *These are malnourished kids,* she thought. *They're harmless innocents.*

'It depends on what you mean by strange.' Victoria picked up some sheets of drawing paper. 'The whole world is strange.'

'I agree,' said Maggie. 'That's why I'm training as a white witch.' That caught everyone's attention.

'You are? We study paganism,' said Donovan.

'Oh, which branch?'

Donovan gave her a blank look. 'What do you mean?'

'Paganism simply refers to any of the pre-Christian religions,' Maggie explained. 'Nobody ever used the term before this century. Most pagan religions express a world view that's pantheistic, animistic or polytheistic, although there are some monotheistic pagans too.'

'Wow,' said Melanie. 'That's so cool. Can you, like, magnetize stuff?'

'No, dear,' said Maggie.

'Bummer. 'Cause our van needs fixing.'

Victoria seemed to reach a decision. 'Here, you can have a look through these if you like. I sketch almost everything I see. I did these of the house.' She handed over the papers.

'I've got a camera but she won't use it,' said Donovan. 'She doesn't draw realistically.'

'I draw what's inside,' said Victoria, tilting her head at the page. 'I studied at Goldsmiths'. When you draw you can see things that don't appear on camera film. You catch the soul. Don't you think that's true, Maggie?'

'I certainly do.' Maggie studied the sketches carefully. The images of the hall were beautifully rendered. Sinister skies roiled around the roof like ocean waves, as if something was about to reach down and snatch the building up into the sky. 'May I borrow some of these for a while?'

'Feel free. We're not rushing off anywhere.'

'Don't you have family?' Maggie asked Melanie. 'Isn't there someone who worries about you?'

'Her father threw her down the stairs and kicked her out into the street when he found out she was pregnant,' said Victoria. 'That's the milk of Christian kindness for you. She nearly lost the baby. She needed love and understanding, not violence. We're her family now.'

Maggie thanked Melanie for the tea and climbed back out into the rain.

42

CHAIN OF FOOLS

May found Monty wandering about the kitchen, getting in the way of Mrs Janverley. With the huge plaster stuck over his right ear complementing the ones on his head and the bandages around his neck, he was looking increasingly like a St John's Ambulance practice dummy.

'Don't you want to come up and wait with us?' asked May.

Monty looked at him as if he was mad. 'What, and risk getting shot again? I'm staying down here, away from the windows. And away from you.'

'And he's in *my* way,' the housekeeper complained. 'I'm not used to cooking. Mrs Bessel's got family. We had to let her go back to Crowshott. It wasn't fair to keep her here.'

'But we told you specifically not to let anyone leave,' said May, exasperated.

Mrs Janverley busied herself with something brown and contumacious in a huge ceramic bowl. 'I didn't expect anyone to still be with us. Now I have to find food for them all. It's going to be potted meat tonight. I'm sorry, I know there are troubles but what's going on up there on your floors has nothing to do with us down here.'

'How can you say that?' asked May. 'Mr Parchment is dead.'

'I wish you'd stop calling him that now.' She punched at the dough. 'His name was Prabhakar, Ernest Prabhakar, but the old lord couldn't pronounce it. Insulting it is, to change a man's name.'

May tried another gambit. 'I heard that a maid was once murdered in the house.'

'Whatever happened to her was probably because of her own foolishness,' said Mrs Janverley uncharitably. 'They throw themselves at the boys, and never do what they're told. You think I'm being harsh but I've seen these young girls come and go. It was worse when the old lord was still with us.'

'What do you mean?'

Mrs Janverley harrumphed a little obviously. 'The usual shenanigans,' she explained. 'When men of a certain age get among young girls. Especially when they're paying their wages. I don't mind telling you, I'm not going to miss this place. It can't go too soon for me. I'm off to my sister's in Margate. Keep your hands out of that.' She slapped Monty's hand, which was straying towards her dough. 'It's going to be a simple menu tonight. It wouldn't be respectful serving a traditional dinner after a death in the house.'

'I'll be glad to get back to London,' said Monty. 'Your forensic wallahs were supposed to be here by now. Where are they?'

'I don't know,' May admitted. 'The phone still isn't working.' He picked up the walkie-talkie Alberman had found for him and used it to call Bryant. 'Where are you?'

'Hello. Come in. I can hear you. Over. Sorry, not over, I haven't finished.'

'Take your finger off the button. Take—'

'I've gone down to the road to see if it's still flooded. If it is I'll push on to Crowshott and call London. I'll get us airlifted out of here tonight if I have to. Can you hear me? Over.'

'You can't get all of us out, Arthur. It'll mean splitting the group up and losing our killer.'

'Perhaps not. "They are all guilty." But they're not though, are they? Over.'

'What do you mean? Over.'

'Not all victims are innocent, and not all murderers are guilty. Over.'

'I have absolutely no idea what you're talking about. Has that strange woman gone?'

'You forgot to say over. I'll call you on this thing when I get back. Over.'

'Wait, are you going to talk to London?'

'I'm going for a pint. Thinking is thirsty work and I'm spitting feathers. I won't be long. Over and off.' He released his button, leaving May staring at the walkie-talkie, dumbfounded.

The saloon bar of the Goat & Compasses was even emptier than usual, except for the one stool occupied by Celeste. Bryant felt his heart lift upon seeing her.

'Oh, there you are. I thought you'd gone back to London,' she said carelessly, indicating her empty gin glass to the barman with her own personalized silver swizzle stick.

'I still have your car,' he said.

'I wondered what I'd done with that. Don't worry, I have others.' She tapped out a cigarette. 'My husband collected them. He liked them almost as much as his wives. You've got soot in your ears.'

'Yes, I got stuck up a chimney.'

'We usually have someone in for that. How's it going up at Murder Manor?'

'It looks like we have to stay a little while longer.' He ordered himself a pint of bitter.

'So you're no closer to nailing your culprit?'

'Well, I think I know what's been going on.'

'So what are you doing in the pub?'

'I need tangible proof before I can make an arrest.'

'And how do you go about getting that?'

'I have some ideas.' He turned to her. 'One of the guests is a crime novelist, Pamela Claxon.'

'I know her. Rather spiky, wears too many Jaeger jumpers. She lives just up the road.'

'She keeps reminding me that her fictional detective would be able to solve the case. She's right; it feels like one of her murder mysteries.'

'Perhaps that's what you want it to be,' said Celeste, sipping her fresh gin.

'You're probably right,' sighed Bryant, gulping his beer. 'I read too much. Even before anything had happened I was looking for suspects.'

'You of all people should know that nothing is ever as tidy as it is in a novel. Real life is messy and incomprehensible. You wouldn't think such peculiar things could happen.' She turned to study him. 'I was reading about Charles Manson this morning. Did you know he used to babysit Grandpa Munster's children? True story. You can't make up that kind of illogic.' She looked over to a table where two old men were playing dominoes. 'I suppose you have to discover where the chain of events began.' She smoothed out his lapel.

'You mean find the first domino and the rest will fall into place. Celeste, you're a marvel.'

'I know.' She winked at him.

Five minutes later Bryant left the pub and rang Gladys again. The sergeant assured him that the forensic experts were finally on their way. They had agreed to take over the investigation, leaving him and May to concentrate on shepherding Monty back to London. The sergeant had some other news, even less palatable.

A sense of catastrophe flooded over him.

It was doubly galling to realize that where the PCU had failed, Canterbury Constabulary would probably succeed.

The hall's claustrophobic atmosphere prevented him from thinking clearly. He knew this was his last throw of the dice, and he had to make it count. Hanging up, he was about to set off, but decided to make one last call.

In order to get back to the hall Bryant needed to bypass the flooded lane, which meant that he was forced to stumble through swampy fields that sucked at his shoes. His *Student Prince* trousers had gone the way of his *Hay Fever* turn-ups. He would have to resort to something fantastical left over from *Salad Days*.

He passed beneath a funereal line of crows hunched on sagging telephone wires. *I hate you,* he thought, *watching me with your impassive, beady little eyes.* Having arrived at the hall with an almost open mind, he had now come to loathe everything about the countryside. By the time he reached the house the clouds had darkened, and there were only candles to be seen in the windows.

He found everyone huddled miserably in Iris surrounded by out-of-date newspapers, unread books and dirty teacups. The enervated guests and their hosts barely bothered to look up when he entered. They reminded him of characters from a Buñuel film, unable to pass across thresholds and sunken into lassitude.

'Look here,' said Monty, who had been forced to vacate the kitchen before Mrs Janverley threw something serrated at him, 'is anyone turning up to look at these corpses or are we just going to leave them lying around? It's indecorous and unhygienic. And you still haven't found the rest of the groundsman. The housekeeper's frightened to open a cupboard in case he falls out. We can't stay here indefinitely.'

'It was raining too hard to conduct a proper search,' said Bryant. 'You'll be pleased to know that the forensics unit is finally on its way to us.' A feeble, sarcastic cheer went up, a further slap in the face. 'Until they get here, I suggest we all stay in the same room. I can have some blankets brought down.'

'I'm going to my suite,' said Lady Banks-Marion. 'I am not "dossing" here like one of those hippies in the garden.'

'They're good people, Mother,' said Harry, stroking Malacrida. 'They've just lost their way.'

'They've lost their minds,' she sniffed. 'And as for that pig, it should be put where it belongs, either tethered in a pen or rashered on a breakfast table. As for you two' – she stabbed a digit at the detectives – 'you weren't even invited here. You've done nothing but cause trouble from the moment you arrived. You brought all this filth with you, tracking it in like mud. From the city into our house.'

No one was listening. Lady Banks-Marion had lost her power to command. Now she was just an old lady querulously complaining to anyone who might show a flicker of interest.

Bryant tapped his partner on the shoulder. 'Before I forget, there's something else I have to tell you. We've been fired.'

May reeled. 'What are you talking about?'

'Roger Trapp went crackers when he found out what was going on here. It's not Gladys's fault. She had to tell him the truth. He called someone from Head Office. They're kicking us out whether or not we still manage to get Monty to the Law Courts in time to testify. There'll have to be a public inquiry, so it looks like our careers are over. As of tomorrow, you and I are free to seek new employment.'

'Thank you for that,' said May. 'You've just completed my day. This has been the worst weekend of my life.'

'You're right,' said Bryant. 'It's my fault. I waited too long to do what comes most naturally to me. I've been a fool. I should have acted earlier on my suspicions. I'll have to make up for it now. I need to put this right.' He rose and wandered vaguely from the room with his hands in his pockets.

'Does he always take things so personally?' asked Claxon.

'I don't fully understand how he reaches his conclusions but they take time,' said May. 'Unfortunately that's the one thing we don't have.'

43

CARDS ON THE TABLE

May found Bryant pacing before the shelves in the library. In times of great stress he always defaulted to books. On an oval mahogany table he had laid out the invitation cards that had been arranged in the hall upon everyone's arrival.

'It's not your fault,' said May. 'You did what you could. We should get Monty packed and ready to leave.'

Bryant ignored the comment. 'Look at this. This is how they were.' He picked up each of the cards in turn, studying them. 'The invitations. The guests left them on the hall table, remember? Monty said it's a country house tradition. In fact, these are the replies mailed back to the hall, each signed by its recipient. Apparently they stay here so that no one has cause to forget anyone's name over the weekend.'

'What of it?'

He pointed to each of the cards. 'They were laid down in the order of arrival, so Donald Burke and his wife were the first. But they weren't greeted by Lady Banks-Marion, or by Harry. None of us were.'

'So?'

'So it must have been Alberman who let them in, except that he says he didn't. Then who did?'

'I don't know. Parchment? Are you saying it had something to do with his death?'

'No, but it was where the weekend started. Celeste put an idea into my head, that if you find the first domino you'll see how they all fell.'

'Who is Celeste?'

'The lady I met at the pub.'

'So you've been out drinking and picking up women while we've been trapped in here.'

'Look at them.' Bryant studied the invitations. 'The first domino. What happened right at the start?'

May gave a shrug. 'Lady Banks-Marion decided to hold a weekend party.'

'No, before that. Go back to before these invitations were laid down. The old lord died, leaving behind no money for the upkeep of Tavistock Hall. Lady Banks-Marion didn't know what to do. Her son had no interest in saving the house – he was off on a voyage of self-discovery. She became tired of being unable to pay the staff and having to put buckets everywhere to catch the rain. She let the servants go one by one. She hired Fruity as the new groundsman because he'd been badly injured and was therefore cheap, but it wasn't enough to keep everything going. It was clear that they were fighting a losing battle. So when Harry suggested they looked for a buyer, she was reluctantly forced to agree. With me so far?'

'Yes, that much is obvious,' said May.

Bryant removed the invitation reply signed by Toby Stafford. 'Harry met the lawyer. Stafford had a wealthy client who was looking to open a business academy outside London. Stafford hadn't even met this chap – to be fair, he didn't need to as his transactions are routinely handled over the phone and he and Burke were based in different parts of the country – but he had a feeling that Burke would be interested in the house. However, there was a problem. Burke didn't like holding his financial meetings in person, so Stafford came up with a solution. "Come down to Tavistock Hall and look it over," he suggested. "They'll hold a weekend party to provide you with some cover. You can come and go as you please. You don't have to meet anyone else. Just assess the investment and leave whenever you like. I'll take care of the rest." Harry attempted to make the house presentable, and emptied the family bank account in order to put on a spread. There was no time to get rid of the ashram and besides, he had no inclination to give his girlfriend and her pals their marching orders.'

Bryant removed the second invitation inscribed with Donald Burke's signature.

'Mr Burke was to be accompanied by his wife, Norma. She was used to acting as his intermediary. By her own admission she wasn't much use on a business trip but she could smooth things over, something she'd become used to doing since her husband's breakdown. Coincidentally Norma had a friend living in a nearby village, whom she asked if she could invite – Pamela Claxon.'

He picked up another card.

'Arthur, where are you going with this?'

'Bear with me. Burke had put in another request, probably through Toby Stafford, for Vanessa Harrow to attend. It all seemed terribly civilized between Norma and Vanessa. Harry didn't know who she was but anyone Burke wanted to bring was fine.' He removed Harrow's reply from the table.

'Who does that leave? Well, appearances must be kept up and a vicar was always invited, so along he came, Trev the Rev, just to keep everything normal. And Slade Wilson wangled an invite from Norma because somebody had to work out what on earth to do with the place once it was purchased.'

He took Trevor Patethric's invite from the table along with the one signed by Slade Wilson.

One card remained. 'So – who does that leave us with?'

'Monty.'

'How did he get his invite?'

May shrugged. 'Through Toby Stafford, of course.'

'Indeed. The lawyer was always at the centre of the circle. Monty pulled the old pals' act on him. But why was he so desperate to come?'

'Because he thought he might be able to get some money from Donald Burke.'

'For the purpose of . . . ?' Bryant teased.

'Buying Charles Chamberlain's company and wooing back Miss Harrow.'

'And what happened?' Bryant sailed the card before him. 'To Monty's horror Burke was found dead, leaving him with nothing. So in desperation he stole the painting.'

'Never underestimate the power of a pretty girl,' said May, who knew about such things. 'The poor goon is utterly lovestruck. In fact, quite a few of them are.'

'What do you mean?' It was Bryant's turn to look puzzled.

May was exasperated. 'Don't you notice anything? Monty's still in love with Vanessa Harrow, hippy Melanie is crazy for Harry, and Slade Wilson had his eye on the vicar.'

'Good Lord, how did I miss all that?'

'Because, my dear fellow, to understand the heart you have to look at people instead of listening to them. So where does this domino theory of yours take us?'

'I was just coming to that. You might be annoyed with me.'

May's voice had an edge. 'Why, what have you done?'

'Ah, there you are,' said Maggie, drifting into the room with a candle in her hand. 'I just introduced myself to the guests. Lord Banks-Marion was very excited to see me again.'

'Did you talk to the commune?' asked Bryant.

'I feel sorry for the flower children,' said Maggie wistfully. 'They just want what the rest of us want.'

'Without having to work for it,' said May.

'We're not all as well equipped as you,' said Maggie.

May looked down at his trousers in puzzlement.

'For life,' she added. 'They're lost.'

'No, they're at the end of the garden.' May was growing increasingly agitated by this strange little woman with wild red hair. It was clear that she brought all of his partner's most irritating traits to the fore. 'They may also be involved in ritual slaughter,' he said testily. 'Did you ask them if they'd heard of the Manson murders?'

'Of course not.' She was horrified by the thought. 'That's not a good way to get a friendship off on the right foot.'

'You're not supposed to be friends with them,' said May. 'They're present at a crime scene.'

'Very much so, which is why I brought you these.' Maggie handed over Victoria's watercolour sketches. 'One of the girls in the ashram has been drawing everything. They may be able to help.'

May dropped them on to the table dismissively. 'Arthur, why am I going to be annoyed?'

'Nobody's coming today,' said Bryant.

'You don't know that.' May looked at his watch. 'It's nearly one. The road's probably passable now – why, what have you done?'

Bryant looked at them both with such wide innocent eyes that they knew he was guilty of something. 'I rang them from the pub and told them to stay away even if the road was navigable.'

'This', said May, 'is the final, *final* straw. If we were putting everything at risk before, you've now destroyed our last chance.'

'You don't have much faith in me, do you?' said Bryant.

'I did, but you didn't come up with anything that made sense.'

'I have now.' Bryant tapped at the side of his head. 'I wasn't thinking clearly before.'

'About what?'

'The cause. You know the problem? It's too simple. I over-complicate everything. Conan Doyle said, "There is nothing more deceptive than an obvious fact." Alberman said, "They are all guilty." I know the answer, John.'

'You know you told me to tell you when you were being annoying?' said May.

It was then that a crash shook the floor of the room above, sending down a light dusting of plaster.

44

NOWHERE MAN

They took the stairs two at a time, accidentally slamming a surprised Alberman against the landing wall. 'Where did it come from?' shouted Bryant.

'Mr Hatton-Jones's room,' replied the butler, trying to right himself.

'He was under orders not to leave Lavender.'

May threw his shoulder against the bedroom door, which was unfortunate timing as Monty was just opening it. 'What's happening?' May shouted as Monty was knocked backwards.

'Someone's here in the room – over there!' Monty yelled, swinging an upturned candlestick at his invisible foe.

The afternoon gloom had dimmed the bedroom, but May had learned to keep a torch with him at all times. He could see a figure clearly outlined by the window. 'Stop,' he called, slamming the door behind him and leaving Bryant on the wrong side.

For a moment nobody moved. The figure darted left and bounced into the chest of drawers.

'He has a knife,' said Monty.

May dropped low and lunged. He grabbed a leg but a boot

stamped down on his shoulder, forcing him to let go. When he swung out, trying to connect, he saw a glimmer of metal and felt a sharp sting streak across his left arm. It had the delayed effect of a shaving cut, and he realized that their assailant was holding an open razor.

As May staggered to his feet, there was a slam of wood and the room was suddenly emptier. His torch had been knocked from his hand and had rolled under the bed. Groping for it, he flicked it back on. Monty was on all fours on the carpet, smeared with blood. There was no one else, and the bedroom door was still shut. When he managed to get it open, Bryant fell in.

'No one came out,' he said. 'Where's he gone?'

'The servants' passage,' replied May. 'It has to be accessible from this room.'

'You're bleeding.'

'It's not deep. Monty's taken another bashing.'

May peered out into the corridor, checking the passageway.

Bryant helped Monty to his feet. 'I was having a lie-down and when I looked up he was standing there beside the bed,' Monty said. 'I threw my brandy in his face but he still got me.' He felt around his hairline and showed Bryant the damage like a schoolboy revealing a cut to his mother.

'That's not so bad,' said Bryant. 'It's just a scratch.'

'That's what you said when I got part of my ear shot off.'

'Well, this is on the other side so it balances out. There'll be cotton wool and bandages in the kitchen. You know the drill. Then what happened?'

'I fell off the bed and sprained my wrist.'

'Over here,' called May. 'Some of these panels have been replaced.'

Alberman arrived as the pair searched for an access door. 'Did you know the closed parts of the servants' passage had been reopened?' Bryant asked.

'They've been closed off as long as I've been here,' replied the butler. 'One goes the full length of the house, right through the middle of it, and another runs behind the sealed-off windows, but they weren't used much after the old staff left.'

May knocked on the walls again, tracing the path of what he hoped were hollow panels. He ran his fingers around the borders but could find no catch, so he gave up and kicked at it, attempting to split the wood.

Bryant reached over and gently pressed the panel on its right-hand edge. The door popped open. 'Obviously your father never put in his own kitchen cupboards,' he said, taking up an oil lamp and climbing inside.

'Be careful,' called May. 'He has a razor.'

The passage was filthy and barely wider than his shoulders. *Servants must have been poorly fed in Victorian times to scurry about in here,* Bryant thought, raising the lamp. He was at the far end of the corridor, so was forced to turn around and make his way back.

Lights showed through the cracks in the boards at his feet but there was only one other doorway into a first-floor room. Stairs ran in both directions, even narrower, their tread-boards bent from a century of use. He made his way down, pausing to listen for any other movement. *So I'm wedged in a secret passage with a razor-wielding maniac,* he thought. *That's one for the memoirs.*

The stairs disappeared into darkness. On the wall beside him was written in neat penmanship:

1st Floor Willow Larch Elm Oak Beech Mulberry
Ground Floor Snowdrop Lavender Rose Lupin
  Primrose Iris Hawthorn

It was how staff delivered breakfast trays from the kitchen. He wondered how many of the rooms connected with each other for the purpose of illicit liaisons.

Somewhere below a door slammed, setting him off at a pace.

May stood in the darkness of the first-floor landing and listened intently. He could hear his partner thudding about inside the walls, but where was Monty's attacker? Whoever it was had to be returning downstairs to provide an alibi. He ran to the central staircase.

The others were still where he had left them. He conducted a panicked head count that left only Monty, Alberman and Mrs Janverley unaccounted for. There was nobody else. The ashram! It had to be someone from there. The members of the commune were hitting back at the titled occupants in charge of their fate. There were eight in all, Melanie, a tall girl, a child, that boy Donovan, others . . . but which of them?

'It's not an Agatha Christie at all, is it?' said Pamela Claxon, making him start. She had an odd smile on her face, as if she knew a secret.

'No,' he agreed, 'there's no dagger in the library.'

'You've cut yourself. All this—' She seemed about to tell him something, but changed her mind and closed her mouth.

They sat in the basement kitchen, among the racks of copper pots and pans that hung in descending order like percussion instruments. The long-suffering Monty had his right arm in a makeshift sling. Mrs Janverley examined the cut on his head and tutted. 'What a palaver you're making! It's barely more than a barber's nick. You only need a couple of stitches.'

'I'm appearing in court tomorrow.'

'If you want to make a decent impression on the judge you'd better wear a hat.'

'I'm not in the dock, you stupid woman, I'm a witness! I came here for a civilized weekend and I'll be going home looking like I've been in a Peckham gang fight.' Monty twisted about trying to see what she was doing. 'Do I really need stitches?'

The housekeeper opened the drawer of her kitchen table and pulled out a small cardboard box. In it were darning needles and thread.

'Wait, you can't just do that! There's no proper light in here.'

'I've worked in lower light than this before. Hold still.' She swabbed some alcohol on the cut.

'At least give me something to drink.'

'Don't be such a baby. It won't take long.'

'I'm serious,' warned Monty. 'I need a glass of brandy, a big one. I threw my last one in somebody's face. I have a terror of needles.'

Mrs Janverley released one of her patented weary sighs. 'Very well, I have some rum in the still room,' she said, hauling herself to her feet. 'Honestly, I've never known such a fuss.'

Monty lay back and closed his eyes while she went to find a bottle. The weekend had turned out to be infinitely more disastrous than he had feared, on top of which he had made a ridiculous fool of himself over a girl who wasn't even remotely interested in him.

He heard the bottle go down on the table behind his chair and was about to sit up for his tot of rum, but the figure that had appeared in his bedroom a few minutes ago was once more standing beside him, and before he knew what was happening had reached forward and put icy hands around Monty's throat.

Monty threw out his arm and found the handle of a saucepan on the hob beside him. It seared his palm but he still raised it and swung, slamming it into his attacker's face, showering them both with boiling water and over-salted carrots.

45

I FOUGHT THE LAW

'Monty,' said May, arriving in the kitchen at the same time as his partner. 'Do you have to keep doing this?'

Hatton-Jones was clutching his scalded face. The floor was slick with water and footprints. A dented copper pan lay on its side.

'You morons, he was right here!' cried Monty. 'I hit him with a saucepan full of carrots.'

'Carrots?' said Bryant, unerringly selecting the only unimportant word in the sentence. 'Where did he go? Wait, the still room. I heard the door slam.'

They ran for the rooms at the far end of the flagstone walk, torch beams illuminating a moth-eaten stag's head and a display of rusted swords. May tried to pull one free but it was securely bolted to the wall.

'Have you got any kind of weapon on you?' asked Bryant.

'I've got a steel comb,' said May.

They reached the still room and tried the door but it was stuck fast in the jamb. 'It's me,' called Mrs Janverley. 'Somebody shut me in. Mr Hatton-Jones is alone in the kitchen.'

They left the cook and ran across the corridor. Bryant's torch, already dim, faded out. 'You didn't put new batteries in when you came away?' asked May, looking back. 'Unbelievable.'

'I didn't know it was going to be this dark during the bloody day, did I? I thought the countryside would be more like Hyde Park.'

Stone steps led up to the wide-open back door. Rain was blowing in and pattering on to the flagstones. Monty stumbled out of the kitchen, pointing. 'Well, go after him!'

'Who was it?'

'Will you stop asking me that? I can't see in a bloody basement without lights, can I? Someone with thick arms, stocky and strong – probably Pamela Claxon.'

'Come with me.' Grabbing Monty by the arm, May frogmarched him upstairs to Iris while Bryant released the housekeeper with another enthusiastic kick of a door handle.

They were now all together in one place, in the reception room. Monty, shot at, bludgeoned, burned and half-strangled, was starting to feel the strain of the past forty-eight hours and all but fell on to an ottoman.

'Alberman, I don't want anyone leaving this room until we're through, do you understand?' warned Bryant. He looked around the room at eight drawn faces half-lost in the gloomy afternoon shadows. Vanessa and Lady Banks-Marion looked cold. Slade Wilson was anxiously biting his nails. Toby Stafford seemed more alert than the others, and was writing in the notepad perched on his knee. Pamela Claxon sat beside Norma Burke, comforting her. Lord Banks-Marion was a picture of sleepy befuddlement. Only the Reverend Patethric was missing. Even Maggie Armitage found herself a seat and settled beside the detectives.

Bryant turned to address the group. 'I need to ask you some final questions.'

'We deserve some answers,' said Lady Banks-Marion.

'And you'll get them, I promise. I'll tell you everything I

know.' He called to the door. 'Welcome back, Reverend, you're just in time. I'm glad you could join us.'

'I thought I should look in.' Trevor Patethric, still in his cassock, nodded awkwardly to the others and took his place among them. Alberman closed the door and stood in front of it. The scene had a ghostly chiaroscuro, actors waiting for a rising curtain.

Bryant first addressed the lawyer. 'Mr Stafford, am I right in thinking that you never met your client, Mr Burke?'

'That's right,' said Stafford, 'we spoke on the phone and wrote to each other. I'm based in Bristol. It was not convenient to meet.'

'You recommended Mr Burke to Lord Banks-Marion?'

'That is correct.'

Bryant turned to Lady Banks-Marion, who watched him warily. 'Your ladyship, I understand it's customary to greet the weekend guests upon their arrival, but neither you nor your son did so.'

'That was the old tradition,' she said stiffly. 'If you must know, we were having an argument.'

'About the sale of the hall and its possessions, is that right?'

'I had no desire to stay in the house while some businessman was poking about placing a value upon everything we own.'

'But your son convinced you to remain.'

'I wanted my mother to witness the signing of the contract,' said Harry. 'I thought she should be here.'

'The end result was that neither of you welcomed Mr Burke or his wife to Tavistock Hall. Miss Harrow.' Bryant walked over to her. 'How were you invited by Mr Burke?'

'By letter.' She took a cigarette from Pamela Claxon's packet and lit it, exhaling nervously.

'Why did you accept?'

'I wanted to meet him.'

A murmur went around the room.

'You're saying that – forgive me – not only were you not his lover, but you had never met Mr Burke?'

'That's right. We only ever spoke through his intermediary, Mr Stafford.'

'Who had not met him either. Mr Wilson, did you meet Mr Burke?'

'Well . . .'

'Tell the truth.'

'Not exactly.' The interior decorator fidgeted uncomfortably. 'Where is any of this getting us?'

'Please,' said May, now realizing where his partner was going with the line of questioning, 'hear him out.'

'Monty, you never met Mr Burke either. Yet at one point or other in the weekend nearly all of you said you'd met him or at least implied that you had, including you, Reverend.'

'I wanted to be sure of securing funds for our roof,' said Trevor. 'Our parish needs—'

'Your parish needs a new vicar,' said Lady Banks-Marion, 'preferably one who doesn't strip the place bare to feed a drug habit.'

'Then why did you all imply that you knew him?' asked Bryant. 'Because it suited you all to have the approval of the millionaire. Which just leaves Miss Claxon and Mrs Burke.'

'I met him many times over the years,' said Claxon. 'And of course Norma was married to him, so I don't know where you're going with this line of questioning.'

'Alberman wrote a card saying "They are all guilty",' Bryant replied. 'But there was one person he couldn't have known about. Miss Claxon, would you say that it's common for writers to work under a pseudonym?'

'Quite common, yes,' Claxon admitted.

'Why do they do that?'

'For several reasons. One is because female writers are not always taken seriously by male publishers, so they use their husband's names. They may be writing about subjects of a personal nature, or they may simply be producing too quickly and need more than one identity.'

'Is Claxon a pseudonym?'

'You sound as if you know it is, Mr Bryant, so why don't you tell us?'

'Your real name is Pamela Burke, is that correct?'

'Yes.'

'You are related to Donald Burke?'

'I am his sister. I'm three years younger than him.'

'You chose not to volunteer this information.'

'It's in the front of my first book.'

'I know. I saw it in the library.' He turned to Norma Burke. 'What can you tell me about the *Silver Thread?*'

'It was the name of my husband's yacht,' Norma explained.

'But I imagine you chose the name. You're Kentish born, after all.'

'Yes, I did choose it. But I don't understand—'

'Where was it moored?'

'On the River Medway.'

'So that's where it was in the summer of 1962?'

'I imagine so, I really can't remember.'

'But that was the year of your husband's breakdown, wasn't it? Let me remember for you. In 1962 Donald Burke took you sailing. Mrs Burke, would you like me to guess what happened on that trip, or will you tell us in your own words?'

An uncomfortable silence followed, during which only the falling rain could be heard.

'What happened that day was not my fault,' Norma Burke said finally.

'No,' Bryant agreed, 'but you're the cause of much that has occurred this weekend.'

Realizing there was no point in trying to deny the truth, she lit a cigarette with unsteady hands. Pamela moved closer to her.

'He was not an easy man to live with,' Norma said, glancing up at her sister-in-law. 'He could be very cruel. And he was certainly not as clever as everyone thought. When his business empire started to collapse I helped him to save it, not that he ever gave me credit. To Donald, I would always be "the little woman", the wife in the kitchen. I could have graduated from the London School of Economics with a first-class degree. He didn't consider any female the equal of a man. I was allowed to keep my own money but there were many things I couldn't do.'

'So financially your hands were tied.'

'That's right. If I wanted to buy something I needed my husband's signature to do so. Until very recently all wives did. Donald's latest business venture had failed, and he was very stressed about it.'

'How old was he?'

'He had just turned fifty-seven. On the day we took the boat out there wasn't a cloud in the sky. Pamela came with us. She's an expert sailor. It was the day everything changed.' She caught Bryant's gaze and held it. 'But you know, don't you? It was the day my husband died.'

46

YESTERDAY

The oil lamps supplemented the watery light from the French windows, casting jaundiced patches across the faces around the room. Everyone waited for Norma Burke to speak.

'It's an odd thing,' she said finally, nervously pulling at her cigarette. 'People often insisted that they'd met my husband even when I knew they hadn't. I suppose in certain financial circles he was famous. People liked to promote the idea that they were associated with him. If you'd been talking to Donald it meant you were someone important. But I think he saw himself as a failure.'

'What happened on the yacht?' Bryant asked.

'We sailed out past Gillingham, past Sheerness and into the Channel. It was terribly hot. Pamela had taken the helm while Donald went to get himself another whisky. He talked about going for a swim. He was rather drunk, but that was nothing unusual. I don't know how long he was gone, but when I looked around he wasn't there. The air was so still. There was hardly a sound. He'd just slipped into the sea and disappeared. We looked in the water for ages but we couldn't see him.'

'I was going to radio for assistance,' said Pamela.

'I told her not to.' Norma passed her cigarette from one hand to the other. Smoking did not come naturally to her.

'Why did you tell her not to get help?' asked Bryant.

'I don't know. There didn't seem to be any point. It wasn't going to bring him back. I knew he wasn't out there somewhere just bobbing about in the water. I just thought I could manage without him.' She batted smoke away from her face. 'For the next seven years I made the world think that my husband was alive. I wasn't allowed access to funds without his signature. I simply carried on investing his money and opening bank accounts. It wasn't as hard as you'd think. Forging letters was the easiest part. I told people that he'd been ill and could no longer come to meetings. I gave myself power of attorney. It's surprising how accommodating everyone was. Whenever I needed an approval, Pamela impersonated him on the phone. On the rare occasions that he absolutely needed to be seen in public, she dressed like him – they have the same facial features – and she allowed herself to be photographed from a distance, usually shielding herself with a hat.'

'I didn't think it was a good idea to leave fingerprints,' said Pamela, 'so I started wearing white gloves. The germ phobia was my idea. Once people got used to seeing him in the gloves, that was all they needed to see. It's like airline pilots – you see the jacket and cap but not the face. They only saw his hands.'

'I dealt with the banks by letter or phone,' said Norma, 'and while I rebuilt my husband's businesses, I made sure that he legally transferred his stocks to me.'

'If she had told the truth – that Donald had either committed suicide or accidentally drowned – she would have lost everything,' Pamela added.

'When I decided that he should die, I enlisted Pamela's help again, because she's a crime novelist,' said Norma.

'Why did you want to end the deception?' asked May.

She ground out the cigarette with distaste. 'For a long time the system worked without any problems. Nobody minded so long as the money continued coming in. I was very good at making a profit. Then the tax regulations changed and more security checks were required. It became increasingly difficult to make Donald's absence convincing. He couldn't attend a shareholders' meeting or a bank manager's dinner because he was away on a trip, or ill, or busy, or had missed his train. They were all men, you see, they expected to get together every now and again. I started to run out of excuses, and the shareholders became suspicious. In order to buy the hall this weekend Donald had to be seen here, so I made sure that Pamela was with me.'

'On Friday afternoon, soon after we arrived, we went for a walk around the grounds,' said Claxon. 'Norma told me that Donald needed to put in an appearance. We tried it out a couple of times. I put on his old suit and a grey hairpiece, and made sure we stayed some distance from the house. Norma could go off to get the deed signed, and we hoped Mr Stafford would accept it. But I had my doubts. I felt sure he would want to see Donald. So, we were out walking, and when we reached the big oak I saw something lying in the bushes. I pushed apart the branches and knew I was looking at the handle of the sledgehammer covered in flies. There was a man's body lying in a sack at the base of the tree, half-buried under the leaves. I looked inside and saw for myself. His head had been split apart like a pomegranate.'

'You're not writing a novel now,' said Bryant. 'Just tell us who it was.'

'We thought it was a vagrant,' Pamela explained. 'We'd spotted the hippy tents nearby, and of course we'd both read about the Manson murders. I mean, who hadn't? I had an awful feeling they might have killed some poor tramp for the fun of it.'

'But you also realized it was the perfect time for Norma to get rid of her phantom husband.'

'Yes, I just needed time to think it through, to make it fool-proof. I asked myself: What would Inspector Trench do? We were terrified that someone would find the body and report it before we'd come up with a plan. It occurred to me that a house like this would have a septic tank and a way of treating sewage, but we didn't find the barn until Saturday morning.'

'We hauled the body to the barn easily enough,' said Norma. 'There was no one nearby and it hardly weighed anything. The block and tackle allowed us to get it over the macerator. I added the wedding ring. I could identify the body and Donald would finally be declared dead. The whole thing only took a few minutes. We needed a lookout, so I sent a note to Vanessa, asking her to come down to the barn. I didn't explain why. I'm afraid she unwittingly covered for us. Pamela said it needed to look like an accident, so she sawed through the handrail and broke it. She didn't reckon on you two deciding that it was murder.'

'All police officers are naturally suspicious,' said Bryant. 'I didn't believe for a second that a germ-phobic man would go near the barn. That was the first mistake you made. The second was Pamela not fitting her brother's clothes. Millionaires wear hand-made suits. There were other errors.' He thought back to the conversation he had overheard between Norma and Pamela masquerading as her husband, and filled in the blanks.

It's gone too far. We'll be found out. Vanessa can't be trusted.

You must stay away from her.

I don't want to do this any more, Norma.

But it was your idea in the first place.

I'm leaving as soon as the deeds are signed.

They know you're not well, so it won't come as a shock.

'Pamela, you shouldn't have taunted us,' said Bryant. 'You said that "nobody really knew Donald Burke", and Norma, you forgot to take away Vanessa Harrow's water glass.'

'I knew that as soon as you all started attacking Vanessa she would admit that she had never met Donald,' said Norma.

'We had to stop her talking for a while, so we thought it would be a good idea if she just slept for the afternoon. We didn't know she had her own supply of sleeping pills as well.'

'It's a good story,' said Bryant. 'Cruel husband, ignored wife who helps him make his fortune, he cracks under the pressure of work and drowns himself, you take over the business. There's only one problem with it all. The *Silver Thread*.' He turned to the others. 'My knowledge of English history is largely confined to London, so it was lucky that I also found this in the library.'

He raised the book and showed them its cover. '*A Guide to English Miracles, Myths and Legends*. That's where I read the story.'

'For heaven's sake, what story?' asked Trevor Patethric.

'Hang on a minute, I marked the page.'

Bryant had always possessed a flair for the theatrical. He opened the book and read aloud:

'In 1171 a boy from Rochester drowned trying to catch frogs. While he lay lifeless on the bank of the Medway, his mother measured him from head to foot and promised to give a silver thread of equal length to St Thomas. A miracle occurred and the boy came back to life.'

He closed the book. 'It goes on to say that around this part of Kent, the legend of the silver thread is very well known. I think it was you who named the boat, Norma. You planned to kill him all along, and bring him back to life.' He let that sink in for a moment. 'But there's more. My friend Maggie here has turned up another surprise. Maggie, do you have the sketches that your hippy friend made?'

Maggie rose and handed over the pages.

'I'm afraid you're all in for another shock.'

Everyone was preparing for this when the French windows exploded.

47

COMMUNICATION BREAKDOWN

John May was the first one out of the room. Even so, it took him a minute to realize that a shell had landed in the middle of the lawn. It must have been powerful because the crater it had left behind was immense and the ashram's yurt was blown flat. The hippies had been blasted awake and were sitting up in various states of undress and bemusement. May ran over to check on them.

'Wow,' said Donovan, pushing down his hair and pointing to the smoking pit. 'Ley-line energy.'

'It's a full moon tonight,' said Melanie wistfully.

Something was pattering down on to the lawn and the patio beyond. Assorted pieces of amphibians and lily pads had been blasted from the ornamental pond.

Bryant had got his rain of frogs.

Inside Iris, the reception room's heavy brocade curtains had caught nearly all of the flying glass. Unfortunately the whole lot had then come down, tearing the brass rail from which they hung out of the ceiling. This brought with it a spectacular cascade of plaster, filling the room with choking dust. A further part of the ceiling cracked and fell in.

'I take it that's not the shock you meant,' said Monty, dusting himself down. He had the good grace to be barely surprised by the latest turn of events. 'That couldn't have been the army. They've packed up.'

'Everyone stay inside,' warned Bryant, holding up his hands for calm, but as a failed student of human nature he had reckoned without the survival instinct that brought everybody out into the garden.

'Stay off the lawn,' May shouted. 'There could be other devices.'

'We're under bombardment now?' asked Pamela. 'This sort of thing would never happen in an Inspector Trench novel.'

'It'd be better if it did, just to wake the reader up occasionally,' said Maggie Armitage, who was following the serial confessions with unfeigned delight.

As the smoke cleared, the chatter gave way to an ominous silence. Bryant turned around, trying to see what they had spotted. Someone in a knitted cap and combat fatigues was standing in front of them with a stick grenade in his left hand.

'Who on earth is that?' asked Harry, squinting over his granny glasses.

'Fruity Metcalf,' said Bryant.

'No, that's not Fruity,' Harry replied vehemently. 'We employ a jolly good groundsman called Fruity Metcalf, utterly reliable, but that's not him. Fruity only has one arm and one leg.'

He was right. The man standing before them possessed the full complement of limbs. But he was certainly the man with whom Bryant had been to the Goat & Compasses.

'Hand him over to me,' said the man with the grenade.

'Who?' asked Pamela, not unreasonably.

'Hatton-Jones. He is coming with me.'

'I knew it,' said Monty, turning to Bryant and May. 'I said there could be somebody on the inside but you didn't believe me.'

'I'm confused,' May admitted.

The others were distancing themselves from Monty, backing away until only he and the detectives still stood on the far side of the crater.

'I'll count to three. If you don't hand Hatton-Jones over by then, I'll just kill him, and probably both of you.'

'That's not in your brief, though, is it?' said Bryant. 'You're only supposed to terrify him. That's what Charles Chamberlain wants you to do, so that Monty won't testify tomorrow. If you kill him you won't get paid.'

'One.'

It was a standoff. Monty pulled himself free of May's arm. 'I told you Charles was behind this. I'm not going with that fellow, he's a nutter.'

'Two.'

'Monty, you have to go with him for now,' said May. 'We'll make sure you're all right. It's the only way to stop anyone else from getting hurt.'

'*We'll make sure you're all right?*' Monty scoffed. 'Forgive me if I don't invest a huge amount of trust in that promise.'

'Three.'

The assassin raised his grenade higher. Everybody ducked. Just then an unearthly, bone-trembling roar filled the air. Heads tilted up towards the source of the noise. A second roar was even louder.

'It roars twice as a warning,' Celeste had said, 'but if you hear it a third time you know it's right behind you, about to attack.'

Walking delicately along the largest branch of the hawthorn tree that grew behind the grenade-clutching murderer was a slender black creature with shining yellow eyes and a twitching tail almost as long as its body. It roared again, revealing fearsome incisors.

'The Beast of Crowshott!' cried Maggie, her eyes like saucers.

'It's a panther, you silly woman,' said Bryant.

'The army,' said Toby Stafford. 'I heard they blew up a couple of sheep and accidentally shelled the wall around the safari park. The landlord at the Red Lion told me the police were still trying to round up animals.'

The panther stretched itself forward, each huge front paw wavering before carefully planting itself further along the branch. Nobody dared to move. As it crept nearer, the branch began to bend.

A third and final roar turned into more of a yawn. The animal flopped down on its branch, which splintered beneath the sudden weight.

The panther fell on top of their assailant in a thunderous cascade of leaves, knocking him flat and swiping away his woollen headgear. Having been stared at through bars for most of its life, the animal decided it had had enough and bounded off towards the ashram, scattering hippies in every direction.

As the man who had taken Fruity Metcalf's place searched for his cap, the detectives saw that the top of his head resembled a badly stitched baseball.

48

RUNAWAY

Monty made a run for it. Everybody screamed. The hippies proved excellent at climbing trees. May threw himself at Cedric Powles, the stitch-headed arch manipulator late of Broadmoor Hospital, and knocked the stick grenade from his hand. The thing somersaulted through the air like an Indian club and Pamela Claxon caught it with the finesse of a baseball outfielder.

Lady Banks-Marion witnessed the mayhem with increasing incredulity, and was somehow reminded of the drunken parties they had held on the lawn before the war. She watched as Powles pulled himself free and hurled himself across the lawn with Bryant and May in pursuit.

Powles raised his arms across his face, punched his way through a wall of hedge and fell out into the road in a shower of leaves.

Harry turned to Norma Burke. 'Don't even think of moving from this spot,' he warned. 'Alberman, lock her in the still room until we get this sorted out.'

'What about me?' asked Pamela Claxon.

'You know where the law stands on your participation in

this better than we do,' said Harry. 'Think of it as research for your next novel while we wait for the Canterbury Police.'

Lady Banks-Marion studied her son and frowned. It was the first time she had ever heard him sound authoritative. Perhaps there was hope for him yet.

As Powles pounded up the wet lane the two detectives were hard on his heels. May's legs were longer and carried him further, but he still proved too slow. Bryant was slipping in mud and already running out of breath.

If Powles reached the tree cover beyond the property border they knew they would lose him. Moments after he vanished around a bend in the road, they heard a screech and a loud thud. They followed the curve to find that their quarry had been knocked on to his back on the tarmac. Next to him was a Rolls Royce Silver Ghost with its engine running and its driver's door opening.

'I didn't mean to bash into him,' said Celeste, climbing out. 'He just came charging out of nowhere. I normally only hit rabbits.'

Cedric Powles looked up at this glamorous vision, then closed his eyes and allowed his head to sink to the tarmac, wishing he was back in hospital.

Celeste pulled a silver hip flask out of her jacket.

'Don't revive him!' warned Bryant.

'Darling, this is for me,' she said, helping herself to a tot of brandy.

Bryant explained everything else when they had all returned to the shattered reception room. Powles was still groggy and lay on the floor. He had been trussed up like a Christmas goose by Alberman, who had spent enough time in the kitchen to know knots.

'The man you found smashed up in the garden wasn't a vagrant, Pamela, it was poor old Fruity Metcalf. That's why he was so easy to lift; he was missing two limbs. He lost them during the war. Didn't you notice when you looked inside the sack?'

'God, no,' said Claxon. 'I saw flesh and bone and a lot of spongy red stuff, and shut the thing back up as quickly as possible. I can't stand the sight of blood. We carried the sack over to the macerator and emptied it out.'

'The gentleman on the floor is a mentally deranged hit-man,' said May. 'It would appear he offered his services to the fellow Monty is facing in court tomorrow morning. He was paid to watch Monty carefully and scare him out of testifying. Powles was sent here and seems to have overreacted somewhat. I imagine he was challenged by the real Fruity and killed him. Then he strapped up his own right arm to impersonate him, picking up the rest as he went along.'

'Somebody must have noticed it was a different man,' said Pamela disbelievingly.

'Why would they? Fruity wasn't allowed to set foot in the house, and nobody ever came out to see him except Lord Banks-Marion who – forgive me, your lordshipness – is in a permanent stupor due to the enormous amount of drugs he ingests. The barman at the Goat and Compasses said, "You newcomers are always in such a rush." He included Fruity in that statement. But Fruity told me he came to the pub all the time. So why didn't the barman recognize him?'

'I had a couple of joints to relax, is that so wrong?' said Harry. 'I can get us all one if you want. Donovan sells them.'

'We're police officers,' May reminded him. 'Let my partner finish.'

'So – poor old Parchment was outside in the garden when Monty was attacked,' Bryant continued. 'He looked up and saw Powles on the roof, pushing the gryphon with *both hands*.'

'Why didn't he say anything?'

'Because he's a servant. It's ingrained in him not to speak

out, no matter what he sees. One of the hippies was watching, too. Victoria was drawing the house. She sketched a man with both of his arms intact. She was lucky; this sutured Frankenstein only focused on the valet, and went after him. He had trouble getting to Monty because we made sure that Monty was hardly ever left alone. But then he saw Pamela here using the servant passages that allowed "Burke" to come and go, and did the same. There's a trick to the panels. If you see someone else do it, it's easy to copy. When I went to see Toby Stafford I saw the whole of the old servants' passage drawn in on his floor plans of the house.'

'You had an idea about what was happening and kept it to yourself,' said May accusingly. 'You should have told us earlier.'

'I needed proof,' Bryant replied. 'But it's true that I became suspicious early on. The pig, Malacrida, had fresh blood on its hoofs and snout, but the remains of the body in the macerator were contained inside a waste-pan. The pig had found *Metcalf*, not Burke. I dare say the contents of her stomach will confirm that. I can't imagine anyone will want to eat her now.'

They waited for the waters to subside, making periodic raids on the kitchen to keep their spirits up. Alberman continued to stop anyone from leaving long after he had been instructed to stand down. Cedric Powles was kept under supervision, but remained mostly asleep.

Norma Burke's composure finally buckled under the stress of the weekend. She sat on the kitchen chair with sore red eyes, trying not to look upset. 'I'm relieved that it's over,' she told May. 'I didn't kill him. He chose to die. I keep thinking about that. He chose to die rather than hand over power to me.'

'Perhaps one day soon women will be better recognized in industry,' said May, even though he knew that most working females were still secretaries, bookkeepers and primary school teachers.

'A verdict of suicide would have left me with nothing.' Norma wiped her eyes. 'His family would have taken every penny I earned for him. Once I'd made the decision to keep him alive there was no turning back.'

May seated himself beside her. 'I can't imagine the strain you were under.'

'At first it was easy. I was so invisible, you see. I walked into Donald's boardroom and his employees thought I'd arrived to take the tea order. Everyone dismissed me. Not pretty enough to draw attention, not smart enough to do a man's job. But I had always done a man's job, first looking after my family, then looking after Donald. When he and I were out together his colleagues saw a captain of industry and a housewife. They never imagined that one could be the other.'

'You committed fraud, Norma.'

'If he was legally allowed to sign for his wife, why couldn't I do the same for him? All I did was continue to make money for my husband, just as I always had.'

'You hadn't let the law catch up with you,' May said.

'It's caught up now.'

'We're not the law, we're an academic unit. We can report the details of the case in a way that we see fit.' He was determined not to give her too much hope. 'All I can do is have a word with my partner.'

The sky had finally cleared, and a headlamp-bright moon had appeared above the treeline. The air smelled of wet hay, cows, marijuana and explosives.

'What shall I do with the grenade?' Pamela Claxon was still dazed by the revelations of the weekend. She weighed the weapon in her hand as they stood on the steps of the house looking out across the silent fields.

'Keep it as a souvenir,' said Bryant. 'Maybe leave it on the desk in front of you as you write. That's what I would do.'

'Are you going to have us arrested?' Her question was studiedly casual.

'What would be the point?' Bryant shrugged. 'I can't prove that Mrs Burke drowned her husband. He could have had an accident or decided to kill himself. From what I've heard about the pressures of his business, I suspect the latter. The choice of the boat's name might just have been as she says, a coincidence. You had us fooled when "Donald Burke" disappeared from the library. We were looking for a secret passage that wasn't there.'

Pamela looked pleased with herself. 'Oh, *that*. I only used the closed passageway once or twice. Usually it was enough to just snatch off the wig and tie – it's a clip-on. That's what I did in the library before stepping outside.'

'Powles was outside doing his Fruity Metcalf and must have seen you, but it wasn't in his interests to say anything,' Bryant pointed out.

'I'm afraid I started enjoying myself a little too much,' Claxon admitted. 'Is Vanessa going to press charges?'

'You could have killed Miss Harrow. She says she's prepared to leave you alone if you do the same. You also committed forgery and fraud, although you did it to claim back the money Mrs Burke earned for her husband in the first place. There's more at stake than you realize; the Equal Pay Act is currently making its way through parliament, and the last thing anybody wants is for that to be derailed. So perhaps we have to be content with the arrest of Powles.'

'You're being very generous,' said Claxon, looking sheepish. 'I'm not sure Inspector Trench would have done the same thing.'

Monty turned to Lady Banks-Marion. 'I'm sorry I tried to steal your painting, your ladyship,' he said, attempting to present a reasonably believable vision of contrition.

She fixed him with a cold eagle eye. 'That's all right, it was a cheap imitation. Rather like you, Mr Hatton-Jones. Typically, you stole the wrong part. It's the frame that's valuable, a rare Louis XIII gold setting with three bands of carved laurel leaves, worth an awful lot more than the painting.' She turned away from him and headed back inside the house.

'She's a piece of work, isn't she?' said Monty admiringly.

'A word with you, my lord?' May requested.

'Hmm?' Harry actually seemed cheerful. Malacrida trotted around him, her face permanently fixed in its strangely human grin.

'Mr Stafford tells me you're going to keep Tavistock Hall.'

Harry leaned towards him in cheerful confidence. He reeked of patchouli and marijuana. 'We've come to an agreement, he and I. I'm giving him the east wing for Mrs Burke's business institute, and the paintings.'

'And the necklace?' Bryant asked with wide, innocent eyes.

'Oh, that.' Harry looked sheepishly down at his piglet.

'Perhaps you want to pop it back into your mother's jewellery box just to save any embarrassment, what with us being police officers and all.'

'Of course,' said Harry hastily. He knelt to unclasp the diamond necklace from Malacrida's pink throat. 'Well, thank you for a most entertaining weekend. It was a lot more fun than shooting partridges and playing contract bridge.'

'It was very pleasurable meeting you.' Bryant handed Celeste the keys to her yellow Mini. 'Perhaps our paths will cross again.'

'I rather doubt it,' said Celeste. 'You're a little young for me, Mr Bryant. My men tend to be more mature, and I'm not sure you're quite ready for rich, bored widows.'

'Your husband's not dead.'

'No, he's in Cardiff.' She turned the car keys over in her hand.

'I'm maturing quickly,' said Bryant proudly. 'I'm already starting to lose my hair and my waistcoat buttons are going to go any minute.'

'Really?' She gave him a look of great seriousness. 'Perhaps I should move back to the city. Buy myself a little mews cottage in Marylebone. I'm a little too fast for Kent. One can come and go as one pleases in London.'

'If you do, perhaps you'll allow me to take you out to dinner, at least,' Bryant offered.

'There would be no one to scandalize.' She weighed up the idea. 'I'll tell you what.' She held her hand over his palm and released the keys to the Mini. 'Why don't you hang on to the car for now. Use it as a runabout. I'll send you the log book. He's called Victor, by the way. I expect great things of you, Mr Bryant. Perhaps we'll meet again. When you're feeling a little more . . . grown-up.'

'I can't say I'm sorry to lose the commission,' said Slade Wilson. 'Harry wants the colour scheme to be pea and prune with mustard highlights. Oh, I nearly forgot.' He dug into a brown paper carrier bag. 'Mrs Janverley wanted me to have this, but I think it would look better on you, Mr Bryant. There's some blood on it but you can get that out with a little salt and half a lemon.' He handed Bryant an immense red and yellow striped scarf. 'It's the one Parchment had just finished knitting when he was killed.'

He lovingly wrapped it around Bryant's neck and patted it into place. 'There you go. Just try not to think about the needle that knitted it.'

49

HELLO, GOODBYE

It turned out that the Canterbury team, feeling that they had been mucked about enough, decided to ignore Bryant's cancellation message and turn up at the hall anyway, so they had the satisfaction of taking Powles away with them, although they were rather confused by the swift turn of events.

The detectives drove back to London in Victor. Bryant hunched over the wheel while May kept an eye on Monty, who had been wedged with considerable difficulty into the tiny back seat.

'I never thought for a second that it was about you doing the right thing,' said May. 'I was pretty sure you wanted to be there to pick up the remains of Charles Chamberlain's company after you'd destroyed it. There had to be a reason why you were so determined to meet Donald Burke, to ensure you had guaranteed capital.'

'It's not rocket science, being a detective, is it?' said Monty sourly.

Victor sped towards Covent Garden, and Bow Street. The Sunday-night traffic was light and Bryant drove with reckless abandon, repeatedly whacking Monty's plastered head as he bounced over the cambers at junctions.

As he pulled up outside the unit, he studied their passenger in his rear-view mirror. 'Lady Banks-Marion was right. You dragged London crime into her house. If you hadn't told everyone you were heading for Tavistock Hall, Cedric Powles wouldn't have got there ahead of you and taken Fruity Metcalf's place.'

'Something bothers me,' May added. 'Your concrete sample.'

Bandaged, bloodied, bruised and generally bashed about, Monty looked as if he'd fallen down several flights of stairs. 'What about it?' he asked exhaustedly.

'Why would you provide your own sample? Why not wait until the court asks for one and sends an official representative to collect it?'

'I thought it would prove more helpful if I had one at hand,' Monty said quickly.

'It was important enough to take away with you on a weekend in the country.' He caught his partner's eye. 'It doesn't match the ones your factory makes, does it? It wasn't just Charles who came up with ways of saving money in the production of new homes. Chamberlain's designs might have placed the construction rods further apart, but it was your people who changed the cement formula. The fault is with your concrete mix, am I right? You knew it was faulty and did nothing about it because of the expense. Your firm prefabricates the building sections and bolts them together on site.'

'It's more cost-effective that way,' muttered Hatton-Jones.

'There's a reason why the new manufacturing process employed by your plant is so cost-effective, Monty. The cement is no good.'

'That's not true,' said Hatton-Jones, now anxious to get out of the car. 'You wouldn't understand. Our mixes contain things called polymers. They're resins that form strands that bond the cement. I didn't want our formula to get into anyone else's hands, so I kept it with me.'

'I read your company brochure, but it's taken me a while to

realize exactly what you're up to,' said May, ignoring him. 'You shouldn't let your lab scientists write your sales documents. Surely your polymers would degrade at different speeds depending on the acidity of the mix.'

'I wouldn't know,' Monty maintained. 'I'm an entrepreneur, not a scientist.'

'You thought you'd entirely got rid of the need for steel rods. Chamberlain knows nothing about the molecular structure of your products other than what your development team tells him. Which is why you agreed to testify, to head off the blame before it reached you. It's why you brought a doctored sample with you, to make sure the court wouldn't put you in the dock. Then, after the dust had settled, you could buy Chamberlain's company. Except that the plan was scuppered when Donald Burke turned out to be dead.'

'Good luck proving that,' said Monty. 'Ours is a perfectly good product.'

'I don't doubt it. But when the judge hears that you knowingly let Chamberlain incorporate it into untested new designs, he may decide it was your fault that those children in Hackney died, not his.'

He climbed out of the car and pulled forward the seat. 'I'm locking you in a cell overnight, Monty. For your own safekeeping, you understand. You might as well get used to the experience.'

When the detectives went up to their office and Bryant emptied out his overcoat, he found six tightly rolled joints in one pocket, a gift from Donovan. He kept them sealed in a tobacco tin as a reminder of what could go wrong – and right – in an investigation, and finally smoked them, strictly for his incipient arthritis.

He rarely returned to the countryside, and on one of those trips he only stayed overnight because he was trapped in a snowstorm on Dartmoor.

*

They got Monty Hatton-Jones to the court on time on Monday morning, of course, although, annoyingly, he wasn't called as a witness that day or on Tuesday. When he finally made it to the stand on Wednesday afternoon, the detectives began to get a sense of what would actually happen.

The defence quickly dismissed Monty as a credible witness, citing his unreliable history, his litigious past, his current state of distress caused by his injuries and, not least, his ongoing involvement in a murder investigation. As the detectives had suspected, the defence detailed further difficulties involved in assigning responsibility for the manufacture of Sir Charles Chamberlain's buildings. The tape recording was ruled inadmissible. The Westminster Council official left the court without a stain on his character, although two years later he was charged with accepting a bribe from a building contractor. Pleading mental stress, he was granted a deferred sentence.

The case against Chamberlain began to unravel.

The prosecution attempted to introduce new evidence but was overruled, as it did not pertain to the case under review. As the old boys' network sprang into action, a phenomenal number of highly respectable character witnesses were introduced. Two days later the trial was halted. What shocked Bryant most was that nobody at court appeared angry or even surprised. Everyone seemed to have forgotten the young Hackney family whose lives had been snuffed out when their dream home collapsed about their ears, except for a handful of exhausted-looking people who sat outside the law courts with placards demanding justice. One of them was Arthur Bryant's mother, Mary.

The trial's collapse allowed for a new, entirely separate case to be prepared concerning the hiring of Cedric Powles by Sir Charles Chamberlain. Consistent with the topsy-turveydom of the legal process, Monty Hatton-Jones now found himself portrayed as the slighted plaintiff.

During the preparation of the trial, Cedric Powles hanged

himself in prison over an entirely unrelated incident, and the second case collapsed. However, in a private suit brought by the families of the deceased (including Ernest 'Parchment' Prabhakar's stepbrother in Kenya), Chamberlain was voted out by his board of directors and left the country to work in South Africa. It was the case that hardened the detectives' antagonistic attitude towards the legal process, and the year that changed the way they saw their future. They decided to concentrate on developing a singular set of skills that would make the Peculiar Crimes Unit truly unique, and leave the parts they could not control to others.

Swinging London evaporated so completely that it seemed to have never existed. It became a wonderful, dazzling mirage, fondly remembered but impossible to pin down. For a brief shining moment it really had felt as if singers, inventors, designers and models would set trends around the world. The term 'youthquake' summed it up; students were invited to sit on college boards, and careers began early – photographer Gered Mankowitz was just twenty-one when he took his celebrated shots of Jimi Hendrix – but the novelty of youth slipped quietly away as the old guard fought its way back. In Sheffield, Manchester and Nottingham there were still children without shoes and slums with no running water. A campaign to encourage everyone to buy British products, 'I'm Backing Britain', failed abysmally, its Union Jack T-shirts having been manufactured in China.

And the country continued to change. By the end of the decade abortion was legalized, the rules governing divorce were remodelled and the Equal Pay Act was ratified so that women like Norma Burke got a fairer deal. Things were better than before; they just didn't feel quite as exciting any more.

John May dated Vanessa Harrow for five months, until she grew tired of the demands made upon his time by the unit and married a professional gambler more than twice her age in Monte Carlo. She persevered with her singing career, and her single, 'Riviera Romeo', reached number 82 in the UK Top 100.

Monty Hatton-Jones gave up his company and became a property developer, selling homes to wealthy clients in Knightsbridge. In 1979 he went to jail for defrauding patients in the Great Ormond Street Children's Hospital and trying to bribe the judge in the case. Upon his release he founded Brit-Out!, an organization dedicated to removing the country from Europe, which he ran from his cottage in Somerset.

Roger Trapp resigned from the PCU at the end of 1969, complaining of nervous exhaustion. He took over a fruit and vegetable smallholding in Broadstairs, where he was much happier.

Gladys Forthright's daughter, Janice Longbright, eventually joined the London Metropolitan Police and became the PCU's longest-serving member of staff.

Pamela Claxon wrote a series of romantic thrillers featuring a codebreaking alcoholic martial arts instructor called Leticia Goodbody. Critics unanimously declared them awful. She moved to Hollywood and became a successful scriptwriter.

Norma Burke gave nearly all her money away to children's charities, and was subsequently awarded an OBE.

Reverend Trevor Patethric was caught trying to steal the 1530 petition from the English clergy asking Pope Clement VII to annul Henry VIII's marriage to Catherine of Aragon, housed in the Vatican archives. How a lowly Kent vicar managed to inveigle his way in there was never fully explained. He was defrocked and subsequently moved to India with one of the girls from Lord Banks-Marion's ashram.

Melanie gave birth to a daughter who grew up to become one of the world's most successful recording stars.

In 1973 Toby Stafford had gender reassignment surgery and became an air hostess for Qantas.

Slade Wilson did not care for the muted shades of the seventies. He gave up his career as an interior designer after meeting a samba instructor in Rio de Janeiro. They set up a school teaching colour coordination to carnival dancers.

Captain Debney was hospitalized after being attacked by a traumatized ostrich, and left the army to run an animal sanctuary in Sussex.

The Burke Better Business School went bankrupt. Plans to turn Tavistock Hall into a National Trust property fell through, and it was sold to developers who transformed it into flats. The paintings, statues and other fittings all went to overseas collectors. The stained-glass window of Herne the Hunter was bought by an American hamburger chain for its flagship outlet in the King's Road.

Alberman and Mrs Janverley were paid the wages they were owed in full, and retired. Mrs Bessel became a successful television chef.

Lady Banks-Marion and Harry moved to Knightsbridge, where they bought one of Monty's apartments, and in 1972 Harry died of a heroin overdose. Three years later Lady Banks-Marion passed away. Some said that leaving Tavistock Hall was a tragedy from which she never recovered, and that she died of a broken heart. Among the few belongings she took with her were some photographs showing Tavistock Hall in its heyday, faded sepia images of shooting days, costumed nights, picnics and fayres – and snapshots of the young lord with whom she had fallen in love. They were all outlived by the pig, Malacrida.

Celeste made headlines when she became the first female manager of the Hong Kong National Basketball Team.

It took four years for the families who lived in sub-standard accommodation constructed by Sir Charles Chamberlain's company to be rehoused.

Maggie Armitage remained a lifelong friend of the Peculiar Crimes Unit, where she was sometimes employed as a kind of spiritual drainage expert.

Arthur Bryant looked back to the night he sat with

Donovan the hippy, and wondered what would have happened if he had not tried marijuana in a Mongolian yurt covered in tie-dyed sheets in the back garden of a Kentish country house. He should really have told his partner the truth: that it eased the pain in his joints, and it sometimes helped him to follow a different mental path. Although explaining why he had a marijuana plant growing underneath his office desk never got any easier.

The long-buried memory of Lord Banks-Marion fishing a false moustache from a bowl of porridge gave Bryant fresh ideas about the transference of DNA. He began to plot a new future for the unit that would keep them safe from closure. The offices of the PCU were shunted from Bow Street to Savile Row before ending up in Mornington Crescent, and then King's Cross. Bryant rented a second-floor flat in a run-down house in Notting Hill from an Antiguan landlady called Alma Sorrowbridge, and kept Celeste's custard-yellow Mini Cooper, Victor (187 TWR). He wore Mr Parchment's knitted scarf until the day he died.

John May married and had a son, Alex, and a daughter, Elizabeth. His wife Jane developed mental health problems and was taken into care. His granddaughter, April, worked at the unit before moving to Canada. May continued at the PCU for many, many years, working with his oldest and greatest friend. His life was often painful but never boring.

One further incident warrants a mention. It had been a fine, fresh night, that Sunday in September 1969, when the detectives drove Monty Hatton-Jones back from Tavistock Hall to London in Celeste's old Mini Cooper, Victor.

They passed great crowds leaving an anti-nuclear march, waving brightly painted banners as they dispersed from their gathering point in Greenwich Park. As they crested the hill at Blackheath they could see the lights of the city glowing before them. They pushed on into London, heading for Waterloo Bridge. So many women had worked on the new concrete crossing over the Thames that for a time it had become known as 'the Ladies' Bridge'. A soft grey mist lay on the olivine waters, and in places had curled itself over the road.

As he reached the centre of the bridge, Bryant looked out and saw two elderly men, one tall and upright, the other shorter and more rotund, dressed in a hat and scarf, leaning on a walking stick.

For a moment he thought they looked familiar. They were standing at the balustrade on the bridge's eastern side, calmly surveying the city, somehow looking as if they owned it and were simply checking that everyone was being taken care of.

Then the van behind him hooted and the moment passed. Bryant looked in his mirror to try and catch another glimpse of them, but they had dissipated, ghosts of a London yet to come.

50

ALL YOU NEED IS LOVE

'I've never had a jellied eel,' said Simon Sartorius, looking apprehensive. 'What do they taste like?'

'I can get you some if you want, my shout,' offered Bryant as they entered Manzes' pie and eel shop, purveyors of fine working-class fare, on London Bridge Road. The black and white tiled interior of the café was crowded with office workers and children from a nearby school.

Simon peered over the counter, looking at a steel pot filled with green bubbling liquid. 'Ah, I think I'll stay with a pie, thanks. What is that?'

'It's liquor.'

'Not – alcohol?'

'No, parsley sauce. It slips down a treat with pie and mash.' Bryant waved aside a small boy in a backward baseball cap and lowered jeans. 'Let me through, I'm a pensioner.'

'Sod off, Granddad,' said the child, standing his ground.

'How would you like a broken nose?' Bryant offered, raising the steel-studded handle of his walking stick.

'That's an offensive weapon,' said the boy.

'You're an offensive child,' said Bryant.

'I'll report you.'

'I'm a copper, I'll report myself. Pull your trousers up.'

'Arthur!' called John May, pushing open the door. 'You only gave me half the address. This is the third pie shop I've visited. You must be Mr Sartorius, I'm Arthur's partner, John.' He shook the publisher's hand. 'I'm sorry I'm late.'

'Oh, that's quite all right,' said Simon magnanimously, 'we were late too. Mr Bryant got trapped in an escalator.'

'It tore off the front of my boot.' Bryant pointed at his big toe, which was peeking from the toecap of his right shoe. 'Is it pies all round?'

They squeezed into a table beneath an art deco mirror and tucked into their plates of mash. 'I take it this was Arthur's idea,' said May.

'Mr Bryant thought it would do me good to have a change from French cuisine.' Simon raised his mash-coated fork uncertainly. 'He probably told you that we're hoping to publish some more of the unit's memoirs.'

'That reminds me,' said Bryant, digging into his briefcase, a hard trick to pull off as they were bunched so tightly together on a narrow bench. 'Here you go.' He whacked down 330 pages of typed paper. 'There's your memoir. I'd have got it to you earlier but I thought I'd wait until we had lunch together again.'

'But I only saw you last week,' marvelled Simon as he picked up the manuscript and turned it over. 'I thought you were joking when you said you had a book for me.'

'There's a cover note,' said Bryant with a sparkle in his eye. 'John, why don't you take a look?'

May removed the folded sheet clipped to the front of the manuscript and opened it out. He read aloud:

Dear Mr Bryant,

I believe I once told you that after my son died I could not countenance the thought of bringing back my fictional detective, dear old Inspector Trench. I never did return him to print, and after the failure of the *Leticia Goodbody, Martial Arts Codebreaker* series, I moved to Beverly Hills to pen the Percy Pig movies.

I'm not sure why I decided to write about our experiences at Tavistock Hall over that very strange weekend in September 1969, but I thought I would make you and Mr May the protagonists, rather than relaying events from my point of view. As I understand you are planning to embark upon a series of memoirs, I thought you might find it useful to have this account, to do with as you please. I have entitled it *Hall of Mirrors*. It's the only way I can say thank you for the kindness you showed us. Norma and I did not mean anyone any harm. The last thing we had ever expected was to stumble across a real-life murderer, or to meet you and Mr May.

I tried to find a way of squeezing Leticia Goodbody into the story but there were quite enough larger-than-life characters in there already. I hope you will not think I took too many liberties. I spiced it up a bit.

Pamela Claxon

PS Perhaps it would be best to do a few rewrites and use your own name on the book's title page. After the critical reception of *Leticia's Ghastly Surprise* I'd rather not draw any more attention to myself.

'I've read it through,' said Bryant, 'and I can promise you, every single word of it is the absolute truth.'

He caught John May's eye across the table, and it was all his partner could do to keep from bursting out laughing.

Bryant and May will return.

A Q & A WITH THE AUTHOR

Q: What attracted you to setting a mystery novel in the 1960s?

A: The mid-1960s in Great Britain had no name until America defined it. To *Vogue* and *Time* magazine, London became 'the most swinging city in the world', signified by political activism, sexual liberation, youth and spending power. Unfortunately I was at school and managed to completely miss it.

Q: So how did you learn about it?

A: I had osmotically absorbed all the details – how could you not when it was all anyone talked about at school? You look to older role models. By the time I left school and was ready to hit the town the sixties had been replaced by the gruesome horrors of the strike-ridden, impoverished seventies. And disco.

Q: How did you do the research?

A: That part was easy; everything was already in my head although mostly unusable, otherwise the whole book would have been peppered with Monty Python jokes about fascists and philosophers, and lurid scenes from Ken Russell films. I talked to some of the people who were there and read around a dozen volumes dissecting the era, many quite contradictory.

They all agreed on certain points: that it was easy to get a job if you showed initiative, and good fortune was on the side of youth. It was by all accounts a great time to be young.

Q: Wasn't it a little perverse, having the whole of this period to draw on and then marooning your detectives in a country house?

A: I knew I could get bogged down in too much period detail if I just had them rattling around in Swinging London for the entire book, partly because Swinging London was a mindset as much as a movement. Any one element, like the political agitation of the time, could have filled a whole volume and would have been more a history lesson than a crime novel. Besides, I've read most of the country house crime novels and wanted to tackle one myself. I wasn't interested in their heyday so much as their demise.

Q: Did it feel strange writing about your elderly detectives as young men?

A: It made a pleasant change. They needed to behave in an immature fashion, so I could have them excitedly bounding about, playing silly games, making mistakes and being athletic. They also realize that most of their suspects are older than them, and are therefore more daunting to deal with. They feel disrespectful but need to obey the behavioural codes of the time.

Q: Does the reader require any knowledge of the previous books to read this one?

A: Not at all. The Bryant & May novels are not one long serialized adventure; they are really all the crime stories I ever wanted to write, and they can be read pretty much in any order. This is the third period novel I've tackled in the series.

Q: Did you miss not having the usual team of PCU officers and misfits to fall back on?

A: No, because in order to be true to the country house murder mystery I needed a good range of suspects, and there's only so much room for characters in one fifty-chapter story.

Q: Speaking of which, why does every Bryant & May have fifty chapters?

A: It seems to me the ideal length for this kind of novel. I like a bit of structure to my writing; writers love rules. Crime novels shouldn't outstay their welcome.

Q: Looking back at the 1960s, what makes it so important to you?

A: It was out of reach to a schoolkid in suburban London, and therefore still has a talismanic effect on me. It took me years to appreciate the influence the era exerted on us; it may not have been as widespread as we like to imagine, but one thing was clear: it profoundly changed the country and had an effect on the whole of Europe. Most crucially, it gave the young a voice. It's a lesson we would do well to relearn. The sixties was when our modern tolerance for others was born. This particular element was the one that most fitted with the Bryant & May ethic.

ACKNOWLEDGEMENTS

As ever I owe a debt of gratitude to my agents Mandy Little and James Wills, who exhibit the kind of calm patience I can never find in myself, and to my valiant editor Simon Taylor, whose good nature I have tested in the opening pages of this volume.

Kate Samano and Richenda Todd inject some well-needed common sense into the proceedings (I have a particular problem with timelines that they always help me unravel) and Sophie Christopher gets the word out. Thanks of course to Pete, without whom I could not keep up the pace. A hug to Jan, Porl, Maggie, Martin, Jo, Joanna, Darrell, Lesley, Sally and everyone who accepts my friendship in the understanding that *books come first*.

As is my usual wont, there are several Easter Eggs hidden in the book. Not all of the chapter titles come from before 1969; they're meant to provide a soundtrack of the period – all except one, that is. Provide the explanation on my website, christopherfowler.co.uk, and I'll send you something as a reward. You can also find me on Twitter @peculiar.

CHRISTOPHER FOWLER is the award-winning author of more than forty novels (fifteen of which feature the detectives Bryant and May and the Peculiar Crimes Unit) and short story collections. The recipient of many awards, including the coveted CWA 'Dagger in the Library', Chris has also written screenplays, video games, graphic novels, audio plays and two critically acclaimed memoirs, *Paperboy* and *Film Freak*. His most recent publication is *The Book of Forgotten Authors*, drawn from his 'Invisible Ink' columns in the *Independent on Sunday*. Christopher Fowler lives in King's Cross, London, and Barcelona.

To find out more, visit www.christopherfowler.co.uk or on Twitter @Peculiar